MORE PRAISE FOR CORDELIA STRUBE

"Canada's best bet to succeed Alice Munro."

—*Toronto Star*

"Strube deftly navigates around the human heart in a way sometimes reminiscent of Carol Shields. The writing is so effortlessly accomplished that it makes me wonder where Cordelia Strube sprang from."

—*Books in Canada* on *Alex & Zee*

"Strube's comic sense is like a perfectly mixed martini: exceedingly dry and potent."

—*Toronto Star* on *Dr. Kalbfleisch & the Chicken Restaurant*

"Often witty and pointedly observant in the face of pain and absurdity."

—*Newsday* on *Alex & Zee*

"Filled with wry and shrewd observations about the agony of growing up."

—*Chatelaine* on *Lemon*

"A remarkable literary feat."

—*Maclean's* on *Blind Night*

"Strube's sure way with words, her mordant punchlines and equally sharp assessments of urban life on the edge of normal make this familiar story a compulsive read."

—*Globe and Mail* on *Alex & Zee*

"[Strube] tells a loopy story in clear, unadorned prose and with gentle irony. Despairing Milton is given just enough hope to keep him going and to make us care deeply about whether he gets there. Anyone comfortable with laughing in the dark will be, too."

—*Montreal Gazette* on *Milton's Elements*

"*The Barking Dog* is a rare achievement, an unstintingly honest, hilarious and dreadful delight."

—*Globe and Mail*

"Her portraits of characters caught in urban angst are riddled with laugh-out-loud humour. . . . Strube's rueful insistence on contemplating human darkness is tempered by a certain wistfulness, a yearning for something finer, a flicker of hope that is never quite extinguished. . . . A book that crackles with anger, righteousness and a strange kind of passion for living."

—*Edmonton Journal* on *The Barking Dog*

"The bare-knuckled prose, reminiscent of early Margaret Atwood novels, is entirely free of metaphor or lyricism."

—*Toronto Star* on *Teaching Pigs to Sing*

"A heart-wrenching and daring subplot that leaves the reader shuddering . . . Strube knows very well those on the edge often have superior insight into what makes people tick."

—*National Post* on *Blind Night*

"Strube's novel achieves that marvel, instilling a belief that, despite everything, there is a reason for living."

—*Waterloo Region Record* on *Dr. Kalbfleisch & the Chicken Restaurant*

"Crisp, edgy, wincingly real. This is an exciting new talent."

—*Books in Canada*

"Most writers can either create great characters or propulsive plots: Strube nails both, with gusto, and then does her best to save the planet along the way."

—*Ottawa Citizen* on *Blind Night*

ON THE SHORES
OF DARKNESS,
THERE IS LIGHT

a Novel

CORDELIA STRUBE

ECW PRESS

For Carson

To Homer
By John Keats

Standing aloof in giant ignorance,
    Of thee I hear and of the Cyclades,
As one who sits ashore and longs perchance
    To visit dolphin-coral in deep seas.
So thou wast blind;—but then the veil was rent,
    For Jove uncurtain'd Heaven to let thee live,
And Neptune made for thee a spumy tent,
    And Pan made sing for thee his forest-hive;
Aye on the shores of darkness there is light,
    And precipices show untrodden green,
There is a budding morrow in midnight,
    There is a triple sight in blindness keen;
Such seeing hadst thou, as it once befel
To Dian, Queen of Earth, and Heaven, and Hell.

BEFORE

"There's a baby stuck in a car." Harriet waves anxiously at the crowd of parents watching T-ball. They don't notice. She runs back to the SUV, across grass turned to straw. It hasn't rained in six weeks. Smog chokes the city.

The baby, mottled pink, purplish around the eyes and mouth, is strapped to the car seat. Wailing, she jerks her chubby arms and legs, her cries muted by the latest technology in road noise reduction. She looks like the baby Harriet pictured when her mother told her she was pregnant: a cute baby with a normal head and curly blonde locks. Harriet presses her nose against the window, causing the cute baby to stare at her as though she is the one who trapped her. "Don't blame me," Harriet says.

Just this morning, her mother blamed her for losing the plastic pitcher for bagged milk. "Why can't you put things back in their place?" When it turned out Harriet's little brother used the pitcher to shower his plastic animals, her mother didn't apologize to Harriet. Or scold Irwin. There's no doubt in Harriet's mind she'd be better off without her little brother. She should have snuffed him when she had the chance, after they took him out of the incubator and handed him to her, all red and wrinkled, with his stretched head and veins pulsing weakly under his see-through skin.

"Say hi to your brother," her mother said. She no longer looked like her mother because she'd stopped eating and sleeping when Irwin was cut out of her. The furry-lipped nurse who'd helped Harriet put on the sterile gloves said, "Your brother is a miracle baby." Harriet didn't see why.

The cute baby trapped in the car seat has stopped wiggling and isn't pink and purple anymore, just pale. Harriet tries the doors again before scrambling back to the crowd of parents. She pushes her way to the front of the pack, where her mother and her mother's boyfriend, Gennedy, coach Irwin as he swings wildly at the ball balanced on the T.

"Keep your eye on the ball, champ," Gennedy says, bending over, revealing his butt crack above his track pants. He claims he was a jock in high school and consequently unable to kick the track pants habit. He has a shred of Kleenex stuck to his chin from a shaving cut. Harriet considered telling him about it this morning but decided to see how long it would take to drop off.

Harriet's mother, in short shorts because, according to Gennedy, she's got great legs, fans her face with her hand and says, "Try again, peanut, you can do it." The other parents pretend they don't mind Irwin getting extra turns because he's developmentally challenged. They order their unchallenged kids to be nice to him, and Irwin thinks people *are* nice because everybody acts nice around him. But they never invite him for playdates, so he is in Harriet's face 24/7. *Harry, check on your brother. Harry, help your brother with his buttons. Harry, be a sweetheart and wipe your brother's nose.*

She squeezed toothpaste into his slippers this morning, but he went barefoot.

"Good swing, champ," Gennedy calls.

What Harriet knows about adults is that they say one thing while thinking something completely different. For this reason she doesn't believe a word any of them says. She won't have to deal with them anymore when she gets to Algonquin Park. She has $248 in her bank account but, because she's only eleven, her daily withdrawal limit is $20. Emptying her account requires thirteen withdrawals, and she's worried the ladies at the bank might rat on her because Harriet's mother worked there before Irwin was born. She'd often pick Harriet up from daycare and take her to the bank to finish up paperwork. As the doors were closed to the public at six, Harriet was allowed to sit at a big desk and draw with an assortment of pens. After Irwin was born, Lynne quit working at the bank and lived at the hospital. She came home on weekends to do laundry. Trent, Harriet's father, sat in the dark absently plucking at his eyebrows, until he started going to farmers' markets and met Uma.

Harriet tugs on her mother's arm.

"Bunny, please don't do that, you're not a two-year-old."

"There's a baby stuck in a car."

When Harriet's parents divorced, her mother went back to work at the bank until her breakdown. Harriet loves the bank and plans to work in one when she grows up. She craves the quiet, and the soft sound of bills being counted, the clicking and sliding of metal drawers, the tapping of keyboards, the dependability of safety deposit boxes, the finality of stamp pads. Everybody's polite at the bank and nobody shouts or swears. She tugs on her mother's arm again. "Somebody's forgotten their baby."

"I'm sure that's not true. The baby's probably just napping."

"It's not."

Irwin bats the ball and it bounces feebly to the side. Gennedy applauds. "Way to go, champ! That was awesome!" Other parents jerk into phoney smiles while Irwin chortles, bobbling his big head.

Harriet sewed some rags together to make a voodoo doll of Gennedy that she sticks pins into daily. Last Christmas she asked her mother why he moved into the Shangrila with them. "You wouldn't understand," her mother said, but Harriet kept pestering her for an explanation until Lynne slumped on a kitchen chair, fiddled with a busted angel decoration and said, "Because when he says he won't leave me, he means it." Harriet understood then that she was doomed to cohabit with Gennedy, the shouter and swearer, who calls her uncooperative, and who can't even cook a decent tuna casserole. When her mother's at the hospital, Harriet lives on Lucky Charms.

"The baby *isn't* sleeping," Harriet repeats, more loudly this time even though her mother hates it when she's loud.

"Harry, it's none of your business. I'm sure the parents are here somewhere and keeping an eye on the car."

"They're not."

"What's the problem here?" Gennedy wipes sweat off his nose. The Kleenex is still stuck to his chin.

"No problem." Lynne swigs on a water bottle.

"There *is* a problem," Harriet says. "There's a baby stuck in a car."

Irwin stumbles towards them. Gennedy grabs him and swings him up in the air. "How 'bout some burgers, big guy?"

"Wowee, wowee, burgers with cheeeezze!" Irwin squeals, causing other parents to stare and jerk into phoney smiles again.

"There's a baby stuck in a car!" Harriet shouts.

"Harriet." Her mother grips her arm but Harriet jerks it away and shouts even louder, "There's a baby stuck in a car! Right over there." She pushes through the crowd and points at the SUV.

"Fuck my life," a rumpled man in a Blue Jays cap cries before charging to the SUV. He gropes frantically in his pockets for his remote, repeating, "Jesus fucking Christ" and "Fucking hell." His T-ball player son chases after him, hooting and flapping his arms. Finally the man unlocks the car. "Tessy," he croons in a baby voice as he ducks in and frees the listless infant.

Darcy, on her tummy on the couch, finishes painting her nails black. She spreads her fingers to admire her handiwork. "Swag."

Harriet sits in the armchair Darcy's mother keeps covered in plastic to protect it from cat hair. "Did you shoplift that polish?"

"Damn straight. No way I'm paying eight bucks for this shit." Darcy flashes her fingers at Harriet. "Like it? Black is dope, dude." She sucks the straw on a can of Diet Sprite. "I'm going on a date later. I am single and ready to mingle like a Pringle."

Darcy moved into the Shangrila a month ago. She's twelve and knows how to give blowjobs, suck on bongs and inhale fatties. Harriet has no interest in blowjobs, bongs or fatties, but she feels flattered that an older girl wants to be her friend—although, in her experience, friendships don't last. Eventually the new friend finds out Harriet has no other friends, can't text because she doesn't have a cell, or an iPod, or an allowance, plus a freak for a brother. Darcy's mother rips ladies' hair off with wax. She doesn't shout or swear and lets Darcy eat junk food, go on Facebook, Twitter and Tumblr, and watch whatever she wants on YouTube. Gennedy only permits Harriet an hour of computer time per day, and he's constantly looking over her shoulder to make sure she isn't frittering away her time on useless pop culture. He shouted at her when he caught her watching the Brazilian cab driver singing "Thriller" just like Michael Jackson. Harriet didn't know anything about Michael Jackson, except that he died a long time ago and looked creepy. But Darcy showed her the "Michael Jackson Best Moonwalk Ever!" video, and Harriet was impressed by his footwork. Gennedy caught her practicing moonwalking while watching the cab driver from Brazil. "How is this improving your mind?" he demanded.

According to Harriet's mother, Gennedy is the only criminal lawyer in history that's broke. If he works at all, it's doing legal aid, defending drug addicts, thieves and vandals. Lynne could have done better than Gennedy, Harriet thinks. Men have always ogled her mother. Construction workers and loiterers whistle and snicker "Nice ass," "Come to papa" or "Whatever you need, I'll give it to you, baby." When Harriet was little she'd turn on these pervballs and shout, "Stop looking at my mother! Leave my mother alone!" She doesn't defend her mother from pervballs anymore because she's figured out her mother likes the attention.

Darcy flaps her hands to dry the polish. "The Shangrila is a downer, dude. How can you stand living here? It's, like, seven floors of seniors—a freakin' old people farm. My mom says the carpets haven't been replaced since man wiped his dirty feet on the moon. She says they're moon carpets and she's going to split her head open tripping over a crater." She sniffs the polish in the bottle before screwing the lid back on. "Want to go to Shoppers World?"

"You just said you had a date."

"Before that."

"Not really." Monte, the cat, gnaws on the plastic covering the armchair. Harriet nudges him away so he won't choke.

"Come on, H, let's go to the mall. Don't be such a douchebag."

"Do you even know what a douchebag is?"

"It's a bag, duh, to put douches in."

"Do you know what a douche is?"

Darcy pulls on Monte's tail, causing him to dart across the moon carpet. She hates the cat because she has to feed him and clean his litter box.

"You don't even know what a douche is," Harriet says, "so why are you always calling people douchebags?"

"LOL, so what is it then, Miss Super Brain?"

"It's a nozzle women shove up their snatches to clean them out. The douchebag has water in it, and other stuff. When you squeeze the bag, the stuff squirts up."

"Cool story."

"It's true. My dad's girlfriend squirts herbs up her hoo-ha to make her mucous friendlier to my dad's sperm."

"Yuk!" Darcy flaps her hands again. "Oh my god, would you shut up, that is so gross. That is like . . . nobody does that. That's sick."

"I just think you should know what a douchebag is before you call people douchebags."

"Okay, fine, thank you, Einstein."

Darcy moved into the Shangrila because her parents got divorced. Her mother, Nina, has what Darcy calls mad-nice red hair, the same as Darcy's. "What's so mad-nice about it?" Harriet asked.

"Au naturel, woman. No box job for these dames."

Nina is being fucked over by her ex, Buck. "Buck's fucking me over," she often says. Harriet has adopted this phrase and consoles herself, when alone, by muttering that . . . *fill in the blank* . . . is fucking her over. Lynne doesn't say Trent is fucking her over, although, since he cut back on child support to pay for Uma's expensive infertility treatments, Lynne has been referring to him as the asshole.

Darcy starts painting her toenails black. "I wish my dad was here. He'd take us to the DQ." Harriet likes Buck because he calls her the Lone Ranger and drove them to Canada's Wonderland in his Mack truck, bought them entrance passes and candy floss. But, according to Nina, Buck's a pothead and thinks with his dick. This is why she divorced him. Harriet's not sure why *her* parents divorced other than her dad freaking over Irwin, and meeting Uma and deciding she had a brilliant mind. He wouldn't have met Uma if Irwin hadn't had a seizure at the farmers' market.

"I'm going to post these on my wall," Darcy says, taking photos of her toes with her phone. "Bee tee dubs, you reek. Have you been dumpster diving again?"

"I found some wood, not warped or anything." Harriet paints on primed plywood or stiff cardboard because she can't afford canvas. Tom Thomson sketched on wood. Uma, when she first started dating Trent, took Harriet to a Group of Seven show. The painters' worn wooden paintboxes and palettes fascinated Harriet. Tom Thomson's box was small, just a rectangular box. Frederick Varley's was fancier, with compartments. Even though Tom Thomson died too young to be officially part of the Group of Seven, Harriet thinks of him as her favourite of the group. She was mesmerized by his small, simple box, imagining him hiking through Algonquin with the box stuffed in his backpack, entranced by a piece of sky or water or a tree and sitting down to paint them. She imagined him taking out the box, balancing it on his lap, rubbing his hands together to warm them and resting his wooden sketch board against the box's lid. She longed to watch him pick and mix his colours and make his first stroke, touching his brush to the board. She felt if she could sit quietly behind him, he wouldn't mind. He was so handsome, even though he smoked, and she loved it that he never went to art school. "Harriet," Uma huffed, "we're here to look at the paintings, not the paintboxes." Harriet memorized the colours on Tom's palette, determined to recreate them at home. It seemed as though the lights dimmed when she moved away from the boxes, and the studio paintings held none of the vibrancy of the sketches he made in the wilderness. She couldn't feel Tom in the studio paintings the way she felt him in the paintbox, palette and the sketches. She wanted to understand why he died at Canoe Lake, why he let that happen when he could paint like that. She couldn't imagine letting herself drown if she could paint like that. In her room, she tried mixing the colours but they were lifeless on the board and it occurred to her that maybe Tom Thomson let himself drown because he could no longer paint like that.

Darcy unwraps a piece of Dubble Bubble and pops it into her mouth. "One of these days you're going to get the flesh-eating disease from a dumpster and die."

With Darcy busy with her nails, Harriet takes the opportunity to search for the capybara video on Darcy's laptop. Darcy blows a bubble then pops it. "Let me guess. You're looking at the giant hamster again."

"It's the world's largest rodent."

"Gee wow, who gives a fuck?"

"They don't bark. My mother won't let me have a dog because it barks and my brother's allergic."

"I thought you hated dogs."

"Just Mrs. Schidt's." Mrs. Schidt is eighty-one, lives down the hall in 709 and pays Harriet $14 a week to walk her skinny white dog with yellow eyes. She's been paying Harriet $14 a week for three years, and always has to scrabble around in bowls and drawers for toonies and loonies to make the fourteen.

"I bet giant hamsters shit busloads." Darcy pops another bubble. "You'd spend all day stooping and scooping ginormous hamster turds."

"You can house-train them, and you don't have to walk them." Harriet avoids dog people because all they talk about is dogs, and they act snarky when you don't let their dogs jump on you, lick your hand and sniff your crotch.

The capybara's lady owner holds a green Popsicle and the capybara nibbles it. The lady lifts the Popsicle just out of the capybara's reach. The world's largest rodent taps the lady's shoulder gently with its paw to signal it wants some more. Repeatedly the capybara and the lady exchange pats for nibbles on the green Popsicle. This looks like so much fun to Harriet.

"What kind of name is Harriet anyway? I mean, it's, like, an old lady name."

"It's my father's mother's name. And my grandfather's name is Irwin. My parents named us after them thinking it would make them forgive them for eloping. They're rich, and my parents keep hoping they'll give them money, or drop dead and leave them money. But they'll never die."

"Everybody dies."

"Not mean and cheap people, they live till a hundred. Look at Mrs. Butts." Mrs. Butts lives next door in 712 and sends Harriet on errands for a quarter. She's fat, eighty-two, humpbacked and addicted to painkillers and sleeping pills. When she wants Harriet to do something, she smiles and puts on a nice little old lady voice, but if Harriet brings back Minute Maid orange juice with, instead of without, pulp, or beef-flavoured, instead of chicken-flavoured, Temptations for her cats, Mrs. Butts turns into a mean junkie.

The word among the seniors at the Shangrila is that Harriet will go down to Hung Best Convenience for a quarter. Mr. Shotlander in 506 has her picking up the paper on Fridays for the TV listings, and Harriet suspects she's underpriced herself, but at least the errands get her away from Gennedy.

What she can't understand about her mother shacking up with Gennedy is why Lynne has to be with somebody in the first place. Harriet prefers to be by herself than with anybody. Around people she feels bound in one of Gran's pressure stockings. She also doesn't understand why Gran is nice to her but mean to her mother, even though Lynne cleared the junk out of her house when Gran was evicted for health violations after Grandpa died. Lynne furnished Gran's new place with nice things from IKEA, but still Gran complains about her: *Where'd that know-it-all mother of yours put my muffin tins? Where'd that high-and-mighty mother of yours put my electric frying pan?*

It seems to Harriet people are better off by themselves and not caged together in apartments and houses. When she escapes to the back woods ranger cabin she won't have to talk to anybody. Lost Coin Lake is isolated from road and canoe routes, and the marshy shoreline is unsuitable for swimming. Nobody goes there. This makes it perfect.

Two

In the lobby, the seniors congregate under the broken chandelier. Propped up on the shabby, leatherette furniture they discuss the weather, physical ailments and lottery losses. When they see Harriet, they dig in their pockets and purses for quarters. She carefully writes the individual orders on Post-its and puts them, with the cash, in Ziploc baggies, one per customer. She prints the amount of cash they give her in big numbers on the Post-it, because often they insist they gave her a twenty when they gave her a ten.

Mr. Pungartnik nudges Harriet towards the dusty plastic palm and pushes a twenty at her. "Export A's," he whispers. Mrs. Pungartnik tries to dye Mr. Pungartnik's hair auburn, but it turns out orange.

"I can't buy you cigarettes, Mr. Pungartnik. I'm only eleven."

"I'll give you a buck."

"Mr. Hung won't sell me cigarettes until I'm eighteen."

"Tell him it's for me."

Mrs. Pungartnik dyes her hair too, which also turns out orange. She stomps up and pinches Harriet's arm. "Is my husband trying to get you to buy him cigarettes?" She has a cast in one eye and consequently looks as though she's looking away even when she's staring right at you. "Don't buy him cigarettes." She wags an arthritic finger at Harriet. "No matter what he pays you, understand? That's assisting suicide, you could go to jail for that, you hear me? *Jail.*"

"What do you want me alive for, anyway?" Mr. Pungartnik demands. "My pension?" He holds his fifty-year-old transistor radio against his ear to block out Mrs. Pungartnik.

On the sidewalk outside Hung Best Convenience, Mr. Hung practices his golf swing. He can never take time off to play golf but practices his swing anyway. After they've filled the seniors' orders, Mr. Hung offers Harriet an Orange Crush. He often gives her day-old muffins, dented chocolate bars, crumbling date squares, but an Orange Crush with no best-before date is unprecedented. His generosity baffles Harriet because he doesn't seem to like her, never feigns interest the way other adults do. The Hungs had a dry cleaning business, but the chemicals made his wife sick. Their math-brain son studies engineering and never helps out at the store. Harriet does because she enjoys wrapping Mrs. Hung's baked goods in Saran Wrap and setting out the buckets of flowers. And Mr. Hung always saves the best cardboard and packaging for Harriet's mixed-media projects.

He arches his back with his hands on his hips.

"Is your back hurting?" She pops the tab on the Orange Crush.

Mr. Hung works sixteen-hour days, seven days a week when Mrs. Hung's lung condition makes her too sick to mind the store. Harriet thinks it would be better for his back if he worked at the bank. "They even have stools now," she told him, "for the tellers." Mr. Hung didn't respond, which didn't bother Harriet. Most people talk too much.

She sucks on her straw. "Is it true they put cats in Chinese food?"

"Only at very best restaurants."

"It's just meat, I guess. I mean what's the difference between a cat and a chicken."

"Both good in dumpling."

She's never sure when Mr. Hung's joking. Most people introduce jokes with nervous titters or smiles. Mr. Hung stays poker-faced, which means Harriet isn't obliged to laugh at his jokes, if they are jokes. Gennedy gets cranky when he thinks he's being funny and no one's laughing. *Am I the only one with a sense of humour around here?*

Mr. Hung has never admitted if it bothers him that the seniors joke about how he is hung. Mr. Shotlander frequently croaks, "Hey, Harry, go on down to Hung Best, or is he hung worst, and get me some barbecue chips." Harriet tries to respect the seniors but she won't tolerate them making fun of Mr. Hung. "He'd knock you flat in an IQ test," she told Mr. Shotlander.

"That Chinaman?" Mr. Shotlander was tugging up his polyester trousers. His pants constantly fall down because belts give him tummy trouble. Mr. Chubak wears suspenders and advises Mr. Shotlander to do the same, but he refuses. *What am I, a farmer?*

When Harriet asked Lynne why there are so many old people in the Shangrila, Lynne said, "That's what you get with low-cost housing. Seniors and single mothers."

"You're not a single mother. You live with Gennedy."

"It's not official." Gennedy tapped his index finger against his nose to indicate that their living arrangements were top secret.

"If anybody official-looking asks about Gennedy," Lynne said, "just say he's your uncle."

"So it's okay to live with your brother but not your boyfriend?"

"Bunny, just mind your own business for once, okay? On the books I'm a single mom. That's how we get financial aid."

"Doesn't he pay rent?"

"I help out," Gennedy said. "That's a little different."

"And your asshole father with his sterile so-called intellectual is not making his payments."

Harriet hopes that someone official-looking will demand to inspect the apartment and discover Gennedy, preferably in his tightie whities. She imagines the official-looking person taking him away in cuffs.

Mr. Hung offers her a bag of damaged Doritos then spits.

"Why do you spit?" Harriet tears open the packet.

"Everybody in China spit. Good for lung."

She crunches a Dorito. "Do you know what a capybara is?"

Mr. Hung inspects the bananas, collecting the rotten ones for Mrs. Hung's muffins. "Capybara. Animal?"

"It's the world's largest rodent."

"Good for Chinese food."

Harriet decides he's joking. "I should get back to the seniors."

They complain if she made substitutions. Mr. Chubak, gripping his red suspenders, insists he asked for Alfonso Tango Gelato when he asked for Mango Tango, but Harriet calmly sets them straight, one baggy at a time. In the elevator she counts her quarters. She's made $2.75.

Lynne and Gennedy are having their usual how-can-a-criminal-lawyer-be-broke argument. They're not watching Irwin. He's scraping toothpaste out of his slippers with his fingers and laughing. "Haarreee, look, I got toothpaste in my slippers."

When Irwin was a year old he couldn't sit up or crawl, but he could laugh. Dwarf quintuplets shared the ICU with him during one of his continuous EEG monitoring stays and one of the dwarves could laugh too. Staring at the dwarves, Lynne whispered to Harriet, "Look how lucky we are." Meaning, at least Irwin wasn't a dwarf. But the doctors weren't sure if Irwin would live, or walk, and Harriet didn't see how not being a dwarf when you might not live or walk was something to celebrate. She admired the dwarves. They didn't have stretched heads or unformed ears. They were just tiny, resembling crabby old men, except for the one who laughed all the time. Harriet filled a sketchbook with dwarf drawings, but it was impossible to capture what was really going on beneath the skin of the laughing dwarf, or Irwin; it was as though they were under some kind of spell. She's concluded that the water sloshing around Irwin's brain and bloating his skull insulates him, preventing him from noticing how mean and unfunny people are, enabling him to laugh. He holds up his slipper. "See, toothpaste. How did that get there?"

"Beats me." She closes her door with the *NO ENTRY* sign on it and stands at her easel. Her portrait of Gennedy has been irking her all day. The beak is not right, nor is the left talon. She has painted many portraits of Gennedy, although no one knows they're Gennedy. No one looks at her paintings anymore, anyway. Before Irwin was born, Lynne referred to Harriet as "my little artist" and bought her art supplies for her birthday. Now she buys her girly clothes displaying brand names. Harriet removes any sewn labels with nail scissors, sometimes tearing the fabric. "Most girls would kill for those labels," Lynne cries. "Why do you have to be so difficult?" Difficult is a word she often uses to describe Harriet. "She's a difficult child" or "She can be difficult."

What Lynne doesn't know yet is that Harriet has taken scissors to her *People* and *Us Weekly* magazines, cutting off Jennifer Aniston's head and gluing it on Angelina's neck, and gluing Angelina's head on Brad's body. She put Brad's head on Obama and Obama's head on Lady Gaga, and Lady Gaga's head on George Clooney. She put George's head on Kate Middleton's neck but then couldn't decide what to do with Kate's head. In the "Who wore it best?" feature, Kate was in a gaudy orange dress beside a shot of Madonna in the same gaudy orange dress. Harriet trashed the original Kate head then cut out the one on the gaudy orange dress, as well as Madonna's, and switched them. She performed this surgery in front of Irwin, who she was supposed to be watching in case he seized. Irwin loves it when Harriet cuts up Lynne's magazines: his eyes bulge and he bounces, laughing and pulling on his deformed ears. Actually, they look almost normal now—slightly Spockish—but Lynne asks the barber to go easy around them, allowing hair to cover their tips.

Her mother knocks on her door. "Come have dinner."

It's the proportion of Gennedy's left talon that is particularly bothersome, and the light on his beak. Harriet refers again to the photo of the bald eagle in her *Majestic Birds* book, trying to figure out what she's done wrong. She has always painted with loose, underhand strokes, starting from shadow, which makes rendering talons and beaks challenging. At school, Yannick Picard draws with a tight grip and gets A-pluses from Mrs. Elrind for his artwork because he starts with a recognizable outline of his subject then fills it in. Yannick Picard, in Harriet's opinion, isn't actually seeing what he's drawing, just drawing what he *thinks* he's seeing. In the same way people decide they are looking at a house because they are familiar with things that look more or less like houses. This is what enables people like Yannick Picard and Mrs. Elrind to say that the particular house they are looking at is a big house, an ugly house, an old house, but when Harriet paints and draws she has no conditioned responses to her subjects, and begins with the shapes she *actually sees*. She observes how light interrupts her subject and curves into shadows. Sometimes the shadows look like hamsters, or the African continent, or a sleeping cat without a tail. She stays focused on each shape, one after the other, until the subject emerges from the shadows. It seems to her people rarely understand shadows; they forget that they're part of the light. She has always drawn this way, upsetting Mrs. Elrind who gives her C-minuses.

Gennedy pushes the bowl of carrots at her even though he knows she doesn't like boiled carrots. "So what did you get up to today?" he booms. When Gennedy first started hanging around, Harriet asked her mother why he talked so loud. Her mother said, "It's the litigator in him." Harriet looked up litigator, disappointed to learn it bore no relation to alligator.

All year Harriet endures Gennedy demanding, "How was school today?" And all summer, before Uma's infertility treatments meant there was no money for day camp, Gennedy would ask, "How was camp today?" Harriet hated camp with its organized games and crafts, ADHD boys and disinterested counsellors on cells. She is free this summer to make escape money, and has stopped rolling her coins for deposit but instead changes them into bills she can hide in her art books. She has been staking out the bank, making note of the tellers' shifts, to work out a system for withdrawing the remainder of her balance. The ATMs are in plain sight of the tellers but if Harriet makes $20 withdrawals when ladies who don't know her are working, she should, by October, have enough cash to escape. She is determined to get to Algonquin for the fall colours.

Gennedy raps his knuckles on the table. "Knock, knock, who's there?"

Irwin guffaws, spewing chewed carrot. "*I'm* here."

"Not you, champ. I'm trying to engage your sis in conversation."

"Knock knock, who's there?" Irwin giggles, bouncing.

Lynne wipes up Irwin's spewed carrot with a napkin. "Harry, please answer Gennedy."

"What was his question?"

"He asked what you did today."

"Nothing."

"Nothing?" Gennedy booms. "You were out all day—you must have done something. I hope you weren't garbage-picking. Mr. Shotlander saw you climbing out of the dumpster again yesterday."

"Mr. Shotlander should mind his own business." Harriet will have to blackmail the old buzzard, tell him she won't pick up his TV listings if he keeps informing on her.

"I wish you'd stop doing that, bunny." Lynne cuts up Irwin's fish sticks. "Dumpster diving is dangerous, and what happens if you can't climb out?"

"I don't go in if I can't get out. I use Mr. Hung's milk crates. It's easy."

Gennedy shakes his head and snorts. "All so you can glue garbage on cardboard. Unbelievable."

"Look at your hands, Harriet," her mother says. "I mean, seriously, baby, there's paint and glue under your nails, and in the cracks of your skin. It's not healthy. Lord knows what's in those tubes. Not to mention the glue. Please tell me you're not sniffing the glue."

Gennedy spoons more carrots onto Harriet's plate even though she hasn't eaten any. "Why don't you go outside and play in the park like other kids? It's summer, for chrissake, get out in the sun. When I was a kid, you couldn't pay me to stay indoors."

Gennedy and Lynne have this idea that Harriet will meet nice kids in the park, even though cigarette butts, syringes and used condoms litter the patchy grass.

"Bunny, did you talk to *one* person your age today?"

"Just Darcy." If she admits she was at Darcy's watching YouTube, Gennedy won't let her go there.

"Who's Darcy?" Lynne spends days away from home doing bookkeeping for dubious businesses that pay cash, so she's not up to speed regarding Harriet's social life.

"Darcy," Gennedy announces, "is the new girl on the block. Moved in four floors down. I've chatted with her mother in the laundry room. Apparently Darcy is sexually active."

"So?" Harriet helps herself to another fish stick.

"She's twelve."

"Lots of people are sexually active at twelve," Harriet says.

"Am I really hearing this?" Lynne grips her forehead.

Irwin bounces. "What's sexshally active?"

"Can we take a time out here?" Gennedy booms. He frequently says this, like anybody cares. All Harriet wants are time outs.

They eat listening to Gennedy chomp like a horse and scrape his plate with his fork to clean up every scrap of food so nothing's wasted. Leaving the carrots on her plate, Harriet pushes her chair back. "May I be excused?"

Gennedy's cloven hoof isn't giving off the right feeling either. Harriet will have to let the talon and the hoof dry for a week, paint over them and start again. Or burn the painting, although Mr. Shotlander is bound to rat on her. He caught her burning some mixed media behind the building and immediately reported the incident to Gennedy, who took Harriet's glue gun away.

She tries some blending on his beak to fix the light problem and digs around in her box for Chromatic Black. She's running out of blacks, as well as Burnt and Raw Umber, Burnt Sienna, Indian Red and Raw Sienna. The big tubes cost $10.95 plus tax, and she has to buy bus tickets to get to and from the store. Buying the smaller and therefore cheaper tubes of dark oils ends up costing more as her paintings are primarily dark except for the occasional accent of a burning tongue, a gaping wound or a gouged eyeball.

Her mother pushes open her door, despite the *NO ENTRY* sign, and waves the *People* and *Us Weekly* magazines. "Why do you do this?"

"Why do you read them?"

"Oh, is that what this is about? You disapprove of my reading material? How would you feel if I came into your room and cut up your stuff? It's disrespectful. That's just like your father." She frequently accuses Harriet of being just like her father, and her father frequently accuses Harriet of being just like her mother. They both make it sound as though resembling the person they married, and swore not to leave until death did them part, is the worst thing that could happen to Harriet.

Lynne sees the portrait of Gennedy and covers her mouth with her hand. "Oh my lord, what *is* that?"

"A painting."

"You really should be seeing somebody. I mean, we can't afford it but this . . . this is disturbed. I have to talk to your father. These are *sick* pictures, Harriet. They're nightmares. Why do you paint nightmares? Is there nothing in your life that makes you happy?"

Harriet starts cleaning the brushes she picked up at the open studio. Rich kids too lazy to clean brushes leave them behind. Once a month Harriet pretends to look for her "big sister" at U of T and sneaks into the studio to collect discarded brushes. Even if they're dried solid, soaking them overnight in Varsol softens them up.

"Seriously, bunny, answer me, does nothing make you happy? What would make you happy?"

She can't say a dead brother, or life the way it was before Irwin was born, when she had a father who played Scrabble with her and a mother who was always there, life before Trent discovered farmers' markets and Uma's brilliant mind, and before Lynne would settle for a loser because, when he says he won't leave her, he means it.

Lynne tucks Harriet's hair behind her ears. "You've become so sullen. A dark little cloud. What's the matter, baby? Where's my bright little girl? When did you last wash your hair? It's getting darker, isn't it? You'll end up a brunette like me. Do you want me to wash your hair?"

Harriet longs to feel her mother's fingers massaging shampoo into her scalp, and the caress of warm water as it trickles from her head into the sink.

"Babe?" Gennedy calls.

"What is it?"

"He's having one."

"How long?" And she's gone. The two of them will turn Irwin onto his side to prevent him from inhaling mucous. They'll pull down his pants and inject Diastat up his rectum, and pad the area around his head with cushions to avoid head banging. They'll hover anxiously, waiting to see if the drug will work or if he'll start to turn blue or have difficulty breathing. Lynne will log the exact start time of the seizure in her notebook. If the rigidity, tremors, twitching, nystagmus and repetitive movements don't begin to abate in five minutes, they will call an ambulance and he will be rushed to the hospital for the loading of medications to stop the seizure. Always there is the fear that this is the Big One, and always Harriet hopes that it is.

Three

The only upside to Irwin's visits to the emergency ward is Lynne gives Harriet money for a treat at the hospital's Second Cup. Harriet usually orders a large Italian strawberry soda and a slice of red velvet cake, even though she's not supposed to eat red dye because it makes her hyper. She prefers having a table to herself but, if it's crowded, people sit at her table without asking. A woman with a pile of golden hair that looks too young for her face grabs a chair. "Is this in use?"

Harriet shakes her head. The woman smells of cigarettes and talks loudly on her cell about somebody dying. Harriet searches for signs of grieving in the woman because Harriet intends to appear grief-stricken when Lynne rushes through the elevator doors to tell her it was the Big One.

But it is Gennedy who tracks her down. "You okay?"

"Fine."

"They're trying a new cocktail on him."

They're always trying new cocktails on Irwin, and his liver doesn't like it. Sometimes he pukes his guts out and turns yellow.

Gennedy looks at his watch. "They're going to keep him here for a while.

Your mom's staying with him in case he comes to and has a meltdown." Irwin has meltdowns if Lynne isn't directly in front of him. Gennedy has to distract him when Lynne sneaks out to do bookkeeping for cash. If Irwin sees her leave, he gets hysterical, which can cause a seizure.

Her mother staying at the hospital with Irwin means Harriet will have to return to the apartment with Gennedy.

"I want to stay with my dad," she says.

"Your mum called him. He and Uma are in the middle of a cycle right now."

A cycle means that Trent and Uma rush to the infertility clinic every morning where doctors inject Uma with fertility drugs and look up her hoo-ha to see if she's ovulating. If she's ovulating, Trent jacks off into a specimen container so they can squirt his sperm up her snatch. Uma explained all of this in too much detail to Harriet when she explained about douchebags.

All Harriet wants is to be with her mother. "Can I go see Irwin?"

"You know how crazy it is in ICU." Gennedy checks his phone. "We'll come back tomorrow."

"I want to stay with Gran."

"You know your mom doesn't want you staying with Gran."

"Let me phone my mom." Harriet reaches for Gennedy's cell, knowing he won't let her have it.

"She's stressed to the max right now, Harriet. Anyway, her phone's turned off."

"No it isn't. Then *you* wouldn't be able to call her." Harriet darts out of the Second Cup and into the lobby to a pay phone. She takes two quarters from her jeans and dials her mother's cell. Lynne picks up right away.

"Mummy, please don't make me go home with Gennedy."

"Oh for god's sake, Harriet, do you have to do this now?"

"Please can I go to Gran's? She hasn't burned any pans since she figured out how to use the timer. And anyway, I know how to use the fire extinguisher. I read the instructions. I even practised taking it off the wall with Gran."

When Irwin was three he put plastic dinosaurs in Gran's microwave. Harriet smelled the smoke and called 911. Gran, who'd lost her sense of smell and wasn't wearing her hearing aids, didn't notice anything until the fire trucks showed up. Ever since, Lynne has forbidden overnight stays.

"Please, Mummy, I don't want to stay with Gennedy. It's summer. Can't I have a holiday? Gran and I can make Rice Krispie squares and stuff. I'll keep an eye on the stove, I promise. And I'll help her clean." Lynne despairs over her mother's grime, filth that Gran can no longer see. When she could see, she wasn't much of a cleaner anyway, unlike Lynne who wipes all surfaces regularly with bacteria-killing cleansers.

"Bunny, I'm so worn out, I don't have the energy to fight you on this. I mean, I'm so scared. Irwin's really sick, and I'm . . . I'm having trouble thinking straight right now."

"I understand that, and I won't be any trouble. If I stay at Gran's, Gennedy can help you think straight at the hospital because he won't have to look after me." This is a brilliant ploy, Harriet realizes, because her mother loves boohooing on Gennedy's shoulder.

"Okay," Lynne says.

"Really?"

"Don't let me think about it too long. Where's Gennedy?"

He's right behind Harriet, spying as usual. She hands him the phone. He listens and says "okay" several times and "I love you, babe." The *babe* word sickens Harriet. Her mother is a grown woman.

He hangs up. "You win. Let's go."

They have a key to Gran's apartment because she can't hear the buzzer. Dirty plates, cups and Kleenexes litter the place as usual. Coffee stains dot the IKEA sofa. Harriet warned Lynne not to buy light-coloured furniture, but it was the best sofa for the price and only came in parchment white.

"Gran?" Harriet says loudly. Gran not answering the phone didn't concern her because, if she's not right beside it, she can't hear it. But finding the galley kitchen and small living/dining area empty sends jolts of anxiety through Harriet. Mr. Kotaridis in 114 died in his bathroom. "Just up and died taking a shave," Mr. Shotlander told everyone a thousand times while tugging up his polyester trousers. "At least he wasn't taking a shit, god rest his soul."

"Gran?" Harriet picks up Gran's container of heart pills that always seems to have the same amount of pills in them.

"I'll check the bedroom," Gennedy says.

"Can you check the bathroom first?"

"I'll check the bedroom and the bathroom. She's probably gone out."

Gran rarely stays out past nine because she falls asleep. She has trouble sleeping in her bed but can fall asleep in a restaurant or on the bus. Usually, by ten, she's on her sofa, falling asleep in front of the television with the volume set so high the neighbours complain.

"Gran!" Harriet shouts.

"Settle down," Gennedy says, returning from the bedroom. "We'll wait a bit."

"I'm not going back with you. I can wait here by myself."

"Is that so? And what am I supposed to tell your mother?"

"Don't tell her anything."

"You know I can't do that."

"Yes you can. She doesn't care. All she cares about is Irwin."

"I can't believe you said that. That is so infantile, Harriet. I wouldn't have expected that from you."

"Expect this," Harriet says, flipping him the finger. Darcy flips everybody the finger, repeating the verb in their last sentence and adding *this* as in *eat this*.

"All right, that's it." He moves towards her but she scoots around the sofa, forcing him to jog after her, hitching up his track pants. They run in circles, and Gennedy starts shouting at her. "You ungrateful, selfish little bitch, your brother's fighting for his life and all you can think about is yourself!"

"Go back to the hospital," Harriet screams. "I don't need you here! Leave me *alone!*"

"Hush," Gran says, stepping in from the balcony, "you'll scare the parrot."

Both Gennedy and Harriet stop. "What parrot?" Harriet asks.

"Come see. He likes bananas."

On the balcony, a large bird perches on the railing. Harriet can't make out its colours in the dark. "Are you sure it's a parrot?"

"He sings 'Tutti Frutti.'" Gran starts to sing, "A-wop-bop-a-loo-mop alop bam boom."

"Mads," Gennedy booms. Gran's name is Madeline but everyone calls her Mads. "Mads, can I speak with you privately for a moment?"

Gran winks at Harriet. "Keep an eye on Polly."

How wonderful, Harriet thinks, to have a live tropical bird to paint. She can't wait to see it in daylight. She hears Gennedy using the patronizing tone he saves for the elderly. No doubt he is writing a list for Gran about what's required re: Harriet—no food products containing red dye, make sure she brushes and flosses, changes her underwear, don't leave her unsupervised around the stove. Harriet has figured out that Gennedy writes lists to feel empowered. List in hand, he appears to be a man of purpose—and not the only criminal lawyer in history that's broke.

He pokes his head out the balcony door. "It's all set. I'll call you tomorrow."

Don't bother, Harriet wants to say but instead attempts to appear contrite so he'll buzz off. After Gran sees Gennedy out, she steps back onto the balcony. "Hokum bokum, that no-goodnik gets his knickers in a knot."

"How long has the parrot been here?" Harriet asks.

"A couple of hours." Gran fluffs her white hair. "I kept waiting for him to fly away, but then I thought, maybe he's hungry. That's when I thought of bananas, him being a jungle bird."

"How do you know it's a he?"

"The girls don't get to be that colourful."

"He might be older than you, you know. Parrots can live past a hundred."

"Is that so? Well, at last my prince has come. He poops on the balcony below. Don't know how those grumblers feel about it. Smokers anyway, serves them right." Gran abhors smokers because Grandpa was one and died on her. Not that she liked him much, but her survivor pension is a quarter of what she got when he was alive.

"How's that high-and-mighty mother of yours?"

"She's worried this is the Big One."

"What else is new? Has she started smoking again?"

"Probably. When Gennedy's there she'll take smoke breaks. Have you given the parrot any water?"

"What's that?" Gran cups her hand around her good ear.

"Water," Harriet says loudly. "We should give the parrot water." She pours water into a bowl and carefully sets it on the patio table close to the parrot. "I wonder if he's lost, or if he just ran away."

"Maybe he got sick of staring at the same old faces and places." Mads regularly complains about this.

"Maybe he was abused and that's why he ran away."

"Doesn't look abused to me."

Harriet steps back slowly, not wanting to scare the parrot. "Lots of abused people don't look abused. Mindy in 408 was beat up by her husband and nobody knew about it until the police came."

Mads peers at the parrot. "You got bruises under those feathers, mister?"

"They like eye contact."

"Well, he's been giving me the eye since he got here. Sing 'Tutti Frutti' again," she tells it then starts singing "Tutti Frutti" and wiggling her hips.

The parrot only stares at her.

"Maybe he's tired," Harriet says.

"What about you? You want me to fry us up some hambangers?"

"We ate already."

"Butterscotch ripple?"

"Yes please."

Jed, who lives down the hall, drops by to tell them Floyd from the Legion died. "The diabetes got him finally." Whenever an acquaintance of Jed's dies, he seems pleased with himself, as though out-living the victim is an accomplishment. Mads puts up with him because she needs a dance partner, but she insists they're just friends, even though she calls him Jedi. "Old Jedi doesn't make my heart go pow," she told Harriet.

"Who makes your heart go pow?"

Gran squinted as though trying to read a menu.

"Did Grandpa make your heart go pow?"

"Uckety puckety, no, no, no."

"Then why did you marry him?"

"He asked me to. You had to get married in those days."

"Why?"

"Everybody was doing it."

None of this made any sense to Harriet. It makes even less sense that Gran puts up with Jed just because she needs a dance partner. Harriet suspects Gran is still waiting for a man to make her heart go pow because, when they go out for doughnuts, Gran wears high heels even though she has to wear a back brace, and chats up the old men sitting at the counter doing crosswords to determine if they are "eligibles." She says she wants a widower with money in the bank.

Jed taps Harriet's shoulder. "So what's the plan, Harry-o?"

"No plan."

"Oooh la la, you got to have a plan, otherwise things can't go wrong."

"I want to paint the parrot, if he's still here."

"Why wouldn't he be here?" Gran asks. "He's got crackers, water, a banana."

"He might fly home."

"Pish tah."

After Jed leaves, they watch *Dancing with the Stars*. Mads' eyelids droop and suddenly Harriet doesn't want to be alone. She checks the balcony to make sure the parrot's still there, then plops heavily on the sofa to alert Gran, but the old lady is sinking into sleep.

"Gran?" Harriet says loudly. "Gran?"

"What is it? How'd *you* get here? Oh for goodness' sake, of course you're here. Want me to fry us up some hambangers?"

"No, I just wanted to talk."

"Fire away."

Harriet doesn't know what to talk about. She turns a sofa cushion over in her hands, trying to think of something to say before Gran falls asleep again. "Do you love my mother?"

Gran purses her lips as though pondering a very difficult question. "Who's asking?"

"I'm just curious because I'm not sure she loves me."

"Of course she does."

"Sometimes it seems like she loves Irwin more."

Gran kicks off her pumps. "Well, you see, that's why having two is a gamble because there's always a chance you might like one better than the other."

"Is that why you just had Mum?"

"The truth is your grandpa wasn't one for nookie, and when he did get down to it, he was firing blanks most of the time. I didn't have your mama till I was forty-four. Not that I minded. I wasn't much for mothering. Your great-grandma had eight and it killed her."

"Did your mother like your brothers and sisters better than you?"

"You betcha." Gran massages her bunions.

"Did she like you at all?"

"Not one bit. And you know what? I've out-lived every one of those bloodsuckers."

"Why didn't she like you?"

Gran purses her lips again. "Didn't do what I was told."

"*I* do what I'm told, most of the time. And Mum still doesn't like me. She's always having rests when I'm around. I tire her out just by existing."

"Well, mugsy, it's her loss."

The most difficult question—the question Harriet most wants to ask—teeters on her tongue. She tugs on the sofa cushion's buttons. "Do *you* think she loves Irwin more than me?"

"I think she loves you different. There's no law saying everybody has to love everybody the same."

"I think if Irwin dies, she'll want to die."

"For a while, mugsy, but then she'll move on. She'll have to."

"There's no law saying she has to."

"No, but folks do. They take a good long look at death, get real personal with it then decide they've had enough. It wears you out."

"A-wop-bop-a-loo-mop alop bam boom," the parrot shrieks.

After Gran's gone to bed, Harriet lies stiffly on the IKEA sofa, imagining what's happening to Irwin. He'll be hooked up to an IV. They'll have put electrodes on his head to monitor his convulsions and tubes up his nose and penis. They'll monitor his breathing and put a clip on his finger to check his blood pressure. His eyeballs will roll around under his lids, and he'll chew even though he isn't eating. Sometimes he'll become rigid, other times he'll have tremors or twitching.

It would be so great if he died.

Harriet's heart seems to be beating higher than normal, as though it's trying to force its way up her throat and out her mouth. Ever since Gran's bypass operation, Harriet's had heart trouble, particularly when she's trying to sleep. She has to calm her heart, talk to it like one of the seniors, or it will leap out of her. Sometimes she feels it stop and has to jump around to get it moving again. She doesn't trust her heart.

She must make sure Gran takes her pills. She'll sneak them into food like they do with Irwin, or Mrs. Schidt's dog. Mrs. Schidt stuffs Coco's antidepressants into cheese and he gobbles them up. Who's going to walk Coco while Harriet's at Gran's? Darcy saw an ad for dog walking, $16 per hour for a group walk, $22 for a private walk. Darcy says Harriet is being hosed by Mrs. Schidt and should demand a raise. Maybe if Mrs. Schidt is forced to hire an expensive dog walker, Harriet will be in a good negotiating position when she gets back.

Her heart stops again and she hops around, worried she is being punished for wanting her brother dead.

"A little song, a little dance, a little seltzer down the pants," the parrot shrieks.

Four

In the morning the parrot is gone and Harriet no longer feels constricted by a pressure stocking, but that she is loosening in all directions. Her hands flop on her wrists and her feet dangle from her ankles. She spills milk and drops the Cap'n Crunch. Not only has the parrot fled, but Lynne hasn't called. Her mother has forgotten about her again.

Gran, in her turquoise sequinned peaked cap, announces that Jedi is driving them to the Scarborough Town Centre. "He's going to treat us to lunch in that nice food court. You can get anything you want there— Chinese, pizza, burgers, you name it."

Jed drives in both lanes at the same time. Drivers honk but he doesn't seem to notice. He's more concerned about whether or not he has the necessary documents to get his passport renewed. His daughter, in Boston, has been trying to get him to visit for two years. Harriet stares at the strands of white hair stretched across his pate, trying to figure out why his daughter wants him to visit. In Harriet's experience most family members don't like each other, although they pretend they do. The only family members she's met who truly like each other are Filipino and always cramming into Mr. Rivera's in 313. Even after Mrs. Rivera died, the Riveras' children and grandchildren, nieces and nephews continued to crowd around the karaoke machine singing golden oldies. Mr. Rivera invites Harriet to sing with them when she buys him bananas from Mr. Hung's, but she's too shy, despite the Riveras' encouragement. Mr. Rivera says one day Harriet will sing "My Way" with him.

The light turns green, but Jed doesn't notice. "My daughter's lonely south of the border. Too many Yanks." The car behind them honks.

Gran pulls the visor down to check her lipstick in the mirror. "Why'd she move there then?"

"Opportunity."

"What's she do?" Harriet asks.

"She's a doctor."

Gran flips the visor back up. "What's stopping her being a doctor here?"

"She makes more money in the U.S."

"Money isn't everything," Gran says. This is a lie, considering Mads' hunt for a widower with money in the bank.

"Why doesn't your daughter visit you here?" Harriet asks.

"Says she's too busy."

Harriet's father said he was too busy to take her to the Abstract Impressionist show at the AGO. Harriet figured out this was another adult lie. She suspects the doctor isn't too busy either; she just doesn't want to see her father. That Jedi can't figure this out makes Harriet envy him.

He drops them at the entrance to Sears before heading for the passport office. When Harriet pleads with the two of them to arrange a meeting time and place, Gran says, "Pish posh, don't be such a ninny. Jedi'll find us. Let's have some fun." Harriet never has fun in the Scarborough Town Centre. She constantly gets lost and has to retrace her steps to find her bearings. Mads is no help because she wanders wherever she pleases, heedless of who is tagging along behind her. Harriet must keep a constant eye on her, a challenging task because Gran has shrunk due to osteoporosis and easily disappears behind displays.

"Let's get us some perfume samples," Mads says, charging into Cosmetics.

The smell of cologne gives Harriet a headache but she enjoys looking at the bottles and the light shining through their exotic contents. While Gran spritzes perfume behind her ears and on her wrists, Harriet fondles the bottles, soothed by their smooth, rounded surfaces in hues of gold, yellow, bronze and apricot. Her favourite is a combination of smooth and textured glass, draping from a cylindrical cap like a lady's evening gown. "Isn't this beautiful?" she asks before turning to where her grandmother was seconds ago. "Gran?" Mads is nowhere in sight and Harriet feels herself coming undone again. "Gran!" she calls, causing the heavily made-up women behind the cosmetic counters to stare at her.

"Have you seen an old lady in a turquoise hat?" Harriet asks.

The heavily made-up women shake their heads. "Try paging her from Customer Service," one of them says. "It's on the third floor."

Leaving the first floor would mean losing any chance of finding Gran. Harriet scours the main floor behind stacks of shoes, shelves of handbags, scarves and hats. Her heart pushes at her throat, and she keeps swallowing to force it back down. Periodically she thumps her collarbone to restart it. She pauses in Jewellery because she can see above the display cases. A saleswoman with an angular haircut watches her. "Can I help you?"

"I'm just waiting for someone."

"Don't lean on the display cases."

"Sorry."

"Are you lost?"

"No."

"If you're lost, you should go to Customer Service on the third floor."

Harriet checks her watch every few minutes to make it appear as though she is waiting for someone. If Gran's gone to Dollarama to buy lilac-scented soap, Harriet will never catch up with her. Dollarama is on another tentacle, near the Walmart. Maybe Gran's gone into the Walmart to look for shoes.

After fifteen minutes in Jewellery, Harriet takes the escalator to Customer Service where she waits at the counter until an ample woman, wearing clothes that look too small for her, asks if she can help her.

"I've lost my grandmother. Can you page her, please?"

"Name?"

"Madeleine Stott."

"*Your* name?"

"Harriet Baggs."

"Relation?"

"She's my grandmother." Harriet said this already. "Please tell Madeline Stott that her granddaughter is waiting for her at Customer Service on the third floor."

The woman picks up the phone and says, "Madeline Stott, please go to Customer Service. Your granddaughter's looking for you."

"Please tell her it's on the third floor."

"On the third floor."

"Can you say the whole thing again a little louder? She doesn't hear very well."

The buttons on the woman's too-small blouse strain as she sighs and says, louder, "Madeline Stott, please go to Customer Service on the third floor."

"Your granddaughter, Harriet, is looking for you," Harriet prompts.

"Your granddaughter, Harriet, is looking for you." She slams the receiver down. "Okay, you can sit over there while you wait." She points to a row of metal chairs.

"Thank you." Harriet takes a seat beside a mother and child. The mother chews her chipped nail polish, reading the same issue of *People* that Harriet cut up for Lynne. Dressed in pink, the little girl repeatedly pushes a picture book at her mother and asks her to read it. The mother, without putting down the magazine, says, "You can't just read about fairies and princesses all the time, Jessica," then takes a call on her cell.

The little girl in pink gnaws a corner of her book about fairies and princesses while staring at Harriet. Every second that Harriet waits, she feels Gran orbiting farther away from her.

The little girl steps cautiously nearer. "Do you have a glass eye?"

"No."

"My brother has a glass eye and my mom has to put moisture in it at night so it doesn't dry up. When he blinks it's like a windshield wiper."

The mother grabs the girl's arm and yanks her back to her seat while yelling into her cell. "What did I just say? Use the fucking gift certificate and forget the coupon."

Harriet takes the escalator to the main floor, exits the Sears and looks for arrows pointing to Walmart. Shoppers bump her with bags and strollers. A man in a bear suit waves at her. Harriet still can't see a sign for Walmart but doesn't want to attract attention by asking for directions. As she walks she peers in store windows, scouting for the turquoise hat. Outside a camera store, a crowd watches a demo for a video camera. Trent bought a video camera years ago to record Irwin's first arrival home from the hospital. Everybody else had video cameras, so Harriet thought her dad buying a video camera meant her family would start being like everybody else's. When Irwin had to keep returning to the hospital, Trent put the video camera in his closet.

Finally she spots a sign pointing to Walmart and picks up her pace, pushing past an old lady using a walker who demands, "What's the hurry?" A well-fed family munching on waffle cones lingers in Harriet's path, but they don't look happy. She doesn't know if anybody really *is* happy because people lie. She has seen her mother, barely conscious due to lack of sleep and food, assure people she's "fine." Gennedy tells people things are "tootin'." Her father tells Harriet he loves her even though he won't let her stay with him because he and Uma are in the middle of a cycle. Harriet's not sure why he doesn't like her anymore, whether it's her fault, Uma's or the bicycle's. Maybe all three but certainly the new bike has something to do with it, consuming her father's time as he participates in bike meets with other forty-something men in bicycle shorts, tight nylon T-shirts and helmets that hide their thinning hair.

Last year when Harriet asked if she could have a new bike for her birthday, Trent said there was nothing wrong with her old one, that they should wait for her to grow a little more before they replaced it. Already he'd adjusted the seat as high as it would go, forcing Harriet to hunch over the handlebars. Then he went and bought himself a new bike even though he'd stopped growing and already had a perfectly good bike.

A whiskered old man in a Walmart smock grabs her arm. "Where are you off to, little miss?"

"I'm getting my grandmother. She's buying shoes."

"You're going the wrong way, munchkin." He points in the opposite direction.

"Thank you."

She checks both aisles of the ladies' shoes section but does not see Mads. Her loose joints wobble as she sits on a bench. "Imagine" plays on the sound system and resignation seeps into Harriet. She is lost, Gran is lost. She feels like she did when she fell from the tree, calm, even though she knew she was dying. She travelled backwards in time as she lay staring up at the rustling leaves, to before Irwin was born, when her parents took her to Niagara Falls to stay at the Americana. Under the tree, she felt no pain—it was as though she were floating in the pool at the Americana, with her arms hooked around a noodle, looking up at the cloudless sky and thinking how wonderful everything was because, after swimming, the three of them would walk down Lundy's Lane and order club sandwiches with fries. She could have chocolate fudge cake, ice cream, whatever she wanted. It was heaven as she lay unmoving under the tree, feeling as though she were floating in the Americana's pool, and she didn't fear death until pain knifed up her leg and into her back, pain so severe she must have started screaming because her father was suddenly above her, looking as though he didn't know what to do. This scared Harriet because he usually knew what to do.

A mother on a smartphone sits her little boy on the bench beside Harriet and pushes his feet into running shoes. "How do those feel?" she asks. The boy stays focused on his Game Boy and the mother says to the phone, "It had *philosophy*. That's what I loved about it. I mean, they showed shoes being made by *children* in Vietnam." She finishes tying up his shoes. "Walk around, Cameron. See how they feel." The boy hops off the bench and trots up and down the aisle, still riveted to his Game Boy.

"How do they feel, Cammy?"

The little boy shrugs.

"Let me feel your toe."

Harriet is no longer floating at the Americana but trying to remember the last time her mother felt her toe. Gennedy takes her shoe shopping and always checks prices before she can try anything on.

After she fell from the tree, her mother looked at her as lovingly as she looked at Irwin. While they waited in Emerg, the pain subsided but Harriet pretended it still hurt. Her mother stroked her hair and rubbed her back, calling her "my precious angel." She didn't once mention Irwin. Until X-rays revealed nothing was broken.

People of all nationalities and sizes crowd the passport office. An elderly man in a uniform asks Harriet if she's looking for someone.

"An old man," she says. "He came to get his passport renewed. He was with my grandmother and now I can't find her so I'm trying to find him."

The elderly man scans the waiting area, scratching behind his ears. He looks Filipino, which reassures Harriet because Filipinos don't make her feel stupid. Mr. Rivera tells his relatives that Harriet is very smart and an artist. He pestered her to show him her paintings until, finally, she brought down a portrait of Gennedy. Mr. Rivera raised his eyebrows and said, "*Ganun!*" and "*Galing!*" which are words that mean *awesome* in Tagalog.

"Can you tell me his name?" the man in the uniform asks.

"Jed. I don't know his last name. He's friends with my grandmother." Harriet can see that Jed is not sitting in the waiting area but hopes that the man in uniform will be able to page him in a corridor, or maybe even the toilet. Jed makes frequent toilet stops.

"Not to worry," the Filipino says. "You sit here and rest." He points to his chair and walks to a counter to speak with a Chinese lady, who scrutinizes Harriet then nods and picks up a phone. "Is there a Jed waiting here, please?" she inquires. "Would *Jed* please come to reception immediately, please?" The Chinese lady and the Filipino scan the waiting area. She repeats the message, and they glance around again before looking at each other, then at Harriet. She knows they are about to report her to someone who will call her mother. This will get her and Gran into even more trouble. She bolts for the elevators.

Back in the concourse of the Scarborough Town Centre, she tries to blend with the moviegoers. They all belong to somebody. They separate to buy popcorn, or use the washrooms, but are soon drawn together again like magnets.

She hasn't been to a movie since Irwin seized at *Harry Potter and the Half-Blood Prince*. They had to stop the movie. The adults in the audience tried to look as though they felt sorry for Irwin, but the kids booed, called him Frankenstein and stamped their feet. Harriet shouted "Shut up!" at them until Lynne grabbed her arm and said, "Just ignore them." Lynne always advises Harriet to just ignore cruel, rude and ignorant people, as though they can be ignored.

She counts her quarters; not enough for a drink, but at least the theatre lobby is air-conditioned.

While Irwin was convulsing in the aisle, with Lynne and Gennedy on their knees beside him, a blubbery woman, clutching popcorn, wouldn't stop staring. Harriet barked at her.

"Please don't bark, Harriet," her mother said. "Just ignore her."

Harriet curled her hand under her chin and flicked it at the blubbery woman the way Mr. Tumicelli in 305 taught her. "Oh for Pete's sake," the woman said.

"Him too." Harriet flicked her hand again and waved her arms to push back the gawkers. "We need air here, move back." An usher who looked like a boy but was wearing aqua, sparkly nail polish joined her in the arm waving. His nails glinted and Harriet decided to match their colour later. It was while she was mixing the aqua that it occurred to her that during seizures the real Irwin was trying to free himself of Irwin's body. The real Irwin didn't want to stay cooped up inside a stick body with a ballooning head. If they let Irwin die, the real Irwin would be free to join other spirits in the transmigration of souls, just like Mr. Bhanmattie in 410 said. Mr. Bhanmattie is from India and meditated with the Beatles. "The soul, after death," he explained, "can be reborn in the body of another human, an animal or some other creature, once, repeatedly or infinitely, according to the quality of the life one has lived. It is a give-me-another-chance doctrine." Irwin's soul is probably tired of Irwin's body and wants another chance in a bird or a deep-sea creature.

When Lynne came home from the hospital on weekends to do laundry, she recounted other patients' tragedies. The parents of a hydrocephalic baby girl with a malignant brain tumour wouldn't let her die. They agreed to every medical intervention, making the baby's last days torment. When her heart repeatedly failed and the medical team asked the parents if they should keep trying to resuscitate her, the parents said yes. The baby's ribs were broken by the hand compressions, and she was bloated unrecognizably from steroids. When her kidneys stopped functioning, she needed an immediate surgical intervention to connect her to a dialysis machine. The mother was screaming, "My baby! My baby!" Even after the baby's heart stopped beating for twelve minutes, the parents wanted them to keep compressing her chest. "They should have let her go," Lynne said. Like it was that easy, like she could ever let Irwin go. Harriet told her father this story, hoping to remind him how lucky he was to have a healthy daughter. "Why does your mother tell you stories like that? It's morbid."

"She says it gives us perspective on Irwin's condition."

Trent, wrench in hand, was leaning over his new bike, adjusting gears. "Well, I'm going to have to talk to her about that." He always says he's going to talk to Lynne about things. He never does.

"She wants us all on donor lists."

"She what?"

"She's seen so many sick kids. She thinks everybody should be on donor lists." Harriet likes the idea of her organs continuing on without her body to save a life. She asked Mr. Bhanmattie if being on a donor list would ruin her chances of becoming an albatross in her next incarnation, and he told her it would not affect her soul's transmigration.

All the movies have started. She is the only customer in the lobby. An usher with one side of his head shaved asks her who she's waiting for.

"My mom. She said she'd pick me up here."

"You mean, like, after the movie? Why aren't you watching a movie?"

"I'm not feeling well. I thought the movie might make me dizzy. The 3D and everything. I'm just going to wait out here for a bit."

"Which movie? Can I see your ticket?"

Harriet feels around in her pockets. "That's weird. I had it a minute ago."

"You can't loiter here, miss."

"I'm not loitering."

"I have to follow procedure. If you're loitering, I have to call security."

"Maybe I dropped it in the washroom. I'll go look."

She practises her moonwalk in the washroom mirror, and attempts some Michael Jackson moves from "Speed Demon" that she saw Mr. Rivera's family imitating on their Nintendo Wii console. She crouches down then jumps up and scampers across the tiled floor with an elbow crooked at shoulder height and the other arm stretched behind her. She tries Michael Jackson's side step with the knee bounce, and jerks up her elbows in a chicken dance, pulling her knees together and swinging them back out again.

The usher knocks on the washroom door. "If you don't come out, miss, I'll have to call security. I have to follow procedure."

Five

She phones her father, knowing his cell is probably turned off. He works in IT and clients constantly call him, disrupting his concentration. He used to work for the same bank as her mother but he quit "that corporate vulture." Now he has no health insurance and many different clients who take months to pay him. He constantly tells Lynne he's waiting for a cheque.

Uma answers the home phone because she never goes out but sits with her laptop on beds, couches, stairs and her yoga mat, working on her thesis. Sitting at desks hurts her back but all other surfaces seem to be fine for thesis writing.

"Is my dad there?"

"He's biking."

"Do you know when he'll be back?"

"I have no idea. Is everything all right, Harriet? Has something happened to Irwin? Lynne told us he's back in the hospital."

"It's not Irwin. I'm at the Scarborough Town Centre. I was hoping my dad could pick me up."

"We already told Lynne we're mid-cycle. It's not a good time for a visit."

"I realize that. The thing is, I came here with Gran and I lost her and now I don't have enough money to get back."

"What do you mean you 'lost' her?"

"She was looking at perfumes and then she was gone."

"She left you *alone* at the Scarborough Town Centre?"

"Not on purpose."

Uma doesn't speak but Harriet knows she disapproves of Lynne and Gran. She has heard her refer to them as white trash. "Where did Dad go biking?"

"Stouffville. He'll be gone for hours. I really don't need this right now. Did you call Gennedy?"

"He's not answering." This is a lie. She would rather die than call him.

"What about your mother?"

"She's busy with Irwin. Did my dad take the car?"

"Why would he take the car if he's on his bike? What are you angling for, Harriet?'

"I was wondering if *you* could pick us up."

"You know he doesn't like me driving the Rover."

The Range Rover was built in England and has a manual transmission. Trent doesn't like Uma driving it because she burns the clutch. He has pampered and protected the Rover for years, although one of Irwin's puke stains could not be removed from the leather upholstery.

"You *can* drive it though, can't you?" Harriet asks. "It's getting late and I don't have any money." She pictures Uma clenching her jaw, considering Trent's reaction when he finds out she left his daughter in a mall, and checking a website on her laptop for more information. Uma never makes decisions without first checking her laptop.

"Where are you exactly in the centre?"

Harriet knows she's searching Google Maps. "I'll wait outside the theatre."

"Wait inside the lobby."

"I can't wait inside. The security guard thinks I'm loitering."

"Is he there? Let me talk to him."

Uma believes in conflict resolution. For this reason Harriet never reveals any of the unresolvable conflicts in her life. "I'm in the mall, at a pay phone. I'll wait for you inside the doors to the food court."

"Not inside the doors, Harriet. It's not safe. Sit in the food court near the door. I'll find you."

"What about Gran?"

"What about her?"

"We have to find her."

"Let's worry about you for now. Don't go anywhere or talk to anybody. Wait for me. I don't know how long I'll be. It depends on traffic."

"Okay. Thank you." There is no way Harriet is leaving the mall without Gran. She might have upped and died like Mr. Kotaridis. Harriet doesn't mention this to Uma because she suspects she wouldn't mind if Mads upped and died.

It makes no sense that they want a baby. Babies consume every hour of every day. Uma would have to abandon her laptop, and Trent his new bike. Uma has explained to Harriet that eggs on ovaries after thirty-five start to rot. At thirty-nine, Uma's eggs are seriously rotting. This didn't seem to concern her until she went on a yoga retreat and met a blind Buddhist mother of six who convinced her that giving birth would open new channels and help her live in the eternal present. Harriet knows all this because Uma explains things in detail that she thinks Harriet needs to understand. "What you need to understand," she has said on several occasions, "is I'm not trying to be your mother. More like your sister. Or just a friend." Harriet would prefer she not try to be any of those.

When Harriet asked Trent why he wanted another baby, he said, "Uma feels she needs a radical change in her life."

"Maybe she needs to be alone," Harriet suggested, "away from you, I mean, to discover her true potential." Mr. Chubak reads horoscopes and they're always advising people to discover their true potential.

"I need you to be nicer to her, Hal. She needs a friend right now. Her thesis is taking a lot out of her."

Uma's thesis is very demanding. Harriet isn't clear what it's about but knows it has something to do with Women's Studies because that's what Uma hopes to teach after she finishes it.

There are no empty tables near the door of the food court. Harriet stands by the trash bins.

"Harriet Baggs, fancy meeting you here." Mrs. Elrind pushes her patchy red face in Harriet's line of vision. "Are you alone?"

"I'm waiting for someone."

"Your mother?"

The last time Mrs. Elrind saw Lynne was at a meeting arranged by Mrs. Elrind to discuss Harriet's behavioural issues. Lynne avoids Harriet's parent/teacher interviews unless a teacher requests a meeting. The teachers advise her that Harriet doesn't work well in groups and that her behaviour needs improvement. Lynne responds, "Tell me something I don't already know."

Mrs. Elrind did more than complain about Harriet's behaviour. She called her belligerent and suggested she had Oppositional Defiant Disorder because Harriet refused to follow instructions. Mrs. Elrind referred to an incident in which she had instructed the class to work with three geometrical shapes and Harriet insisted on working with six. "Your daughter is deliberately disobeying me."

"So what do you want me to do about it?" Lynne demanded. "You explain to me how to make my kid do your stupid-ass projects."

Mrs. Elrind, according to Lynne, became miffy, commenting that "clearly, the acorn did not fall far from the tree." She recommended a psychological workup for Harriet.

"Go fuck yourself," Lynne said.

Harriet had expected Lynne to be angry when she returned from the meeting, but her mother just told her what was said, delighting Harriet, who imagined Mrs. Elrind's red face getting even patchier and her shrill voice becoming even shriller. "So there you go, Mizz Harriet," her mother said. "It's your life. Your choice. I can't fix it for you."

And now, in the food court, Mrs. Elrind is faking concern for Harriet. "Why don't you join us while you're waiting? You shouldn't be unaccompanied in a place like this." She puts her doughy arm around Harriet's shoulders and guides her to a table already occupied by a man whose face is so puffy, Harriet can barely see his eyes.

"This is Mr. Elrind." Mrs. Elrind pushes her into a seat. "Harriet is the student I told you about. The abstract artist."

"Is that right?" Mr. Elrind says. "I hear you've been giving my wife the runaround."

"Now, Earl," Mrs. Elrind cautions.

"I was the same at your age. Only learned what the rules were after I'd broken them." Scaly skin covers Mr. Elrind's hands, and his fingernails are yellow. Combined with the puffy slits for eyes, he resembles a reptile. Harriet decides to paint him later.

Mrs. Elrind crosses her doughy arms the way she does before asking the class a challenging question. "Now why would your mother leave you alone in the food court?"

Harriet knows she's snooping around for a reason to contact Children's Aid. Mrs. Elrind notified them about Tiffany Bussey's mother slapping her and calling her a slut in training. Tiffany had a psychological workup, and Children's Aid took her away from her mother to live with her aunt in Mississauga.

"My mother didn't leave me alone. She's at the hospital. My brother's sick again."

Mrs. Elrind must be aware of Irwin's condition because all the teachers were asked to watch for seizures and, to the best of their ability, ensure that he doesn't eat all his snacks at once like the other kindergartners. He needs to eat small amounts regularly or food becomes blocked by scar tissue in his bowel left behind by repeated surgeries. Lynne numbers his snack containers with felt marker, and draws little clocks on them—even though he can't tell time—to indicate when he should eat them.

"I'm sorry to hear that, Harriet. Who's here with you?"

"My grandmother."

"And she left you alone in the food court?"

"I'm waiting for my father's girlfriend to pick us up."

"Your father's *girlfriend?*" Mrs. Elrind looks at Mr. Elrind picking his teeth with his yellow fingernail.

"My parents are divorced. He's allowed to have a girlfriend."

"You're right there, pardner," Mr. Elrind says.

"Earl, stay out of this." Mrs. Elrind offers Harriet her New York Fries.

Harriet loves New York Fries but doesn't want anything touched by Mrs. Elrind.

"Astonishing how many of my pupils' parents are divorced," Mrs. Elrind says to no one in particular. Mr. Elrind takes several of her fries even though he still has a slice of pizza on his plate. Mrs. Elrind nibbles a fry. "Well, I think it's high time we called your mother. What's her cell number?"

"I don't know. She just changed it."

Mrs. Elrind looks at her the way she did when Harriet lost the school field trip forms her mother was supposed to sign. She didn't really lose them. Pinning Lynne down to sign forms when Irwin's in the hospital is nearly impossible. For the trip to the ROM, Harriet forged her signature and stole the ten bucks from Gennedy's track pants while he was in the shower.

"How old are you, sailor?" Mr. Elrind asks.

"Eleven, captain."

"What do you want to be when you grow up?"

"I'm going to work in a bank."

"A financier, eh? Move over, Mr. Trump."

"If you hope to work in a bank," Mrs. Elrind says, "you would do well to memorize your multiplication tables." Her thumb is working speedily on her cell. Harriet fears she's looking up the Children's Aid Society.

"My father's girlfriend should be here any minute."

"Well, why don't we call your father? Do you know *his* number? Or did he change his number too?"

"He's biking to Stouffville."

"He's what?"

"He bikes a lot, long distances."

"Holy mac," Mr. Elrind says. "Stouffville? That's got to be fifty kilometres from here."

Mrs. Elrind clasps her hands under her bosom. "Harriet, let me make sure I understand you correctly. Your mother is in hospital with your ailing brother, and your father is bicycling to Stouffville."

"That's correct." Harriet glances at the glass doors for signs of Uma.

Mrs. Elrind holds up her hands as though she's under arrest. "Is it just me or is this an utterly appalling situation?"

And then Uma bustles through the doors. Harriet hurtles towards her and throws her arms around her. "Take it easy, Hal," Uma says. Normally Harriet resents her using her nickname but now she feels only surges of affection for Uma, who is always home. "Who were you talking to?"

Mrs. Elrind steams towards them. "Do you have any idea how long this child has been unaccompanied?"

Uma, a head taller than Mrs. Elrind, looks down at her. "Is that any concern of yours?"

"As her teacher, it most definitely is. She needs a stable home environment, obviously. I have half a mind to report this incident to the authorities."

In the parking lot, Uma grips Harriet's hand so hard it hurts.

"We have to find Gran."

"Your grandmother is perfectly capable of looking after herself. She's probably in a doughnut joint flirting with the gents."

"What if she isn't? What if she had another heart attack?"

"Then she'll be rushed to the hospital and your mother will be notified. This is a public place. People notice when old ladies have cardiac arrests." She opens the passenger door. "Please get in, Harriet. This isn't good for my hormone levels."

Harriet climbs in but doesn't fasten her seat belt. "Couldn't I just ask at the information desk?"

"Do you even know where the information desk is in this consumer ghetto?"

"Yeah."

"You're lying." Uma starts the Range Rover. "Let me explain something to you. Trent and I are at a critical stage in this cycle."

"Is that why he's biking to Stouffville?"

"If you're going to be adversarial, I'm not talking to you. I don't need this." She starts to back out of the parking spot but stalls the Rover. "Fucking stick." *Stick*, Harriet knows, means the manual transmission.

"Please, Uma? I could just run in and ask. It'll take two seconds." Her father always says "it'll take two seconds," which means at least twenty minutes.

Uma burns the clutch some more. "Absolutely not. Listen to me. What you need to understand is I have two follicles maturing. If I am stressed, it raises the cortisol levels in my blood, which could jeopardize ovulation. If those follicles don't release the eggs in the next twenty-four hours, they will have to give me an injection of another hormone to prevent the eggs from becoming post-mature. All of this costs money none of us want to waste. So please, spare me a sob story about your grandmother who abandoned you in this retail urban disaster."

"She didn't abandon me."

"Then what do you call it, Harriet? You're a child. She is supposed to be responsible for you."

"She forgot."

"Oh. That makes it okay then." A car honks as Uma stalls the Rover again. "Fucking stick." She restarts the engine and cruises towards an exit only to find it blocked by several cars and a school bus.

"There's Gran!" Harriet shrieks, pulling at the car door.

"Don't get out while the car's moving."

"It's Gran, by the bus."

Forced to stop due to the lineup of cars, Uma stalls the Rover. Harriet charges over to Gran. "Gran! What happened?"

"Oh there you are. Me and Jedi have been looking all over for you. Poor old Jedi backed into a school bus."

"Is he hurt?"

"No, but the cops aren't too happy about it. They're talking about taking his licence away. He says the bus blocked him. But some no-goodnik witnesses say the bus was moving when he hit it."

Uma strides towards them, shaking out her hands the way she does after she's been working on her laptop. "Hello, Madeleine."

"Who're you?"

"She's my dad's girlfriend."

"You gotta be kidding," Mads says.

"You met her at Irwin's birthday party," Harriet reminds her. "She's come to pick us up. I thought you were lost."

"I'm never lost. Where'd *you* go?"

"Madeleine," Uma interjects, "it would appear that you were leaving without Harriet."

"We're not going anywhere now."

"Harriet, let's go."

"I want to stay with Gran."

"Out of the question. You'll talk it over with your father when he gets home."

"But you said you don't want me staying with you because of your eggs."

"*I've* got eggs," Mads says.

"I want you safe, Harriet. You are not safe with an old man who backs into school buses and an old woman who deserts you in the Scarborough Town Centre."

"I didn't desert her."

"If you say so. Let's go, Hal."

Harriet waits for Gran to insist she stay with her, but Mads has her eye on an old duffer behind the wheel of an antique Jaguar. He rolls down his window and asks what's going on. Mads adjusts her turquoise cap, sidles over to him in her high-heels, and leans in the window kicking her leg back the way she does when she wants eligibles to notice her legs.

"Harriet," Uma warns, "the Rover's still running. All we need is for it to get stolen."

Uma cooks rigatoni primavera. Her laptop sits on the kitchen table. "Is it all right if I use your computer?" Harriet asks.

"Go ahead." One of the good things about Uma is that she lets Harriet use her Mac. Trent gets hysterical if Harriet touches his because client information is on it and Irwin corrupted thirty-six files. "But I'm not Irwin," Harriet argued.

"We're all dependant on this tool, Hal. It's not a toy."

Harriet eats the noodles and vegetables with gusto. She enjoys Uma's cooking because she uses fresh ingredients from the farmers' market, although Harriet doesn't like fennel, leeks or the weird greens Uma puts in her salads. Trent does: that's how they met—they were both searching for arugula and radicchio when Irwin had the seizure.

Uma holds the pepper grinder over Harriet's plate.

"No thank you."

"Are you worried about your brother?"

"Not really."

"He'll pull through." Uma offers Harriet a wedge of Parmesan and a cheese grater, another good thing about Uma. At home they eat tasteless Parmesan from a can. "What do you need the Mac for?"

"Photos of reptiles. I want to paint one. I like this one." She turns the screen towards Uma.

"The Tarentola gigas," Uma reads. "Wonderful." She often says "wonderful" but never as though she means it.

Harriet points at the reptile. "See his hands and feet. Four digits on each."

Uma grates Parmesan over her rigatoni. "Harriet, there's something you need to understand."

"It's a tiny lizard, but fat. I want to paint a fat one." She tries to look busy with her noodles to avoid hearing what she needs to understand.

"You know my parents were killed by a transport truck when I was nineteen?"

"Yes." Trent told her the truck was transporting fuel and that Uma's parents burned alive, belted into their seats. "That's why you get to live in this house," Harriet says, "because it belonged to your parents." Harriet lost her house in the crash of 2008. When she works in the bank, she will buy her own house that nobody can take away from her.

"Actually, I tried to sell the house, even had some offers, but I couldn't do it. It's all I have left of my parents."

"It's a nice house." It has a big front yard with trees and flowering shrubs. If Harriet hears the woodpecker, she scoots under the huge oak and watches the bird hammering away at the bark. She tried to draw him but couldn't get the neck right.

"It contains a lot of memories," Uma says. "But no parents. Harriet . . ." She leans over the table and gently closes the laptop. "Did Trent ever tell you I had a brother?"

"No." Harriet tries to imagine a male Uma.

"My brother drowned trying to save *me* from drowning. He was fifteen. I was your age. It took him four days to die in the hospital. Do you know what my parents said to me? They said, 'We told you not to swim to the rock.' Then they stopped talking to me."

"Forever?" Harriet would love it if her parents would stop talking to her forever.

"After the funeral they started saying the necessary day-to-day things but, no, it took a year before conversation flowed easily between us."

It never occurred to Harriet that she could drown Irwin. It would be difficult because Lynne buckles him into life jackets. She pushes some leek slices to the side of her plate and grates more Parmesan on her noodles.

"My parents *stopped speaking* to me, Harriet. Can you imagine how isolating that would be for a little girl?"

Harriet spears a rigatoni with her fork. "Why weren't you wearing a life jacket?"

"I was a kid. I wanted to swim to the rock like my big brother."

"What was his name?"

"Otto."

"Where was the rock?"

"In a quarry where we swam when we visited my grandparents." Uma sits very still, looking a bit like a baboon, and Harriet tries to memorize the shapes of the shadows on her face.

"What I'm trying to make you understand, Hal, is I identify with the isolation you feel when your brother is in the hospital. All the love and attention is turned on Irwin and that must be very painful for you. You can't help but resent that."

Harriet forks zucchini slices into her mouth, and then a mushroom. She knows if she doesn't say anything, Uma will go on explaining things.

"What you need to understand is that you have two parents who love you very much, they just don't always show it because your brother's condition is all-consuming."

"My father doesn't visit my brother."

"He doesn't like to visit your brother when your mother is present and, as you know, she is always there. What you have to understand is that we're all under a great deal of stress right now. Your father is trying to support two households while getting T. Baggs Consultants off the ground. Your mother claims to be unemployable due to her mental health and your brother's condition, and Gennedy, well, I'm not sure what the problem is there. The point is . . ."

"*You* could work."

Uma sits straighter and tucks her baboonish chin into her neck. "I do work, Harriet. I work very hard."

"I mean for money. You could get a job to help pay for infertility treatment. You could work as a greeter at Walmart. Mr. Bhanmattie got a job as a greeter and he has no retail experience. Then Dad would be able to pay us what he used to."

"Since when do you know how much your father pays?"

"I don't. I just know Mum's always complaining he's not making his payments. And when he does, it's not what the court ordered."

"It's very difficult to make regular payments when you go freelance."

"Mum says he shouldn't have gone freelance. If he'd kept his job, your fertility drugs would be covered by insurance."

"How wonderful that she keeps you so well informed." Uma tosses the salad with sharp, convulsive movements. Shreds of weird greens tumble on the table.

"It just seems to me," Harriet says, "if your thesis stresses you out, and my father's work stresses him out, maybe you should be doing something else."

"One day, Harriet, you will grow up to discover that the path of least resistance is not always the most rewarding."

"What's rewarding about *your* path?"

Uma jerks her head as if a fly has landed on her nose. "I really don't need this right now." She starts to clear the dishes even though Harriet hasn't had any salad, not that she wants any.

Harriet eats an olive. "Trying to have a baby when you're stressed out all the time doesn't make any sense. Babies are stressful. My great-grandmother had eight and it killed her."

Uma, dishrag in hand, begins to tear up. Her tendency to start crying for no good reason irritates Harriet because suddenly everybody has to pay attention to Uma and tell her it's okay to cry. Not Harriet. "If I was stressed out all the time, no way would I have a baby."

"You can't possibly understand. You're a child."

"I could understand if you had a good reason."

Uma wipes her eyes. "It's impossible to explain."

"Which means you don't have a good reason. A good reason wouldn't be impossible to explain."

Uma turns on her, her face almost as red as Mrs. Elrind's. "I want my *own* family, Harriet. I *lost* my family. All I have is Trent. You have two parents, two stepparents, three grandparents and a little brother. I have *no one*." She leans against the counter as though she needs it to stand.

"My family is nothing but trouble." This what Mrs. Butts says about Harriet when she buys Minute Maid orange juice with pulp, or beef-flavoured Temptations for her cats instead of chicken.

Uma, red-eyed, stares at her as though eels are coming out of Harriet's mouth. "I can't believe you said that. Please go upstairs until your father gets home."

"Can I take the Mac?"

"No!"

In Uma's old room, Harriet opens the box of acrylics her father bought her and begins her portrait of Captain Elrind the Tarentola gigas. She prefers the translucency of oils to the flatness of acrylics but her parents think oils are toxic. She closes her eyes, remembering the shapes of the shadows on Mr. Elrind's scaly hands. Below, Uma slams drawers and cabinets, and Harriet wonders what this is doing to her hormone levels. As she mixes reds, browns and yellows, visualizing the Tarentola gigas' eight fingers and eight toes, she tries to think of ways to drown Irwin. It would have to look like an accident. But then she could have his room—it has better light than hers—and use it as a studio until she gets to Lost Coin Lake. She called Greyhound and a child's one-way fare to Mattawa, including tax, is $84.73. This is more than she budgeted for. She'll need at least $400 for supplies. She plans to arrive the day after Thanksgiving, when Algonquin closes the backwoods cabins for the season, making her break-in easier.

Shadows start to take shape in her mind, and she touches her brush to the plywood.

Uma must have liked violet because everything in her old room is painted violet, except the buttercup yellow walls. A poster of a bare-chested nineties rock star with a mushroom cut and high-waisted pants is on one wall, and two photos of Uma with her parents. Harriet has studied these carefully. Now that she knows Uma drowned her brother, they make more sense. In the photos Uma stands slightly apart from them, almost as though they're strangers. The parents look surprised, and Harriet would like to know who took the shot, and what they did to surprise the parents. Uma doesn't look surprised in the photos, just worried—the way she always looks. It's as though she thinks worrying will bring her brother and parents back to life. Harriet doesn't understand why Uma doesn't move on. Mindy in 408 says she has to move on every time her ex beats her up. Harriet has sat with her on the fire stairs and listened while Mindy, sucking hard on cigarettes and holding ice packs over her bruises, insisted she would move on. She never does though, and Boyd comes back and beats her up again.

It's hard to imagine what Uma and Trent's baby would look like. Nobody seems concerned that it might have a stretched head like Irwin; they say his condition is congenital, which Harriet looked up and learned means nonhereditary. Still, what kind of baby would grow from a rotting egg and middle-aged sperm?

Just before her breakdown, Lynne did in-home pregnancy tests whenever her period was late. She and Gennedy tried to get pregnant for over a year. Harriet knew this because they discussed it with her and Irwin at the DQ. "Bunny, how would you feel about a little sister or brother?"

"I already have one," Harriet said.

"Wowee wowee." Irwin bounced on his stool. "I want a little brother. Boys only!"

"Gennedy loves you guys but he's always wanted a child of his own. I'd like to give him one." She made it sound as if she could wrap a child up and hand it to him. "Harriet? How would you feel about that?"

Harriet knew it didn't matter what she felt, so she shrugged and spooned more of her Blizzard. For months she heard them humping more than usual through her bedroom wall. Gennedy became super friendly and bought Nintendo games that held no interest for Harriet. "Harreee . . ." Irwin would call, "come check this out, this is soooo cooool!" When he traded five Nintendo games for Voytek Bialkowski's giant pencil, Gennedy shouted at him. Harriet had never heard him shout at Irwin before. "No trading at school, understand? Do you know how much those cost? Jesus fucking Christ, how could you be so stupid? What the fuck do you want a giant pencil for anyway? A giant pencil costs a buck. Who is this Voytek Bialkowski kid? I'm calling his parents." Gennedy turned on Harriet. "Do you know this Voytek kid?"

"No." Of course she knew him. He was famous for swindling the kindergartners.

"Why don't you ever look out for your brother? Jesus fucking Christ. From now on, we're following a strict no-trading policy, understand?" Irwin, trembling from the Gennedy assault, nodded slowly, looking like E.T. After Boyd beats up Mindy, sometimes she asks Harriet to watch *E.T.* with her because she watched it as a little kid and it makes her feel safe. The only criminal lawyer in history that's broke contacted the school regarding the giant pencil swindle and hounded Voytek Bialkowski's parents until he eventually got the games back. But Irwin didn't want to play them anymore. A week later he got an infection in his tubing and had to go to the hospital. When he returned home, stick thin with a fresh surgical wound on his abdomen, Lynne stopped going out except to buy cigarettes to smoke on the balcony. Harriet no longer heard them humping through the wall.

Her father has returned and she can hear him and Uma having a heated discussion downstairs. He always starts out taking Harriet's side but in the end caves to Uma. With Lynne he would storm out and she'd shout after him, "That's good, just walk away from it. That's real constructive." Gran calls Trent "a spineless no-goodnik." When Irwin was in the incubator with a collapsed lung, Trent found excuses to avoid the hospital. In those days Harriet was keen to visit Irwin because she believed he would turn into a normal baby brother. "When will he come out of the plastic box?" she kept asking, but no one would give her a straight answer. She stood on the footstool beside the incubator and talked to him about what fun they would have when he got better. She even told him about the Americana, convinced that this would give him a reason to live. When he was four months old, he started to breathe on his own. Lynne phoned Trent in tears and he came to the hospital right away. Harriet remembers her parents clinging to each other as though they were in a hurricane. When Irwin stopped breathing again, the doctors asked Lynne and Trent if they wanted Irwin back on the ventilator, or if they should let nature take its course. "Save him!" Lynne wailed. "Save my baby, you fuckers, or I'll sue your asses." They didn't do hand compressions and break Irwin's ribs because his heart and kidneys were functioning. Still, it seems to Harriet, the situation wasn't that different from the hydrocephalic baby's whose parents insisted the medical team keep resuscitating her, forcing her to die a torturous death.

After Lynne screamed at the doctors, nobody in the ward was nice to them. The nurses no longer called Irwin a miracle baby. When he turned six months, they wanted him out of there. Trent bought a car seat and a wedge of foam he cut into a U shape to support Irwin's ballooning head. The foam was bigger than Irwin. It was becoming undeniable to Harriet that her brother would never turn into a normal baby. In public places, she kept her distance from him and her parents.

At home Irwin watched her. Lynne laid him on a sheep shearling mat on the floor wherever she was because he couldn't go anywhere. While other babies rolled around and crawled, he just lay there. If Harriet came into the room, she felt Irwin's eyes fix on her. She tried not to look at him because sometimes he'd smile goofily and she'd start hoping he'd get better, even though experience had taught her that he wouldn't. He still can't hold his swollen head up properly. It always lists to one side.

With a fine brush, she paints the suspicious eyes of Captain Elrind the Tarentola gigas.

Six

Her father knocks on the door. "Hal?"

She runs to him. He lifts her up and she wraps her legs around his waist, pressing her forehead into his neck. It smells of bike sweat but she doesn't care.

"It's okay, Hal. He's still in status epilepticus."

She knows this means Irwin is hooked up to the IV and still being monitored. "Did you go see him?"

"I did. Lynne's holding up pretty well although she's not too happy Gran lost you."

"She didn't lose me."

"She's old, Hal. With a few screws loose. Anyway, what happened here with Uma?"

"Nothing."

"Really? Because she's pretty upset."

"Why?"

"Well, I was hoping you could fill me in a little."

Harriet knows he'll pretend to listen to her side of the story but, after she spills her guts, he'll still blame her. She won't play this game. "I don't know what she's talking about."

"She told you about Otto. And her parents."

"I knew that already. You told me that's why you get to live in this house."

"Did I? Anyway, she feels you lack compassion. Do you know what compassion is?"

"Of course." She's not absolutely sure but doesn't want to look ignorant. She knows it has something to do with feeling sorry for people. She doesn't understand why anyone wants people feeling sorry for them. Harriet doesn't want anybody feeling sorry for her.

Her father sits on the bed, removes her arms from his neck and sets her beside him. "Do you think you lack compassion, Hal?"

"Of course not. Why are there no pictures of Otto anywhere?"

Trent looks around. "That's a good question."

"Maybe she hated him and is pretending she loved him. It's easy to love people when they're dead."

"Wow."

Harriet's figured out Trent says "wow" when he can't think of what else to say. "If she really loved him, she'd want pictures of him all over the place. She hardly has any pictures of her parents either. Just those." She points to the two shots of Uma looking worried and her parents looking surprised.

Trent stands and studies the shots. "I've never noticed these before."

"Do they look like they love each other to you?"

"They were German."

"So?"

"She says they weren't very demonstrative."

"Maybe they hated her."

"Harriet . . ." He only calls her Harriet when he's annoyed with her. "Why do you always have to be so negative?"

"She drowned their son by swimming to the rock when she wasn't supposed to. Why wouldn't they hate her?"

"Because she's their daughter."

"Just because you're related to someone doesn't mean you don't hate them."

"Whoa, can we start over here for a second?" Her father frequently asks if they can start over here for a second, as though it's possible to delete what has just transpired. "It's not a good idea for you to stay here, Hal. Not right now."

"Oh please, Daddy, I'll be positive. I could go with you to the infertility clinic and wait in the waiting room. I won't bother anybody."

"You say that now, but if things don't go your way you'll start barking or something."

"I promise I won't bark."

Trent runs his hands through his hair flattened by the bike helmet. "I really want you guys to like each other."

"I like her."

"Then why don't you tell her that? She says you're confrontational with her."

Adults say she's confrontational when she doesn't agree with them.

"You upset her, Harriet. Why would you tell her to get a job at Walmart? Don't you realize she's a little overqualified for that?"

"What's she qualified for?"

He bends over to untie a knot in his bike shoelaces. "She's an intellectual. She has a brilliant mind. Can you undo this knot for me, Hal?"

An expert at knots, she unties it in seconds. "Is it okay if I stay with Gran?"

"Wow. I can't believe you're even asking me that."

"I don't upset Gran."

"That's because she's deaf and not that bright." Trent scratches his thigh under his bike shorts.

"She loves me," Harriet insists although she's not sure if this is true.

"Of course she does, we all love you, Hal. We just need you to be a bit more understanding."

Harriet daubs vermilion onto Captain Elrind the Tarentola Gigas' face.

"Is that a dragon?" her father asks.

"Yeah," Harriet says to avoid having to explain that it isn't.

"Your mom wishes you'd paint some happy pictures."

"The dragon's happy." Harriet slashes a grin across the "dragon's" face.

"Another option, kiddo, is you can stay with Harriet and Irwin. You haven't seen them in ages." He means his rich parents who despise Lynne because she eloped with their only son and gave birth to a weirdo and a freak.

"Please, no, Daddy, they hate me. I hate going there."

"They don't hate you."

"They think I'm strange and don't know how to sit still. There's nothing to do there. Please, Daddy, I'll be nice to Uma, and I won't bark or anything."

Trent sighs and scratches his other thigh under his bike shorts. "Let me talk to Uma."

Harriet wants to scream, "Why do you always have to ask Uma?" Instead she focuses on transforming *Captain Elrind the Tarentola Gigas* into a happy picture. She starts lightening the shadows to make it look the way people think a dragon looks. She tries to paint it the way Yannick Piccard would paint a dragon.

It seems like hours before her father comes back. First he and Uma talk below then clomp up the stairs to continue their deliberations in their bedroom. Harriet loathes the dragon painting. Trent leans against the violet doorframe and stares at it. "Wow. I like the flames."

"He's blowing flames because he's happy," Harriet explains. "Sad dragons can't blow fire."

"Wow. Show it to Uma. I think she'll really like it."

"I don't want to bother her."

"You won't bother her. She really wants to talk to you. She's in bed, go have a chat."

"About what?" She knows he wants her to apologize. "Did she say I could stay?"

"She said you can come to the clinic and then we'll see."

"See what?"

"How things go." Trent nudges her towards the door. "Go on, show her the dragon. She'll love it."

Uma pats the bed beside her. "Come talk to me. Oh, is that what you were working on? Let me see." Harriet shows her the grinning, brain-dead dragon. "Wonderful," Uma says. "I used to draw dragons. And castles and wizards. Do you ever draw those?"

"All the time."

"I loved the Harry Potter books. I know grown-ups aren't supposed to read them but I couldn't put them down."

Harriet found the good versus evil simplicity of the books tedious. She was forced to listen to them because Gennedy—a Potter-maniac—bought the books on CD and played them while they drove to Florida. When they arrived in Orlando, Lynne noticed what looked like a tumour protruding from Irwin's gut. She and Gennedy freaked out in the Holiday Inn Express parking lot because they didn't have health insurance. They drove back to Canada, listening to Harry Potter. It turned out the subcutaneous shunt going from Irwin's skull to his stomach had broken. The fluid was collecting under his skin, forming a lump. The fluid had to be drained and the shunt revised.

"I bet you've read all the Harry Potter books," Uma says.

"Every single one."

"Voldemort got what he deserved, don't you think?"

"Totally."

Uma adjusts a pillow behind her head. "I want us to be friends."

"Me too. I didn't mean to hurt your feelings."

"I know that, honeybun." Harriet hates it when Uma calls her honeybun. "I need to explain something to you." Uma rubs night cream that smells of moth balls on her face. Harriet shifts a little farther down the bed.

"When I was a little girl," Uma says, "all I wanted was to be a mommy. Then Otto died and I didn't believe I deserved to be a mother, or even to be loved for that matter." Harriet doesn't understand why Uma adds "for that matter" to the ends of sentences. "I immersed myself in my academic pursuits. A lot passed me by. But then I met Trent and it was like the world opened up to me. I felt things I didn't know I could feel. I felt reborn. Loved." Harriet doesn't look at her but can tell from the crackling in her voice she's getting teary again. "Being loved is the greatest gift of all, Harriet. But you know what the toughest part about being loved is?" Harriet shakes her head, staring at the dragon painting. "It's letting yourself *be* loved. I know sometimes you feel unworthy of love, Hal, and that's why you act out. Let yourself be loved, honeybun. You *deserve* to be loved." She stretches her arms towards Harriet but can't reach her. Uma slides down the bed and strokes Harriet's back the way she strokes the neighbour's cat.

Many dejected women and a few men sit in the waiting area of the infertility clinic. Filipinas in lab coats summon the women, one at a time, behind a partition to draw their blood. Harriet suspects the men slouched around the clinic reading newspapers and checking smartphones are waiting to find out if, like Trent, they must jerk off into a specimen container. Uma explained that her blood results and an ultrasound will determine if she's ovulating. "Infertility treatment requires the patience of a saint," she said. Nobody in the waiting area looks like a saint. Some of them lean back in chairs, closing their eyes. Some drink Starbucks coffee. Uma tugs on Trent's sleeve. "Can you get me a grande non-fat sugar-free extra-hot no-foam decaf vanilla latte?"

"Coming up." Trent kisses Uma's forehead. "You want anything, Hal?" Harriet has been on her best behaviour, never saying what she means but only agreeing and nodding when spoken to. "Hal? You want anything?" She would love a hot chocolate with whipped cream but fears it might be too extravagant at this hour.

"May I please have an orange juice?"

"Of course. Do you want to come with me or stay here with Uma?"

Harriet looks to Uma for some indication of the appropriate move. Uma gives a saintly nod. "Go with your dad. I'll be fine."

The lineup at Starbucks extends almost to the door. Trent takes her hand. "You okay?"

Harriet nods, thrilled that he took her hand. She can't remember the last time they held hands. "Do you remember when Mummy was pregnant she'd lie down and rest her Starbucks mug on her belly?"

"I do."

"When I was little I thought that was why Irwin had a stretched head. I thought the mug had flattened it." Harriet wishes her father would say something. Hand in hand, it's almost like before Irwin was born.

"Hal, your mother said something about Irwin having a hard time in show and tell. Do you know anything about that?"

"He told the class about the shunt breaking in Florida. He said he had to have a ball cut out and they thought he meant he had his ball cut off. So they were teasing him about having only one ball."

"Kids can be cruel." He releases her hand to pull a twenty out of his wallet, slides the wallet back in his pocket but doesn't take her hand again. "Do you stick up for your brother at school?"

Harriet wants to say, *Do you stick up for your son, ever?* but she understands that if she says what she means, he'll call her confrontational and negative and send her back to Gennedy. "He's in kindergarten. I hardly ever see him."

"When you do see him, does he seem all right?"

Irwin never seems all right. "Sure."

"You see him at lunch, don't you? Apparently the school has a zero-tolerance-for-bullying policy." A zero-tolerance-for-bullying policy holds no meaning in the schoolyard. That adults believe policies change things astounds Harriet. At five, Irwin has yet to feel the full brunt of school bullying. The kindergartners play in a separate yard. In the fall he will be in grade one, in the big yard and defenceless. Harriet will be in middle school a bus ride away.

"Uma feels you're preoccupied with money. What I pay in child support shouldn't concern you. Your mother shouldn't be speaking to you about it."

How can it not concern her when she is one of the children being supported? It bugs her that adults pretend money isn't important when it's all they ever talk about, and yet when Harriet mentions that her father has been defaulting on child support payments, suddenly she's preoccupied with money. This is why, when she gets a job at the bank and buys her house, she will never marry. She will never support or be supported by anyone.

Ahead of them, a wiry woman holds up a compact mirror and smears mauve lipstick over her meagre lips. Harriet decides to paint the wiry woman's snaky mouth later. She knows her father will continue to default on his payments. He will avoid her and Irwin and jack off into plastic cups so doctors can squirt his sperm up Uma. Her father is a spineless no-goodnik. She no longer wants to hold his hand. "*Hindi bale*," she mutters which means "it doesn't matter" in Tagalog.

When the ultrasound reveals that Uma's follicles have released two eggs, she becomes all creepy smiles and touches, sighing wearily as though she has accomplished something that required great effort. That normal women ovulate every month without even thinking about it doesn't seem to occur to her. She is the mothership.

Trent disappears into a room marked *PRIVATE* while Harriet tries to look engrossed in a magazine ad that says *Science has never looked so sexy!* The ad claims that CelluScience can reduce cellulite in forty-seven days. Harriet didn't know what cellulite was until Darcy showed her the cellulite-busting cream Nina uses on her thighs. Darcy rubs it on her waist where she insists she has cellulite although it just looks like fat to Harriet.

"Honeybun, why are you reading about diet products?"

"There's a bazillion ads for them. This one says it's America's strongest female fat burner. You can lose twenty-five pounds in three weeks."

"Harriet, if anything, you're too thin."

"I was looking at it for a friend of mine."

"Your friend's body-image issues shouldn't be your concern." She looks at the door marked *PRIVATE*. Harriet flips through the "Hollywood's Hottest Couples" feature, wishing she had a pair of scissors to cut off their heads.

"Does insemination hurt?" she asks.

"There's some minor discomfort when they push the catheter through the cervix."

Uma has explained, on a previous occasion, that the doctors open her vagina with a metal speculum and inject the sperm into the cervix through a plastic catheter. Harriet turns to a photo of Angelina as a teenager. Angie sits on a couch with her brother, James, who has the same big lips, stubby nose and staring eyes. "Did Otto look like you?" she asks.

"I can't talk about him right now, Hal. I have to relax."

"Sorry." She looks at a shot of Angie and James with their mother, who also has the stubby nose but not the big lips. The mouth must come from their father. "Do I look like Irwin?"

"A little."

"How?"

"Same nose. Your dad's nose."

"If Irwin were dead, they'd have called us, right?"

"Irwin isn't dead. He's been through worse. He'll get through this. He has a warrior spirit."

Uma has referred to Irwin's warrior spirit before. Harriet wanted to ask what kind of spirit Uma thought she had but suspected Uma would say her spirit is evil, which Harriet fears it is. Mr. Rivera's family believes in evil spirits that make tik-tik sounds that grow quieter as they approach, fooling the victims into thinking the spirits are farther away when in fact they're about to stick their proboscises down the victims' throat to suck out their heart, liver or unborn babies. The Riveras lower their voices if they sense one of these vampire-like witch ghouls is present so they can hear the tik-tik. Mrs. Rivera warded off not just *aswangs* but *multos* and *manananggals* by staring them down. She'd notice an evil spirit before anyone else. "*Aswang* is here," she'd whisper. The rest of the family would flee but Mrs. Rivera would stay in her armchair and give the shape-shifting spirits the evil eye. Mrs. Rivera was very brave and wise, and Harriet never stops missing her.

She puts the magazine down. "Filipinos believe in an evil spirit called *aswang* that enjoys eating unborn babies, sucking them out of the mothers while they're sleeping. They always have bloodshot eyes from staying up all night feasting on babies."

Uma blinks several times. "Why are you telling me this?"

"They ward off *aswang* with vinegar which they call *suka*. It wouldn't hurt to spray some *suka* around the house."

"Thank you for sharing. No more talking please."

Trent, flushed, exits the *PRIVATE* room and hurriedly hands his specimen container to a lab-coated Filipino who takes the specimen container behind a swinging door.

"Where's he taking it?" Harriet asks.

"To the lab to be washed."

Trent kisses Uma's forehead again. "Now we just have to wait till they're ready for you, Oom. How are you doing?"

"Trying to relax. Please take Harriet somewhere."

"Why, is she giving you a hard time?"

"If talking about Filipino demons that feast on unborn babies qualifies as giving me a hard time, yes."

"Harriet?"

"I was just trying to be helpful. They ward it off with vinegar. It wouldn't hurt to try. It's good for cockroaches too, although mostly they swat those with flip-flops which they call *chinelas*. *Chinelas* is a way nicer word than flip-flops."

Uma closes her eyes again. "Take her away, please. I need some tranquility."

Trent and Harriet walk around the College Park mall, where office workers scurry to fast food outlets then hunch over tables, shoving pizza and burgers into their mouths. Her father calls Lynne but she doesn't answer. Harriet spots an ATM. "Would you mind if I use the bank machine?"

"Since when do you use a bank machine?"

"Since forever. Mum taught me how."

"What do you need money for?"

She can't say to escape to Algonquin Park. "I want to buy a birthday present for a friend."

"Sure. Whatever." Trent seems distracted, which makes sense, given the circumstances. Harriet is having difficulty banishing images of him jiggling his penis from her mind. Mr. Frogley in 515 was often seen lurking around the elevators jiggling his penis before his son put him in a home. Once, while he was jiggling, he accused Harriet of stealing his newspaper. Harriet barked at him and he ran away. Mr. Chubak told her that Mr. Frogley was a war hero who survived for five weeks on a life raft after his submarine got torpedoed. Harriet stopped barking at him after that.

She pulls her debit card from her jeans pocket, inserts it into the machine and enters her PIN, presses *withdrawal* then $20. A shiny bill slides out of the slot. She folds it carefully and slides it into her front pocket.

"Harriet, why would you talk about baby-eating demons to Uma?"

"I thought it might help. The vinegar, I mean. It works for them. They have lots of babies. There's ninety-three million people in the Philippines."

"Uma's very delicate right now. You have to be careful what you say."

She always has to be careful what she says to Uma. "I'm sorry."

He pulls out his iPhone. "I've got to deal with these clients." This means he'll be on the cell for hours. She feels the twenty in her pocket and pictures herself hiking through the woods ablaze with crimson, tangerine and citron yellow. Mr. Chubak gave her his compass last Christmas and taught her how to map out coordinates. She knows exactly where she's going and which trails to take. She just has to convince the Greyhound bus driver to let her off at Bissett Creek on his way to Ottawa. She'll buy her final supplies in town before heading south. Lost Coin Lake is only seven kilometres from the park boundary. Already she is collecting bear-resistant coffee tins to fill with food and hang from trees.

Seven

Nobody talks in the Rover. Trent, when he isn't shifting the stick, rests his hand on Uma's thigh. Uma pushes her seat into the reclining position, cramping Harriet's knees. Trent asks Oom if it's okay if he listens to the news, and Harriet can't believe he has to ask. Uma nods, closing her eyes. The lead-in is about an eight-year-old plane crash survivor. She and a university student were ejected from the plane, still belted into their seats. They sat in the freezing tundra while the plane burned behind them. The eight-year-old seemed unaware that her little sister was still in the plane. She said to the university student, "This is my first plane crash. Can you tell me what to do?" The university student talked to the girl about horses until help arrived.

"I can't listen to this," Uma says, and Trent immediately turns off the radio. Harriet quietly hums "These Boots Are Made for Walkin'," one of Gran's favourite tunes, but Uma says, "Harriet, please don't hum." Harriet can't move her legs with Uma's seat in the reclining position. She's afraid to mention this because she senses she is very close to being shipped back to Gennedy. She watches her father's anxious eyes in the rear-view mirror. His son could be dying, but all he's worried about is Uma's eggs. Harriet hates him for this, and for all the times he has let her down, all the times she has sat waiting for him to take her to African Lion Safari. All the times she has listened to his excuses then said, "It's okay," because reproaching him was what her mother did and it never worked. During Lynne's breakdown, he insisted on organizing a birthday party for Harriet even though she didn't want one. He printed out party invitations decorated with balloons. Harriet invited her whole class, even the boys, because she was afraid no one would show up. On the invitation it said it would be a make-your-own-pizza party with a special guest. "Who's the special guest?" Harriet asked.

"It's a surprise."

As Lynne's oven fit only four small pizzas at a time, the kids had to wait in line gripping raw dough. "This is so totally lame," Katie Bosley said. "Like, why would you have a make-your-own-pizza party if you only have one puny oven?"

The special guest turned out to be Uma dressed as a magician, performing dumbass tricks like transforming her wand into a bouquet, or finding coins behind kids' ears. Harriet hid in the bathroom until Kester Hubble pounded on the door, announcing he had to take a dump. In the kitchen, her father—wearing an apron with *I swear to tell the trout the whole trout and nothing but the trout so help me cod* printed on it—was talking in the goofy voice he reserved for children. "Are you guys telling me you've never heard about Rubik's Cubes? No way! Say it ain't so!" The kids stared at him. Roger Brocoli had his finger up his nose. "A Rubik's Cube," Trent continued, "is only the most *awesome* toy ever invented. I won a Rubik's Cube contest when I was ten. It's been downhill ever since." Harriet knew he was making a joke but the partygoers, clutching raw dough, did not.

And now these adults think they can be parents.

He drops them off in front of the house before driving into the garage. Uma climbs regally up the steps. Harriet follows at a respectful distance, hoping Oom will cook noodles but Uma ascends to the bedroom and closes the door. Harriet hurries to the kitchen to see if Uma's laptop is still on the table. She grabs it, along with two granola bars, and scampers up to the violet room to watch clips from *Hogan's Heroes*. She clicks "The Best of Schultz," and when Schultz says, "I see nothing. I was not here. I didn't even wake up this morning," Harriet says it too. Her viewing is interrupted by her father howling as though he is being mauled by a bear. Harriet charges downstairs and out the sliding doors to the deck where Trent sits hunched on the steps. "Dad, what happened? Are you hurt?"

"My bike's gone."

Harriet glances at the side of the garage where her father habitually leans his bike before locking it in with the Rover.

"Some fucker stole my bike. I can't fucking believe it!"

Uma appears with her hair mussed from lying with her butt and legs propped up to make it easier for sperm to reach her eggs. "What's going on here?"

Trent, head in hands, sobs.

"Somebody stole his bike," Harriet explains.

"From the garage?"

"No," Trent says with a venom Harriet has never heard him use with Uma. "I forgot to put it in the garage because I was marching to your fucking ovulation drum and rushing to the fucking jerk-off clinic!"

"Don't be so reactive, Trent. It's only a bike."

"It is *not* only a bike. It is *my* bike that I have *customized* to make into my perfect bike."

"So, you'll fix up another one."

"I can't just 'fix up' another one!" Trent wails. "Do you know how hard it is to track down quality parts? Everything's made in fucking China."

Uma sighs heavily and shakes her head. "You shouldn't form attachments to things. They're inanimate objects. They don't live and breathe, they don't die."

Trent stands and jerks his arms around like a robot. "You don't get it, do you? You're so wrapped up in this baby bullshit a fucking tornado could spin me off the planet and you wouldn't notice until sperm drop-off time."

Uma strikes a baboonish pose and Harriet expects her to bare her teeth and snarl. Instead she says, "I can't talk to you when you're like this," and steps back inside, closing the doors behind her.

"That's good," Trent yells, jerking his robot arms. "Walk away from it! That's real constructive." Harriet considers pointing out that this is exactly what Lynne used to say when he walked away from arguments, but her father resumes sobbing so hard that, from behind, it looks as though someone is punching him repeatedly in the gut. She has never seen her father cry, not even when he sat in the dark plucking absently at his eyebrows because Irwin had to keep returning to the hospital. And now Irwin might be dying and her father is sobbing uncontrollably over the loss of a bike. This must be what Lynne means when she says Trent has the emotional maturity of a five-year-old.

Harriet climbs back upstairs to search for the dancing inmates video where Filipinos dance to "They Don't Care About Us" by Michael Jackson. Next she watches "Maglalatik," a Filipino folk dance. Harriet wishes she could go to the Philippines. When Mrs. Rivera looked like a skeleton and could no longer get out of bed, she told Harriet she missed the Philippines because everybody there wants to have fun and dance and sing karaoke. She asked Harriet to sing and dance for her. "Don't be shy, *anak*. Try it, you'll like it." Mrs. Rivera attempted to wave her arms to suggest dancing but she was too weak. Harriet tried to think of a song or a dance because she wanted to please Mrs. Rivera. All she could think of was the "Hokey Pokey," and there was no way she was singing that. Her feet felt duct taped to the broadloom, and she was certain an evil spirit was squatting on Mrs. Rivera's commode. She waited for Mrs. Rivera to stare down the *multo*, but she'd fallen asleep again.

She hears Trent trudging up the stairs and down the hall to the bedroom, probably to beg forgiveness from Oom.

Harriet searches "Moymoy Palaboy," a video with two Filipinos lip-syncing to the Gypsy Kings' "Volare." Their fake moustaches come unstuck and their curly black wigs slip. One of them strums a broom while the other waves his hands like a flamenco dancer.

Next she searches "Yosemitebear double rainbow." She listens to the guy shout "Oh my god!" and "What does this mean?" over and over as he films the double rainbow. She's not sure if he's laughing or crying, maybe both. And then, of course, she looks at the capybara nibbling the Popsicle again.

"Harriet?" Uma knocks on the door. "Do you have my laptop in there?"

"Yeah. I thought you were resting."

"I still have to work. Please don't remove my laptop from the kitchen table. I always leave it on the kitchen table so I can find it when I need it."

"Sorry."

Uma takes the laptop and returns to her room, closing the door firmly behind her. Harriet smears black all over the dragon painting, and eats the two granola bars but is still hungry. Downstairs she finds her father drinking the Steam Whistle beer he buys because one of his bike buddies works there. He sticks his fingers into four empty bottles and rolls them around on the table. Harriet fears they'll slide off his fingers and crash to the floor.

"That's too bad about your bike," she says.

"It is."

"At least you've still got the old one."

Her father makes a sound like air escaping an inner tube. She looks around the kitchen for signs of food preparation but the counters are bare. "Dad, is Uma making dinner?"

"Uma doesn't cook on insemination day."

"Are *you* going to cook?"

"What did you have in mind?"

"I don't care."

"Oh yes you do, Harriet. You care very much. You have very fixed ideas about what you want, and when you don't get it, you torture the rest of us. You're just like your mother."

He has never accused her of torturing before. She thinks of the Spanish Inquisition, or anyway, Monty Python's version of it, with a man in a black robe shouting, "Nobody expects the Spanish Inquisition!" and beating people watching telly with a cushion. "I could make grilled cheese," she says. "Do you have any cheese slices?"

Trent stares at her as though she has asked if he has any crack cocaine. He begins to laugh as hard as he cried, and Harriet has no idea what to do. He beckons her with limp hands. "Come here, sweetheart." His words sound gooey. "You're a funny one." He pulls her to him. "Cheese slices." He starts guffawing again, reminding her of Irwin. His breath smells of beer and he's holding her so tight it hurts. "How 'bout some hambangers like your grandma makes? Nothing like fried, greasy, hormone-saturated cow. That would get Uma off her ass."

"I want to call Mum." Harriet breaks away from him and grabs the cordless. Her mother doesn't pick up, probably because she thinks it's Trent. "Did she call you today?"

"She did, your majesty, mostly to check up on you. The prince is still in status and the queen is suitably distraught. What would your mother do without the drama of the sick child? No one suffers like your mother." He swigs more beer.

"Irwin suffers."

"Yes, well that's the point, isn't it?" He waves his beer bottle around. "*Why* should Irwin suffer? A boy who will probably die before he gets to high school? *Why* is he being made to suffer? Because his mommy saved him, that's why. Saved him from what?"

Harriet has heard Lynne brag about saving Irwin, saying the doctors were ready to give up but she insisted they keep him alive. "My sweet boy," she says. "They would have let my baby boy die. Where would I be without my sweet boy?" This is all about her, not Irwin. Maybe if Lynne hadn't saved him he'd be flying high in the sky, or swimming deep in the ocean. Instead he is trapped inside a stick body with tubes running in and out of him.

She watches her father open his sixth beer. "Do you think Mum should have let him die?"

"Who knows, Hal? All I know is it's not going to get any better and there's been a lot of collateral damage."

"You mean the divorce?"

"And you, kiddo, why are you so freakin' messed up? Why are you painting hell? You're eleven for fucksake, you're supposed to be painting rabbits and butterflies." He lines the empty bottles up and stares at them as though searching for hidden meaning. "What's hard for you to understand," he says, rubbing his fingers into his eyes, "is that I loved your mum. Very much. She was the absolute love of my life." Harriet worries he's starting to cry again. "We should have stopped at you, kiddo. We should have counted our blessings." He drops his head onto his forearms on the table.

"What about Uma?"

"What about her?"

"Do you love her?"

"It's different."

"How?'

Her father lifts his head and stares at the row of empty beer bottles again, apparently unable to find words to describe how his love for Uma is different.

Harriet looks in the fridge at weird vegetables, hummus and goat cheese. She finds peanut butter and spelt bread. She pulls out four slices, spreads peanut butter on them then cuts a banana and carefully arranges the pieces on top of the peanut butter. She presses the bread slices together and places a sandwich on a plate in front of Trent. "I'd like to go home tomorrow."

"Are you serious?"

She nods.

"Wow."

"Can you drive me? You'd have to stop drinking."

"I won't drink tomorrow, Hal. I don't get to drink during stud duty so after the dirty deed, I go a little wild."

More adult excuses for bad behaviour. Harriet's not allowed to make excuses. "Don't make excuses," Lynne says.

Trent tugs on Harriet's ponytail. "Are you sure you want to go home? Is it because of Uma? She's a little scatty right now. It's the drugs." More excuses.

"I just want to go home."

"Whatever you say, kiddo."

They sit side by side, ejected on the freezing tundra, while the crashed plane burns behind them.

Eight

The seniors are abuzz under the broken chandelier in the lobby because Mrs. Butts found a snake on her toilet.

"It's those goddamn Japs," Mr. Shotlander insists, tugging up his polyester trousers. "The minute they moved in I knew they were trouble."

"They're not Japs," Harriet says. "They're Filipino."

"Whatever, they party all night and cook stinky fish."

"That's *tuyo*. Dried sardines."

"I don't care what it is, it stinks to high heaven, and now they've brought snakes into the building."

"Who says?" Harriet resists an urge to yank the hair growing out of his ears.

"And where in heck have *you* been anyway?" Mr. Shotlander demands. "Mrs. Schidt's fit to be tied."

"Has anybody been walking Coco?"

"Mindy in 408 was supposed to take the mutt out but then her nutjob husband showed up. The dog's shitting on the balcony. Mrs. Schidt's going to have your hide."

Mrs. Pungartnik—with her crazy eye and orange hair—shuffles

towards Harriet, staring at her and away at the same time. "Are you the one who bought my husband cigarettes?"

"I haven't even been here."

Mr. Chubak, wearing his Che Guevara T-shirt, digs around in his worn corduroys for toonies. "Hey, Harry, I could use a Mango Vanilla Marble fix."

Harriet takes the toonies. "What happened with the snake?"

Mr. Shotlander sits on one of the leatherette chairs and expands his chest, preparing to recount the event. "Well," he begins, "Mrs. Butts had just eaten her Bran Buds when she looked in her bathroom and saw a five-foot python curled up on her toilet seat. She screamed so hard Bhanmattie, who happened to be on her floor, knocked on her door to find out if she was being murdered. Meantime Mrs. Butts had the good sense to close the bathroom door so the snake couldn't get away. Bhanmattie takes a gander and, what do you know, the python was in the bathtub. He said it was big and strong like the snakes in Bollywood movies. He figured it came in through the plumbing, up the toilet and pushed open the lid. How do you like that? So he closes the door and calls 911."

"The police are up there now," Mr. Zilberschmuck says, brushing cigarette ash from the lapel of the three-piece suit he wears when he smokes out front. "No need to be alarmed."

Mrs. Pungartnik wags an arthritic finger at him. "Was it *you* who gave my husband cigarettes?"

"Certainly not, Ava, I would never do that to you." Mr. Zilberschmuck is what Gran calls a ladies' man. Whenever he's in the lobby Mrs. Pungartnik, Mrs. Butts and even Mrs. Schidt in her wheelchair fawn over him and play euchre.

Mr. Shotlander takes his finger out of his ear. "The cops said yesterday they found a corn snake in a building two blocks over." He wipes his earwax on his polyester trousers. "They said it must have slid through the wall."

"Heaven help us," Mrs. Pungartnik gasps.

Mr. Chubak scratches his bald spot. "Didn't an escaped cobra asphyxiate two kids a while back?"

"You've got to ask yourself," Mr. Shotlander says, "what this country's coming to when we've got buildings full of snakes. Too many goddang foreigners."

Mr. Bhanmattie in his Walmart smock and Taj, the janitor, step out of the elevator with a Sikh policeman.

Mrs. Pungartnik stomps towards them. "Did you shoot the snake?"

"No, ma'am," the Sikh policeman says. "Animal Services will be here shortly to take care of it."

"Will *they* kill it?"

"Most likely they will take it to a reptile zoo."

"A reptile zoo?" Mrs. Pungartnik clutches her crumpled Kleenexes. "Who ever heard of such a thing? When will they get here? What if it goes down the toilet again and into the plumbing and slithers up somebody else's toilet?"

Harriet hopes the python snakes up her toilet while Gennedy's taking a crap. He reads John Grisham novels on the shitter, even though he complains that John Grisham "doesn't tell it like it is."

Mrs. Schidt wheels out of the elevator with Coco on her lap. "What if the snake swallows my dog?"

Mrs. Butts points her cane at the Sikh policeman. "Or my cats? It could poison Lindy and Lukey."

"We do not believe it is a poisonous snake, ma'am. Most certainly it will not eat your pets. Most likely it will be afraid of them."

"Not of Coco," Mrs. Schidt says, kissing her skinny white dog with yellow eyes before spotting Harriet. "And where have you been, young lady? No call, no note, what am I supposed to think?"

"My brother's in the hospital. I had to stay with my dad."

She wheels up to Harriet. "And you couldn't call? What's the matter with you, you careless and untrustworthy girl. Shirking responsibility as usual."

"I wasn't shirking anything. And anyway, you don't pay me enough." It just slips out. She'd intended to broach the subject carefully, mentioning the ad offering group walks for $16 and private walks for $20. Mrs. Schidt trembles and her lips move but no words come out.

Mrs. Pungartnik pinches the Sikh policeman. "What in heaven's name should we do to keep safe?"

"I would recommend looking first before you go into your washroom. Most likely the python was a pet that was let go. People buy them then discover taking care of them is too much trouble."

Taj, who spends more time on the street selling pirated DVDs than doing his janitorial duties, holds up his hands in an effort to quiet the seniors. "Please, ladies and gentlemen, it is all taken care of. Not to worry. No more snakes." He escorts the policeman out.

"Just cockroaches," Mrs. Pungartnik grumbles. "I killed two yesterday."

"Spray vinegar," Harriet suggests.

"None of this is good for my ulcer," Mrs. Butts says. "The doctor made me go to the drugstore to buy some medicine and it's making me sick to my stomach. I haven't eaten a thing all day and the cats aren't eating either." The other seniors edge away from Mrs. Butts as she rambles on about her cats and her various imagined illnesses. Most of the seniors have chronic illnesses and are desperate for a cure. Mrs. Butts is desperate for an illness. "I put out their special food with the fat in it, and they won't touch it. I even put out fish and chicken. And Lindy won't touch her milk. Now Lindy has a nervous condition but Lukey, I don't know what's gotten into him. He never stops eating but today he even refused chicken-flavoured Temptations. Oh and Harriet . . ." She switches into nice little old lady mode which means she wants something. "My doctor says my iron's low and I should eat prunes. Would it be too much trouble for you to go to the store and get me prunes and kitty litter? Oh and Lukey stepped on the remote again. I don't know how he got to it, I put it up high on the shelf, but there's no stopping him. Anyway I'm hoping you'll reprogram it again." The elevator doors open and Harriet makes a run for it.

It's obvious Lynne has not been home because newspapers, legal pads and clothes are strewn everywhere. Gennedy never puts anything back, even though he reprimands Harriet for never putting anything back. He said he would be home, but the computer is off. Harriet does a quick recon of the apartment to ascertain that she is alone then says, "Hubba hubba," before searching for her glue gun. Gennedy wouldn't have trashed it because he's too cheap to throw anything out. She starts with their bedroom, digging around in the closet crammed with dress shoes Lynne wore at the bank. Harriet tries on several pairs, pulling up her jeans to see if they flatter her ankles. Gran says a good pair of pumps should flatter your ankles. Since she stopped working at the bank Lynne wears Uggs with skinny jeans in winter, and shorts and flip-flops in summer. Gran thinks it's a crime that Lynne never wears skirts and heels anymore. "That girl's got my gams," she insists. "She should show them off. It's a crime."

When she can't find the glue gun in the closet, Harriet rummages through their dresser drawers, avoiding Gennedy's red Speedo that reminds her she almost drowned last summer. Gennedy had the brilliant idea to drive them to Wasaga Beach. His fifteen-year-old Corolla overheated, cutting their beach time short. This turned out to be a good thing because Gennedy was wearing the Speedo. Every other male, young and old, had the decency to wear swimming trunks, but Gennedy was tossing the Frisbee in bikini briefs. Harriet took her noodle far out into the water so as not to be associated with him. Lynne, also in a bikini, looked all right, despite having had two kids. Irwin, masterminding a lopsided sandcastle, suddenly realized Harriet wasn't present and began hollering that she was drowning. Harriet, too far out to hear him, surmised what was going on because Lynne and Gennedy were running up and down the beach with their eyes on the water. Harriet could have waved but she felt sleepy, lulled by the gentle pull of Georgian Bay, and lifting an arm required too much effort. She thought of the people of the First Nations, and birchbark canoes, and what the shoreline must have looked like two hundred years ago before the white man trashed it. She was thinking she was born in the wrong place at the wrong time, but then remembered what Mr. Bhanmattie said. She had been born in her current body for a reason: a lesson had to be learned. It didn't feel like she was learning anything. The same shit kept happening. A wave from a motorboat slapped her in the face and knocked the noodle from her grasp. Pushed under she allowed the water to close over her, enticed by the possibility of drowning—of being free of Gennedy and school and sacks of shit. But her lungs fought back, forcing her to bob to the surface in time to see Gennedy speed-crawling in her direction. He'd been on his high-school swim team, probably in the same red Speedo. She tried to swim away from him, kicking frantically, but her legs tired.

"Grab the noodle," Gennedy bellowed as he splashed towards her. When he reached her, he looked frightened, and Harriet felt sorry for him until he said, "What the hell do you think you're playing at?" He grabbed her with one arm and hauled her towards shore. The noodle bobbed out of reach, but he refused to swim back for it. It rolled on the waves, moving farther and farther away into a new life while Harriet returned to the old. She had never been skin to skin with Gennedy before. At Christmas they would exchange an awkward fully-clothed hug, but feeling his hairy chest heaving against her back, she felt sick and puked. "Keep your head up," he ordered. "Don't swallow any more water."

As soon as they made it to shore Lynne wrapped her in a towel on the beach blanket, rubbing her back to warm her. "My precious angel, you scared me so much, oh my lord, I'm so glad you're safe." She kissed her repeatedly and it was almost as wonderful as when Harriet fell from the tree. Except that Irwin crawled up like a bad puppy and rested his big head on her thigh. "I love you, Haarree. Don't ever do that again, pleeeze don't. That was sooo scary." Gennedy sat down, wrapping his arms around Lynne and Irwin, transforming them into the picture of a happy family. He never let Harriet swim without a life jacket after that. For this reason there is no way she is going to any beach with him this summer. She refuses to be the only eleven-year-old wearing a life jacket.

She searches their bedside tables. Two books sit on her mother's: *If I'm So Smart Why Do I Keep Messing Up?* and *When I Say No, I Feel Guilty.* Face creams and makeup clutter the drawer. Harriet scores some cherry cough drops, forbidden due to the buzz she gets from red dye. She shakes two out of the box and sucks on them while digging through squeezed-out tubes and busted eye shadow containers. Lynne never throws out makeup because she's afraid the new product won't be as good as the old one. Harriet uses her mother's forgotten remnants of lipsticks, blush and eye shadows in her mixed media. She pockets a sparkly fuchsia lip gloss and some moss-green shadow before sliding across the bed to Gennedy's bedside table. The only book on it is *The Four-Hour Work Week.* Not wanting to touch his stuff, Harriet jabs a pen into the contents of his drawer to fish for the glue gun; nothing but socks, aftershave, tightie whities and condoms. Harriet pulls one out of its wrapper and unrolls it, trying to figure out if the condoms mean Lynne and Gennedy are no longer trying to conceive. The box was shoved to the back, suggesting it's old. While she's checking for an expiration date, several condoms fall between the bedside table and the bed. Harriet kneels down to reach for them and spots the handle of her glue gun under the bed. "Tally-ho!" she says, grabbing it. She collects the condoms, stuffs them in the box and shoves it to the back of the drawer. With red dye coursing through her veins, she charges to her room to resume work on *And I Think to Myself, What a Wonderful World*, a mixed-media project she had to abandon when Gennedy stole her gun. She needed it to glue delicate things like pebbles, pieces of broken glass, safety pins and a discarded syringe. She was able to glue the cheese grater and the sieve with LePage's, but making the small objects stick was impossible. She plugs in the gun and waits for the glue to heat, listening for Gennedy. When she doesn't hear him she darts to their bedroom again, takes two more cherry cough drops and hurriedly searches her mother's jewellery box for beaded bracelets. Lynne buys them from street vendors, wears the bracelets for a summer, then forgets about them. Harriet finds three Lynne hasn't worn for at least two summers and takes them to her room to cut and sort by colour in small yogourt containers. She smells the glue melting and says, "Cha cha cha," while digging around in her feather collection. She found a black and white woodpecker feather last week and has been eager to glue it onto *And I Think to Myself, What a Wonderful World*—between the syringe and the cigarette butts. She's not sure where to put the condom and decides to save it. Rushing mixed media can destroy the entire project because, once items are glued, she can't just paint over them. She picks up the gun, inhaling the fumes. It's when she's applying a thin line of glue to the feather that she hears Gennedy's key in the lock.

"Hello? Harriet?"

"I'll be right out." She puts the gun down and scurries out of her room, closing the door.

"So you made it," Gennedy says. "That's tootin'. Sorry I'm late. Things got complicated."

"No worries." Harriet's not sure if she looks as buzzed as she feels.

"I picked up some pizza, are you hungry?"

"Oh yes please."

"Come eat."

"I'll be there in two secs." She hurries back to her room to unplug the gun and hide it under her bed.

"You look flushed, Harriet. Have you been out in the sun?"

"Totally."

"Excellent." He puts a pizza slice on a plate and hands it to her. "Sit down, stay awhile." He sniffs a couple of times. "Do you smell something burning?"

Harriet smells the glue gun. "I don't smell anything. Did you just come from the hospital?"

"I did."

"Can I call Mum?"

"After lunch. What have you got planned for today?"

"Nothing."

"Really? Because I just ran into Nina and she said you're going to the Eaton Centre with Darcy and her dad."

"Not till later."

"Don't you think you might have asked our permission first?"

"You weren't here. Can I go? Please?"

"What do we know about this Buck guy?"

"He's really nice. He took us to Canada's Wonderland, remember?"

"Oh that's right. He's a truck driver, isn't he?"

"Yeah, sometimes he parks in the back. It's got a really big cab. He sleeps in it."

"Is that so? Well, here's the thing. Your mum and I don't understand why you so badly wanted to go to your dad's two days ago and then, all of a sudden, you wanted to come home again."

"He and Uma are mid-cycle."

"You knew that before you went. What happened while you were there?"

Harriet suspects the adults have discussed what happened, how she lacks compassion, is uncooperative and mistreated Uma. The adults go through the motions of asking her what happened but they've already made up their minds. "Nothing happened."

"Harriet, why is it that whenever I ask you about what happened at school or at camp, or anywhere in fact, you tell me 'nothing.' How would you feel if every time you asked me what happened during my day, I said 'nothing'?"

"I never ask you what happened during your day."

"That's because you have no interest in anything but yourself and your own pursuits. Granted you're a child and therefore egocentric, nonetheless, you might try and show some small consideration for others." He is in what Lynne calls litigator mode. Harriet tries to appear penitent as she wolfs pizza. The red dye has made her very hungry. The phone rings and Harriet lunges for it to avoid further cross-examination. It's Mrs. Butts stoned on painkillers and pretending to be a nice old lady.

"Is that Harriet? So sorry to bother you, dear, but do you think you could come over and reprogram my remote? I can't get anything on the TV and Roger's playing." Mrs. Butts is obsessed with Roger Federer, says he looks like a Greek god. She spreads out on her couch, spooning ice cream while murmuring, "Oooooh look at him. He's perrrfect, like a Greek god, ooooooh just perrrfect."

"I'll ask Gennedy." She knows he won't forbid her from helping an old lady. "Mrs. Butts needs me to reprogram her remote. The cat stepped on it. Can I go over?"

"Of course."

"I'll be right there, Mrs. Butts."

"Oh you're a darling, thank you so much."

Harriet grabs another slice and speeds to Mrs. Butts'. After reprogramming the remote she takes the junkie's money to buy prunes and kitty litter. She lingers in the lobby, trawling for more orders.

Mr. Chubak paces, gripping his red suspenders. "Sometimes I wake up, and I turn on the tube and there's *nothing* on. Not one effing thing worth watching. So I turn it off again."

"What a world." Mr. Shotlander smooths down tufts of hair on his head, glancing at Mrs. Chipchase knitting in the corner. Mrs. Chipchase knits baby clothes, slippers, mittens, hats and scarves for the church bazaar. She doesn't have any children and Harriet wonders how it feels to endlessly knit for other people's babies. Mrs. Chipchase taught Harriet to crochet, and even gave her some yarn to make toques for Lynne, Gennedy and Irwin. In way of thanks, Harriet never charges her for going to the store.

"Hi, Mrs. Chipchase, can I get you anything from Mr. Hung's?"

"Oh, how kind of you, sweetheart. I'd like some Life Savers, butterscotch if Mr. Hung has them."

"Hey, Esther," Mr. Shotlander says. "Do you mind telling me what you paid for that walker?"

Mrs. Chipchase goes on knitting. "My nephew bought it at the Goodwill for twenty-five dollars."

"Are you messing with me?"

"I would never mess with you, Mr. Shotlander."

"Do you have any idea what one of those would cost new?"

Mrs. Chipchase shakes her head, still focused on her knitting.

"I'd say new that would run you at least two hundred." Mr. Shotlander pats the walker's upholstered seat. "A nice seat you got here, Esther."

Mrs. Chipchase goes on knitting. Harriet knows she was gorgeous when she was young because her wedding photo hangs on her living room wall. Mrs. Chipchase looks unsure in the picture, although she's smiling. She never talks about Mr. Chipchase but in the wedding photo he looks very sombre.

"Mr. Chubak," Harriet asks, "do you want some ice cream?"

"You bet your sweet bippy." Mr. Chubak introduced Harriet to the sixties comedy show *Laugh-in* on YouTube and insists "they don't make funny like they used to." Mr. Chubak was a protester in the sixties and thrown in jail eight times.

"Mango Vanilla Marble?" Harriet reaches into her back pockets for baggies and Post-its to record the transactions.

"The girl's telepathic." Mr. Chubak sucks the straw on his juice box. Daily, in the lobby, Mr. Chubak eats an orange and drinks orange juice from a juice box to keep up his vitamin C.

Mr. Shotlander feels around in his pockets. "I could use some barbecue chips, and a Diet Coke."

"Only if you stop ratting on me," Harriet says.

"What's that?"

"I'm not shopping for you if you keep telling my mother's boyfriend my business."

"What business?"

"How and what I do with my art projects is *my* business. If you keep squealing on me I will no longer provide you with service."

"You have been told, Shotlander," Mr. Zilberschmuck says. Mr. Tumicelli hobbles out of the elevator, wheeling his oxygen tank behind him.

"What happened to you?" Mr. Shotlander asks.

"I changed my cell number to get some peace and quiet." Mr. Tumicelli is the only senior with a cell phone. His son married a Dominican girl who programmed "*Feliz Navidad*" as Mr. Tumicelli's ringtone. It rings frequently because Mr. Tumicelli, a retired mechanic, has many relatives who need car repairs. "I'm not giving my number to nobody. Just my kids. That's it." He pulls the black overcoat he wears summer and winter around him and sits on one of the leatherette chairs.

"Do you need anything from the store, Mr. Tumicelli?" Harriet asks.

"I could use some Pepto-Bismol. My stomach's acting up."

"You'll never guess who I ran into the other day," Mr. Shotlander says.

"I give up." Mr. Tumicelli responds to most questions with "I give up" because he has emphysema and talking requires too much oxygen.

"Remember that louse with the Kraut car you fixed up? He lived in 504 with a Puerto Rican *chica* he was always screaming at. Finally she took off and he couldn't pay the rent so he got evicted. I figured he'd be dead in an alley over a drug deal but oh no, he's living two blocks over with some other piece of ass who doesn't know any better. How do you like that? I thought I'd seen the last of that sack of shit."

"Tut tut." Mr. Chubak sucks on his straw.

"Must be something in his pants we don't know about," Mr. Shotlander says. Mrs. Chipchase collects her knitting. "Sorry, Esther. I forgot you were there, you're so quiet."

"You never forget anything, Mr. Shotlander. Harriet, dear, can you help me with the elevator?" Harriet presses the button and when it arrives, holds the doors open until Mrs. Chipchase can push in her walker.

"Oh don't go, Esther," Mr. Shotlander pleads, and Harriet feels sorry for him, so visible is his yearning for Esther's approval.

Mrs. Chipchase gives Harriet a toonie and whispers, "For the Life Savers. Keep the change. Bless you, you sweet girl."

After the elevator doors close there is a weighty silence before Mr. Shotlander says, "I can't believe that sack of shit is living two blocks over."

Mr. Chubak tosses his empty juice box into the wastebasket. "It just goes to show. There's ten people in the world and the rest is ghosts and mirrors."

What a good name for a painting, Harriet thinks. She can put the wiry woman with mauve lipstick from the Starbucks in it, and make her half python.

"That sack of shit had tracks up both arms," Mr. Shotlander says. "I was sure he'd be dead by now. I used to hear him beating the daylights out of her and her screaming like nobody's business. Twice I called the cops but she wouldn't press charges, she was too scared of the bastard."

"Each to his own hell." Mr. Zilberschmuck pulls a cigarillo from his suit pocket and heads out for a smoke.

Mr. Chubak starts to peel an orange. "It's a battleground."

"You can say that again," Mr. Tumicelli wheezes.

"What a world," Mr. Shotlander concludes.

Nine

Harriet uses Mr. Hung's phone to call her mother because she doesn't want Gennedy listening. Lynne sounds as though she has no idea why Harriet is calling her. "What is it, bunny, is something wrong?"

"No, I just wanted to talk to you."

"Did Gennedy get you a pizza?"

"He did."

"He thought he'd take you to a movie this afternoon."

"I'm going out with Darcy."

"Who's Darcy?"

"The new girl in the building. Her dad's taking us."

"Do we know her dad?"

"He took me and Darcy to Canada's Wonderland in his Mack truck, remember? His name's Buck. Sometimes he parks out back. He's really nice."

"Okay, well, if it's all right with Gennedy."

"Why does it have to be all right with Gennedy? Why can't it be all right with you?"

"Bunny, he knows more about what's going on over there than I do.

I'm . . . I'm kind of tuned out right now. If he's met Chuck, and he's okay with it, than that's fine by me. What happened with your dad?"

"Nothing."

"It didn't go so well, huh?"

"Not really."

"He's an asshole. And don't get me started on that sterile so-called intellectual."

"I don't understand why she wants a baby."

"That makes two of us." Harriet and Lynne always bond over the awfulness of Uma.

"How's Irwin?"

"Fighting hard, as usual."

"When are you coming home?"

"Soon. But I really need you to make an effort to get along with Gennedy. He didn't ask for any of this."

Lynne always excuses Gennedy by saying he didn't ask for any of this, as though anybody asks for the shit that happens. The fact that Gennedy gets to live rent-free doesn't enter into the equation, or that Irwin was already sick when they shacked up. It's always what a good man Gennedy is because he sticks around.

"I didn't either," Harriet says.

"What, baby?"

"I didn't ask for any of this either." She waits for her mother to call her selfish, self-absorbed and egocentric. In the background the hospital whirrs.

"A little girl died here today," her mother says. "Septic shock. My lord, it happened so fast."

Harriet can hear sharp intakes of breath, meaning Lynne's trying not to cry. "What's septic shock?"

"It's when an infection spreads and gets into the blood and the body can't fight it."

"That won't happen to Irwin."

"I don't know what will happen to Irwin. That's what's so hard. 24/7 I don't know what will happen to my baby boy."

"None of us knows what will happen to us."

"You're right, Mizz Harriet. So you're okay?"

"Sure."

"At least you're getting a break from Irwin surveillance."

Without the shackle of Irwin, Harriet has moments of feeling utterly lost, empty-handed and guilty.

"Oh, bunny, the doctor's here, I've got to go. I'll talk to you soon."

Mr. Hung gently takes the phone from Harriet and hands her a slightly squashed Caramilk bar.

"Thank you." She unwraps it carefully, saving the gold paper for mixed media.

Outside, boys play street hockey while Irwin fights hard—as usual—and a little girl dies of septic shock. None of it makes any sense. "There was a snake on Mrs. Butts' toilet."

"What kind of snake?"

"A python. A five-footer."

"Good for Chinese food."

"Do Chinese really eat chicken feet?"

"Dim sum. Very good. I take you one day."

"That's okay." Harriet breaks off a square of the Caramilk bar and puts it on her tongue, letting the chocolate melt. "Do you think I lack compassion?"

"Why you ask?"

"My mother's boyfriend and my father's girlfriend say I lack compassion." She looked it up: *a feeling of distress and pity for the suffering or misfortune of another.*

"People say things. Don't react, it give them power."

Harriet puts another square of chocolate on her tongue.

Mr. Hung starts unloading the milk crates. "Egyptian man call himself strongest man in world and lock himself in steel cage with lion."

"Why?"

"To boost tourism in Egypt. Everybody want to see man fight lion in steel cage."

"I wouldn't."

"Egyptian has big plan to boost tourism. He pull airplane with his teeth, pull airplane with his hair and be run over by airplane. In between he fight lions."

"Does he kill the lions?"

"So far only one steel-cage fight happen. Hundreds of people wait for fight to start. Egyptian spend twenty minutes in cage. Lion do nothing. Egyptian declare victory."

"How is it a victory if the lion didn't do anything?"

"Egyptian say he fight dogs too, most ferocious breeds. He punch and kick them. He has fighting style he call 'life or death.' He teach children how to chew glass and pull car with teeth. He say he jump from ten-storey building and hang himself many times."

"Maybe he's nuts."

"He don't care what people say. In his mind he strongest man in world." Mr. Hung stacks the empty milk crates. "In your mind be strongest girl in world. Don't care what people say."

On the subway, Buck stares at pretty girls. When the train rolls above ground, Darcy checks her cell to see if her BFF from her old neighbourhood will meet them at the Eaton Centre. Her dismay at the lack of texts from former friends causes her to slouch and pick at her split ends. "It's not like I moved to China. I bet that Caitlin whore's dissing me." Whenever Darcy needs someone to blame for her friends' disloyalty, she blames that Caitlin whore, whose parents are dentists and buy her Lululemon outfits. Caitlin had a party and invited everybody except Darcy, and gave everybody Lululemon headbands that cost twelve bucks each.

Aware that she is Darcy's stand-in friend, Harriet tries hard not to disappoint, so rare is it that she gets invited anywhere. She's not wild about the Eaton Centre—it's just another mall—but she enjoys looking at the goose sculptures suspended in the atrium, and the granite fountain that spurts water like a whale.

"Fucking whore," Darcy says re: her BFF who hasn't texted back.

Buck nudges her. "Is that nice?"

"Why do you call them whores?" Harriet asks. "Do you know what a whore is?"

"It's a slut, duh."

"No it's not. It's a prostitute."

"Which is a slut."

"No it's not. Prostitution is a profession. The world's oldest. Lots of women do it to avoid starving to death." Mr. Chubak's niece in Winnipeg got laid off and went into the world's oldest profession. According to Mr. Chubak she hated herself so much for being a prostitute she started taking drugs. When she got VD her regular johns dropped her. She tried working the streets but her toes froze and she had to have two amputated. She swallowed all her painkillers at once and died. Mr. Chubak believes drugs should be legalized and writes regularly to the Prime Minister about it.

"Oh my god why are you so hung up about the exact definitions of things, I mean, who gives a fuck?"

"Whores do. If I was a whore I wouldn't want every slutty girl named after me."

"Okay, fine, so what am I supposed to call them?"

"Sacks of shit."

"That sounds derpy."

"Mr. Shotlander says it all the time. Try it."

Darcy sighs histrionically then says, "Sack of shit."

"It's got a certain ring to it," Buck concedes.

They join the crowd cramming into the Apple Store to fondle the latest technology. Harriet watches a pear-shaped, mustard-haired man leaning over a laptop. His shoulders angle straight down from his neck, making it look as though he has no shoulders. Every few minutes he reaches back and scratches his butt. Harriet thinks he'd be an excellent subject for *There's Just Ten People in the World and the Rest Is Ghosts and Mirrors*.

A laptop becomes available and Darcy lunges for it to play *Plants Vs. Zombies*. After that she plays *Neopets*, feeding her cyber dog and trying different doggy jackets and booties on him. Beside them two people who look almost identical in big glasses and cargo pants huddle around another laptop. "I think I'm uptight," the woman says. One side of her hair is considerably shorter than the other.

"Why would you say that?" the man asks.

"We did a questionnaire at work to assess how we cope with stress and I scored really badly. It said uptight people suck at managing stress."

The man searches something on the laptop for several minutes before saying, "I disagree. I think you manage stress very well." They both look uptight to Harriet. The man meanders away from the laptop and the woman follows. Harriet hops over to it and searches YouTube for the crazy chicken lady who plays the ukulele, singing like a chicken. Next she finds the lady in Churchill, Manitoba, tossing boiling water from a cup into the freezing air. "This is how cold it is," the lady says as the water turns to icy snow in midair. This looks like so much fun to Harriet.

Darcy puts a tiara on her cyber doggy. "H, I can't believe you're not on Facebook. I would, like, *die* without Facebook."

Harriet did join Facebook, hoping it would make her less lonely but it made her lonelier because few people accepted her friend requests, and the ones that did didn't really know her. They just blabbed about themselves and the boring stuff they did, and posted selfies and photos of themselves with friends doing boring stuff, like smiling at parties or holding their pets. Harriet couldn't think of anything to post that wasn't equally boring. She knew if she revealed who she really was they would unfriend her in seconds. So she deleted her account.

"Goils, check this out." Buck shows them a clip of a fat man he calls the greatest actor of all time. "That's him in *The Godfather*."

The greatest actor of all time says, "I'm gonna make him an offer he can't refuse."

"He put cotton balls in his mouth to make his cheeks stick out like that," Buck explains.

"Craptastic," Darcy says.

"I'm serious. That's how he got the part. He had to *audition* for the part because everybody wrote him off when he got fat. So he shows up for the screen test with his cheeks puffed out. He won an Oscar. A fucking epic comeback."

"Buck's planning a death metal comeback," Darcy says.

"I never left, girlfriend."

In Lululemon Darcy fondles a Sparkle Scuba Hoodie that costs $108. "Caitlin-the-sack-of-shit has one of these in pink."

"What's supposed to sparkle about it?" Harriet asks. "It just looks like any other hoodie."

Beside them, a scarily thin woman inspects a Live Healthy Wrap while talking on her phone. "What you have to accept is humans are egotistical. We're *different* from animals."

"Swag," Darcy says. "This one's got holes in the sleeves for your thumbs."

"Why do you want holes in the sleeves for your thumbs?"

Darcy checks the price. "A hundred and twenty-eight bucks."

"A steal." Buck winks at an approaching salesgirl.

"Can I help you guys with anything?"

"I believe my daughter's looking for pants, isn't that right, Dee?"

"Perfect," the salesgirl says, hooking hair behind her ears. "Let's talk pants." She surveys Darcy's generous waist, butt and thighs. "Were you looking for a tight fit or something more relaxed?"

Darcy, demonstrating a bashfulness Harriet hasn't seen before, says meekly, "My friend Caitlin has the Wunder Under Pant and they look really cool."

"Perfect. The thing is, the Wunder Under Pants are a Second Skin fit." The salesgirl wrinkles her nose. "Like, really tight. You might want to try something a little more relaxed."

"What about Groove Pants?"

The salesgirl, in what looks like Second Skin fit pants, taps an index finger against her chin. "Perfect. The thing is Groove Pants are also a slim fit. Like, you might want to go for more coverage. What about the drawstring Relaxed Fit? They're totally awesome, and soooo comfortable." She pulls out grey shapeless pants.

"Forget it," Darcy says and plods out of the store. Harriet follows while Buck flirts with the salesgirl.

"I don't think any of those pants are worth a hundred bucks," Harriet says.

"That's because you dress like shit. Do you even *have* another pair of jeans?"

"Goils," Buck calls after them, "are we ready for Sugar Mountain?"

The red dye in the candy apple pushes Harriet into an altered state where everything is amplified and transformed into changing shapes, shadows and colours. After Mr. Shotlander had his hernia operation, the narcotics made him see the Mexican army. "The dang Mexicans were attacking me. There was me bandaged in my bed and Mexicans coming at me through the window with sabres." Harriet isn't hallucinating, exactly, but fake plants seem larger, as though they might be hiding Mexicans. This doesn't scare her. She's ready for a fight. "Try me," she growls to a fern.

Darcy rifles through the merchandise at Ardene. "Check out this bling." She tries on some chunky rings and thick plastic bangles. "Swag."

The mall air conditioning is making Harriet shiver. "I don't wear jewellery."

"You don't say. How 'bout a tank top, two for ten bucks? We could each buy one. What colour do you want?" Harriet never wears tank tops, prefers to hide behind baggy T-shirts. "I want the pink," Darcy says. "Get something different. I don't want us looking like twins, yo."

"Why do you say *yo* at the ends of sentences?"

"Because it's coolio, hoolio." She holds a pale blue tank top against Harriet who understands that if she hopes to continue to be invited places with Buck and Dee, she had better make a purchase. But she's been saving up for a tube of Cadmium Red Deep. It costs $24.99 and is crucial for the gouged tongues and bleeding wounds in her paintings.

"You go, girl. Try it on." Dee pushes her into a changeroom. The mirror is wide and full length, providing an excellent opportunity to practice Michael Jackson moves. Harriet turns sideways and practices her moonwalk then tries some knee bouncing and swinging.

Darcy bangs on the wall dividing the changerooms. "What are you doing in there?"

"Nothing."

"How's it looking, yo?"

Harriet pulls the tank top over her head. The pale blueness of it makes her think of Irwin's eyes, and how he went temporarily blind because they had to give him so much oxygen. Lynne was screaming and grabbing her forehead and wouldn't sit down. Harriet was afraid to move in case Lynne started screaming at her.

Darcy knocks on her door. "Check this out, yo. Does it make me look fat?" Her girth bulges beneath the tank top.

"No."

"Sometimes skinny fits make me look thinner. Whassup wich you, girl? Awks, you need a smaller size. It should fit tighter."

"I don't want it tighter."

"H, it's hanging off you. It looks retarded. Woman, you dress like that and I'm leaving you by the highway. Try extra small."

The extra small pale blue tank top reveals the outlines of Harriet's nipples.

Darcy shakes her head, making tsk sounds. "It's time you got a bra, dawg. You wear that with a decent bra and a pair of skinny jeans, you'll have *serious* street cred."

LaSenza Girl is having a buy-two-bras-get-one-free sale. Darcy hands Harriet a bra with leopard spots, trimmed with pink lace. "If we each buy one, I get one free. Try it on, girl."

"I don't have money for a bra."

"What about all that canine cash?"

"I haven't walked her dog this week."

Dee pushes her into a changeroom. "FYI, I saw Clayton the mutant walking it."

Clayton lives on the ground floor with his obese mother and their ferret. Mrs. Rumph lolls in a lawn chair in front of the building and lets the ferret crawl all over her. Clayton listens to rap so loud Harriet can hear it coming out of his earbuds, and wears baggy jeans halfway off his ass, plus a snap-back with the brim turned sideways.

"I guess that's why the old bag hasn't called you," Dee says. "You've been out-sourced. A low blow, girl."

"I shouldn't have asked for more money."

"Oh yes you should have, girlfriend, you're no Third-Worlder. She can eat it."

"I don't have any income though."

"You've got your senior lobby racket. Those sacks of shit depend on you. How's the bra?"

The leopard-spotted bra makes Harriet look as though she has breasts. She tries some Lady Gaga moves, swivelling her hips and twitching her shoulders. "It's okay. How's yours?"

"Sexyfine. Let's buy'em. Buck will lend us the dough."

"I don't want to spend ten bucks on a bra."

"Let me see it." Darcy pushes at the door. Harriet opens it. Darcy whistles. "You look shit hot, *chiquita*. This is your supernova moment, seriously, you've got to buy it. Dad never makes me pay him back anyway because he wants Mom to think he's loaded."

Buck is leaning on the cash desk chatting up a salesgirl. "You could be a supermodel. I kid you not."

"Pops? We need you to pay for these."

"Anything for you, princess."

With the red dye wearing off, colours fade and the Mexicans retreat. Harriet can't understand why being invited out by Darcy and Buck is so important to her. It must be because she enjoys blending with the crowd. When she goes out with her family, people stare. Nobody looks twice at Buck and Dee. She'd like to have Buck for a dad, even though he thinks with his dick, because at least he pays for stuff and doesn't fuss about computer time or junk food.

"So, goils, are you ready for some grub?"

"Preach it, daddy-o." Darcy gives two thumbs-up. "Let's dip outta here. I'm in a chicken teriyaki state of mind."

Both Darcy and Buck are adept with chopsticks but Harriet fumbles, longing for a fork.

"So, princess, is Nina seeing anybody?"

"Like I would tell you that."

"We're best buds, you tell me everything. How am I supposed to get in the good books with her if you don't give me inside info?"

"These are the questions that haunt me." Darcy expertly chopsticks chicken.

"Seriously, Dee, don't you want Mom and me to get back together?"

"She thinks you're a dick. There's no way she's getting back together with you."

Buck picks at the label on his beer bottle.

"Maybe you could date *my* mother," Harriet suggests, astonished that she hadn't thought of this before. "She still looks good in a bikini."

Darcy shakes her head and wags her chopsticks. "Your mother's with that derp."

"She's only with him because he says he won't leave. If Buck meets her and says he won't leave either, she might boot out the derp. You're way better looking than him."

"Which isn't saying much," Dee says. "*And* she's got a retarded brother. Like, really retarded."

"He's not retarded, just slow with buttons and stuff."

"Seems legit."

"He's not retarded," Harriet insists. "He goes to regular school." Last week Lynne asked Harriet to teach him some spelling. He spelled everybody *evry buddy*. Harriet didn't have the heart to correct him because in his world everybody is a buddy.

"Gee wow, like he can't even tie his shoes."

More noodles slip from Harriet's chopsticks. "Lots of five-year-olds can't tie shoes."

"Why are you defending him? You hate his guts."

Buck grips a piece of sushi. "Hey, take it easy. It's not like I'm available."

"Of course you're available. Mom wants you the fuck out of her life."

He drops the sushi. "She said that?"

"That's all she ever talks about, how Buck fucked her over."

"Now that's not fair, I've totally changed."

"Cool story, bro."

"I learned my lesson, Dee. I want to be with you guys."

"Then how come you're chasing tail?"

"Since when am I chasing tail?"

"Duh, like, since everywhere we go."

"No way."

"I have a witness. H, is he or is he not all over every hottie in groping distance?"

Harriet has been caught in divorce crossfire before. There is no winning at this game. She shrugs as a bean sprout slips from her chopsticks.

"Seriously, Dee, like when was I all over some hottie?"

"Gee wow, let me think, how 'bout at every store we've been to."

"You mean with the salesgirls? We were just talking."

"Well, it's your 'just talking' that makes Mom want to rip your nuts off."

Back at the Shangrila, two policemen push Mindy's crackhead husband into a cruiser. Mr. Shotlander and Mr. Chubak shake their heads and resume playing checkers. "Jump you and jump you again," Mr. Chubak says.

"No fair. I was distracted by the crackhead." Mr. Shotlander squints hard at the board. "I'm red, right?"

In the elevator, Dee says, "Anybody who tells Mom what I ate is a dead man."

Mindy's seeking refuge at Nina's. They're both drinking spritzers.

"If I could kill the fucker, I would," Mindy says. "I'd blow his fucking brains out." Nina pours more wine. Buck sets Darcy's purchases on the table. "Anything I can do to help?"

Nina flicks her mad-nice red hair out of her face. "What could you possibly do to help?" Already Buck is eyeing Mindy, whose breasts are pushed up in a bra like the one Darcy forced Harriet to buy.

"So what's the story, Min?" Dee asks. "How come Romeo didn't give you a black eye this time?"

"Is that nice?" Buck says.

Dee checks the fridge for carbs. "The whole building's going to be talking about it, might as well get the facts straight. Did you try the move I showed you?" Darcy has been practising self-defence moves she learned online.

Mindy wipes smeared eyeliner off her cheeks. "I didn't get a chance, it all happened so fast."

"That's where they get ya," Darcy says. "You've got to be ready." She holds her hands up and bends her knees in a demonstration of readiness. "Rock 'em and sock 'em."

Buck sits next to Mindy, resting his arm across the back of her chair.

"Buck," Nina says, "what do you think you're doing?"

"I was hoping we could talk."

"Buck, get the fuck out."

"When are you going to get through this anger stuff?"

"Not in your lifetime. Fuck off. I mean it. *Now.*" And he does and Harriet admires Nina's ball-busting powers. She wishes Lynne was a ball buster and not a hottie who settles for a derp because he won't leave. Darcy jerks her thumb at her bedroom. "H, let's investigate this further in the situation room."

Harriet follows. "Investigate what?"

Darcy pulls out her Ouija board, sets it on the Barbie table and places her right hand on the pointer. "Come on, woman, let's do this thing."

"What thing?" When Harriet told Mr. Rivera about Darcy's Ouija board, his eyes widened and he warned her that it might release evil spirits. "If *multo* tells you to come," he said, "don't go. Even if it says if you don't, you will be possessed by the devil." Last time Darcy and Harriet did Ouija, it took all afternoon for the pointer to spell *A part of you will change*. For a week Harriet kept checking to see if a part of her had changed. When she told Darcy no part of her had changed Dee said, "Duh, genius, it doesn't have to be on the outside. It could be on the inside. Like, you could be growing a tumour or something."

"Do you have anything red I can wear?" Harriet asks.

"Say what?"

"I'm not doing it unless I can wear red. Mr. Rivera says red wards off evil spirits."

"Hell's bells." Darcy tosses a pair of red shorts at Harriet. She slides them over her jeans.

"Now concentrate," Darcy orders, switching the lights off. "Hand on pointer. No talking till we make contact."

Mindy and Nina, livened by spritzers, can be heard through the wall discussing how they'd like to watch their exes die. "Electrocution, totally," Nina says. "Real slo-ow. Starting with his balls." They shriek with spooky laughter.

Dee closes her eyes with her hands on the Ouija. "Is anybody there? Is there anybody in the room with us?" The pointer shifts slightly, pointing towards *Hello* on the board.

"Touchdown," Darcy says. "So glad you could make it, dear sir or madam. May I ask to whom I am speaking? Are you by any chance related to Harriet?"

"Why does it have to be related to me?"

"Shh . . . I feel it moving." The pointer points towards *Yes*.

"Bam," Darcy says.

"You're moving it."

"No way. Like I really want to ask questions I have to answer myself."
She closes her eyes again. "If you are a madam, would you by any chance be
Harriet's dead grandmother?"

"Both my grandmothers are alive."

"Oops, scratch that, what about your grandfathers?"

"One of them's dead."

"What was his name?"

"Archie."

"Sir, would you by any chance be Archie?" The pointer indicates *Yes*.

"Touchdown," Darcy says. "Now we're cookin'. So, Archie, what do
you want to tell us, sir? Do you have a message for Harriet?" The pointer
indicates *Yes* and Harriet feels herself tightening because she misses
Grandpa Archie. He taught her how to pick locks and lent her his staple
gun even after Lynne forbade her from using it.

"Archie," Darcy says, "I'm going to cut to the chase here and ask if
Harriet's little brother is going to kick it."

"Don't ask him that."

"Why not? Don't you want to know? I would. Archie, are you there?
Don't be afraid to spill the beans, dude, we can take it. Is Irwin going to die?"

"Everybody dies," Harriet says.

"Okay, let me rephrase that. Arch, is her little brother going to, like,
check out this week?"

Nina and Mindy are singing "How Can You Mend a Broken Heart"
really loudly.

The pointer indicates *Yes*. Darcy gasps.

"You moved it."

"Like why would I do that?"

"To scare me."

"Get serious. I've got better things to do with my time."

"So do I." Harriet pushes the board away and heads for the door.

"Take it easy, H."

"Nothing's easy. Ever."

She takes the elevator to the lobby to see if she can make escape money.
Mr. Hoogstra, who owned a yacht once and still wears a grubby captain's

hat, points at his teeth. "Food gets stuck in the gums. I take a toothpick on dates so I can dig 'em out. Chicken's the worst."

Mr. Shotlander tugs up his polyester trousers. "Since when have you had a date?"

"Wouldn't you like to know." Mr. Hoogstra tips his hat at Harriet. Mr. Tumicelli's cell rings "*Feliz Navidad*" even though he changed his number to stop people calling for car repairs. He pulls it out of his black overcoat and wheezes into it in Italian, except for car-part words like struts.

Mr. Shotlander digs his finger in his ear. "Harry, just the person I want to see. I got hacked again." He always thinks he's being hacked. "What's with the red shorts? You going to clown school?"

Harriet forgot she had on Darcy's shorts.

"It's all the rage in Paris." Mr. Chubak scratches his bald spot. "Everybody's wearing them."

"Now that's a Kodak moment," Mr. Hoogstra says.

Harriet pulls off the shorts and stuffs them behind the dusty plastic palm. "Does anybody need something from Mr. Hung's?"

Mr. Shotlander trails her. "Harry, this is serious business, I can't get my emails. My son sent me an email two days ago and I didn't get it."

"That doesn't mean you were hacked."

"What's it mean then? I can't get into the goddang account. Some hacker's messing with me."

"Were you using the right password?" He forgets his passwords.

"Of course I was using the right password. I need you to open me a new account."

Harriet usually charges the seniors a loonie to help with their computers but it's time for a raise. "Only if you pay me a toonie."

"For the love of Mike, what are you, some kind of IT expert all of a sudden?"

"I've got expenses. Last call for Mr. Hung's."

"I could use a treat." Mr. Chubak digs around in his corduroys. "See if he's got some Raspberry Devil."

Mr. Hoogstra hands her a five. "A carton of 2%. Check the date. The last one you bought was two days past the best before."

"That was the only 2% he had."

"That Chinaman is always selling rotten goods," Mr. Shotlander says.

"What do you mean 'always'?" Harriet demands. "When has he sold you something rotten?"

"Why are you so pro-commie all of a sudden?"

"You try working sixteen-hour days, 24/7."

"God dammit," Mr. Hoogstra says. "I got something in my eye."

"Use your finger to get it out," Mr. Shotlander advises.

"It's like somebody poured acid in it," Mr. Hoogstra says. "Dammit and dammit again."

Mr. Chubak starts peeling an orange. "Try pulling your upper lid over your lower."

Mr. Shotlander tramps over to Mr. Hoogstra with his dirty fingers. "Let's have a look."

Harriet speeds to Mr. Hung's, thinking she never asked for any of this.

Ten

After her deliveries, she counts her profits in the elevator and stuffs them in her pocket, where Gennedy can't see them. He'll be angry because she's late for dinner. She hears Mrs. Butts' cane tapping behind her in the corridor.

"Harriet, dear, could you do something for me?" Mrs. Butts has the pickled stare she gets on painkillers. "It'll only take a minute."

Harriet, hoping there's money in it, follows the old lady into her apartment. "My back's bad. I don't know what I did, but I can't lift the litter box. Would you be a dear and empty it for me and pour in some fresh. I ordered the large bag because it's cheaper but I had no idea it would be so heavy. They should have told me it was so heavy when I ordered it. I'm a regular customer, they should know better, they know I'm not well."

"If you pay me."

"Excuse me?"

"I need money for a trip and Mrs. Schidt has hired another dog walker."

"Why would she do that?"

"Because I asked for a raise. She's been paying me fourteen dollars a week for three years. That doesn't even cover inflation." Lynne used to say this about the raises she got from the bank.

"But Harriet, you're a child."

"I'm being exploited." Lynne also said this.

"My, my. All right then, I'll pay you a quarter."

"Fifty cents."

"Fine, fine. I don't know what's got into you. Sometimes you can be so disagreeable." She leads Harriet to the litter box. "Lukey bit me. Look." She pulls up the sleeve of her food-stained cardigan. "Do you see that? Toothmarks. Thank goodness I've had my shots." Lukey winds around her legs. "You're a bad cat, yes you are, a *bad cat*. And Lindy's breath smells funny. I think that's why she's stopped eating. I felt her neck and tummy and there's some swelling. I don't know what I'd do if something happened to Lindy." Lukey sharpens his claws on the furniture. "Shoo." Mrs. Butts waves her cane at him. "Stop that! *Bad cat*."

Mr. Shotlander calls Mrs. Butts "Misery" behind her back. "Here comes Misery," he'll mutter when Mrs. Butts comes tapping through the front doors. All the seniors avoid her monologues about her imagined ailments and her cats. Mr. Hoogstra says an overdose would be a merciful end for Mrs. Butts. At Seniors' Reading Night, where Harriet serves beverages for fifty cents a glass, Mr. Chubak read from an ancient Greek play. Harriet liked some of the words and wrote them down for a mixed-media project:

> *Never to have been born is best,*
> *But once you've entered this world,*
> *Return as quickly as possible to the place you came from.*

Harriet wishes she could return as quickly as possible to the place she came from, even though she doesn't know what or where it is.

"Harriet, be careful, you're spilling it. What a mess. I'm not paying you a nickel until you clean that up. I don't know what's gotten into you. All this talk about money. A girl your age. It's not right."

Grandpa Archie must have been in a hurry to get back to the place he came from, probably because of Gran nagging him about smoking and just about everything else. He took refuge in his workshop. He and Harriet used to work side by side, hammering and sawing for hours, speaking only when they had something to say.

"Put the bag down, Harriet, or you'll drop it. I can't get over how heavy it is. They should have told me. I'm going to complain to the manager. He knows me, I'm a regular customer. He should know better."

Harriet drops the bag and cleans up the mess. Back in the corridor Clayton Rumph, wearing his snap-back sideways and his pants halfway off his ass, is dragging Mrs. Schidt's dog by a leash. Harriet never leashed Coco until they were out of the building.

"You're scab labour," Harriet tells him.

"And you're a cunt."

Harriet raises her hands in self-defence readiness as per Darcy's instructions, and starts bouncing on her feet, punching and kicking the air in what she imagines to be the Strongest Man in the World's Life-or-Death fighting style. When Clayton just stands there, slack-jawed, she snarls like a lion in a steel cage, causing Coco to yap. Clayton grabs him and scurries to the stairs instead of waiting for the elevator. "Die, bitch!" Harriet roars at his retreating back.

"Where the hell have you been?" Gennedy demands.

"I told you. I was with Buck and Darcy."

"You were with Buck and Darcy for part of the day. There remains hours of the day unaccounted for."

"I was at Darcy's."

"Don't lie to me, Harriet. I phoned them. Nina said you left a couple of hours ago."

"I was doing errands for the seniors."

"Do you have any idea how humiliating it is for us to have you running around scamming the elderly for quarters?"

"I don't scam."

"Shotlander tells me you were trying to charge him a toonie to help him with his computer."

That's it, no way is she getting that snitch any more Diet Cokes or barbecue chips. "My time is money."

"Listen to yourself. Where does this come from, this miserly behaviour? Not from your mother or me, that's for sure."

"Maybe if *you* got paid I wouldn't have to run errands for seniors, and Mum wouldn't have to work for sketchy businesses. If you weren't the only criminal lawyer in history that's broke, I could have an allowance."

"What a spiteful child you are."

"I'm only saying what Mum says."

"She also says you're an expert on infertility expenses and how this is affecting your father's child support payments. Where would we be without you to keep us informed, Harriet?"

"In a shithole worse than this one." She sees his crummy tuna fish sandwiches on the table. He never puts enough mayo in them. "I'm going to my room. I'm not hungry."

"Really, and why's that? Could it be because you're full of junk food you mooched off your new best friend? She dropped this off, by the way. Didn't know you wore push-up bras. I'm sure your mother will be thrilled to hear her eleven-year-old is dressing like a slut. Leopard spots no less. You know what they say about leopards. Seems appropriate given that you continue to be selfish and greedy and self-absorbed." His cell rings. It must be Lynne because nobody else calls him. "Everything's fine, darlin'," he tells her. "Harriet's right here, safe and sound."

Harriet waits for her mother to ask to speak with her.

"We're just about to have tuna sandwiches," Gennedy says. "How are things at your end?" He stares at the craters in the moon carpet. His speechlessness suggests the news is not good. Maybe Irwin is dead already. This possibility sends a charge through Harriet, compelling her to scamper to her room to resume work on *And I Think to Myself, What a Wonderful World*. She digs in her drawer for the stiff leather glove she picked up off the sidewalk that looks like it still has a hand in it. She plans to glue this beside the shards of broken Christmas ornament and the sparkly glass gemstone she found in the parking lot. But the glue gun is no longer in the shoebox hidden under dirty laundry at the bottom of her closet. She searches her drawers and under the bed, even though she's certain she left it in the shoebox. She hears Gennedy consoling her mother, and telling her he loves her and they'll get through this, darlin', they always do. Harriet moves stealthily to their bedroom and gropes under the bed. No glue gun. She tries all the drawers and rummages in the closet. She works fast, expecting Gennedy to barge in because she no longer hears him talking to her mother. A fury spins inside her. She cannot live without her glue gun. It's not fair that the derp has taken it again. How would he feel if she took his things? She grabs his digital clock, strides to her room and shoves it under her chest of drawers. Sitting on the bed, staring at her mixed media, she tries, as she has many times before, to think of a way to get rid of Gennedy. She has expounded to her mother about other kids' fathers who have real jobs and take their families on vacations. On Father's Day, Mrs. Elrind invited several of them to come to school to talk about their professions. The dads were businessmen, computer programmers and lawyers who got paid. Timo Krings' father, a doctor, described how he makes apple strudel, stretching the dough to make it flaky. Harriet thought pointing out that men exist who make strudel and earn a living would indicate to Lynne what a raw deal she has with Gennedy, who can't even make a decent tuna fish sandwich. But Lynne didn't seem to be listening, and Harriet's throat was so sore it hurt to talk. She didn't tell her mother about the sore throat. She knew her illnesses didn't matter because they couldn't. Irwin's mattered.

Still no sounds from Gennedy. Usually he makes noise, squishing around the apartment in his Crocs, phoning people who never return his calls, boiling the whistling kettle for endless cups of tea that leave dirty rings and drips on countertops and tables. Usually he talks to himself, although technically he's talking to the foes responsible for making him the only criminal lawyer in history that's broke.

Harriet's rage at the injustice of it all creates an implosive pressure in her body. She jumps up to practise some rock 'em sock 'em moves. He has no right to steal her glue gun. She bounds to the living room, jabbing her fists and kicking, ready for a fight. Gennedy is slumped on the floor beside the bamboo plant that's supposed to bring good luck but always seems to be dying.

"They're coming home tomorrow," he says. "He's lost more weight but he's okay. When he woke up he asked for you, Harriet. That little guy adores you. You don't deserve it."

"I don't deserve any of this."

"You got that right." He rests his elbows on his bent knees and his head in his hands. "Why him? That's what I can't figure out. Why *him*?"

Harriet takes this to mean why not her. "I want my glue gun. You have no right to take it from me."

"You have no right to set this building on fire."

"I left it on *once*, once in my entire life."

"Once is enough."

"You can't boss me around, you're not even legit. I could notify the authorities and you would be out of here."

"What authorities do you have in mind?"

"Official people."

"Go for it, I'm sure they'll get right on it. You know, at the start of all this I really tried to like you, told myself your eccentricities were cute, that your moodiness was acceptable considering the circumstances, but now I don't buy any of it. Your brother's just been to hell and back and all you care about is your fucking glue gun. What's the matter with you? I've never even seen you cry. What kind of kid doesn't cry when her brother's almost dead in the hospital?"

"You just said he's okay."

"He'll never be okay. You know that better than anyone."

"It's *my* gun. My grandfather gave it to me. I want it back."

"Yeah, well, we all want a lot of things. I'm not caving to your whims like your mother. You've met your match here, young lady." When he starts to get up off the floor she lunges at him, knocking him down and straddling him. She digs her fingers into his pasty face, mashing it like clay, trying to obliterate it so she never has to look at it again. He tries to push her off but she remembers one of Darcy's moves and jams her knuckles into his neck just below the jaw.

"Ow!" he yawps. "You little bitch!"

She jumps off him and tears out of the apartment, down the corridor to the fire stairs. She takes them two at a time; the slapping of her sneakers echoes off the concrete walls. She will never go back while he's there, ever. She slams through the back entrance, bounding into the parking lot.

"Hey, Lone Ranger," Buck shouts from the cab of his truck. "The fuzz on your tail?"

"Can I climb up?"

"Sure thing." He opens the passenger door. The cab smells of weed. Harriet loves Buck's truck. If the bank doesn't work out, she plans to become a Mack truck driver. It would mean she could escape whenever she wanted. Buck's cab has a bed, a microwave, a mini fridge, a sound system with an iPod dock, and even a little TV. A curtain divides the sleeping compartment from the front of the cab. If the curtain's drawn, Darcy advised Harriet, it means Buck's going at it. The curtain isn't drawn and Buck seems genuinely pleased to see Harriet.

"What's up, Ranger?"

"I got locked out. I forgot my keys."

"Nasty. Who do you want to call?" He hands her his phone.

"Nobody. I'll just wait for somebody to come home. Are you leaving soon?"

"Nah. It's my night off. I'd hoped to spend some quality time with my family but, hey, who am I kidding."

"It's too bad Nina's so mad at you."

"Tell me about it."

"I think my mum would like you a lot." Hooking up Buck and Lynne would be a way to get rid of Gennedy. "She's really pretty. And nice. And my brother isn't retarded. He just has hydrocephalus."

"What's that?"

"Water on the brain. He has a shunt under his skin that drains it to his belly."

"Nasty."

"It messes up his balance and coordination and he has trouble with buttons and stuff, but he's not retarded. Everybody really likes him. My mother says he lights up a room."

"Nice."

Maybe Buck could drive her to Algonquin in his truck, then she could take her easel. He selects a song on his iPod; eight-year-old Michael

Jackson belts "I Want You Back." Buck sings along, reaching into his mini fridge. "Want a Pepsi?"

"Yes please."

"That kid had everything going for him. What the frick happened that made him so freakin' weird?" Harriet has seen the Jackson Five on YouTube and she can't figure out what happened to Michael Jackson either, except that he grew up and discovered people were sacks of shit.

Buck flips the tab on the Pepsi and hands it to her. Gennedy appears at the side of the building, looking stealthily one way then the other. Harriet slides down in her seat, out of sight.

"Here's what I don't get," Buck says. "I'm an awesome dad, seriously. I'm always where I say I'm going to be. I never stiff her on child support. You should meet the deadbeat dads I know, totally useless buttheads, like, to them kids are a burden. They're always complaining about the stuff they have to do with their kids."

Harriet peeks out the window and sees Gennedy creeping around the opposite end of the parking lot. Hitching up his track pants, he turns abruptly, heading in their direction.

"Could you take me to my grandmother's?" she asks. "I know she'll be home and she'd probably cook us some dinner, if you're hungry."

"That's really nice of you. A home-cooked meal would be sweet."

"Then floor it."

"Right on, Ranger."

Harriet leans on Gran's buzzer—knowing she won't hear it—hoping that someone will exit or enter the building, presenting an opportunity to grab the door. Buck, playing air drums and talking about his death metal comeback, doesn't notice that no one is answering the buzzer. Finally Jedi's scratchy voice comes through the intercom. "Go away. We don't want any."

"It's me, Harriet. Can you buzz me up?"

"Harry-o, what a treat. Come on up."

They've moved the coffee table to make room for ballroom dancing. Harriet smells peach fuzzes and sees the vodka bottle on the kitchen counter. Gran sashays towards her, waving the silky scarves she wears for tangos. "Mugsy, it's sooo good to see you. I thought those numbskulls would never let you come see me again."

"They can't stop me."

"That's the spirit." Jedi raises his fists.

Gran swishes a scarf in Buck's direction. "And who's this handsome gent?"

"His name's Buck. He's my friend's dad. I got locked out of the apartment so I asked him to drive me here."

"Isn't that nice of him. Are you hungry? Want me to fry you up some hambangers?"

"Yes please," Harriet says. "And do you have any sweet potato fries?"

"Of course I have my favourite granddaughter's favourite food."

"I'm your only granddaughter."

"Who's counting?"

Jed holds up his peach fuzz. "Can I get you one?"

"Why not?" Buck says.

As the adults slip into drinking mode, their movements become delayed and clumsy. This pleases Harriet because sauced they won't wonder why no one's looking for her. She unplugs the phones and pours herself some orange juice.

Jed salutes her when she returns to the living room. "What's the plan, Harry-o?"

"No plan."

"Oooh la la, you got to have a plan otherwise things can't go wrong."

"They go wrong anyway." She picks up the framed photo of Lynne with Irwin as a baby. "That's my mother."

Buck whistles.

"And that's my brother when he was a baby."

"Why's his head so big?"

"Hydrocephalus, I told you."

"You didn't tell me he had a big head."

"That's what happens. The skull fills with water and stretches."

"How big is it now?"

"Not that big."

"It's big," Gran says. "Nobody's supposed to say so—we're all supposed to tiptoe around like he's normal but he ain't."

Harriet puts the photo back on the mantle. "He's not retarded."

"Says who?"

"He's *not*." The three tipsy adults ogle her.

"Take a chill pill, Harry-o. We're all friends here."

Gran tosses beef patties into her electric frying pan. "Don't know why she's so protective of him all of a sudden, she hates the little bugger."

"I don't hate him."

"Could've fooled me, mugsy."

She doesn't hate him, not all the time anyway. When he can't sleep and lies with his head on her chest, listening to her heartbeat, she doesn't hate him. Ever since he was a baby, Harriet's heartbeat has put him to sleep. She lies very still, not wanting to disturb him, feeling his heart beating much faster than hers. She doesn't have heart trouble when Irwin falls asleep on her chest.

Harriet takes the sweet potato fries out of the freezer and arranges them on a cookie sheet.

"So, Buck," Jed says, "what business you in?"

"I drive a transport truck."

"How romantic." Gran gestures grandly, still holding her empty peach fuzz glass. "Travelling the open road. I always wanted my deceased husband to go into that business. Thought we could see the Grand Canyon together, but he was a homebody from start to finish. I've always fancied a travelling man."

Harriet slides the cookie sheet into the oven, trying to figure out how to stop Gran from flirting with Buck. It gets worse over burgers when she talks about Lynne having her gams and that it's a crime she never shows them off. Jed looks worried, pulling on his nose more than usual, and suggests they play Charades. Harriet acts out *heart trouble* by clutching her chest and pretending to pass out. She hopes to remind Gran that she has heart trouble, is in her seventies and shouldn't be flirting with Buck, but Gran shouts, "Heartache!" Harriet shakes her head and feigns heart failure again. "Broken heart," Gran shouts. She always shouts during Charades.

"Lovesick," Jed offers.

"Heart attack?" Buck says.

"Sick at heart," Gran shouts.

"Young at heart," Jed says.

"Heart disease," Buck says.

Harriet points to her heart again then mimes shaking pills out of a container and swallowing them.

"Heart pills!" Gran shouts. She wobbles in her heels to the kitchen and Harriet thinks she's about to take a heart pill, but instead she swats the counter with a rolled up newspaper. "There's another one of those buggers. I was up half the night spraying the little critters with Lysol. I got a whole army in here. Where'd they come from? I got so many ants I dreamed they got in my mouth, woke up spitting."

Jed squashes ants with his thumb. "You must've been spilling relish juice on the counter again. They like the sugar."

"Pish tah." Gran pulls condiments from the fridge and slaps them on the table. "Who wants what on their hambangers? Help yourselves."

Harriet eats two burgers while the adults drink more peach fuzzes and discuss what motivates flashers. "It's the shock factor," Buck says. "I did it in high school. There's nothing like flashing your jewels at the prom queen."

"There is a child present." Jed settles on Archie's old La-Z-Boy.

"That's no child," Gran says. "Mugsy knows more about life than the two of you combined."

Harriet sips her orange juice. "There's a flasher in the dog park. He pulls down his running shorts and asks the dog people to slap his ass."

"Yeow!" Buck says. "And do they?"

"They call the police but he always gets away on his bike. If he asked me, I'd slap his ass really hard. I'd wear rubber gloves though."

"He'd like that," Buck says.

Harriet can't get over how easy it is to talk with Buck. She can say whatever she wants and he doesn't get upset. The neg is the pot smoking. Lynne thinks potheads are lazy, says they consider rolling a joint an accomplishment.

"Anybody for Scrabble?" Jed asks. They play for a while but Gran uses words that aren't in the dictionary. As she doesn't have a dictionary, they can't prove her wrong. After butterscotch ripple Jed falls asleep in the armchair and Gran puts Frank Sinatra on her record player to teach Buck the foxtrot. She tells him to hold her close and feels him up while adjusting his position. Buck doesn't seem to notice because he's busy looking at his feet, trying to get the steps right. Gran's apartment isn't air conditioned and sweat patches spread across Buck's T-shirt. It has two vertical arrows printed on it. The one pointing up says THE MAN and the one pointing to his crotch says THE LEGEND.

Harriet's ingrown toenail throbs. She's been trying to ignore it because she knows better than to bother Lynne with minor problems. But it's really starting to hurt, and she pulls off her sneaker and sock to examine it. It's swollen, and pus oozes from where the nail digs into her skin. When this happened before, she felt sick and had to go on antibiotics to stop the infection spreading through her body. She wonders if this is what septic shock is, and if it will kill her. She plugs the phone in and calls her mother at the hospital. "I'm at Gran's."

"I figured." Lynne's voice quavers. "I've been calling for hours. Where've you guys been?"

"We went for doughnuts. We had a really good time. Gran's really happy to have me here."

"Let me talk to her."

"She's asleep. I don't want to wake her. You know how hard it is for her to get to sleep."

Lynne sighs. "Bunny, you can't just run out like that."

"He stole my glue gun."

"It's a dangerous tool."

"Grandpa Archie gave it to me and I've never burnt anything and I only left it on once."

"I want you to come home tomorrow. Irwin needs you. He keeps asking for you."

If that really was Archie telling Harriet that Irwin will die in a week, it means in seven days Harriet will be free. She belts this secret deep inside her.

Gran cranks the volume, and Buck says whoops every time he screws up a step.

"What's that noise?" Lynne asks.

"The TV. She can only sleep when it's really loud."

"Gennedy's a good man, Harriet. I wish you'd learn to appreciate him."

Harriet squeezes more pus out of her ingrown toenail and wipes it with one of Gran's cocktail napkins.

"There's a mother here," Lynne says, "whose husband died when her daughter was five." Harriet knows Lynne is telling her this to make her learn to appreciate Gennedy. "She's been raising her child on her own for sixteen years and the girl's gone completely sideways—like sex, drugs, the whole deal. Now the girl's got something wrong with her brain because of herpes."

"What's herpes?"

"A sexually transmitted disease. All her mother talks about is how this wouldn't have happened if her husband were still alive. Bunny, you have two fathers who love you very much and all you do is alienate them. Why?"

There's no point arguing that they don't love her, they love themselves. "I'm not coming back unless I get my glue gun."

"Oh, Irwin's awake, say hi to him."

"Haarree?"

"Hi."

"I miss you sooo much."

Harriet puts her sock and sneaker back on.

"Harry, guess what, we're coming home tomorrow."

"I heard."

"Will you be there?"

"Maybe. I'm at Gran's right now. She kind of needs me. She's having trouble with her back."

"Is she going to be okay?" Irwin's concern for other people's health always astounds Harriet.

"Sure, I'm just helping her out. In fact, I've got to go, she's trying to lift some groceries."

"Tell her to be careful."

"I will. See you later." She hangs up and unplugs the phone.

Buck ambles into the kitchen. "Is that a plug-in phone? Fuck me. I didn't know anybody still had those."

Gran sidles up to him and puts her arm around his waist. "How 'bout another cocktail?"

"You're a dangerous woman. I'm driving."

"Sleep over. I won't tell."

Harriet wants to shout at her to keep her hands off him but instead says, "You should get back to your truck, Buck. I'll show you where it is."

"Why's he got to go?" Gran says, reaching for the vodka. "We're just getting started."

"I've got to drive Harriet home."

"What for? She hates that place, don't you, mugsy? She's staying here."

"Gran, Buck has to work tomorrow."

Gran waves the bottle. "One more for the road."

Harriet grabs Gran's keys from the hook by the door. "Wake Jed, Gran. You know how bad his hip gets if he falls asleep in the La-Z-Boy." She makes eye contact with Buck and jerks her head towards the door.

"Oh, you're so right," Gran says. "He'll be hopping mad." She wobbles over to Jed and starts shaking him.

Outside heat radiates off the tarmac even though the sun's gone down. Buck pulls off his T-shirt and wipes his armpits. Harriet wishes her mother could see his muscles. Gennedy's meagre muscles are covered in pasty white skin. Trent's legs are muscular from biking but his gut spills over his bike shorts.

"Want to cool off in the cab, Ranger? It's got air con. We'll have us some Pepsis."

"Sure." High up in the cab, she feels untouchable.

"Do you think I can park here tonight?"

"It says visitor parking and you're a visitor."

"Yeah, but some places have psycho supers who don't want trucks in the lot."

"I don't think there is a super here."

"Sweet. Mind if I smoke a weedie?" He starts rolling one without waiting for her reply.

For Lynne to like Buck, Harriet needs to make him cut down on weed. "Studies show that potheads' IQs drop by ten percent a year."

"Yeeow, that must mean I'm pretty stupid because I've been smoking for a lo-ong time. It's why I don't get sick. Other drivers get bowel trouble, migraines, back pain. I don't get any of that because I take my medicine." He winks as he hauls on the joint. It occurs to Harriet that if he's stupid, he'll make an even better Gennedy replacement. Gennedy thinks he's smart because he went to law school, and Uma thinks she's smart because she's working on her thesis. They both get hysterical about dumb shit nobody cares about. Buck doesn't get hysterical about anything. Inhaling second hand weed smoke, Harriet leans back in her seat, resting her feet on the dash, and imagines her world free of adults who get hysterical about dumb shit nobody cares about. "Do you have 'Thriller'?"

"Are you kidding me? It's my ringtone."

"Can you moonwalk?"

Buck hops out of the cab and moonwalks better than anybody Harriet's ever seen besides Michael Jackson.

"Wicked," she says.

He climbs back up, hands her a Pepsi and scrolls through his iPod till he finds "Beat It." They sing along really loudly when Michael sings "beat it."

"My mother also loves Michael Jackson." Harriet doesn't know if this is true. Since Irwin was born, Lynne stopped playing music because she was afraid she wouldn't hear him if he seized.

Buck takes a call on his cell and tells the caller not to get excited. "My phone's been acting up . . . No worries, baby . . . Oh you know how it is, no talking when I'm driving. Seriously, baby, I gotta go. I'll call you tomorrow." He puts the cell back in his jeans pocket.

"Why do men call women 'babies'?"

Buck pulls on a clean T-shirt that says DON'T STEAL, THE GOVERNMENT HATES COMPETITION. "Good question. Never thought about it."

"It's patronizing."

"Is it? Fuck me. I think we mean for it to be, like, affectionate or something, sexy even."

"Babies aren't sexy. Except to pervballs."

"Too true."

"Are you seeing somebody seriously right now?"

"You mean, like, a woman?"

"Yeah. Like the one who just called you."

"I think maybe *she* thinks we're serious."

"You don't?"

Buck pushes his seat into the reclining position. "She says she likes me because I'm 'emotionally available.' She says a lot of guys expect women to figure them out then get pissed off when they get it wrong."

Harriet wonders how long it will take the woman to figure out Buck thinks with his dick. "What does 'emotionally available' mean?"

"What you see is what you get with me, Ranger. No mind games."

Lynne would appreciate this. She hates mind fuckers. She calls Uma a mind fucker.

Harriet touches the baby shoes dangling from the rear-view. "Did these belong to Dee?"

"The one and only."

"Nina thinks you screw around because you want to spread your seed even though you don't want any more kids. She said that's just part of male psychology, and that once a woman isn't fertile anymore you're not interested. She said that's why you chase girls twenty years younger than you are."

Buck stares out the windshield as though looking at something very far away and not the back of a dingy apartment building. "That woman's got me so wrong." He sucks hard on his fatty.

"Do you think if you met the right woman, you wouldn't want to spread your seed anymore?"

"Totally." His cell rings "Thriller" again. He looks at it then puts it back in his pocket.

"*I* believe in true love," Harriet says, even though she doesn't. "I believe we're all destined for one person, and sometimes it takes years to find that person, even though we don't realize we're looking for them, and then suddenly they're just there, in the laundry room or someplace, like, where you'd least expect to meet the love of your life."

"Sounds like a movie I want to see." Buck flicks ash out the window.

"You just have to open your mind to the possibilities. Nina doesn't want you back, Buck. You broke her trust. I've heard her say it, 'Fucking Buck broke my trust.'"

"No shit, she said that?"

Harriet nods sagely. "It's time to move on."

"You're making me sad, Ranger, way too sad."

"I'm just being realistic." This is what Trent told Lynne when they argued about Irwin. "You shouldn't be sad, Buck. You're still young enough to start another relationship, just not young enough to have babies, but you don't want babies anyway."

"Oh you're wrong there, Ranger. I wouldn't mind a baby. I *love* babies. Their teeny tiny fingers and toes, and the way they look up at you with those big goo-goo eyes, oh man. Babies are soooo cute."

If Lynne couldn't get pregnant with Gennedy, it's unlikely she'll be able to have babies with Buck. Her eggs are probably rotting like Uma's. "Babies are stressful and cry all the time. Mindy in 408 keeps trying to Ferberize hers."

Buck squints through smoke at her. "What's that?"

"You're supposed to leave them to cry for longer every night until they get conditioned."

"Conditioned for what?"

"To cry themselves to sleep. It takes forever. Mindy's babies cry all night for months and she doesn't get any sleep, and drinks Brown Cows, and talks about killing herself." She has discussed possible methods with Harriet, including putting a plastic bag over her head while inhaling on a helium tank. Mindy says you can rent a tank for blowing up balloons at Toys "R" Us. Harriet wouldn't want to die this way because, if she tried to talk, she'd sound like Porky Pig.

"Is Mindy that sexy chick who was chilling with Nina?"

He's thinking with his dick again. "Yes. She's seriously messed up. Her husband shows up and beats her, even with a restraining order against him." Harriet tries to squash her empty Pepsi can between her palms. "I *never* want babies. My great-grandma had eight and it killed her."

"It's a bit early to decide that, don't you think, Ranger? Especially with you believing in true love and all that."

"True love has nothing to do with babies."

"Whatever you say, boss."

"It's time for you to grow up and find a life partner." Uma calls Trent her life partner. "Otherwise you'll become a lonely, dirty old man. Mr. Fishberg in 314 is always sitting out front with his shirt unbuttoned, watching the girls and talking dirty. The other seniors don't want anything to do with him."

Mrs. Rivera, when she could still leave the Shangrila, would scold Mr. Fishberg and chase him inside with her *chinela*. If he resisted, she'd give him the evil eye and talk about the *multo* making his *tong tong* shrivel up and drop off. If Mr. Fishberg saw Mrs. Rivera coming, he'd button up his shirt and scoot into the building. As soon as she died, he was back on the bench out front with his shirt open, sometimes with his hand down his pants.

"Dirty old men don't deserve to live," Harriet says, still trying to squash her Pepsi can. She hands it to Buck because she wants it crushed for *And I Think to Myself, What a Wonderful World*. But Buck has passed out from the peach fuzzes. She takes the roach from between his fingers and pitches it out the window. She leaves both windows open a crack, turns off the ignition, locks his door then climbs down from the cab and locks the passenger door before closing it. She jumps on the Pepsi can until it's flattened.

Eleven

Jed's left and Gran's asleep on the couch with the TV blaring. Harriet turns
it down slightly before rifling through Gran's recyclables. Gran forgets to
take the bags stuffed with newspapers, ice cream containers, toilet and
paper towel rolls, milk cartons, Kleenex boxes and soda bottles downstairs.
These materials thrill Harriet because they are the building blocks for
papier mâché sculpture. Gennedy won't let her make papier mâché at
home because it's too messy. She digs around in Gran's cabinets for flour,
cornstarch and the big mixing bowl. She pulls out Archie's toolbox from
the broom closet and finds wire cutters, wire and duct tape. After stirring
three teaspoons of sugar into a cup of Sanka, and eating six Peek Freans
with red centres, she starts to work on *The Leopard Who Changed Her Spots*,
cutting the recyclables into shapes and wiring or taping them together.
"Hot diggity dog," she says.

It takes hours to construct the body, and she can't get the tail right.
It's four in the morning before she mixes the flour and water. The ticking
of Gran's smiley face clock keeps distracting her. She climbs onto the
counter, takes the clock down and removes the battery. Time stands still
and she senses Mrs. Rivera. In science class, Mrs. Elrind showed a video

explaining that matter never really goes anywhere, just moves around and changes shape. Which means people, even when they're dead, never really go anywhere. So feeling Mrs. Rivera in the kitchen doesn't frighten Harriet. She attempts to sing what words she can remember from "Billie Jean" to please Mrs. Rivera. She moonwalks and does the chicken dance. If only Harriet had discovered Michael Jackson before Mrs. Rivera died, she could have demonstrated her new moves and made Mrs. Rivera laugh. She stopped laughing at the end, and the morphine flattened her eyes. She wasn't really seeing Harriet anymore. Before she got really sick, Mrs. Rivera made Harriet feel whole. She realized only after Mrs. Rivera was dead that she never felt whole anymore.

But now in the kitchen she can hear Mrs. Rivera saying, "You are special, *anak*," and nodding and smiling at *The Leopard Who Changed Her Spots*.

When the cancer treatment didn't work and they cut out Mrs. Rivera's colon, Harriet began to despise healthy people walking around free of pain and suffering, clueless as to how incredibly lucky they were to be able to walk, shit and complain about dumb stuff like phone bills and bad movies. The doctors pulled a piece of intestine through the skin of Mrs. Rivera's abdomen for shit to come out. Mrs. Rivera had to regularly measure, cut and glue a ring of plastic to her skin around the piece of intestine, then attach a plastic pouch to the ring to collect her feces, and fasten a clip to secure the plastic pouch's opening. It was a complicated procedure and often shit spilled from the intestine before she was able to get the ring glued properly, or the pouch attached with the clip. The shit would spurt all over Mrs. Rivera's surgical wound, the bed, the plastic ring and the pouch. If Harriet was there, she'd try to stop the stream of green and slimy feces with a towel. At first she thought it would be embarrassing for Mrs. Rivera to accept help from a child, but soon it became obvious that all Mrs. Rivera cared about in those distressing moments was containing the shit leaking out of her. Harriet became adept at cutting out the ring and gluing it over the stoma, as well as re-dressing the wound because she'd watched her mother clean and dress Irwin's surgical wounds countless times. Another stoma on the other side of Mrs. Rivera's abdomen drained post-surgical fluids. This stoma required a pouch and changing too, but didn't leak with the same urgency. A few months after the surgery the fluid-draining stoma closed up, leaving another scar on Mrs. Rivera's abdomen. She had as many scars from surgeries as Irwin. Harriet did a painting called *The Tree of Death*. The trunk combined Mrs. Rivera's and Irwin's scarred torsos. The tree burst into blossom above their mutilated bodies and reached into a Prussian blue sky dotted with silver stars. The painting upset Lynne. She asked Harriet to put it in her closet.

Harriet also hated healthy people because they were able to spend money on fun things whereas Mr. Rivera's earnings paid for medical supplies. Harriet would see surgical supply store boxes stacked on the table, with receipts for hundreds of dollars taped to them. The Riveras still had karaoke parties, ate pork intestines and played *pequa*, bingo and Texas hold 'em. They'd bet up to $20, and the winner would laugh at the losers then toss his or her winnings at the children, who'd scramble to collect the loonies, toonies and quarters. Rice was always cooking in the cooker. It came out white and fluffy, not dry and yellow like Gennedy's. When Harriet works at the bank and has her own house, she will buy a rice cooker.

She knows her time is running out, that Gennedy will charge in with his key and drag her back to the apartment to entertain Irwin. For this reason she must finish *The Leopard Who Changed Her Spots* before morning. She eats more red-centred Peek Freans and shreds more newspaper to mix with flour and water. Without the clock ticking she is able to focus and, with the help of a wire hanger, get the tail right.

When Mrs. Rivera could still get out of bed, she and some old aunts prayed together in the living room, always inviting Harriet to join them. They knelt in a circle, fingering their rosary beads, while Mrs. Rivera led them in a prayer for whomever she felt needed one. She'd say, "Together we pray now today for our sister, Vivette, may God grant her health and a long life and make sure she's okay and her family is happy." Then they'd meditate on sorrowful mysteries like the agony in the garden before saying the Lord's Prayer. Next Mrs. Rivera would say, "Hail Mary, full of grace, the Lord is with thee, blessed are thou amongst women and blessed is the fruit of thy womb, Jesus." The other old ladies would chime in, "Holy Mary, mother of God, pray for us sinners, now and at the hour of our death, amen." They'd repeat this ten times then move on to the next sorrowful mystery. None of this made any sense to Harriet but she felt calm kneeling with the old ladies, and they always offered her *pan de sal* and Fita crackers afterwards. Mrs. Rivera worried that Harriet was too thin and made her drink Ovaltine. Harriet liked the malty flavour, especially with SkyFlakes. She loved the contrast of the salty crackers with the sweetness of the Ovaltine.

While smoothing papier mâché on the leopard, she hears Mrs. Rivera saying a novena to her patron saint, Saint Joseph, and blessed Mother Mary, and the sacred heart of Jesus. When Harriet asked what a novena was, Mrs. Rivera explained it was a petition for a cause, direct to God through his son, Jesus Christ, or Mother Mary or any saint.

With all that petitioning going on, it didn't seem possible that Mrs. Rivera would die. She tried to stay ambulatory and would occasionally go to Mr. Hung's with Harriet. But after her pouch burst at Mr. Hung's, she was ashamed to be seen by him. "It wasn't your fault," Harriet insisted.

"No, *anak*, I should have emptied it before we left."

As Mrs. Rivera got sicker, the old ladies started praying at five in the morning—to three or more saints at a time—especially Saint Jude and Saint Peregrine. None of this made any difference and confirmed Harriet's suspicions that there is no God.

Mrs. Rivera gave her a small crucifix to put in her bedroom. It's in the closet, glued to the back of *The Tree of Death*.

She wakens to the screech of the fire alarm. "Gran?" She grabs the fire extinguisher from the wall but can't see any flames, just the electric frying pan smoking. She unplugs it, runs cold water in it and turns on the stove fan. "Gran?" She's not in the living room. Harriet slides open the balcony doors to enable smoke to escape. She finds Gran in the bedroom banging the phone against her bedside table. "Phone's not working."

"Gran, you left the frying pan on. Didn't you hear the alarm?"

"Is that what that was?" She shakes the receiver and holds it against her ear. "That damn phone company."

"I'll fix it." While Gran's fluffing her bedhead in the mirror, Harriet plugs in the phone then hurries to the kitchen to plug in the one there. "Is it working now?"

"How'd you do that, mugsy? You are so smart. Don't know where those brains came from. Not from your father's side of the family, I'll tell you that. How 'bout I make us some pancakes? Just let me call my hairdresser."

"The pan's got to cool off first. You can't leave the kitchen when it's on. When you put the frying pan on, stay in the kitchen."

"I always do. I just had to call Barb to get my hair done. Big night tonight at the Legion. Got to look my best—you never know when an eligible might turn up."

Harriet writes with felt marker on a piece of cardboard *DO NOT LEAVE KITCHEN WHEN FRYING PAN IS ON!!!!!!* and tapes it to the wall behind the counter. She pulls Eggo waffles from the freezer and slides them into the toaster.

Gran, patting her hair, looks around at the mess. "What you been up to?"

"Mum and Gennedy will put you in a home if you keep forgetting to turn the frying pan off."

"I'd like to see those numbskulls try." She spots the leopard. "Aha, a sculpture." She steps back and squints at the leopard, closing one eye, then the other. "Is it an earthquake? Wait, don't tell me, it's *after* an earthquake, when all the roads are lumpy and twisted up."

This is what Harriet loves about art; it can be anything to anybody. "It does look like after an earthquake."

"What happened to Mr. Happy Face?"

"The ticking was bugging me." Harriet fits the battery back in the clock and climbs on the counter to hang it on the wall. "What's the clock on the stove say?"

"Ten twenty."

Harriet resets Mr. Happy Face.

"Don't know how a clock ticking can bug you, mugsy. High strung is what you are, just like your grandpa. You want some Sanka?"

"Please."

"You didn't sleep at all did you? There'll be hell to pay with your mother."

"Don't tell her."

The Eggos pop and, while Gran pulls the syrup and butter from the fridge, Harriet sneaks a heart pill into her waffle.

"You must've scared the ants." Gran squints at the counter. "I don't see any of the little critters."

"Just don't drip any syrup."

The phone rings and Harriet grabs it, suspecting it's her mother.

"Where have you guys been?" Lynne asks. "I've been calling and calling."

"We've been busy."

"Well, Gennedy's on his way over."

"What about my glue gun?"

"What about his digital clock?"

"I'm not coming home unless I get my gun."

"I told him to give you back the gun."

"What if he doesn't?"

"Oh for god's sake, Harriet. There are more important things in this world than your glue gun."

Gran grabs the phone. "Quit doing what that lazy-assed boyfriend of yours tells you to do. You're a grown woman and she's *your* daughter. Give her back her gun or I'll buy her another one." Gran picks up her waffle, dripping syrup on the floor. While she listens to Lynne she winks at Harriet. "Yeah, yeah, yeah, we all know you know what's best for everybody. That's why your daughter comes running here every chance she gets . . . No need to shout." She holds the receiver away from her ear while munching waffle. Harriet starts on her second Eggo and pours herself orange juice. Gran, still holding the phone away from her ear, yawns. Lynne sounds distraught and Harriet considers taking the receiver and consoling her, but she's angry about the glue gun. Gran says loudly into the phone, "Mark my words, that good for nothing loser will be the end of your daughter. One morning you'll wake up and she'll be gone and it won't be to my place. Find yourself a decent man, for goodness' sake—enough of this half-wit." She hangs up then lifts the receiver off the hook and drops it on the table. "Beats me why she wastes her time with no-goodniks. She's still got the gams, she could have anybody she wants if she put on a skirt and some decent pumps."

"Why does she have to have a man at all?"

"Everybody has to have a man."

"No they don't. Lots of women don't have men and do just fine."

"It gets mighty cold between the sheets, mugsy. You'll find that out." The phone beeps, indicating it's off the hook. Gran stuffs it in her tea cozy. "What a fug." She starts stomping on the ants crawling in the dripped syrup. "Uckety puckety."

The apartment door swings open and Gennedy booms, "What the hell's going on here? I smell smoke."

"It's the neighbours' barbecue," Harriet says.

"Like hell it is. Mads, did you leave something on the stove again?" He puts his hands on his hips the way he does when he scolds Harriet.

Gran eyeballs him. "Who pissed in *your* Sugar Puffs this morning?"

"You're a threat to yourself and everyone in this building."

"Then get out of it." Gran stomps on more ants. Harriet wets paper towel and starts mopping up the syrup.

"Enough of that, Harriet, we're leaving."

"Says who?" Gran demands. "She's doing fine here."

"You can set yourself on fire, Madeleine, but I won't let you kill our daughter."

"*Your* daughter? Don't make me laugh."

"Come on, Harriet. Your brother and mother need you."

"Where's my glue gun?"

"On your bed."

"How do I know you're not lying?"

"You don't." He stares at the leopard. "What the hell is that?"

"A sculpture. I'm taking it with me."

"Not a chance. It'll mess up the car."

"I'm not leaving without it."

Gennedy sighs, gripping the bridge of his nose between his thumb and forefinger to indicate that nobody suffers like he does. Harriet picks up Gran's phone and calls Lynne. "Is my glue gun on my bed?"

"If he said it's there, it's there."

"I want you to check."

"Oh for god's sake."

"I'm not going with him unless it's on my bed."

"Fine, give me a second." As her mother walks to her bedroom Harriet hears Irwin singing his ABCs. "Yeah, it's here. Please come home, bunny. I'll make grilled cheese for lunch."

Irwin squeals, "Haarree! Pleeeeze come home! I miss you soooo much!"

"I'm not leaving without my sculpture. He says it will mess up the car. I'll wrap it in a garbage bag and it won't mess up anything."

Gennedy grabs the phone. "For once can you not undermine my authority by giving in to her?" He turns his back on Harriet as he listens to Lynne. Harriet sticks out her tongue. "I just don't think it's right," Gennedy says then listens again, periodically saying, "I understand, darlin'," and "I know he does," and finally, "All right. Whatever you say. You know best." He hangs up and turns to Harriet who is already fitting the leopard into a garbage bag.

"What's it supposed to be anyway?" he asks.

"Whatever you want it to be."

"I want it to be gone. History. I'm sick of your messy garbage that nobody gives a shit about."

"And I'm sick of *you* that nobody gives a shit about." Harriet watches his face redden and his shoulders edge towards his ears. She knows he wants to thwack her. "Why don't you get your *own* wife and your *own* family and leave mine alone?"

"Hear, hear," Gran says.

He looks at her as though he wants her eaten by *manananggals*. "I'll be waiting in the car."

They don't exchange a word until he drops Harriet in front of the Shangrila and says, "Go straight up and see Irwin. And take that catastrophe with you." She carefully lifts the leopard from the back seat and heads for the lobby. The seniors mob her. "Where in heck have you been?" Mr. Shotlander demands. "My computer's on the blink again. I can't turn the dang thing off or on. I checked all the wires. Nothing doing."

"I am no longer in your employment. I don't work for snitches."

"Snitches?" Mr. Shotlander smooths his tufted hair. "What are you on about?"

"You tell my mother's boyfriend everything. You're a no-good spy, and I'm not going to help you anymore."

"I'm no spy. He asked if I'd seen you. What am I supposed to say?"

"You say nothing. You shut your big yob."

Mr. Chubak, in his Che Guevara T-shirt, feels around for change in his corduroys. "Harry, some bad news this end. Wouldn't you know it, I've been rooked by Bell again. If I give you a toonie, could you call those nice folks in India for me?"

"Maybe later."

Mr. Hoogstra tips his grubby captain's hat. "What you got there, Harry?"

"A sculpture."

"No kiddin'. I'm crazy about sculpture. Henry Moore, have you seen that guy's stuff down at the AGO? Terrific, all those big women. You got to love that guy." He lifts one end of the garbage bag. "Can I take a peek?"

Because no one ever asks to see her art, Harriet pulls the garbage bag off the leopard.

Mr. Hoogstra stands back to admire it. "Now that's a Kodak moment."

"For the love of Mike," Mr. Shotlander says. "What *is* that?"

"It's abstract art, Shotlander." Mr. Zilberschmuck slides a pack of Dunhills into his suit pocket. Mrs. Pungartnik, her orange hair frizzing out of control, tromps towards him, clutching a crumpled Kleenex.

"Was it you who gave my husband cigarettes?"

"I did not, Ava, I assure you."

"God will punish you." She points to the ceiling. "He sees everything." She stops in front of the leopard, staring at it and away at the same time.

Mr. Chubak, gripping his red suspenders, approaches the sculpture. "Is it a sign of the zodiac?"

"It's abstract," Mr. Zilberschmuck repeats. Harriet presses the elevator button.

"I'll bet you money it's Libra," Mr. Chubak says.

Mr. Hoogstra jabs a toothpick into his gums. "Looks like it's got a tail."

"Could be a hose," Mr. Tumicelli wheezes, pulling his black overcoat around him.

Mrs. Chipchase, knitting quietly in the corner, says, "It's a leopard."

"Are you kidding me?" Mr. Shotlander pokes his finger in his ear.

"Are you going to give her spots, Harriet?" Mrs. Chipchase asks.

"It's the leopard who changed her spots," Harriet clarifies.

"Of course," Mrs. Chipchase says.

"A leopard, eh?" Mr. Hoogstra circles the sculpture, observing it closely. "*I* can see that. A leopard. Terrific."

Harriet steps into the elevator.

When she lets herself into the apartment, she smells scrambled eggs and suspects her mother and Gennedy have been force-feeding Irwin. She makes a beeline for her room, but then sees her brother on the couch, thinner than ever, struggling to do up his belt. His helplessness weakens her, forcing her to set the leopard on the coffee table. Irwin stands and reaches for her, causing his pants to drop. She pulls them back up, cinching his belt to the last hole. "We've got to put a new hole in your belt, buddy." He wraps his arms around her waist, holding tight. He smells of hospital and she tries not to think about what he's been through. He grips her hand and guides her to the couch. "Look," he points at some stick figures made from pipe cleaners. "A nice lady gave them to me. She said all her grandkids make pipe cleaner people." Irwin's pipe cleaner people are lopsided, with disproportionate arms and legs and big, sloping heads. "Want to make one, Harry?"

"Sure. Maybe I'll make an animal."

"That would be sooo coooool!" Irwin sits so close she can feel the bone of his thigh. "What kind of animal, Harry?"

"What kind do you want?"

"A rabbit?" Irwin's favourite story is *The Velveteen Rabbit* because, as harrowing as it is, the boy gets better in the end. Harriet has read him this story many times. She begins to twist rabbit ears out of the pipe cleaners. Irwin's laboured breathing suggests his lungs might be filling with fluid and he could die within the week. Lynne and Gennedy start arguing in the kitchen, probably about Harriet. She can tell they're trying to keep their voices down so as not to upset Irwin. "Just a sec," she tells him. He tries to grab her as she slips off the couch. "Be right back."

The glue gun is on her bed. "Hallelujah," she says, immediately hiding it on the windowsill between the drawn blind and the pane. She reaches under her dresser for Gennedy's clock, grabs it, dashes down the hall and sets it on his bedside table.

"Haarreee?"

"Coming."

As per Irwin's requests, she makes a pipe cleaner rabbit, a dog and a lion. While twisting the lion's mane she notices her brother's head listing more than usual to one side. He leans heavily against her. "Are you okay, bud?"

"They're fighting."

"I know."

"Will you snuggle with me?"

"It's morning. You can't go to sleep yet."

"I'm really pooped. Please, can we snuggle?"

Harriet doesn't want to do this. She wants to work on the leopard and make escape money off the seniors to get away from Lynne and Gennedy. "Okay." She lies back, making room for him on the couch, adjusting cushions around his bony frame.

"They never fight at the hospital," he says. "How come they fight here?"

"They'll stop soon. Go to sleep."

He rests his head on her chest and immediately she feels his speedy heart beating into her ribs. Her knotted heart loosens slightly. His breathing slows and it occurs to her that he might be dying right this second, and what a gentle way this would be to go, not shaken by a seizure, with eyes rolling, foaming at the mouth—shitting himself—but gently coasting into another form of matter.

Twelve

They wake Irwin for grilled cheese but he doesn't eat much. Lynne and Gennedy exchange worried looks. Lynne cuts off the bread crusts and holds a piece of sandwich in front of Irwin's mouth.

"He's not hungry," Harriet says.

Lynne doesn't lower her hand. "He has to put weight back on."

"Then let him eat what he wants. What do you want to eat, buddy?"

Irwin, uneasy at the centre of conflict, tries to sit straighter and chew the sandwich. "I like this."

"No you don't," Harriet says. "Too hard to swallow, right? How about some chocolate pudding? Do you want me to get some from Mr. Hung's? With marshmallows?"

Irwin looks apprehensively at Lynne to determine if this is allowed.

"There is no nutrition in instant pudding," Lynne says. "Please try to eat a little more, peanut, just another bite for Mummy."

"He doesn't want it," Harriet says. "You're making him sick."

"Why don't you mind your own business?" Gennedy booms.

"He *is* my business. He's my brother."

"Oh, so suddenly you care. Get out the Hallmark cards."

Lynne slams her hand on the table. "Can you two stop bickering for *one* second?"

"You two were bickering all morning," Harriet says. "Are only adults allowed to bicker?"

"Where did you learn this disrespect?" Gennedy demands.

"You get what you give." Harriet stands up. "I'm not hungry either."

"Haarreee, pleeeze don't go!"

"I have to. Mr. Shotlander needs my help with his computer." She has no intention of helping the old snake.

"Will you come right back?" Irwin clings to her wrist.

Gennedy glowers at Lynne. "So that's it? You're just going to let her go?"

"It's easier when she's gone. Let her go if she wants."

Being talked about as though she is not in the room, and being referred to as she who is better gone, squeezes Harriet's heart but she pulls her hand free from her brother and keeps pushing one foot in front of the other.

"Haarreee!"

"I'll be back soon."

Hands on hips, Gennedy says, "Be back here for dinner, young lady."

Mrs. Butts is waiting for her. Harriet believes the old biddy hears everything through the wall dividing their units and times her cane-tapping forays into the corridor accordingly.

"Harriet, you won't believe what happened. I was so upset. I was having my glass of scotch the way I do every now and then. And I'd just poured it out, and must have looked away for a second, and when I looked back, Lukey'd knocked the glass over. I was so upset. That scotch costs eighty-nine dollars a bottle. It's my treat. Every now and then I buy myself a bottle of scotch and that cat, that devil, knocked it over and I can't bend down to clean it up because of my back. Heaven knows what it's doing to the carpet. I'll never get the smell out. This is not good for my ulcer. Can you get some soap and water and scrub it?"

"For five bucks."

"Five *dollars?*"

"Take it or leave it." Harriet heads for the elevator.

"You are incorrigible. I don't know what's gotten into you. All this talk about money."

"Money talks."

"All right then, all right."

Harriet follows her into the apartment crowded with knickknacks and Christmas ornaments Mrs. Butts never takes down because it hurts her back. Usually the apartment smells of cat piss but now it stinks of scotch. Lukey winds himself around Mrs. Butts' legs. "Bad cat. Yes you are. You're a *bad* cat. Badsy, badsy. Now shoo." She leads Harriet to the spilled scotch. "He just wants to make trouble. It's all a game to him." Lukey meows at her, opening his mouth wide. "I don't want to talk to you. You're a bad cat. Shoo. I should give you away is what I should do. But who would have you?"

Harriet finds a dishrag, a bucket and a bottle of Mr. Clean under the sink. She fills the bucket.

"What happened to your shoe, Harriet?"

"I cut a hole to make room for my toe. It's swollen." Her toe is turning purple and leaking more pus. Kneeling on the carpet to scrub the scotch puts pressure on it but Harriet endures the pain for the five bucks. That's almost half the price of the mongoose bristle paintbrush she needs for blending.

"Oh, *I* had a swollen toe once." Mrs. Butts sits in her wingchair covered in cat hair. "I went to see so many doctors and not one of them could tell me what was wrong with me. Some of them even had the nerve to tell me my toe wasn't swollen, that it looked normal. Can you believe it? There I was with a swollen toe, and I couldn't get *one* doctor to help. I am the *patient*, I told them, *I* know what my toe should look like and it shouldn't look like this." Lukey winds around her legs again. "Shoo, *bad* cat, I don't want to talk to you, go away, you're a devil. I don't know why I put up with you." Lukey sharpens his claws on the wingchair. "Stop that! You're a terror. *Bad* cat. Well, I certainly wasn't leaving the hospital until I had an X-ray, I *requested* an X-ray to see if anything was broken. Can you believe the doctor never even called me with the results? I went all the way down to the hospital and waited in line for an X-ray, and the doctor didn't have the decency to call me and tell me the results. I was so upset I called his office and demanded answers. Well, you know what his secretary said? She said if there'd been a problem they would have called me. Can you believe it? They think they can treat me poorly because I'm a senior. I wrote a letter to the head of the hospital."

"Done," Harriet says.

"Already? Did you sniff it?"

"Doesn't smell anymore. Five dollars please."

"Goodness gracious. You don't waste any time, do you?"

"Nope."

"Well now, just a minute." Mrs. Butts peers intently at the wet spot on the carpet, poking it with her cane and sniffing. "Are you sure it doesn't smell?"

"Positive. I have to go."

"Why are you always in such a rush?"

"My brother's sick. I have to get him pudding."

Holding Coco on a leash, Clayton Rumph scratches his balls by the elevator. He flips Harriet both fingers. "I'm da shit between da bun, yo. I'm da *hot sauce*. You're nothing, yo. Yo da grease on da grill, bitch."

"Back up, mothafucka," Harriet says. "Or I'm gonna rock yo shit."

He jangles what Harriet surmises are Mrs. Schidt's loonies and toonies in his pocket then points to his crotch. "She's into me, bitch."

Harriet takes the fire stairs. Mindy's smoking in the stairwell, drinking a Brown Cow. "Hi, hon." She is the only person who calls Harriet hon. It makes her feel special.

"You really shouldn't be smoking in the building."

"I can't leave the kids long, and Bhanmattie goes bat shit if I do it on the balcony." She pats the stair beside her. "Take a pew. You don't look too good." Mindy puts her arm around her, and Harriet relaxes into her warmth, even though she stinks of cigarettes and Kahlúa. "Hon, sometimes you remind me of the little match girl. Do you know that story? She's always looking in people's windows. You remind me of her."

"She freezes to death."

"I don't mean you *are* her, hon. It's just you're so skinny and on the run all the time. What's with your toe?"

"I have an ingrown toenail."

"It looks bad. Are you putting disinfectant on it?"

"It's no big deal. I get them all the time."

"Then how come you look so sad, hon. Here." She takes a pink scarf from her neck and drapes it around Harriet's. "You look pretty in pink.

Why won't you let me do you a makeover?" Harriet has refused Mindy's makeovers in the past because nothing bores her more than putting on makeup. But today she would like someone to take care of her.

"Okay," she says.

Mindy's apartment is furnished primarily with large stuffed animals Boyd, her crackhead husband, won at the Ex. The whole family goes every year, and Boyd is an expert at hitting targets. He grew up in Detroit and shot squirrels. He thinks Canada is full of candy asses who can't shoot for shit. In the photos of Boyd and Mindy at the Ex, Mindy looks adoringly at Boyd while he stares grimly into the camera as though he'd rather be shooting squirrels.

"Just a sec, hon. I have to make sure Brianna's asleep."

Mindy's sons, Conner and Taylor, sprawl in front of the TV playing Xbox. Harriet's never seen them not riveted to a TV or computer screen. Conner's a year older than Irwin, and Taylor a year younger. Irwin told Harriet they hold juice boxes against their crotches in the kindergarten yard and ask the girls if they want to suck their straws.

"Okay, beauty." Mindy rubs her hands together. "Let's do it." She leads Harriet into the kitchen and starts pulling tubes and tiny jars from her makeup bag. "What kind of colours do you like?"

"Dark."

"But you're fair. We can't go too dark. When did you last wash your face?"

"Can't remember."

"It shows. Let's start with a cleanser then use a clarifying lotion." Mindy worked at the cosmetic counter at Shoppers Drug Mart. When her boss got tired of her getting beat up, he cut her hours. She's never been officially laid off; he just doesn't put her on the schedule.

Mindy drags a stool to the kitchen sink. "Sit," she says and starts lathering Harriet's face. "You've got good skin so far. Wait till serious puberty starts." Harriet closes her eyes, enjoying Mindy's gentle circular motions. "Okay, rinse it off." Harriet bends over the sink, throwing water on her face. Mindy hands her a towel. "Pat dry, never rub."

Conner and Taylor start fighting. Mindy runs into the living room. "Shut it!" she screams, which wakes Brianna, who bawls. Mindy carries her into the kitchen and pushes her into the high chair. "Want some Goldfish, Bree?" She shakes some of the tiny fish-shaped crackers into a plastic bowl. "Yum, yum, Goldfish, sweetie." She sets the bowl in front of Brianna, who grabs it and empties it on the floor. "Very funny," Mindy says, draining her Brown Cow. "I swear to god, if I'd known what I was in for, no way would I have had kids." Mr. Shotlander says she's always got a bun in the oven because she's after baby bonus cheques from the government. As Conner and Taylor continue to squabble, Mindy ups the volume on her iPod speakers, and Brianna tosses the plastic bowl across the room. "Bad girl," Mindy says, slapping the baby's hand, causing her to howl. "Throwing bad, Bree. Eat your fish." She pops a fish into Brianna's gaping mouth, looks at her phone and texts.

"I should go," Harriet says.

"Not on your life. This is girl time. Conner, Taylor, come and get your sister. Sherry's taking you to the park with Fraser. She's waiting downstairs."

"Oh Mom," they both whine.

"*Now*. Take Bree out or no gaming tonight."

Conner reluctantly lifts the baby out of the chair and carries her on his hip. She quiets, sucking on her pacifier as she watches Taylor push the stroller into the corridor.

"I want you guys out of the house for an hour." Mindy hands Taylor a baby bottle. "I mean it, stay outside with Sherry. You're starting to look like vampires." She closes the door after them and leans against it as though worried they might try to get back in. "I need a smoke." She hurries to the kitchen and turns the speakers down. "Put your ear against the wall. Can you hear Bhanmattie's radio?"

Harriet presses her ear against the wall then shakes her head. Mindy turns the volume back up: Taylor Swift sings about how some guy did her wrong.

"Okay, I'm going for it." Mindy grabs her cigarettes and heads for the balcony. "Be with you in a flash and we'll make you gorgeous." Harriet doesn't want to be here anymore but doesn't know where else to go. She eats several Goldfish, listening to Taylor Swift drone. Mindy's playlist includes women moaning about searching for the right man, or losing him. Harriet can't understand why she listens to this when she's been stuck with the wrong man for years. Just like Lynne can't lose Gennedy, Mindy can't lose Boyd. She comes back in, rubbing her hands together again. "Okay, beauty, you ready? Time for some foundation. We're talking peaches 'n' cream for you, missy." Mindy's makeup sponge feels soft against Harriet's skin. "You've got circles under your eyes, hon. Aren't you sleeping?"

"Not last night."

"You need sleep, otherwise the hormones go crazy. Take Gravol or Benadryl—it'll knock you out. Okay, show me those peepers." Harriet looks at her. "We'll do soft accents, peachy and taupy." Already Harriet feels painted and wants to rub it off.

"Seriously, hon, you've got great bones. And you're model skinny. You should check out those modeling ads. They start them so young now. They're, like, past it by the time they're twenty. You're in your bloom now, beauty."

Harriet wants to change the subject. "Has Boyd been around?" She knows he has because she saw the cops pushing him into the cruiser.

"Yeah, he came by to see the kids, but then he wanted to get it on, like, right when I'm in the middle of cooking dinner and getting Bree ready for bed. He's, like, all over me in front of the boys. I told him to fuck off, then the boys started going at him. It was nuts. Bhanmattie called the cops again. He just doesn't get it. None of those old buzzards do because their gonads dried up a long time ago. Boyd *loves* me. He keeps coming back because he can't get over me. That's called love. If he quit using, we'd still be together. He's a good man."

Just like Gennedy. More excuses for no-goodniks.

"One of these days you'll fall in love, hon, and you won't know what hit you. Okay, what's next? Mascara. Look up." Mindy combs mascara onto Harriet's lower lashes. "Okay, look down." She combs it onto Harriet's upper lashes. "Now a touch of blush, nothing too coral." She picks a colour and brushes it onto Harriet's cheeks.

They hear banging on the balcony. "It's Bhanmattie," Mindy whispers. "Pretend we're not here."

"I know you're in there," Mr. Bhanmattie shouts. "No smoking on the balcony. I have asthma."

Mindy's cell rings Taylor Swift singing "Love Story." She looks at it and puts the phone down. "It's Boyd. I don't want to talk to him. I told him I'm changing the locks. Okay. Lips. Just a hint of pink." She brushes lip gloss onto Harriet's lips. "Gorgeous. Go look at yourself in the bathroom." Her cell rings again. "Oh for fuck's sake. If I don't take it, he'll just keep calling."

Harriet almost doesn't recognize herself in the bathroom mirror. This could be her disguise, she realizes. She's concerned that the Greyhound bus drivers might think she's too young to travel alone. If she wears the leopard bra with pink lace and the pale blue tank top, plus Mindy's pink scarf, they'll think she's older, although this would mean she'd have to pay adult fare. She removes the scarf and uses it to wrap up some of Mindy's makeup samples piled in a basket by the sink. Mr. Bhanmattie continues to bang on the balcony doors. Harriet uses one of Mindy's hair clips to twist her hair up the way Mindy does. She puts on Mindy's cropped jean jacket and slides the door open.

"Who are *you*?" Mr. Bhanmattie asks.

"Who do you think I am?"

"Are you the one smoking?"

"I only do chemicals," Harriet says, delighted that he doesn't recognize her. "Mindy's not smoking anymore. You can stop banging." She slides the door closed. Mindy is no longer in the kitchen but in her bedroom, talking dirty to Boyd. Harriet drops her jean jacket on the couch.

"You look shit hot," Darcy says, fondling lipsticks at the cosmetic counter. "What a sassmaster. How come she never offers me a makeover?"

"Maybe she doesn't think you need it."

"Preach it."

Harriet's gripping a packet of Jell-O Instant Chocolate Fudge pudding and some miniature marshmallows she intends to pay for with Mrs. Butts' five bucks.

"If I had money," Darcy says, "I'd totally get liposuction." She sneaks a lipstick into her hoodie pocket. "Did you hear about the shooting?"

"What shooting?"

"Some pizza joint. The kid was wearing red. What kind of lame brain wears red in Crip territory? What a time to be alive." She lines her eyes with black liner. "*I* could use a heater. Clayton says he can get me a strap for a hundred bucks."

"A strap?"

"A gun, duh." She smears purple eye shadow onto her eyelids.

"What do you want one for?"

"Power, yo. Respect."

"That's dumb."

"Who you callin' dumb, girl?" Darcy brushes blush onto her cheeks.

"You wouldn't even know how to fire it."

"It's easy." She points her finger like a gun and presses down on her thumb. "Pow. No more fat girl jokes." Harriet has witnessed boys oinking at Darcy, calling her porky and grabbing at her breasts. Girls call her a fat slob when she wears tank tops.

"You'd have to kill a lot of people," Harriet points out.

"Not once I get a rep."

Harriet doesn't know Darcy well enough to be certain she's joking. All kinds of kids shoot people. Two fifteen-year-old boys were shot dead by a fourteen-year-old just last week. The idea of having a friend with a strap appeals to her. "So why don't you ask Clayton?"

"I need a hundred bucks."

"Get it from Buck."

"Oh, right, like I can say, 'Hey, Pops, I need cash for a gun.'"

"Ask him when he's stoned. I bet he's always got cash on him for a few grams. Tell him it's for some outfit you want to buy." A heater might solve the Gennedy problem, although she'd have to make it look gang related and lure him into Crip territory. She tries to remember if he has any red clothes other than his Speedo. More pus oozes out of her swelling toe. Where the nail cuts into the skin is turning a blend of Phthalo Blue and Burnt Ochre. She imagines the infection spreading up her leg and the doctor telling Lynne he has to cut it off. "Don't you touch my baby!" Lynne would scream. "You save my baby's leg or I'll sue your ass."

Darcy prods her. "You got any dough?"

"Five bucks and some quarters."

"Get some Fuzzy Peaches. I'm starved." She grabs a packet at the checkout and hands it to Harriet. "I'm with her," she tells the cashier, sliding past Harriet with the lipstick in her pocket.

They sit on the busted fountain in the park, chewing on Fuzzy Peaches. "That Caitlin whore still hasn't texted me," Darcy says. "Her wall is, like, totally fake. She's smiling in every shot like she's a nice person. And she's changed her status again, that fucking slut. Her boyfriend looks like a total derp. He's wearing dark glasses and holding a guitar. Give me a break, he probably can't even play."

"Why do you look at her timeline? Just forget about her."

"That's easy for you to say because *you* don't have any friends. *I* used to be popular."

Harriet suspects this is untrue but doesn't question Dee because it might make her stop chilling with her. "Would you be mad if I fixed Buck up with my mother? Then we'd be sisters. I mean, I don't even know if your dad will be into my mom, or vice versa, but I think it's worth a shot, don't you?" When Darcy doesn't respond she adds, "Wouldn't it be cool if we were sisters?"

Dee pops another Fuzzy Peach into her mouth. "These are the questions that haunt me."

"Seriously."

"Seriously there's no way fucky Bucky is going to go for your mother. She's old."

A dad on a bike with a toddler in a kiddie seat stops in front of the fountain.

"It's busted," Darcy tells him. The toddler chortles in the kiddie seat, waving her chubby arms. The dad reaches back and straightens her helmet then bends down to kiss her hands. The gesture is so natural, so casual, Harriet has no doubt the dad takes the toddler for bike rides every single day, and straightens her helmet and kisses her hands. Trent never put a kiddie seat on his bikes.

"Let's think about all the people we'd whack if we had a strap," Harriet says.

"Now you're talkin'." Darcy reaches for another Fuzzy Peach. "At least you don't have to waste your brother since he's dying in a week."

The thought of Irwin dying no longer sends charges through Harriet but weighs on her. "Some people we should just maim," she says. "Like Mr. Shotlander. We'll shoot him in the foot, make him hop around."

"Nice."

It takes most of the afternoon to compile the list and decide which targets should be killed and which maimed. Generally Harriet hesitates to smoke people who pay her for errands, but she makes an exception in the case of Mrs. Butts.

Mr. Fishberg, with his shirt unbuttoned and his hand down his pants, whistles when he sees Harriet and Dee with makeup on. Mr. Shotlander holds the door open for them. "Leave the girls alone, Fishberg." Harriet knows he is making a show of defending them because he wants her to fix his computer.

"Look at you, Harry," Mr. Chubak says, scratching his bald spot. "All grown up looking. Buffo buffo. Almost didn't recognize you." This is what Harriet wants to hear. She presses the elevator button. Darcy snaps open her stolen lipstick and glides it over her lips then offers it to Harriet, who does the same.

"Now that's a Kodak moment." Mr. Hoogstra tips his captain's hat.

"Where did these beautiful dolls come from?" Mr. Zilberschmuck asks, brushing ashes from the lapel of his three-piece suit.

"Harry," Mr. Shotlander pleads. "I'll pay you five bucks if you can fix it."

"Show me the cash."

"Since when do you need cash up front?"

"Since now." She steps into the elevator.

"Okay, okay, okay." Mr. Shotlander pulls out his wallet. "Dang it, I don't have a fiver. You got a fiver, Chubak?" Mr. Chubak feels around in his corduroys. The elevator doors start to close. Mr. Shotlander jams his orthotic shoe between them.

"I got a couple of toonies," Mr. Chubak says.

Taj, the janitor-cum-movie-pirate, suddenly appears. "No feet in the elevator doors. You want the elevator to work, no feet. How many times do I call the elevator company? We have to raise your rent."

Mr. Shotlander removes his foot and the door closes.

"Alone at last," Darcy says. "Come over later. Buck's taking me to the DQ. I'll see if I can set something up with your mom."

"Seriously?"

"That's the buzz, cuz. Text me and we'll work out the deets."

Harriet knows better than to remind Dee that she doesn't have a cell.

The apartment appears to be empty. Harriet rushes from room to room to ascertain that Gennedy is out then checks to see if his computer is password locked. It is, which means they've been gone awhile and could return any minute. She scrambles into the kitchen, pulls out the plastic mixing bowl, measures out the milk, pours in the instant chocolate pudding mix and blends it with the electric mixer. "Presto," she says. Once it's thickened, she stirs in some miniature marshmallows. She eats several spoonfuls before fitting the lid on the bowl and hiding it under her bed with two spoons. She hurries back to the kitchen to clean up the evidence and phone Darcy. "Have you figured out how to fix up our parents yet?"

"Be at the DQ at eight. Get her to put a face on."

The minute Gennedy and Lynne walk in the door, Harriet can tell her mother's been crying again. Red eyes and a puffy face will not turn on Buck. While Gennedy carries the sleeping Irwin to his room, Harriet wraps her arms around her mother and kisses her on the cheek several times to cheer her up.

"What's got into you?" Lynne asks.

"I love you and I'm so happy you're home."

"I love you too, bunny." Lynne holds her at arm's length. "You're wearing makeup."

"Mindy did a makeover."

"Who's Mindy?"

Gennedy returns. "Some white trash in the building." He pours spaghetti sauce into a saucepan.

"*You're* white trash," Harriet says.

Gennedy looks at Lynne. "You see how she talks to me?"

"Harriet, why were you with Mindy? Aren't there children your own age to play with?"

"I went out with Darcy afterwards."

"Who's Darcy?" Lynne sits wearily.

"The new girl in the building of questionable character," Gennedy reminds her. "They went to the Eaton Centre together to purchase the leopard spotted bra with pink lace trim."

"You're so obsessed with that bra," Harriet says, "*you* should wear it."

He waves a wooden spoon at Lynne. "I'm supposed to tolerate this disrespect? You think I exaggerate how she treats me, but I can assure you no exaggeration is required."

Lynne leans her elbows on the table and rests her head in her hands. "Bunny, what's with the bra? You're way too young for a bra like that. If you want a bra we can get you a sports bra that's soft. You don't need a padded underwire bra."

"She needs it to make her breasts look bigger," Gennedy says.

"And you need dick enlargement," Harriet says. Darcy showed her ads for penis enlargement online.

Gennedy waves the wooden spoon again. "See how she talks? Is this acceptable language for an eleven-year-old? She's rude, potty mouthed, disrespectful . . ."

"Respect has to be earned," Harriet says. Mr. Chubak says this. "And I'm not 'she.' I'm right here, in this room, and what I buy is none of your business. It's *my* money. Mum, what's up with Irwin? Is he getting worse?" Suddenly she's worried her mother is crying because he's almost dead already, before Harriet has had a chance to make him happy with pudding. Just as she was too late to make Mrs. Rivera happy by singing "Beat It" and moonwalking.

"He needs rest," Gennedy says. "Do *not* disturb him."

Harriet runs to Irwin's room and stands over his bed, waiting for him to move. She holds a hand in front of his face to feel if he's breathing. She has done this many times, always hoping to feel nothing, but now the soft puff of air against her palm causes giddy relief and she whispers in his ear. "Do you want some chocolate fudge pudding with miniature marshmallows?"

"Am I allowed?"

"Just don't tell. Be right back."

Lynne and Gennedy resume their bickering in the kitchen. Harriet knows it will escalate until Lynne boohoos on his shoulder and he tells her they'll get through it, darlin', they always do. *Get through what?* Harriet wants to shout. There's always more to get through for them. She doesn't want to spend her life getting through stuff. She grabs the bowl of pudding, the spoons and scurries back to Irwin's room, closing the door. "If we're quiet, they'll forget about us." She helps Irwin to sit up, bolstering him with pillows, and hands him a spoon.

He digs into the pudding. "Wowee, wowee, marshmallows."

"They're vitamin enriched. They'll make you strong."

"Cool." He spoons pudding into his mouth. "Yum."

"Chocolate fudge is my absolute favourite."

"Mine too." He spoons more pudding. Knowing this equals hundreds of calories, Harriet feels triumphant.

"They're fighting again," Irwin whispers.

"No, they're just trying to figure out what to make for dinner."

"I don't want dinner."

"Just pretend to be asleep and they'll leave you alone."

"See my new spy handbook?" He holds up a small bound notebook with a clasp. "I can lock it shut. It's got a key."

"Wicked. What are you writing in it?"

"Spy stuff. Top secret. Will you snuggle with me?"

"When you don't want any more pudding. We don't have to finish it. I'll put it back in my room and we can have more later."

"Cool."

He eats eight more spoonfuls. Harriet feels whole, as whole as she felt with Mrs. Rivera.

Thirteen

When Harriet hears Lynne's flip-flops coming down the hall, she shoves the pudding and spoons under Irwin's bed. "Let's see your face," she whispers, wiping the chocolate off his mouth. "Pretend you're asleep or she'll be on your case about eating spaghetti."

"How long do I have to pretend for?"

"Till she leaves. Shhh. I think she's checking my room first."

"She doesn't know you're here?"

"No, shhh, we have to pretend to be asleep. We'll spy on her and you can put it in your spy handbook. Do spoons." Irwin rolls onto his side and she tucks her knees behind his, wrapping her arm around him.

Lynne stands over them for what feels like an hour. Irwin is ticklish behind the knees and Harriet must hold completely still to prevent a fit of giggles. Finally Lynne sits on the rocking chair she rocks Irwin in after seizures, or when he wakes up scared. He frequently dreams that he has to go back to the hospital. When he was little he didn't mind the hospital because he didn't think he would have to return to it again and again. When he was little he thought he would get better because that's what everybody said would happen, especially Lynne. She'd rock him in the chair and tell him what a big boy he was, how smart and brave, and how he was getting stronger all the time. Irwin would beam in these moments, his smile trusting and hopeful, but after he turned three Harriet figured out it was all lies. She started hating her mother not only because Lynne loved Irwin best, but because she lied to him. Grandpa Archie used to say they should call a spade a spade. "Call a spade a spade," she says in her head while her mother rocks on the chair, sniffling. Gennedy squishes down the hall in his Crocs. "You okay, darlin'?"

"Look at them," Lynne whispers. "Aren't they beautiful? My babies. They're so sweet together."

Gennedy grunts.

"He never stopped talking about her at the hospital. He idolizes her."

Gennedy grunts again and squishes over to the rocker. The rocker stops rocking and Harriet hears kissing noises. She feels Irwin wriggle and grips him more tightly.

"I hate it when we fight," Lynne says. "You're so good to us. I don't know what we'd do without you."

"I'll always be here for you, darlin'."

"I know it's hard, but you have to be patient with Harriet. She's been through a lot."

"Not as much as Irwin."

"It's different."

"Tell me about it. Can't believe they're from the same parents. You sure there wasn't a mix-up at the hospital?"

"Very funny." More smooching. Irwin starts to giggle and Harriet knows he's about to blow their cover. She pretends to be waking up, making a show of rubbing her eyes and yawning.

"Bunny, did we wake you? You guys shouldn't be sleeping now anyway. It's time for spaghetti."

Irwin sits up. "Surprise! I'm awake too."

"I've got to put another hole in Irwin's belt," Harriet says. "Come on, Irwin."

"Mizz Harriet, what happened to your shoe?"

"My toe's infected. The shoe was hurting it."

"Let me see it." Lynne pushes off the rocker and examines Harriet's toe. "Oh my lord, Harriet, why didn't you say something?"

"To who?"

Lynne looks at Gennedy, who shrugs. "I was here. She never mentioned it."

"I'm not *she*," Harriet says. "I'm me and I'm in the room now."

"Yes, and pretending to be asleep so you can listen in on a private conversation."

"I *was* asleep."

"You never sleep in the daytime. You hardly sleep at night with all the creeping around and garbage collecting."

"Gennedy, she was asleep. I saw her."

"We were *both* asleep," Irwin insists too loudly because he's a lousy liar.

"Stop copying your sister." Gennedy turns his back on them to face Lynne. "Don't you see how she plays you? She didn't tell you about the toe because she wants to make an issue out of it so you'll feel guilty for not rushing her to emergency."

"Well, that's exactly what we're going to do. She needs antibiotics."

"She needs to soak it in salt water, is what she needs. She doesn't need us to do that."

"Don't tell me what my daughter needs."

"There you go, this is exactly what she wants."

"Who's she?" Harriet demands. "And who are *you*?" She jumps off the bed and pokes his shoulder to make him face her. "Are you married to my mother? No. Are you related to my brother? No. Do you try to hit me when my mother is not around? Yes."

"What?" Lynne covers her mouth with her hand.

"I have never hit her."

"Only because you can't catch me," Harriet says.

"She's framing me, can't you see that? She hates me, always has. She's trying to get rid of me."

"Did you try to hit her?" Lynne asks.

"She attacked *me*. Jumped on me like some kind of wild animal."

"*Did* you hit her?"

"I did not hit her."

"You would have if you'd caught me," Harriet says.

"Oh really? So you can predict the future now."

"Come on, Irwin," Harriet says. "Let's fix your belt." She grabs his hand and tries to pull him off the bed but he vomits chocolate pudding and miniature marshmallows all over the cratered carpet.

East General is not nearly as nice as SickKids. It doesn't have a Second Cup, and Emerg is filled with drunks, drug addicts and sick people who occupy the washroom for hours. Harriet needs to pee but keeps missing her chance as one feeble person exits the washroom and another enters. Her mother sits in the corridor on a plastic chair with her eyes closed and her head tipped back against the wall. She isn't speaking and Harriet's not sure if this is because she's still angry with her, or if she's just been in too many hospitals. A scarlet-haired woman in platform shoes clomps up and down the corridor shouting. Her mouth and one eye are bleeding. When hospital staff pass her, she clutches at them and says, "I hurt soooo bad. I'm dy-ing over here." Some of the staff ignore her, others say they can't give her anything until the doctor sees her. An orderly with cornrows tries to make her sit down but she keeps pacing. Harriet hears the orderly say to another man in scrubs that the scarlet-haired woman in platform shoes is "a frequent flyer."

"Mum?"

"Yes."

"I'm going to use the washroom."

"Come right back. You could be called any minute."

Harriet waits outside the washroom, picturing bacteria spreading. Mrs. Elrind showed them a video about how disease is spread. Each time a cartoon character touched anything, they smeared purple germs. When the next cartoon character touched the same doorknob or elevator button, they smeared purple on a handrail or an ATM. Soon the whole cartoon world was covered in purple smears. The video said you can get sick from someone coughing ten feet away. Lots of people cough in Emerg. Purple clouds and germs engulf Harriet. She tries to breathe as little as possible and to touch nothing. After a man in a hospital gown limps out of the washroom, Harriet grabs the door lever with the bottom of her T-shirt to open it, then covers the toilet seat with toilet paper. Almost immediately someone knocks on the door. "I'll be out in a sec," Harriet says, noticing some of Irwin's chocolate pudding vomit on her jeans. "Are you trying to kill him?" Gennedy shouted at her. "What's the matter with you? Did you not hear your mother say no chocolate pudding? And then you add marshmallows? What kind of sadist are you?" Harriet wasn't sure what sadist meant but assumed it had to do with being sad which she was.

"*I'm* the saddest," Irwin cried, "because you keep fighting."

"He's right." Lynne lifted him up and carried him to the bathroom, leaving Harriet and Gennedy staring at the vomit.

"Clean it up," Gennedy ordered.

"*You* clean it up."

"You made him sick. You clean it up."

"*You* make me sick. You clean it up."

"Both of you clean it up," Lynne screamed from the bathroom so loudly it sounded as though she'd ripped her vocal chords. Harriet thinks this may be why she isn't speaking.

She washes her hands carefully, dries them with paper towel then covers the lever with paper towel before pressing on it. Her mother is still sitting with her head tipped back and her eyes closed. Harriet dashes to the pay phones, digs in her pocket for quarters and calls Darcy. "It's me. Is Buck there yet?"

"Negative. Probably stuck in traffic."

"Okay, well, I'm running a bit late. Can we make it nine at the DQ?"

"No promises. I need my Choco Cherry Love blizzard, yo. TTYL." She hangs up.

Lynne still hasn't moved.

"Mum?"

"Yes."

"I'm really sorry."

"I know you are, bunny."

"Do you think we could do something fun after this? Just you and me?"

"What kind of fun?"

"I was thinking we could go to the Dairy Queen. We never go there anymore. Girls' night out."

"You haven't had dinner."

"I don't need dinner. I had a huge lunch at Mindy's. She's totally into health food."

Her mother looks her in the face for the first time in hours. "Can you take that makeup off please?"

Harriet forgot she had it on. She charges back to the washroom just as an old man in a wheelchair wheels out of it. Under the fluorescent lighting the makeup makes Harriet look old, almost as old as the scarlet-haired woman with the bleeding face. Harriet scrubs her skin with soap and paper towel. The mascara leaves dark rings under her eyes. It takes ten minutes to remove all the makeup. Many sick people knock impatiently on the door.

Her mother slouches in her seat, staring at the floor. She never slouches because she says it makes her gut stick out. Harriet touches her hand. Lynne looks up. "There's my baby girl." She pulls Harriet to her and holds her close. Even though Harriet's nose is squashed against her mother's neck, making breathing difficult, she wants to stay like this forever.

The doctor from Iran is hard to understand. He seems annoyed by Harriet's toe, and talks very fast. When Lynne says, "Can you please repeat that, I don't understand," he talks even faster. Harriet thinks he might be threatening to cut off her leg. He keeps pointing at her leg while talking fast and shaking his head. Harriet expects her mother to lose patience with the doctor and demand to see one who speaks English. She did this on one of Irwin's Emerg visits when she couldn't understand a Chinese doctor. Lynne seems almost afraid of the doctor from Iran. "Very bad," he says, and Harriet doesn't know if he means the toe is very bad, or that Lynne is very bad for not noticing the toe, or if it's very bad that he has to cut her leg off. He scribbles a prescription on a pad and thrusts it at Lynne, who takes it without a word then slumps against the examining table as the doctor speeds to the next patient.

"What just happened?" Harriet asks.

"He wants you on antibiotics. We'll go get it filled."

"After that can we go to the DQ?"

"Oh, bunny, I'm so tired."

"It'll give you energy. Yummy ice cream." She hops off the table and hugs her mother again. All this hugging feels awkward but wonderful. She never hugs her mother when Irwin's around. "Please? Just us? Girls' night out?"

"Okay, well, let me phone Gennedy and make sure Irwin's all right."

Harriet wants to kick the wall but instead sits demurely on the chair. She hears the scarlet-haired woman shout, "Don't talk shit. I hurt soooo bad. I'm dy-ing over here."

"How's he doing?" Lynne asks. "Any temperature?" While listening to Gennedy she tugs at a piece of torn upholstery on the examining table. "Is he keeping liquids down? . . . Did you try giving him a piece of toast or something? . . . Okay . . . I don't know. Harriet wants to go for ice cream." Harriet can hear Gennedy squawking, probably about how she doesn't deserve ice cream; you don't reward a potty-mouthed child who poisons her little brother. "We'll talk about it later," Lynne says. "I just want to make sure you'll be all right with him and that he's stable. Call me if there's any change." Her mother's tone is cooler than usual with Gennedy. This gives Harriet hope for Buck, except that Lynne hasn't put a face on and has chocolate vomit on her tank top.

"Mum, maybe we should go home and change."

"What for? The Dairy Queen? Let's just go."

"Do you have any makeup in your purse?"

"Since when are you so interested in makeup, bunny?"

A stern nurse draws the curtain. "Are you done here?"

"We're done," Harriet says, grabbing her mother's hand.

They stop at Shoppers Drug Mart to pick up the antibiotics. Harriet keeps holding her mother's hand even though she knows it's childish. While they wait for the prescription to be filled, Harriet steers Lynne to the makeup counter. Lynne catches sight of her reflection in a mirror and gasps. "I look a wreck."

"Put some makeup on," Harriet suggests. "Try this colour." She holds out a bright red lipstick called Siren.

"It's a bit bold for me, Hal." Lynne starts examining the makeup samples and within minutes is putting a face on. In Harriet's head, she hears Darcy saying, "Now that's what I'm talkin' about."

Buck and Dee aren't at the DQ. Peewee soccer teams swarm the counter and tables. Harriet grabs a couple of stools by the window. Lynne watches the boys Irwin's age with a broken smile. Harriet knows she's trying to picture Irwin healthy, pushing and shoving his fellow peewees, ordering a large Blizzard and gobbling it all down.

Harriet hugs and kisses her again. "I'll line up. You save our seats."

"Thanks, baby." Lynne hands her a ten. "Nothing fancy for me. Just a cone. Chocolate dipped." This equals messy, not sexy. Harriet doesn't want her mother dribbling chocolate bits in front of Buck.

"You don't want a Blizzard? I thought you liked Mint Oreo."

"Do I? Okay, whatever. You choose."

Standing among the peewees, Harriet tries to imagine what it would be like to have one for a little brother. She'd probably smack his head. At least Irwin's quiet. One of the babies at the hospital cried constantly because he was missing a piece of his brain. "He's got no cerebral cortex," Lynne whispered. "He can't think. That's why he never stops crying. He can't make sense of anything. We're so lucky Irwin's got a brain." Harriet thought of the Straw Man who didn't have a brain. He did all right.

A spiky haired peewee glares at her. "You butted in."

"I did not."

"We were here first."

"You weren't standing in line."

"We were too."

"Quit talking out your ass," Harriet says.

It seems to her Irwin's brain spends too much time on stuff he can't do anything about, like littering. "Why do people litter?" he asks. Or mass murder. Lynne tries to shield him from the news but when psychos kill a bunch of people, Irwin finds out because everybody's talking about it— especially if little kids get murdered. "I don't like this world," he said the last time little kids were shot to death. "Too many people kill each other." He was studying his world records book, sliding his hand over a picture of the great white shark, the ocean's fiercest predator that sometimes kills people. "What if somebody tries to shoot *us*?" he asked. "We should get a gun so we can shoot them back."

The spiky-haired peewee points at Harriet. "I'm telling Coach you talked dirty."

"Shut da fuck up, mothafucka," Harriet says, trying to decide if the Strawberry Cheese Quake has more red dye in it than the Choco Cherry Love Blizzard. She glances back and sees Lynne on her cell again, talking, no doubt, to Gennedy. Her gesticulating suggests she's still mad at him—a good sign. Harriet breaks from the line and steps outside to use the payphone. Darcy takes forever to pick up. "Where are you?" Harriet asks.

"Oh, the 'rents are at it. He's, like, begging her to take him back. It's like he's her bitch."

"Excuse me while my mouth fills with barf."

"Copy that."

"Tell him he has to get to the DQ. My mum's pissed at the derp. The timing couldn't be better."

"Pops?" Darcy says loudly. "Harriet requests an ETA at the DQ."

Harriet hears Nina shouting, "Get the fuck out of my life, Buck!" which pleases her enormously. She pokes her head out of the booth to check on Lynne, who's still on the phone but holding her other hand against her forehead. This could mean she's still mad at Gennedy, or making up.

"Timing is crucial," Harriet says. "You've got to get over here."

"I'm on it."

Harriet gets back in line behind the peewees. When she finally buys the Blizzards, her mother is off the phone but talking to Barney in 507, who came back from Afghanistan nuts. At first he looked normal and all the seniors treated him like a war hero, even when he couldn't get a job. But when he kept trying to strangle his wife in his sleep, nobody treated him like a hero anymore. She left him and he started boozing and working at the car wash. Lynne calls it a modern tragedy and lets him yak at her whenever they run into each other. Harriet doesn't want Barney chatting up her mother. Buck could show up any minute. If he sees her flirting with Barney, it'll turn him right off.

"Harriet," Lynne says, "you remember Barney."

Barney doesn't take his eyes off Lynne. If he were a dog, he'd be drooling. Harriet shoves the Mint Oreo Blizzard between them. "If you're getting ice cream," she tells him, "you better get in line."

"No worries, I just had a cone. I'm trying to lay off the beer."

"Good for you," Lynne says.

Barney turns his ball cap backwards. "There's something about vanilla cones that keeps me off the hootch."

"Oh I love vanilla cones." Lynne licks Blizzard off her spoon. "They're so soothing. I actually prefer them to this fancy stuff."

"Easier on the budget," Barney says.

"And the waistline," Lynne adds. They both laugh at their lame jokes. Harriet looks out the window for Buck's cab.

"We should form a vanilla-cones-only club," Barney suggests.

"Oh, that's a great idea." They both laugh again. Barney has pointy teeth. He sits on the stool beside her mother.

"That's *my* seat," Harriet interjects.

"Harriet," Lynne scolds.

"That's my seat. My mother was saving it for me."

"Take it easy, Hal. I hope you don't mind, Barney, but we were trying to have some girl time. Girls' night out."

"Oh. Gotcha. When the boys are away the girls will play, wink wink. No worries. I'm outta here." He lifts his ball cap. "Till we meet again."

"You take care of yourself," Lynne says.

Harriet sits on the stool. "Was he that stupid before he went to Afghanistan?"

"Bunny, show some compassion." There's that word again. "He probably killed people over there, and saw people getting blown up. I mean, who knows what really goes on over there. Nobody talks about it."

"Because war's stupid."

"It's not that simple."

"Yes it is. If people talked about what really went on over there they'd figure out war is stupid and stop having them." Remembrance Day drives her nuts: everybody acting sorry about dead soldiers when there wouldn't be dead soldiers if there were no wars.

"Mizz Harriet, can we talk about the bra?"

"What about it?"

"I want you to be comfortable with your body, but I just think you might be trying to act older because of peer pressure."

"I'm not going to wear the bra. I only bought it because they had a buy-two-get-one-free sale and Darcy didn't have enough cash."

"I'm hearing an awful lot about this Darcy."

"She's my friend."

"I appreciate that, sweetheart, but one thing I've learned in life is, if you fall in with the wrong crowd, it's really hard to get back on your feet."

"What crowd are you in?" She knows her mother has no friends. She had some before Irwin was born. She and Trent invited them over for dinner. When they split up and sold the house, Lynne went broke and stopped having friends. She tried making friends in a mom and baby yoga group, but Irwin had a seizure and drooled all over the yoga mats.

"Gennedy is my crowd."

"One person isn't a crowd."

"Can't you see what he's done for us, bunny? Who would have looked after you when I had the breakdown?"

"We didn't need looking after."

"He swears he has never hit you. Is that true?"

"He'd hit me if he could."

"Oh for god's sake, Harriet, don't you see how you make everything more difficult? You have to be right all the time. That's just like your father."

Buck's cab pulls into the parking lot, and Harriet is so excited she can't speak.

"Your father is the most judgmental and righteous person I have ever met. It's those parents of his. Nothing he did was ever good enough."

Nothing Harriet does is ever good enough.

"Hal, you have two sets of parents who love you and would do anything for you. You just refuse to see it."

Harriet points to the parking lot. "Look, there's Darcy and her dad. His ex has full custody so he only gets to see Dee if Nina says it's okay." It concerns Harriet that Buck and Dee are wearing jogging shorts. They both look sweaty. Sweat is only sexy in movies. Buck's T-shirt says *IF WE ARE WHAT WE EAT, I'M FAST, CHEAP & EASY*. Darcy's shorts are giving her a wedgie. Harriet waves, beckoning them over.

Darcy acts surprised. "Oh, wow, hey! Long time no see. Is this your mom?"

"It is."

"Dad, this is Harriet's mom."

"Do we have names?" Buck asks.

"I'm Lynne." She offers her hand. He takes it in his sweaty one, covering both their hands with his left as they shake.

"I'm Buck. Good to meet you. I've heard so much about you."

"All good I hope."

"Totes," Darcy says.

"She means totally," Buck says. "Totally all good."

Dee pulls on Harriet's arm. "Come on, H, I need a fix. Dad?" She holds out her hand for cash. "What'll it be, Bucko? A Banana Cream Pie Blizzard?"

"Totes." Buck hands her a twenty. Harriet knows she'll keep the change.

They linger at the counter, even after they have the Blizzards, to watch the Buck and Lynne developments. "This is way better than online dating," Dee says.

"How would you know?"

"Buck's tried it. He has to sit through all the let-me-tell-you-about-myself crap. He totally hates the moment when he's supposed to make a move on her, or ask for her number. The bitches get all testy if he doesn't at least ask, so he puts their numbers in his cell, even if he'd rather throw himself on a sword than call them. Half the time he forgets to delete them and phones them by mistake. There was one chick he really wanted, like a totally together woman with her own couture business. She spent all night telling Buck what clothes would look good on him. He got all excited picturing her sewing him swag jackets. He always buys off the rack and the arms are too short. Anyway, she was hot *and* an entrepreneur. But when he asked for her number she said no. He thought maybe she'd misunderstood his English— she was Japanese—so he asked her again and she said no, then flagged a cab."

"She probably figured out he thinks with his dick."

"I know, right." Dee, spoon in mouth, pokes her head around a pillar to get a better look at the potential lovebirds. "There's definitely something cooking. They're both leaning forward. If Buck's sitting back, I know he's not interested. Okay, let's make the drop then say we want to sit outside."

"Hello, goils. What took you so long?"

"A lineup." Darcy hands him his Blizzard.

"I was just telling Lynne here about our workout routine. Turns out Lynne would like to jog with us."

"Dad, we've only jogged once, like, today."

"It's a start. And the more the merrier, I say. Maybe Harriet will join us."

"I don't jog."

"Why not, Ranger? Running's a lifesaver. I had a friend made it to the provincial finals. Guess what happened?"

"He lost," Harriet says.

"He got rear-ended, smashed his head into the windshield and went blind."

"That's tragic," Lynne says.

"Here's the thing. I knew he'd die if he quit running. So while he was recovering, I joined a running club and trained to be a guide."

"Say what?" Dee asks.

"I learned to guide blind runners. You run beside them and match their stride. They're the star, right, you just keep them in the lane, guide them through the curves. It's *their* race. They have to make the finish line— you just have to keep up."

"That's so amazing." Lynne crosses her legs again. "I mean, that you would do that for a friend." Harriet can tell she likes Buck. She imagines Lynne breaking the news to Gennedy, ordering him to pack his bags and get out. "I had no idea blind runners have guides," her mother says. "But it makes perfect sense. I mean, if running is your life and you go blind, you have to keep running."

"So, is it like a freak show, or what?" Darcy spoons some of Buck's Blizzard. "Do they, like, bump into each other? Like, they don't race with normal people, right?"

"There's races for all kinds of disabled athletes, Dee. If you love a sport you can't just give it up."

"I used to love track and field," Lynne says. "I still miss it."

"Let me guess." Buck points at her. "The long jump."

"How did you know that?"

"Your legs." They both look at her legs and Lynne blushes. Gran was right, she's still got the gams. And Buck hasn't even seen her in decent pumps.

"But," Lynne says, "how do you guide them? I mean, you can't run arm in arm."

"It's a rope tether you wrap around your hand. Here." He takes Lynne's hand and holds his wrist against hers. "You just touch lightly. You're running in sync and the blind guy's got to feel your arm. You sense each other's movements through your arms. Try it, move your arm with mine." Buck and Lynne move their touching arms up and down.

"That's so beautiful," Lynne says. Darcy and Harriet exchange looks.

"Here's what's happening," Dee says. "Me and H are going to chill at the picnic tables." The grown-ups continue to move their arms together in slo-mo. It is a sight to behold. Grandpa Archie used to say this if a Blue Jay hit a home run—which rarely happened—but when it did, Archie would sit back in his La-Z-Boy and say, "That is a sight to behold."

Skateboarders are doing dumbass stunts in the parking lot, flipping boards and swearing every time they screw up. "The blond's cute," Darcy observes, arranging her butt cheeks on the picnic table. Harriet wishes Darcy would stop staring at boys. It's embarrassing. She tries to look preoccupied with her Choco Cherry Love Blizzard.

"So Buck's definitely into her," Dee says. "He'll probably try to get her into the fuckmobile."

"Not if he thinks it's true love. He won't want to rush it."

"Says you with the wealth of experience."

"He knows she's with the derp."

"It's the hitched ones that want quickies because they've got to pick up their kids from karate and shit."

"Well, my mom doesn't want a quickie. It's going to be different with her."

Dee pulls out her stolen lipstick and glides it over her lips. "The blond's checking me out."

"No he isn't."

"Skinny guys like big women."

"Can we talk about something else?"

"Okay. Here's the bad news. Buck gave Nina crabs."

"She doesn't like seafood?"

"Not sea crabs. The little black things that, like, cling to your pubes and lay eggs and itch like crazy. She was going ape shit scratching. Meanwhile my aunt was in town and slept in Nina's bed, so *she* got crabs. The two crazy bitches kept cussing and scratching and smearing crab poison all over their pooters and armpits. They stuffed sheets and underwear and anything else that might be contaminated into garbage bags. A week later, Nina starts scratching all over again. The pharmacist tells her the larvae can hatch up to seven days after the actual crabs are dead."

Harriet considers the consequences of her mother getting crabs. If she gives them to Gennedy, he'd find out she'd screwed around. This might make Gennedy leave. "Does he have crabs now?"

"Sadly I am not privy to that information." Still staring at the skateboarders, Dee leans back against the picnic table and crosses her plump legs. "What a time to be alive. Oh my god there's that Caitlin whore."

"Where?"

"Leaning on my dad's truck."

"Does she know it's your dad's?"

"Fuck no. She just wants the skateboarders to notice her." The Caitlin whore sucks on a cigarette, fanning the smoke like it's somebody else's. "I'll wait till she sees me then I'll put a hurt on her ass."

It seems to Harriet that Caitlin is already looking right at them, and snickering to her friends who are also wearing short shorts and flip-flops. Caitlin is the only one smoking, which is why it's weird she keeps fanning the smoke like it's bugging her. The cute skateboarder rolls up to her and takes a drag from her cigarette.

"Slut," Darcy says. "I can't even look at her she's such a skank."

The cute skateboarder and Caitlin share the smoke until she grinds the butt into the tarmac with her flip-flop.

"She's coming over here," Harriet says.

"Fuck my life."

"We could run inside."

"Are you kidding me? This is *our* turf, girl." Darcy pretends to be fascinated by the Dairy Queen sign but Harriet studies Caitlin, who is the kind of girl Harriet plans to impersonate for the Greyhound bus drivers. She might even steal some of Lynne's smokes, and—before getting on the bus—suck on one and fan the smoke at the same time.

"Hey, Darcy," Caitlin says. Her gum-chewing associates slouch on either side of her. "What are you up to this summer?"

Darcy, disturbingly timid, mutters, "Not much."

"*We're* going to horse camp and are, like, amped to the max."

"Totally," the associates chime.

"I'm allergic to horses," Darcy says. Harriet waits for her to put a hurt on Caitlin's ass.

"Really?" Caitlin says. "Well, there's pills for that. Emmy takes them and they get her high. Right, Em?"

"The non-drowsy kind. It's kind of like taking speed."

"Who's your little friend?" Caitlin asks. Feeling the spotlight on her, Harriet becomes hyper aware of Irwin's vomit on her jeans.

"I'm her babysitter," Darcy says. Harriet, flabbergasted by this lie but afraid to call her on it because Dee might get mad and blow the deal with Buck, drinks the melted ice cream in her Blizzard, hiding her wounded expression behind the big plastic cup.

"Too bad you couldn't make it to my party," Caitlin says. "It was awesome. I posted a bunch of pics if you want to check it out. It was a blast."

"Best party ever," Emmy says.

"Totally," the other associate agrees. Harriet waits for Darcy to say she wasn't invited, but she just scrapes the inside of her empty Blizzard cup with her spoon.

"Gotta run," Caitlin says. "Text me."

Harriet waits for Darcy to tell her she has texted her, and that Caitlin hasn't replied. But all Dee says is "Sure."

Caitlin and her associates meet up with the skateboarders and schlep into the DQ.

"She said she had to run," Harriet says. "She's not running." Darcy pulls the wedgie out of her shorts.

Harriet tosses her empty plastic cup into the trash. "I thought you said you were going to put a hurt on her ass."

"It's all in the timing, H. The timing wasn't right. I'll get her back." This is like an adult, saying one thing and doing something completely different.

Harriet walks briskly into the DQ and prods Caitlin. "She's not my babysitter, and you didn't invite her to your party, and you *never* return her texts. You're a lying sack of shit and if you lie to her again, I will jump your ass." Caitlin flushes a colour Harriet wants to paint later—crimson with a hint of moss.

"Who the fuck are you, bitch?" the cute skateboarder demands.

"My dad's a cop. You better watch what you smoke, you finger-popping asshole." A circle of hostility forms around Harriet, and she fears she will have to resort to a life-or-death fighting style to defend herself, but suddenly Buck is taking her hand.

"She's right," he says. "You're lucky I'm off-duty. I could make things real uncomfortable for you losers. So watch your backs. I never forget a face. Come on, honey."

Harriet flips the bird at the cute skateboarder. "Later, skater."

Buck doesn't release her hand even when they're in the parking lot. His grip feels warm, strong and trustworthy, and she thinks she's falling in love with him.

Fourteen

Lynne doesn't say anything driving home. She turns on the radio and hums to Whitney Houston belting "I Will Always Love You," a song from a movie starring an actor Lynne crushed on until he went bald. Not wanting to appear too interested in the Buck connection, Harriet doesn't ask questions. They're meeting up with him and Dee for a run tomorrow, which is a major step forward. Lynne drops Harriet outside the Shangrila with instructions to go straight to the apartment and check on Irwin. But Mr. Fishberg sidles up to her, asking if he can touch her *tetas*, and Mrs. Rumph, in her lawn chair, with her ferret climbing all over her, shakes a flabby arm at Harriet. "I require some shut mouth from you, young lady. My son told me how you talk."

"Do you know how your son talks?"

"You're just jealous because Mrs. Schidt likes him better than you."

"I don't give a fifth of a fuck about Mrs. Schidt."

"Jealousy is poisonous, Harry," Mr. Shotlander cautions, shaking a pebble from his orthotic shoe.

Mr. Zilberschmuck taps cigarette ash into the flower bed. "Which is exactly why you shouldn't be jealous of Gerhardt, Shotlander."

"Who says I'm jealous of Gerhardt?" Mr. Shotlander shoves his foot back into his shoe.

Harriet has heard them argue about Gerhardt before because he's seventy-six and has a thirty-eight-year-old trophy wife. Mr. Shotlander thinks she's a gold digger but Mr. Zilberschmuck believes Celestia is the autumnal romance Gerhardt deserves after being a bush pilot in Australia for fifty years.

Mr. Shotlander trails Harriet into the lobby. "We're having Seniors' Reading Night tomorrow. Can we count on you for bevies?"

Mr. Chubak stops peeling an orange to feel around in his corduroys. "I got a couple of toonies here, Harry, do you think you could call those nice folks in India for me about the phone bill? I know they mean well but I can't understand a word they're saying." He looks at his watch. "It's daytime over there."

"Sure." Harriet takes the toonies.

"Now hold your horses," Mr. Shotlander says. "You'll call India for that rascal but you won't take a look at my dang computer?"

"He doesn't snitch on me." She presses the elevator button. "Let's go, Mr. Chubak."

When she's old, she wants to be like Mr. Chubak with an apartment full of tropical plants that never die. He decided doors made the apartment feel cramped, and replaced them with beaded curtains. He hangs glass prisms in his windows that create light shows on his walls. Mr. Chubak never married because he says he would never do that to a person. He worked as a social worker in the Arctic, fighting the fallout from what he called the Great White Invasion. "The white man," he explained, "is the scourge of the Earth." He has photos of the Arctic tundra and icebergs all over his apartment. When Harriet gets a job at the bank she plans to spend her vacation pay visiting the Arctic to paint icebergs and seals. Mr. Chubak ate seals to make friends with the Inuit. He says you have to make friends with them or you won't learn anything about the North. The seals taste fishy. Harriet plans to eat whatever it takes to make friends with the Inuit. She wants them to teach her how to carve soapstone.

Mr. Chubak hands her his phone bill. "Ask them why I'd want someone leaving a message with silicon Sally when they can just call me back."

Harriet dials up the Customer Retention department and demands they reverse the charges on an answering service promotion Mr. Chubak did not agree to. Faced with resistance, she becomes aggressive with the Indian on the phone and demands to speak to his supervisor. After twenty minutes another Indian comes on the line that turns out to be just another service rep. Harriet gets even more belligerent while demanding to speak to a supervisor. Mr. Chubak shakes his fists, cheering her on. "Go get 'em, Harry." After another twenty minutes a supervisor comes on, and Harriet lets loose about how Bell takes advantage of seniors, pressuring them to accept offers they don't fully understand. The Indian, sounding weary, agrees to reverse the charges.

"Way to go, Harry. Remind me to nominate you for prime minister. Would you care for cookies and OJ?"

"Yes please." She looks at the photos on the wall of Mr. Chubak's grandparents. They lived in the Ukraine and jumped into the freezing river every New Year's to cleanse themselves of the old year. "They took it a day at a time in those days," Mr. Chubak told her. "It was just plain survival they were interested in. If they had a pig they were happy. Especially after my father bought a freezer and they could store pork all winter. They had a party to show everybody in the village the freezer. Next thing you know they were storing everybody else's pig. That's just the kind of people they were. Sharing came natural to them. You had to look out for everybody. Not like these days."

He hands her a juice box and arranges Chips Ahoy! cookies on a plate. Harriet takes one and points to a photo of a young soldier. "You've never told me who that is."

"Because it's a sad story. That's Oskar, my uncle. The war messed him up real bad, what with shell shock and all that. But he made it through. Four days after the war ended, he stepped on an unexploded mine. Blew him to bits."

Harriet doesn't see what's so sad about stepping on a bomb you didn't know was there if you're messed up real bad. Ka-boom, your suffering's over—you didn't see it coming—*and* you might come back as a bird or a deep-sea creature.

Mr. Chubak stares at the photo, shaking his head. "My grandmother never got over it. 'There's justice for you,' she'd say. She even quit going to church. See that?" He points to a picture of a tiny boy in a grey suit. "That's me in the itchiest get-up ever made. My grandma had a loom and was always weaving cloth that would rip your skin off. Whenever we visited, my mother made me wear it to make my grandmother happy." He pokes the straw into his juice box.

"Did it make her happy?"

"Nothing made her happy after Oskar got blown up."

"So why'd do you have to wear it if it didn't make her happy?"

"Why do we have to do anything? Because it's expected."

"I don't do things because it's expected."

"No, well, Harry, that's because you're a special snowflake."

The phone rings. It's Mr. Shotlander tracking her down. Mr. Chubak covers the mouthpiece. "You've got him over a barrel, Harry. He says he's got a fiver for you. Do I tell him you're on your way?"

Before checking Mr. Shotlander's cables, Harriet demands the fiver. After he hands it to her, she orders Mr. Zilberschmuck off the couch because the outlet is behind it. He is drinking Jack Daniel's and fingering a cigarillo. When he's indoors and can't smoke, he drinks JD. They're still arguing about Gerhardt.

"You're talking about a guy the girls were *crazy* about," Mr. Shotlander says.

"Unlike yourself. As I said, you're jealous."

Harriet points to the computer. "It was on hibernate."

"It was what?"

"You put it on hibernate instead of sleep. When you put it on hibernate you have to press the power button for at least four seconds to get it to start up again."

"Since when do computers hibernate?" Mr. Shotlander rips open a bag of barbecue chips and eats several. "I'm telling you, life was a lot simpler before all this techno nonsense."

"It can still be simple," Harriet says. "Just don't complicate it by doing dumbass things like clicking hibernate or snitching on me."

"Truer words were never spoken." Mr. Zilberschmuck pours more whiskey.

She listens outside her apartment, hoping to hear her mother and Gennedy arguing because Lynne's giving him his marching orders. Gran was always threatening to give Archie his marching orders. Harriet can't hear anything and opens the door quietly, intending to sneak to her room.

"Where the hell have you been, young lady?" Gennedy demands in a hoarse whisper because Lynne and Irwin are asleep on the couch.

"I had to fix Mr. Shotlander's computer, and call Bell for Mr. Chubak."

"No doubt you charged them plenty."

"Is Irwin all right?"

"What do *you* think? Don't ever feed him without our permission again."

Harriet wants to scream in his pasty face that Lynne's met The One and he should start packing. She looks for signs of a fight—deserted dinner plates, unwashed pots and pans—but the kitchen is tidy, even the chairs are pushed neatly into the table.

"Your mother told you to come straight up to see Irwin, but of course you didn't because you never do what you're told."

"He doesn't need me when she's around."

"That's where you're wrong. For no reason I can fathom, he needs you all the time." He pulls a plate of spaghetti out of the microwave. "Your mother wanted me to heat some dinner for you."

"I'm not hungry."

"I told her you'd say that." He pitches the food into the garbage and drops the plate into the sink. "You can starve for all I care."

"Right back at you." Harriet grips the magenta button she found in the DQ parking lot, and moves sluggishly into the living room, dragged down by Irwin's inexplicable and unceasing need for her.

Her mother and brother must have fallen asleep watching TV. Irwin's curled into Lynne and she's resting her cheek against his head. Harriet holds a hand in front of his face to feel if he's breathing.

"What are you doing?" Gennedy hisses. "I told you not to disturb them."

Harriet never curls up with her mother to watch TV. She did before Irwin was born. They'd walk hand in hand to the video store, and Lynne would let her choose a movie. Harriet picked DVDs with dogs on the cover. She dreamed of having a faithful Saint Bernard that would go with her everywhere and rescue her from snow avalanches. The video store went out of business, and Harriet can't have a Saint Bernard because of Irwin.

Gennedy hands her the antibiotics. "Take a pill. Your mother says you're supposed to take one at bedtime. It's late. Go to sleep."

She plugs in her glue gun and shakes the pill container like maracas while waiting for the gun to heat. Untreated the infection will spread and her mother might take her to the hospital again. They might admit her and Lynne might stay with her all night long.

She carefully dots glue on the back of the magenta button and places it between the eyes of *The Leopard Who Changed Her Spots*. "This is your third eye," she tells her, opening the shoebox of squeezed-out paint tubes. She badly needs more siennas.

"Bunny, did you take your pill?" Lynne stands groggy in the doorway, holding a glass of water. "You didn't, did you?" She hands Harriet the glass, takes the pill container and tips a capsule into Harriet's palm. "Gennedy's right, you know, you should soak your toe in salt water."

Harriet takes the capsule but pushes it to the side of her mouth with her tongue. "When are we jogging with Buck tomorrow?"

"He said he'd text Dee and you guys would sort out the deets."

"He's nice, isn't he?"

"Who?"

"Buck."

"He smokes dope."

"How do you know?"

"I know a pothead when I see one."

"He can't be a pothead if he drives a Mack truck. Maybe he's a recreational user."

"A.k.a. pothead."

"I think he's the nicest man I've ever met."

"He's nice all right."

While Lynne catches sight of her reflection in the mirror and adjusts her hair, Harriet spits the capsule into her hand. "Does Gennedy know?"

"What?"

"That you're jogging with another man."

"Gennedy doesn't jog. Bunny, you have to promise me you won't feed Irwin anything without asking me or Gennedy first. It's really important."

Providing treats was one of the few things she could do for Irwin, and now she has to ask permission. "I won't feed him anything. Period."

"What smells? Is that the glue gun? Oh my lord, Harriet, it's after eleven. You have to go to bed. Did you brush your teeth?"

"I will."

"Please don't be difficult."

"I won't." She hopes her mother will hug her again. The boldness she felt earlier that empowered her to initiate hugs has left her.

"So why aren't you turning off the glue gun?"

"I will."

"Do it *now*, please. Otherwise I'll take it to our room. You can have it in the morning."

Harriet turns off the glue gun.

"Thank you. Now go brush your teeth. I'm so exhausted I can barely stand so please cooperate. I'm going to bed."

"With him?"

"What?"

"Aren't you mad at Gennedy?"

"Why would I be mad at Gennedy?"

Harriet would like to say *Because he wants to hit me and shouts at me and is the grossest man alive.* Instead she says, "It's just you were fighting all day."

"Gennedy wants what's best for our family, and sometimes he gets a little emotional."

More excuses. Harriet no longer wants to hug her mother. She pushes past her to the bathroom. Gennedy's just been in there and it stinks. She drops the capsule into the toilet and grabs her toothbrush, trying to make herself feel better by thinking about Buck moving in. He won't be around all the time because of his job. This would mean more computer time for Harriet. And he'd make Lynne laugh, which Gennedy never does. Irwin would love him too, especially if Buck takes them to Canada's Wonderland and buys them cotton candy. Irwin might miss Gennedy but, if he's going to die before the end of the week, it won't matter. And Harriet could make his room into her studio. Already she's feeling better. And hungry. She sneaks into the kitchen to make a peanut butter sandwich and call Dee. "What the fuck?" Dee says. "It's like one in the morning or something."

"It's the only time I get privacy on the phone. Did he say anything about my mom on the drive home?"

"Woman, you need to calm down."

"He must've said something."

"He said she's really nice."

"That's all?"

"What's the problem, yo? We know he wants to do her."

"Yeah, but it's got to be different from the others."

"I got no control over that, dawg."

"You could talk about her, like how great she is."

"I don't even know her."

"Just keep telling him she's not a ball buster like Nina."

"What are you eating?"

"A peanut butter sandwich."

"You skinny-assed bitch. I'm totally starved and my mom's hidden *all* the carbs. She says I'm not supposed to drink Slim Fast plus eat a meal. She says Slim Fast's a meal replacement. I said, 'Bitch, you try living on liquids.'"

"Do you want me to bring you a peanut butter sandwich?"

"Now you're talkin'. With jelly. You go, girl."

At night the building becomes Harriet's domain. Free to search for mixed-media materials without anyone spying on her, she finds treasures. Most recently, a pearl earring she plans to pawn. Outside Mr. Rivera's, she spots a piece of gold-trimmed burgundy ribbon. Through the crack between the door and the floor she notices that his lights are on. She presses her ear against the door and hears Mr. Rivera praying and sobbing, sounding almost as though he's choking, and she considers knocking but then he stops choking and starts praying again. She fears this means Mr. Rivera is sick because, in her experience, Filipinos only pray all night when someone is dying. She stands very still hoping to hear Mrs. Rivera's spirit assure her that everything is all right, *anak*, but all she hears is Mr. Rivera praying.

Dee's waiting outside her apartment. "Get your skinny ass over here." She grabs the peanut butter and jelly sandwich and takes a bite while scrolling through her Facebook newsfeed. "Fun Fact. That Caitlin whore got her tongue pierced."

"Stop reading about her."

Dee holds out her phone. "Check out the whore beast in her Lululemon Groove Pants. What a cam ho."

"Stop looking at her."

"You need to take my profile picture, yo. Mine's a selfie and it sucks. Let's do new pics tomorrow."

Being included in Darcy's plans gives Harriet an unfamiliar sense of self-worth. Dee is including her in her plans, not because she has to, but because she wants to.

Mr. Bhanmattie steps through the fire stairs door and begins slapping the walls with a fly swatter.

"What's up with him, yo?"

"He's on steroids," Harriet explains. "They're for his asthma. They make him see bugs on the walls and ask for pink gin."

"Nice."

Mr. Bhanmattie scuffles towards them. "You see all these insects? Where are they coming from? We must exterminate them. They carry pestilence."

Harriet slaps at the walls with him. "Got 'em."

"My throat is so dry." Mr. Bhanmattie touches his neck. "I require refreshment."

"Go ask Mr. Shotlander," Harriet says, pressing the elevator button. "I was over there earlier and he's got all kinds of drinks. 506. He'd love to see you. And there's no bugs on *his* walls."

"Mr. Shotlander." Mr. Bhanmattie narrows his eyes. "Can he be trusted?"

"Certainly." The elevator doors open and she guides Mr. Bhanmattie in, then presses five before jumping out again.

Dee fist-pumps her. "What a badass. And the way you slapped that Caitlin whore around? You made that ho eat the voodoo, seriously. You rocked it, girl. Bam." Dee's admiration swaddles Harriet, making her feel proud.

"That'll teach her to mess with my crew," Dee says.

"Darcy?" Nina calls. "Who are you talking to?"

"The warden's after me," Darcy whispers. "TTYL, bra."

Gennedy is lurking in the kitchen when Harriet returns but says nothing, just stares at her with eyes dulled by life's disappointments and she knows she has been one of them. She tries not to care, although his loathing has started to burn holes in her. He shakes his head slowly and goes back to drinking milk. This is another thing she can't stand about him. What kind of grown man drinks milk?

"So tell me about your little art projects," he says. "What's the glued garbage supposed to represent, your angst?"

"I'm going to bed now."

"Of course you are."

She lies very still in her bed, pretending she's Tutankhamun in his tomb, surrounded by treasures. Uma, when she was still trying to impress Harriet, took her to King Tut's exhibit at the AGO. That's when Harriet learned that nobody knew about Tutankhamun's tomb because Tutankhamun was a runt pharaoh with one leg shorter than the other. Bigger pharaohs with legs the same length had bigger tombs that were raided for hundreds of years while Tutankhamun lay forgotten and undisturbed. A man with BO beside her said, "The little twerp slipped under the radar." This is what Harriet will do at Lost Coin Lake.

Fifteen

She hears Mrs. Butts' cane tapping towards her while she's waiting for the elevator. "Harriet, I need you to go to the drugstore for me. I woke up this morning and my arm was swollen. Lukey's bite is infected, look." She holds out her forearm.

"It doesn't look infected."

"The last time he bit me the doctor told me cat bites can be fatal. I need you to run to the drugstore and get me some Polysporin immediately. The ointment, not the cream."

"I'm busy. I have to get drinks for Seniors' Reading Night."

"Did you not hear what I said? The doctor told me cat bites can be fatal."

"Call an ambulance."

"What's gotten into you? First you want money for every little thing, and now you're just plain rude." Lukey slips out of her apartment and winds around her legs. "Bad cat. I can't even look at you. You're a horror. A devil."

"Five bucks."

"What?"

"I'll do it for five bucks. It's out of my way—I was just going to

Mr. Hung's." Pop is cheaper at Shoppers Drug Mart than at Mr. Hung's. For the extra five bucks she'll go the extra distance to make a bigger profit on the seniors' drinks.

"All right then, all right. Just a minute." Mrs. Butts taps her way back into her apartment to get the cash. The elevator comes and goes.

"Harriet?" Gennedy calls. "Where do you think you're going?"

"I have errands."

He squishes towards her. "Can you not even have breakfast with your brother? The minute he woke up he ran to your room and you weren't there. He started to *cry*, Harriet."

"That's not my problem."

"Really? Yesterday you said he wasn't *my* business because I'm not related and that he was *your* business because he's your brother."

"I can't help him. He's going to die anyway."

The slap across her face is so swift she thinks she might have imagined it. But the sting spreads to her ear, and she can tell from his startled expression that he has hit her.

Mrs. Butts comes tapping back. "Here's ten dollars. It shouldn't cost more than five so I expect to see some change. Get a receipt. Now hurry up about it." Harriet presses the elevator button. Mrs. Butts turns to Gennedy. "What are *you* staring at? Don't think I don't know what you're up to, living in sin. No wonder this girl is turning into a criminal. You should be ashamed of yourself, taking advantage of that woman and her sick child. I wouldn't put up with you for *one* minute, all that shouting. I have half a mind to call the police." The elevator arrives. Harriet darts inside and presses the close button as Mrs. Butts says, "None of this is good for my ulcer."

In the lobby Mr. Shotlander stops her. "What happened to your face?"

"Nothing. I'm hot."

"You look like you got stung by a bee," Mr. Hoogstra says. His underwear is peeking above his trousers again. "My nephew got stung by a bee and swelled up and couldn't breathe, had to go to the hospital and get hooked up to a pole."

"Did you get stung, Harry?" Mr. Shotlander mines his ear with his finger.

"It might have been a mosquito."

Mr. Hoogstra scratches under his captain's hat. "West Nile is going around again. You should get it looked at, Harry. You can't be too careful with all the crazy diseases out there."

"I don't buy it." Mr. Shotlander grips her arm. "Somebody hit you, Harry. Who was it?"

She tries to wriggle free. "Nobody hit me. I'm going to Shoppers—does anybody want anything?" Immediately the seniors are feeling their pockets for change.

Mr. Shotlander releases her arm to tug up his trousers. "Nobody has the right to hit another human being."

"Or animal." Mr. Chubak hands Harriet a ten. "In the flyer they have a deal on six packs of juice boxes. Can you get me a couple?"

She writes down their orders on Post-its, puts their cash into Ziplocs then looks at Mr. Shotlander. "You don't want anything?"

"I thought I was in the doghouse."

"I'm giving you one more chance on the condition that you don't tell him anything ever again."

"It's him who hit you, isn't it?"

"Nobody hit me."

"That scoundrel. I'll kill the son of a bitch." He digs in his ear again.

"Do I have your word that you won't tell him anything ever again?"

"You have my word. But if he so much as lays a finger on you, he'll have me to answer to." He wipes his finger on his polyester trousers.

"What do you want from Shoppers?"

"See if they have any chips on special. Doesn't have to be barbecue if it's under a buck."

Out in the world, Harriet tries to look like a girl who lives in a nice house with loving parents. Around her, apparently untroubled people glide through the day easily, checking cells, listening to iPods, waiting for busses, sipping coffee out of disposable cups. Small things irritate them like lineups at checkout counters, or slow phones. But nothing really seems to bother them, and Harriet tries to imagine what it would be like if every day wasn't a battle, if she could wake up in the morning and not immediately dread seeing Gennedy, or Irwin, or her mother smoking again. If she could believe that everything will be all right. People say that all the time, "It'll be all right," and they seem to believe it. Whereas Harriet never believes it will be all right. Every day brings new obstacles she must circumvent. And the stormy cloud of Gennedy's loathing has begun to trail her. She thinks he might be right. They might *all* be right about her being difficult, greedy, selfish and without compassion. She forces herself to think about Buck's trustworthy grip, and how she can say anything around him. If she can get him to cut back on fatties, soon this may all be over and Gennedy will be history and Irwin will be dead. A display of Turtles halts her because Turtles are Irwin's favourite food. He laughs as he bites the head off. Buying the Turtles would make Irwin happy. But she's no longer allowed to buy him treats, and suddenly a hurtling sadness spins her into the path of a yoga mom on a cell, pushing a stroller. "Watch where you're going," the mom chides before resuming her phone conversation. "I make my own pepper spray. My husband thinks I'm really smart."

Out in the world, everybody looks as though they belong. Harriet's always on the run, trying to be nowhere, to avoid trouble. Standing in the snack food aisle, checking for chips on sale for less than a buck, she can't run anymore. She stops in front of the Cheetos and sits on the floor while the people who know where they're going bustle around her. When she couldn't sleep last night she glued three of the blue and white antibiotic capsules on the cheeks of *The Leopard Who Changed Her Spots*. "These are your tears," she told her.

She stares up at the snack food packaging: swaths of orange, red and yellow, like William Blake's paintings. His mother beat him for seeing angels in the branches of a tree. He regularly talked to angels, and everybody thought he was nuts. They didn't want him seeing angels where they only saw trees. They wanted him to see exactly what they were seeing, just like Mrs. Elrind, Gennedy, Lynne, Trent and Oom. They want everything flattened, comfortable and predictable. They want a sun to look like a disk hanging in the sky. They think seeing it as a fiery ball of angels means you're crazy. Harriet learned about William Blake at the last Seniors' Reading Night. Mr. Chubak passed around a book of Blake's work and quoted him: "*If the doors of perception were cleansed everything would appear to man as it is: infinite.*" Mr. Chubak said that William Blake thought people who flattened the world based on their past experience were seeing all things *only thro' narrow chinks of his cavern*. Mr. Chubak said those people are doomed to go through the same stuff over and over. "They turn and turn in what Blake calls *the same dull round*." Mr. Chubak was struggling to open a childproof cap on his vitamin E bottle. Childproof caps defeat most of the seniors as they turn and turn in the same dull round. Harriet opens the caps for them, feeling herself turning and turning in the same dull round.

William Blake's paintings were small and filled with angels and demons. She couldn't stop looking at the one called *The Ghost of a Flea*. Harriet had no idea what William Blake meant by painting a flea's head on a muscular man's body. And she couldn't understand why the man/flea was holding out a bucket, or why he was a ghost. But this didn't matter; she couldn't stop looking at it. Mr. Hoogstra, scratching under his captain's hat, told her to pass the book along. She waited for Mr. Hoogstra to be transfixed by *The Ghost of a Flea*, but he just flipped past it, jabbing a toothpick into his gums. "*Satan Calling Up His Legions*," he said. "Now *that's* a painting. Terrific."

Harriet wanted to know what William Blake said to the angels, and what they answered back. It seemed to her that if she could talk to angels and they answered back, everything would be all right.

"You can't sit on the floor here," a boy in a Shoppers Drug Mart shirt says.

"I'm getting up." The boy has a shock of orange hair that flops over his forehead. Harriet tries to figure out what colours to mix to create that burnt orange. She pushes herself off the floor, grabbing hold of the shelving to haul herself up. "I haven't finished my shopping."

"No problem. Just don't sit on the floor."

Why not? she wants to scream. *Why can't I sit on the floor if I'm tired? Why do I have to do what's expected?*

"Do you know where the Polysporin is?" she asks.

"First Aid. Aisle six."

She feels him keeping an eye on her as she heads for aisle six, where she sees Mrs. Schidt, with Coco on her lap, leaning out of her wheelchair to examine corn plasters. Harriet would bolt if she didn't need the

Polysporin. Mrs. Schidt will squint at the tiny print on the corn plaster labels for twenty minutes then demand assistance from "the druggist," who will hurry to her aid because Mrs. Schidt is in a wheelchair. Mrs. Schidt walks fine around her apartment, and only uses the wheelchair when she goes out to make people feel sorry for her. "When you're an old lady," she told Harriet, "use it." She never hesitates to ask strangers for help with packages, doors or getting in and out of cabs. Harriet knows Mrs. Schidt has a mini trampoline in her living room that she bounces on to "get her blood going."

Coco spies Harriet and starts yapping. "Shhh," Mrs. Schidt commands before noticing Harriet. Harriet expects her to say how rude and ungrateful she is, but Mrs. Schidt looks through her. This is worse than if she'd said something mean. Coco keeps yapping and straining against his leash, probably because he expects Harriet to take him to the doggy park. She grabs a tube of Polysporin ointment and stands directly in front of Mrs. Schidt's wheelchair. Mrs. Schidt continues to ignore her, and all the rage Harriet has suppressed during the three years she has been walking Coco for $14 a week blasts out and she shouts, "I'm right here, you stupid old witch. And I know you can walk and bounce on your tramp and are a total fake." Coco yaps louder while Mrs. Schidt tries to back away from Harriet. "You're the stingiest, meanest, most horrible person I've ever met," Harriet says, "and I hope your ugly dog gets fucked up the ass till it knocks his brains out." She doesn't mean this about Coco, she just wants to get back at Mrs. Schidt for treating her like an idiot who can never do anything right. "Get up and walk, you old bag."

Mrs. Schidt's face sags into a pudding, reminding Harriet of Rembrandt's portraits of haggard old Dutch ladies. Harriet nudges the wheelchair with her foot. The orange-haired boy grips her arm. "It's time for you to leave."

At the Shangrila, Mr. Shotlander paces the lobby. "We're going to have words with him, Harry."

"Who?"

"That layabout who hit you."

"Nobody hit me." She distributes the seniors' orders. Gennedy didn't leave a bruise. She checked her face in a mirror at the cosmetic counter.

"Mr. Quigley's going to show you some moves."

"What moves?"

"Self-defence," Mr. Quigley says. His curly white hair springs off his head as he hops around her. The stripes down the sides of his track pants zigzag as he demonstrates fancy footwork.

"I don't need any moves." She hands Mr. Chubak the juice boxes.

"Everybody needs moves." Mr. Quigley air-boxes. "Particularly when you're up against a bigger opponent." Mr. Quigley is five-foot-four but insists he was a professional fighter once. He starts to circle Harriet. "You've got to probe the big guy, circle him in a steady clockwise direction, check out his strengths and weaknesses, flick a jab and move away." Mr. Quigley flicks a jab inches from her face.

"You're giving me a headache," she says.

"Listen to him, Harry. You never know when it might come in handy."

"You stick and slide." Mr. Quigley pretends to throw a punch then slides sideways. "Stick and slide. If things get bad and you're up against the ropes, you get into a protective crouch."

"I thought you were supposed to be at Casino Rama," Harriet says.

Mr. Shotlander sips his Diet Coke. "The lucky bastard won two hundred bucks on the one-armed bandits. How do you like that?"

Mr. Quigley holds his hands and elbows up around his head. "See, you absorb the blows of your opponent, feel his strength ebb and flow. Tire him out."

"Craptastic," Harriet says.

"It's a mind game." Mr. Quigley points at his temple then at Harriet. "It's you and him. In those moments you're the only two people on earth."

Sometimes it does feel as though she and Gennedy are the only two people on earth. Just thinking of the sack of shit's pasty face makes her flick a jab at Mr. Quigley. "That's the stuff," he says, "keep 'em coming, stick and slide." She slides sideways clockwise, flicking and jabbing without actually hitting him. The repeated quick movements flood her with endorphins and she starts to feel like the strongest girl in the world. "Bring it on," she says, sticking and jabbing until a circle of seniors forms around her.

"Way to go, Harry!" they cheer as Mr. Quigley dodges her blows.

Taj is at Darcy's because the toilet is plugged again.

"You put woman things down there," he tells Darcy's mother. "You must not put woman things down there."

"If you mean tampons and pads," Nina says, "we don't flush any of it. We're not stupid. It's a crap toilet. I need a new toilet."

"You don't need a new toilet, ma'am. These are good toilets. Good make."

Nina flicks her mad-nice red hair out of her face. "How many fucking times am I going to have to drag your ass up here before you get me a toilet with a decent flush?"

Dee whispers in Harriet's ear. "See how blotchy she's getting? She's going to bust his balls in a second."

"There is nothing wrong with this toilet, ma'am. Put toilet paper only. Not woman things."

"I am not putting woman things down there, you moron. Are you familiar with the term 'flush' as in flushing power?"

Taj, gripping his plunger, backs out of the bathroom. "It's working now, ma'am."

"Because you've been plunging it for half an hour. It'll be plugged again in no time and you'll be AWOL."

Taj, head bowed as though afraid she might hit him, slinks to the door.

"Don't sneak away from me!" Nina shouts. "I pay over a thousand for this dive, the least you owe me is a decent toilet."

"Nobody else has this problem, ma'am."

"Don't lie to me, little brown man. The geezers are constantly plugging their toilets. Guess I'm going to have to contact your boss and tell him you're never in the building because you're out selling pirated shit. I have photos." She points to her cell. "Lots of pics of you dealing contraband. Even some video. What's your boss' name? Maldonado, isn't it? I'm sure Maldonado would be very interested in my video. Maybe I should put it on YouTube, call it 'Taj the Pirate.'"

"I'll see what I can do, ma'am."

"You've got twenty-four hours. If we don't have a new toilet in twenty-four hours, 'Taj the Pirate' goes viral." She slams the door after him.

Darcy pulls a Diet Sprite from the fridge. "Do you even have any photos or video of him?"

"What do you think."

"Nobody bluffs like Nina Suprema."

"What if he doesn't get you a new toilet in twenty-four hours?" Harriet asks.

"He burns," Dee says. "Come on, H, let's strategize in the Situation Room."

"Why are you wearing so much makeup?"

"Because you're taking my profile pic, yo." Darcy lounges on her bed with one knee up and her head resting in her hand. "Is this a good pose?"

"I can't believe your mom called Taj 'a little brown man.'"

"Why? Isn't he one?"

"That's racist."

"To call somebody what they are? Gee wow."

"My mother would never talk to anybody like that."

"That's why she lives with a derp." She pushes her bust forward. "How's this?"

"Stop trying to look sexy."

"What's wrong with sexy? Oh, I forgot. You're eleven and don't have hormones."

"Any pervball can look at your picture."

"Let 'em look. It's not like they know where I live, LOL." Dee jumps up and starts speedily thrusting her pelvis forward and backwards.

"What are you doing?"

"Showing off my junk in the trunk," she says, pointing to her ass. "*You* got a bubble butt, girl. But *I* got junk in the trunk."

"I thought we were taking your profile picture."

"Right on, dawg." She hands Harriet her phone. "That Caitlin ho bag is smiling in hers. I'm just going to do bedroom eyes." Dee flops back on the bed, crossing one leg over the other and dropping her head slightly then looking up at Harriet with heavy eyelids.

"You look sick," Harriet says.

"How's this?" Darcy puckers her lips.

"Just sit properly and look normal."

"Hell's bells, forgot my boa." Dee grabs a pink feather boa and winds it around her neck. Harriet takes a couple of shots and hands the phone back.

Dee admires the pics. "Don't you just love my smoky eyes? I watched a makeup tutorial to figure out how to do it."

"Does Nina scream at Buck like that?" Harriet sits on the bed.

"Like what?"

"Like she was screaming at Taj."

"Damn straight. Bucko digs it."

"My mother would never shout like that."

"Too bad. Let's hope she's got something else going for her. We'll ask Mr. Ouija." Dee pulls out the board and sets it on the Barbie table.

"I don't want to do Ouija."

"Woman, don't be such a wussy. Personally I want to know what's up so I can strategize."

"Can I look at the capybara after?"

"Oh my god, quit with the mutant rodent."

"That's the deal."

"Fine." They place their hands on the Ouija and wait. "Hello sir, or madam, how do you do? *Bonjour?* Is anybody there?"

"Maybe they're busy."

"Keep your hand on the Ouija or no rodent. Hel-looo? *Qué pasa?* Can you hear us?" Dee gasps and squeezes her eyes shut. "To whom am I speaking? You wouldn't be Harriet's grandpa Archie by any chance?" The Ouija slowly points towards *Yes.*

"You're moving it."

"I'm not moving it. Do you happen to know if Harriet's mom and *my* dad are going to hook up? Be honest. We can take it."

"Take what?"

"Like, maybe Archie's hung up about extramarital affairs and is afraid to talk straight with us. Arch, my 'rents are divorced, so are Harriet's. The derp living with her mother isn't even legit. So no worries. We *want* Buck and Lynne to get it on."

"No we don't. Not that like."

"Like what then?"

"It has to be special."

"Special?"

"A lasting relationship."

"Oh. Right. LOL. Okay, Arch, can you tell us if Buck and Lynne are going to have a lasting relationship?" They both stare at the Ouija. "What a pisser. It stopped."

"Maybe he doesn't know. He can't know everything."

"I think he's afraid to tell us."

"Why?"

"He's afraid you'll be disappointed. Seriously, H, you're pretty amped about this whole deal."

"No I'm not."

"Arch, on a scale of one to ten, what are the chances of Buck and Lynne forming a lasting relationship? Oh my god it's moving."

"No it's not."

"It did it again. Feel that?"

Harriet did feel the Ouija move slightly. Her toes grip the floor. She's not sure she wants the answer to this question.

"Fuck my life," Dee says, "it's pointing to five. That must mean there's, like, a fifty/fifty chance."

Harriet finds Lynne smoking on the balcony. "Mum? We're supposed to go jogging."

"What?"

"We're supposed to meet Buck and Dee for a run."

"Oh. I forgot." Her mother looks as though she just woke up. It's three in the afternoon. Harriet worries she's headed for another breakdown. "Why are you still in your bathrobe?"

Lynne stares down at a Dario's Plumbing truck. "That guy is delivering a toilet. Who's getting a new toilet? Nobody gets new plumbing in this hellhole."

"Mum, they're waiting for us at the track behind the school."

"I really don't think I'm up for it, bunny."

"Sure you are. It'll make you feel better. Way better than smoking."

Lynne glances at her watch. "Okay, well as long as we're back before Gennedy and Irwin get home."

"Where are they?'

"Some superhero movie." Irwin's obsessed with superheroes, charges around with his hoodie hooked over his forehead, squealing "Look at my cape, Harry!"

Harriet takes her mother's cigarette and tosses it off the balcony, hoping it lands on Mrs. Rumph. "You should put shorts on." She guides Lynne to the bedroom and searches drawers for shorts that show off her legs. "Here, put these on."

Lynne holds the shorts as though she has no idea what to do with them.

"Put them on, Mum. Oh boy, bok choy, step on the gas." This is what Mrs. Rivera used to say when she wanted people to hurry up. Harriet finds a sports bra and a tank top that will show off her mother's figure.

"Bunny, did something happen between you and Gennedy this morning?"

If she admits that Gennedy hit her, Lynne won't believe her. She'll insist they wait until Gennedy returns and confront him with Harriet's accusation. It will be Harriet's word against Gennedy's, and she knows how that one goes. "Nothing happened."

"Then why did you leave without saying goodbye to Irwin? He so badly wanted to spend some time with you today."

"I had errands to do."

"You don't have to do any of those errands. You're a child. If you need money for ice cream or something, you can ask me or Gennedy for it. You shouldn't peddle yourself to strangers. It's dangerous. What do you need the money for anyway?"

She can't say art supplies because her mother hates her art. And she can't say escape money. "Mum, put your hair in a ponytail." Ponytails make Lynne look younger. Harriet hands her a hair tie. "We have to hustle."

When they arrive at the track behind the school, Buck is doing one-arm push-ups. Harriet glances at Lynne to see if she's noticed, but Lynne's staring at the ground. "Mum, look. Buck's doing one-arm push-ups. He must be really strong."

Sitting in the grass, scrolling through her newsfeed, Dee sucks on a Diet Sprite.

"Hi, guys," Harriet says.

"They made it." Buck jumps up. "The two most beautiful girls in the 'hood." He's sweaty but it's sexy because he's wearing a muscle shirt. He drinks deeply from a water bottle. "It's another scorcher. We'll have to take it slow."

"Suits me." Lynne pulls at a loose thread on her shorts.

"That's awesome that you can do one-arm push-ups," Harriet says. "Can you do clap push-ups as well?"

Buck drops to the ground and does five clap push-ups.

"Wicked," Harriet says.

Buck jumps up again and swings his arms in circles. "It just takes practice. How 'bout we start with some stretches? Dee, show them the stretches we were doing yesterday."

"No way. They're, like, totally jock."

"They're effective, is what they are, which is why jocks do them. Come on, girl. Let's start with the lunge." He bends one knee and stretches the other leg straight back. Harriet copies him and nudges her mother to do the same. "This one's great for the calf muscles, hams and hip flexors," Buck explains. "And of course the old Achilles tendons. You don't want to start running till those babies get warmed up."

"You really know your stuff," Harriet says. "Mum, did you know about hams, hip flexors and Achilles tendons?"

"Of course."

"Come on, Dee," Buck says, "let's do this thing."

"I'm on the rag."

"No excuses. Stretch."

Dee makes a wobbly attempt at a lunge but Lynne, Harriet notices, is starting to get into it. She puts both hands on the ground on either side of her foot, stretching the other leg farther back.

Buck stares at her legs. "You've still got the flexibility."

"Muscles have memory," Lynne says. "I had this phys. ed. teacher who was always going on about that. It's like riding a bike."

"Nice." Buck puts his hands on the ground beside her, also stretching one leg back. There's no way Gennedy could do this. With Buck distracted, Dee resumes playing *Angry Birds* on her phone. Harriet puts her hands down and stretches a leg back.

"Look at her," Lynne says, "my little rabbit."

Her mother hasn't referred to her as her little rabbit in years. Harriet feels hope swelling inside her.

"Quadriceps?" Buck asks Lynne.

"You got it."

"Lean on me." Buck turns to face Lynne, taking her hand and resting it on his sweaty shoulder. He rests his other hand on her naked one. Almost in unison, they reach behind, grab a foot and pull it towards their ass.

"Oh that feels so good," Lynne murmurs. "It's like the muscles have been asleep for years."

Buck smiles. "Sleeping beauty, your prince has come."

"Give it a rest, Dad."

"Get off your tushie, young woman. Who's the one needs to get in shape around here?"

"It's too freakin' hot."

Buck grabs Dee's hand. "Let's go."

"Yuk, you're sweaty."

Dee and Harriet only manage one lap. Harriet could do more if her toe wasn't throbbing. She sits on the bleachers and studies Buck and Lynne for signs of romance.

"Don't look so worried, H. It's a done deal."

"I don't want him thinking he can just do her. It's supposed to be *serious*. She's supposed to make the derp move out."

"Hmmm, this might require further strategizing." Dee sucks on her Sprite and sits beside her. "Okay, got it, I'm a genius. No need to thank me. Here's the plan. We figure out where they're going to hook up, then set it up so the derp catches them in the act."

"That won't work, the derp would forgive her. She'd get all guilty and teary and he'd forgive her. He's got nowhere to go." Buck and Lynne start another lap. "They look wonderful together, don't you think?"

"If you're into sweat."

"Why are they stopping?"

"Maybe they're having heart attacks." Dee resumes playing *Angry Birds*.

"He's pulling something out of his pocket."

"Uh-oh, here we go."

"What's he doing?"

"Don't ask."

"He's blindfolding her," Harriet says.

"His idea of romance." Dee looks back at her phone.

"Why's he blindfolding her?"

"He's going to tie his horny ass to hers and guide her like she's blind. He was talking about it all the way over here. He said that's how he'll know."

"What?"

"If she's The One."

"I don't get it."

"It means she trusts him, yo. If she lets him blind her and tie her up."

"That's sick."

"You're the one wants them hooked up."

Buck tethers his wrist to Lynne's. She starts walking, tentatively at first. He matches her stride perfectly. Then, as if it were the most natural thing in the world, they begin to run.

Sixteen

Harriet helps Mr. Shotlander set up his living room for Seniors' Reading Night. Tonight's theme is Life and Death and In Between. The more mobile seniors arrive with extra chairs. Mr. Chubak shows up with popcorn and a three-legged stool he bought in Nepal. He squats on it, unfolds a piece of paper and starts reading:

> *To one who has been long in city pent:*
> *'Tis very sweet to look into the fair*
> *And open face of heaven.*

Mr. Shotlander grabs a handful of popcorn. "Chubak, why's everything you read so dang gloomy?"

"That's not gloomy. That's Keats saying maybe dying isn't so bad. Listen to this:

> *O soft embalmer of the still midnight,*
> *Shutting, with careful fingers and benign,*
> *Our gloom-pleas'd eyes.*

Harriet pours Coke and ginger ale into plastic cups. Mr. Quigley brought Gatorade.

"Who says we have to talk about dying in the first place?" Mr. Shotlander says. He usually reads from *The Vinyl Café* in a nasally voice.

Mr. Chubak holds up his piece of paper again. "Listen to the epitaph Coleridge wrote for himself:

> *That he who many a year with toil of breath*
> *Found death in life, may here find life in death.*

"Terrific!" Mr. Hoogstra nibbles a cheese puff because he has to be careful about his gums.

"What in blazes is terrific about it? It's dang depressing."

"What's so depressing?" Mr. Zilberschmuck arranges himself languidly on the only armchair. "He's saying he suffered in life, maybe he won't in death."

"He was a goddang drug addict." Mr. Shotlander sits on the couch beside Mrs. Chipchase and offers her some barbecue chips, but she's knitting.

"Here's one he wrote for an infant who died," Mr. Chubak says.

"Oh, this'll cheer us up." Mr. Shotlander eats several chips.

Mr. Chubak reads,

> *Ere sin could blight or sorrow fade,*
> *Death came with friendly care:*
> *The opening bud to heaven convey'd*
> *And bade it blossom there.*

"Would someone tell me why in heck we're talking about death?" Mr. Shotlander demands.

"Because," Harriet reminds him, "tonight's theme is Life and Death and In Between."

"Let's get to the in-between parts."

"Death is part of life," Mrs. Chipchase says, without looking up from her knitting.

"You're in denial, Shotlander," Mr. Zilberschmuck adds.

Mr. Quigley jogs on the spot, the stripes on his track pants zigzagging. "Wait till you have your first stroke, Shotlander. After his first stroke my buddy Howie's face got lopsided. That's when he started believing in reincarnation. All his life Howie was a straight-up you-die-and-get-buried kind of guy. After the stroke he was planning a comeback."

"As what?" Mr. Shotlander asks.

"A Japanese girl. He saw his Jap parents in his dreams, kneeling and drinking tea."

"Why the heck did he want to be a Japanese girl?"

"It's not like you get to choose. Howie said in a past life he was a platypus and he wanted to be one again because they can survive on land and water and have spurs with venom in them."

"*Mortality weighs heavily on me like unwilling sleep,*" Mr. Chubak reads. "He's saying death is there no matter what.

> *Aye on the shores of darkness there is light,*
> *And precipices show untrodden green,*
> *There is budding morrow in midnight,*
> *There is triple sight in blindness keen.*

"There you go." Mr. Hoogstra reaches for another cheese puff. "*There is budding morrow in midnight.* Terrific! What's depressing about that?"

Mr. Shotlander waves a barbecue chip around. "I just want to have a good time. What's wrong with that?"

"To some people death *is* a good time," Mr. Chubak says. "Or anyway, an easier time."

"It's an escape from human suffering," Mrs. Chipchase clarifies.

Before dinner, Harriet used her glue gun to help Irwin make a flying machine for his plastic animals. They used juice cartons for the cabin, egg cartons for seating and flattened milk cartons for wings.

"Where are they flying to?" Harriet asked.

"To heaven, of course."

"Why, of course?"

"Because that's where everybody goes."

"How do you know?"

"Everybody knows that." His bony shoulders tensed as he struggled to flatten a milk carton. She could see how weak he'd become, and was glad he believed in heaven.

Mrs. Chipchase reads ". . . *village life would stagnate if it were not for unexplored forests and the meadows which surround it. We need the tonic of wildness—to wade sometimes in marshes where the bittern and the meadow-hen lurk, and hear the booming of the snipe; to smell the whispering hedge where only some wilder and more solitary fowl builds her nest, and the mink crawls with its belly close to the ground.*"

Mr. Hoogstra jabs a toothpick in his gums. "*The tonic of wildness.* Terrific!"

"That's Mr. Thoreau," Mrs. Chipchase says.

"You feel like you're right there, don't you?" Mr. Chubak sucks on a juice box. "Crawling around on your belly with all that wildness around you. Notice how he says *wildness* instead of *wilderness?*"

"Terrific."

Mr. Zilberschmuck drinks JD from his mickey. "Thoreau wasn't a drug addict, Shotlander."

"He was a goddang hermit. A freak."

Harriet can still smell body lotion on her clothes. Lynne showered for half an hour after the run, and must have squirted an entire bottle of peach lotion on herself because Harriet could smell it even more than the glue gun.

"Mum's singing," Irwin said.

"Really?" Harriet stopped scissoring and listened to her mother singing the lame Whitney Houston song she'd hummed driving home. This could only be a good sign. Next her mother, stinking of lotion, came and sat on the floor, putting her arms around them. "What are you monkeys building?"

"A flying machine!" Irwin squealed.

Usually Lynne was critical of Harriet's artwork, unable to see how it could be what Harriet said it was. But smiling at the glued cartons, Lynne said, "It's the most wondrous flying machine I have ever seen." Harriet had never heard her use the word wondrous before.

"*I will arise and go now, and go to Innisfree,*" Mrs. Chipchase reads.

And a small cabin build there, of clay and wattles made;
Nine bean rows will I have there, a hive for the honey-bee,
And live alone in the bee-loud glade.

This describes perfectly the peace Harriet will find in her backwoods cabin at Lost Coin Lake.

"Who the heck wants to live with a swarm of bees?" Mr. Shotlander demands.

"Speaking of bees," Mr. Hoogstra says, "did you get your mosquito bite looked at, Harry? You can't be too careful. It was skeeters took down the dinosaurs. The volcanoes just finished them off."

"She wasn't bitten, you jackass," Mr. Shotlander says. "She was hit by that layabout."

"Nobody hit me."

"He wins if you don't make him pay, Harry."

Mr. Zilberschmuck fondles a cigarillo. "It's none of your business, Shotlander."

"Of course it's my business. Harry's my friend."

"Friends don't snitch on friends," Harriet says.

"*I was angry with my friend,*" Mr. Chubak recites,

I told my wrath, my wrath did end.
I was angry with my foe:
I told it not, my wrath did grow.

Listen to Mr. Blake, Harry, he says you have to let it out. Either way you lose if you keep it buttoned up inside you."

"He should know," Mr. Shotlander grumbles, "a goddang lunatic."

"It's time you and Harry kissed and made up," Mr. Chubak says. "It's not healthy the way you two go at each other."

"I don't go at anybody," Harriet says, passing around the Bits & Bites, although she almost went at Gennedy as he sat smugly at the dinner table because he *might* have a client. "Nothing's confirmed," he emphasized. Harriet has heard about potential paying clients before. Gennedy is perennially close to striking it rich via some deep-pocketed criminal or other. He just needs that one high-profile case and all their financial worries will be over. Harriet considered going at him about the extensive evidence proving that he is a useless lawyer no one with brains or cash would hire, but she's done this before and his self-satisfaction is impregnable. Nothing she could say would ever make him doubt his genius. Instead, over tuna casserole this evening, she said, "You should have seen Mum on the track. She was awesome."

"The track?"

"We went jogging with Buck," Harriet explained.

"Who's Buck?"

"Darcy's dad. He's totally built. He can do one-arm push-ups."

"No way!" Irwin squealed.

"And clap push-ups."

"Wowee wowee, can I go with you next time? I want to see him do fancy push-ups."

Gennedy, chomping, turned to Lynne. "Is that the truck driver? Why did you go jogging with him?"

"It's called running, Gennedy, not jogging. I went because he asked."

"I see. What else will you do if he asks?"

"I can't believe you said that."

"What? I'm just asking a question."

"No you're not." Lynne looked at Harriet and Irwin. "Who's coming with me to get freezies?"

"Me me me me me!" Irwin chirped, and off they went. Harriet watched them from her bedroom window. Lynne took an indirect route to Mr. Hung's via the parking lot where Buck's truck happened to be parked, and lifted Irwin into the cab. Irwin sat on Buck's lap with his hands on the big steering wheel. Harriet could not have strategized this better.

Mr. Shotlander offers Harriet his hand to shake. She's thinking about the ear wax on his fingers.

"Come on, Harry," Mr. Chubak urges. "Make peace."

Harriet quickly shakes then surreptitiously wipes her hand on her jeans.

Since he hit her, Gennedy has been avoiding her. But after Lynne and Irwin left, he attempted to reassert his superiority over Buck. "Guess he can't be overemployed if he spends all that time at the gym."

"At least he's employed." Harriet headed to her room to glue the silver ring she found flattened on the tarmac onto *The Leopard Who Changed Her Spots.*

Mr. Shotlander throws up his hands. "What's wrong with a good old love poem? *Shall I compare thee to a summer's day* . . . how's the rest of it go?"

Mr. Tumicelli in his black overcoat, dragging his oxygen tank, comes in wheezing. "She's gone. My wife. She left the building.'

Mr. Tumicelli's wife has Alzheimer's and wanders. Initially he tried to stop her, but she left anyway. His efforts to restrain her bruised her arms. When the police found her, they concluded that the bruises were evidence of spousal abuse. They charged Mr. Tumicelli, and he spent two years in and out of court proving his innocence. The lawyer cost him his savings. He is afraid the police will charge him again if he tries to stop Mrs. Tumicelli from wandering. The other seniors think he should put her in a home with a lock-up but he refuses. So when Mrs. Tumicelli disappears, instead of calling the police, the seniors search for her and coax her back to the building with Smarties.

Harriet collects the plastic cups and chip bowls. She sees the drug addicts' poetry copied out in Mr. Chubak's neat cursive. On the back of the sheet she copies out the cabin poem Mrs. Chipchase has bookmarked. She folds the sheet of paper carefully and puts it in her pocket.

Irwin knocks on Harriet's door. He is the only one who heeds the *NO ENTRY* sign.

"What do you want?"

"They're fighting again."

"Don't worry about it. Couples fight. You want to get in my bed?"

"Can I?"

"Come on." She pulls back the comforter to make room for him. He crawls in and rests his head on her chest. His speedy heart beats into her.

"Are they fighting because of me?" he asks.

"Definitely not." The bickering started in the kitchen while Irwin was having his bath. Lynne told Harriet to watch him. He sat in the water gripping a manatee and an orca, intently pointing them towards each other. This meant the sea creatures were communicating by sonar. Harriet tried to make out what Lynne and Gennedy were saying, but they were keeping it down.

Tucking the comforter around Irwin's shoulders, Harriet hears Irwin's scratchy breathing and pictures his lungs filling with fluid.

"I wish I wasn't sick," he says.

"You're not sick. You just have a condition."

"You'd play with me more if I didn't have a condition."

"I'm way older than you. I don't play anymore."

"What do you do instead?"

Harriet isn't sure. She spends so much time on the run, not belonging, trying to be nowhere to avoid trouble, she's not sure she does anything.

"You do art," he says. "I bet you're going to be a famous artist one day."

"Do you want me to read you some poetry?"

"You mean like nursery rhymes? I'm too old for those."

"No, these are grown-up poems by drug addicts who died a long time ago."

"Cool."

Harriet pulls out Mr. Chubak's piece of paper and reads one of his selections.

"That's pretty," Irwin says. "What's it mean?"

"I think it means death is friendly." She reads another one.

"Is that about dying too?" Irwin asks.

"It could be. Poetry means different things to different people. I'm not sure what *triple sight in blindness keen* means but it sounds wondrous."

"Maybe it's kind of like seeing better without seeing," Irwin suggests. "There's a boy at the hospital who's blind, like, from when he was born. He can see way better than any of us. He knows when the book cart's coming before we even see it. It's like he's got X-ray vision."

"I think maybe dying's like that. You see things you couldn't before."

"Because you're up in heaven looking down. Especially if you get to be an angel, because then you can fly around."

"How do you get to be an angel?"

"By being good, of course. Everybody knows that. The lady who showed me how to make pipe cleaner people told me I'm a shoo-in for angel wings. She told me I must always make sure to fold them properly before I go to sleep. She said some angels get careless about their wings and crumple them in bed. The wings get wrecked but the angels are out of luck, the lady says, because God only gives you one pair of wings. I'm going to take really good care of mine."

"Would you like me to paint a picture of you with angel wings?"

"Wowee wowee. When?"

"Maybe tomorrow. It won't look exactly like you though. I'm not very good at drawing."

"I love your drawings. They're so weird."

Nobody says they love her drawings.

"I wish they'd stop fighting," Irwin says. "I'm scared he's going to leave."

"He'll never leave." She turns over Mr. Chubak's sheet and looks at the cabin poem.

"If you could have a superpower," Irwin asks, "what would it be?"

"Flying."

"I want to be able to breathe anywhere, like, even in outer space. I want to be able to breathe on all the planets. Even Pluto."

"*And I shall have some peace there,*" Harriet reads,

> *for peace comes dropping slow,*
> *Dropping from the veils of the morning to where the cricket sings;*
> *There midnight's all a glimmer, and noon a purple glow,*
> *And evening full of the linnet's wings.*

"What's a linnet?" Irwin asks.

"Some kind of bird." She listens for noises from the bedroom. "I think they've stopped."

"If you could fly, where would you go?"

She doesn't say Lost Coin Lake because, once she's gone, he'll tell them and they'll find her.

"What about the Caribbean?" Irwin suggests. "If I could fly I'd want to go there and have a ship like Captain Jack Sparrow's."

"They've stopped fighting. Go to sleep."

"Can we invent a poem now?"

"A short one. You start."

"*Tomorrow is another day*," Irwin begins. "That's all I can think of."

"*Another day for us to play*," Harriet adds.

"*We'll sing and dance and eat ice cream*," Irwin says.

"*And have lots of time for lovely dreams*."

"That's really nice." Irwin sits up to look at her. "Does that mean you'll play with me tomorrow?"

"I'm going to paint you with angel wings."

"I forgot. That's sooo cool. Wait till I tell Mum and Gennedy."

"Don't tell them. It'll be our secret."

"We'll surprise them." His head, listing to one side, looks too heavy for his skinny neck.

"Go to sleep," she says.

"You're the bestest big sister ever." He rests his head on her chest, calming her heart.

Seventeen

Harriet pours Irwin's Cheerios and reads him *Curious George* even though she thinks he's too old for it. He chimes in whenever the Man in the Yellow Hat appears. Harriet's explained to Irwin that she needs to buy more paint before she can paint him with wings, but he doesn't want her to leave the apartment without him. As usual Gennedy is flicking urgently through the newspaper, as though it's imperative that he read it and that the mere knowledge of world events makes him important. When the paper's late he gets hysterical, like life on planet Earth will end if he doesn't read about it.

"Is Mum getting up today?" Harriet asks, fearing her mother has relapsed into smoking-in-bathrobe mode.

"Your mother went jogging."

"Wowee wowee!" Irwin bounces. "I want to go jogging. Buck said he'd take me and show me one-arm and clap push-ups."

Gennedy looks over the paper at him. "When did you see Buck?"

"Yesterday, when me and Mummy got freezies. He let me steer his truck."

"What?"

"It was parked," Harriet explains.

"Oh, so you're in on this too? Am I the only one who doesn't know about the rendezvous with Buck? What kind of name is *Buck* anyway?"

"What kind of name is Gennedy?" Harriet says.

"Excuse me? Is there something wrong with my name?"

"Shouldn't it be Kennedy, like, what's with the G?"

"Your small-mindedness never ceases to amaze me, Harriet."

"You're welcome."

Irwin waves his spoon. "No fighting."

"You're right, champ. Let's do something fun today. Just you and me."

"Harry's going to paint me with angel wings."

"What?"

Her brother's inability to keep a secret is another thing she can't stand about him. "I have to get paints first."

Irwin bounces. "Please, please, please let me go with you. I love shopping."

"You're just back from the hospital, little man," Gennedy says. "You've got to take it easy. We don't want you traipsing all over town with Harriet."

"She doesn't traipse."

"I do, Irwin. I've got lots of errands. You're better off staying with Gennedy."

Irwin tries to sink the few remaining Cheerios in his bowl with his spoon.

Lynne bursts in, sweaty and energized. "How are my chickadees?" She kisses Irwin's and Harriet's heads.

Irwin flaps his arms. "Cheep cheep cheep."

Lynne runs the tap and drinks several glasses of water. "It's so hot, even first thing in the morning. I've got to take a water bottle with me next time."

Gennedy lowers his paper. "Did you jog with your friend Buck?"

"No, and it's called running. I run, I don't jog."

"I gather you and Buck met up over freezies last night," Gennedy says.

"Actually, it was before freezies."

"And you didn't tell me?"

"Why should I tell you?"

"You let him take our son in his truck."

"The truck wasn't moving, Gennedy."

"That's beside the point."

"What *is* the point?"

Apparently unsure of the point, Gennedy snaps his newspaper.

"You better hurry up and finish reading that," Harriet says. "I'm pretty sure the prime minister is waiting for your call." Her mother, mid-sip, does a spit take.

"Oh," Gennedy says, "I see. So I'm supposed to remain ignorant like most of the population. Amuse myself with online trivia so I won't notice what's really going on."

"How does your knowing what's really going on make any difference?" Harriet asks. "And who believes newspapers anyway? Everybody knows they're controlled by corporate interests." Mr. Chubak says this. He stopped reading the mainstream press when Ralph Nader didn't become president. Still at the sink, Lynne has her back to them but Harriet can tell she's stifling laughter.

"So glad I'm here for your entertainment," Gennedy says, pushing away from the table and taking his paper into the living room.

Harriet knocks on Mr. Rivera's door to see if he wants bananas, but really she's checking to make sure he's all right. Madame Le Drew in 110 lived alone and never talked to anybody. Mr. Shotlander referred to her as Her Imperial Highness. One day she called an ambulance. It kept being redirected to other emergencies and took three hours to get to the Shangrila. Madame Le Drew was dead when the EMS workers arrived.

Finally Harriet hears Mr. Rivera's slippers shuffling towards her.

"*Anak*, how nice to see you." Rosary beads dangle from his hand. He looks tired but not sick. Harriet has learned to recognize signs of serious illness in the seniors.

"I was wondering if you needed bananas." Seeing the apartment empty of relatives causes Harriet to grip the floor with her toes again. "Are you having any visitors over later? Do you need any bananas?"

"You must come to my birthday party tonight," he says. "I'm cooking all afternoon for it. I'm making *pancit bihon* because eating noodles on your birthday makes you lucky. You must eat lots of *pancit*, *anak*. No gift for me, okay, just come. We'll have smoked *bangus* and sing 'My Way' together. My son is ordering *lechon* from a restaurant. You must try it, it is delicious."

"What is it?"

"Roast pig. The skin is crunchy, and everybody fights over the tail."

Harriet can't imagine fighting over a pig's tail, or singing "My Way," but she doesn't want to disappoint Mr. Rivera. "Sure, I'll come."

"Everybody will be so happy to see you."

The thought of people being so happy to see her makes Harriet more self-conscious than usual. She glances down at her throbbing toe poking through the hole in her running shoe.

"So long, mahjong," he says, which is what Mrs. Rivera used to say.

In the lobby, the seniors confer about Mrs. Tumicelli. They found her at McDonald's staring up at the TV. She'd ordered a McFlurry but couldn't pay for it.

"One of these days," Mr. Shotlander says, tugging up his trousers, "Tumicelli's going to up and die from the stress of looking after the old gal, then what happens?"

Mr. Chubak pokes a straw into his juice box. "Take me out and shoot me if I get Alzheimer's."

Mr. Pungartnik corners Harriet. Mrs. Pungartnik hasn't dyed his hair orange for weeks and his white roots are showing. "You scrounge me up *one* cigarette and I'll pay you a buck."

Mrs. Pungartnik, also showing roots, stomps up to Harriet, gripping a crumpled Kleenex and looking straight at her and away at the same time. "Did he just ask you for a cigarette?" Harriet shakes her head. Mr. Pungartnik scuttles out the front doors with his fifty-year-old transistor radio pressed to his ear.

Mrs. Pungartnik wags an arthritic finger at Harriet. "No matter what he pays you, don't give him a cigarette. That's assisting suicide. You could go to prison for that, *prison*." Mrs. Pungartnik tromps out the doors in pursuit of Mr. Pungartnik.

"Does anybody want anything from Mr. Hung's?" Harriet asks.

After filling the seniors' orders, Harriet sets out the baskets of flowers for Mr. Hung because his back hurts. He doesn't admit this but she can tell by his stiff movements.

"Do you want me to wrap Mrs. Hung's baked goods?"

"No bake goods today."

"Why not?"

"Mrs. Hung in hospital."

"Why?"

"She can't breathe."

"At all?"

Poker-faced, Mr. Hung stocks the magazine stand. Harriet knows there's no point in trying to get more information out of him. "I can look after the store if you want to go to the hospital," she says.

"You too young. My son come tonight, after he study." He hands her an Orangina, which is her favourite drink but costs way more than Orange Crush. She feels so honoured, she's scared she'll drop the bottle.

"Sit." He points to the stool behind the counter.

"No, you sit. You're the one with the bad back."

"Sitting no good for back." He cuts dead flowers off the plants in the window. Normally Harriet is comfortable with long silences between them, but with Mrs. Hung in the hospital the silence aches.

The Orangina bottle cools her hands. "Do you miss China?"

"I miss China from my childhood. Sowing rice, harvesting rice. Rice paddies beautiful. So simple. Now more complicated."

"It's like that everywhere, I guess."

"No good. Simple better."

Harriet sucks on her straw.

Mr. Hung puts his hands on his hips and arches his back. "Mickey Mouse come to China."

"When?"

"Long ago. When U.S. make friends with China, they send Mickey Mouse. He stand on Great Wall and wave, and Chinese cheer. The world take photos of Mickey Mouse on Great Wall. Nobody notice Great Wall, just Mickey. That's all China want. They forget thousands of years of civilization to be like U.S."

Harriet's never understood the Mickey Mouse thing.

"Chinese build wall with millions of rocks. Only wall on Earth can be seen from space. But no wall can keep out Mickey. Everybody want SUV. Forget about wall."

Harriet has heard about the pollution over there, that you can't put your hand in the poisoned rivers, or safely breathe the air without a mask in some places. But she doesn't say this because it won't console Mr. Hung.

Dee doesn't answer at first but Harriet can hear the TV.

"Buzz off," Darcy says.

"It's me, H."

Darcy opens the door. "Come and join the party."

"What party?" Harriet sees the cough syrup and liquid NyQuil on the coffee table. Darcy makes cocktails with over-the-counter medications to get a buzz on. She pirouettes clumsily and collapses on the couch.

"When are we going running?" Harriet asks.

"Running?"

"With Buck."

"Oh, fucky Bucky. How should I know?"

"We're supposed to arrange a time I can tell my mom."

"Your mom is so fucking desperate, seriously. It's like all Bucko has to do is look at her and she'll put out for him. She'd blow him in a fucking public toilet."

Darcy turns mean on cough syrup and NyQuil. Harriet usually avoids her when she's drugged, but she needs to contact Buck. "Okay," she says, "*I'll* call Buck. Where's your phone?" Darcy gestures vaguely towards the bedroom. Buck's on speed-dial but unavailable. Harriet sees Dee's laptop on the bed and quickly searches for the "Albatross Encounter" video from Kaikoura, New Zealand. As the birds spread their magnificent wings, she feels a tautness lifting off her chest.

Darcy waddles into the bedroom. "Get your honky ass off my computer."

"I just wanted to check something."

"The giant mutant rodent no doubt."

"Buck's not available."

"You know what, H? There's a world out there, an *entire* universe that doesn't give two fucks about you and your tight-assed mom."

"He said he wanted to meet up for a run today."

"He says a lot of things." Darcy tumbles onto the bed, shoving her face into the pillow. Harriet memorizes Buck's number to try again later.

"I gotta go," she says.

Dee flips over. "Excuse me, I'm in crisis here. You're supposed to be my best friend and all you can think about is my horny-assed father."

"Why are you in crisis?"

"That Caitlin ho bag tagged me in a photo from the DQ." Darcy sits up and signs into Facebook to show Harriet a shot of her wedgied ass.

"You can't see your face," Harriet says. "Nobody knows that's you."

"Can't you read?" She points to the comments: *Hey, Darcy, take it easy on those Choco Cherry Love Blizzards, yo. Time for the fat farm, girl. Oink Oink!!!!!!!!!!* "It's got twenty-six likes." She slams the computer shut. "That's the last onion. I'm going to lay some shit on that bitch."

Harriet knows this isn't going to happen. "I've got to buy paint."

"Are you *deserting* me?"

"You can come with me. I promised my brother I'd paint him."

"Can we stop at Shoppers? I need liquid liner."

As soon as they step through the automatic doors, Harriet is on the alert for the clerk with burnt orange hair. She follows Dee to Cosmetics.

"Quit looking at the security cameras," Dee mutters.

"I'm not. Where are they?"

"On the ceiling, genius."

Harriet looks up.

"For fuck's sake, keep your head down. They're the round glass things. Never look at them. It draws attention." Darcy slips a liquid liner into her hoodie pocket. "Let's dip."

On the street, Dee tears the packaging off the liner. "I want Cleopatra eyes. I saw how to do it on a tutorial."

"One of these days you're going to get caught."

"Not me. I've got a system. You're in, you're out, easy-squeezy. Let's go to 7-Eleven and get Slurpees. Do you have any cash?"

The Slurpees cost $5, leaving not enough money for paint. But Dee is in crisis and won't stop talking about what Caitlin did to her in Guides. "I was a Sprite and she was a Pixie. That ho bag made like all the cool girls were Pixies."

In the parking lot, a man wearing two pairs of sunglasses tells a fat lady that he's not disagreeing with her, even though he keeps disagreeing with her.

Dee sucks on her straw. "Sprites totally rocked it. We did killer stuff like fill condoms with water and pitch them at the stuck-up Pixies. But that twat told on us and we had to write an apology."

"I'm not disagreeing with you," the man in two pairs of sunglasses says. The fat lady fans her face with a pizza slice container.

Dee jabs her straw into the ice in her Slurpee. "Then the skank fucked up my puppetry badge. My mom was too busy to make a puppet with me so she bought a kit I could glue together. Caitlin told Snowy Owl my puppet was store-bought and shouldn't qualify for a badge. 'I still made it,' I said, but Snowy Owl denied me the badge, which was, like, *so* unfair. Everybody knows homemade puppets are made by moms. The girls didn't do shit. At least I *glued* my puppet."

Harriet pulls Dee's phone from her pocket and speed-dials Buck again. This time he answers. "Who dis?"

"Dis is Harriet."

"Ranger, whassup?"

"When are we running today?"

"How 'bout after dinner when it's a little cooler? Eat light. Put Dee on." Harriet hands Darcy the phone.

"Pops, I need cash. Mom won't give me any. She wants me to starve."

"I'm not disagreeing with you," the man in two pairs of sunglasses says. The fat lady fans her face.

"Okay, deal." Darcy pockets her phone. "I got to meet my dad in the Mickydees parking lot. He's taking me to some health food joint." An unexpected yearning wallops Harriet and she badly wants to go with them, to be included, to belong.

Dee drops her empty Slurpee cup in the trash bin. "Catch you later, H.

Text me." A small boy with a Mohawk jumps out from behind a dumpster and aims a stick at Harriet. "This is an AK-47," he says, "and you're iced."

After Mrs. Rivera's last surgery, there were complications and she developed double pneumonia. Drugged, hooked to a respirator, with bags of fluid dripping in and out of her, she lay unconscious. As her temperature soared, her favourite saints huddled around her. "It was like the Last Supper," she told Harriet, "except the table was my bed." Harriet was familiar with the Last Supper painting in the Riveras' dining room. "We had *tinola* together," Mrs. Rivera said, "and *talunan*. Then the Blessed Mother came and held my hand. Saint Jude and Saint Peregrine massaged my feet and gave me a pedi. They painted my toenails with gold, *anak*."

"That's wonderful," Harriet said, although she didn't believe any of it. Mrs. Rivera scared small children when they misbehaved by telling them *momo* could appear at any time and snatch them away. "Sshh, *momo's* here," she'd gasp, pointing to a dark corner. Mrs. Rivera had a very active imagination.

The saints, according to Mrs. Rivera, asked advice about many things, including the best way to cook *adobo*. Mrs. Rivera shared all her secret recipes with them. The saints were extremely grateful and gave her a mani as well as a pedi, and painted her fingernails with gold. They told her she would no longer have to wash the skid marks out of Mr. Rivera's underpants. "You have done your duty," they told her. "You have been a dutiful wife and mother and now you must rest and have *kakanin*." They served her boiled sweet rice with shredded coconut, steamed in banana leaves. Before her last surgery, Mrs. Rivera had been unable to eat white rice or coconut because it gave her diarrhea. But when she was partially dead she ate whatever the saints offered, including *halo halo special*, which, when she was completely alive, went right through her. In those two weeks while antibiotics warred with the bacteria in her lungs, Mrs. Rivera saw her life clearly, and the sacrifices she'd made. She had no regrets, she told the saints, but she was tired and didn't want to do it anymore. She wanted to play the harp in heaven. The saints gave her a glistening golden harp with silvery strings and taught her to play in three days. "My fingers moved like magic, *anak*." The saints asked her to accompany them as they sang her favourite song, "What a Wonderful World." "You have never heard such beautiful voices." Mrs. Rivera pressed her hands together when she said this and closed her eyes as though she were listening to the saints' voices. "Like silk, *anak*."

When the fever broke and Mrs. Rivera slowly regained consciousness and was taken off the respirator, she insisted there'd been some mistake, that she should be on the other side with the saints. Her family tried to convince her that she was meant to be on earth with them. By the time they brought her home, she'd accepted being earthbound and lay docile on her bed as she always had, but Harriet sensed something different about her. She told Harriet not to miss her chance. "You mustn't allow yourself to be crushed by duty, *anak*," she said. "You must become yourself, nobody else." The saints helped Mrs. Rivera to "get to the bottom of everything." As Harriet urged her to drink clear fluids, Mrs. Rivera said, "I understand everything now." Harriet didn't ask her to explain everything because she was weak and talking wore her out. But Harriet understood the longing to go back inside a dream or a memory. She wanted to go back to before Irwin was born, to float in the pool at the Americana under a cloudless sky. She played rummy with Mrs. Rivera but never pushed her to speak or eat as her relatives did. Harriet knew that Mrs. Rivera was waiting to die so she could return to the saints.

Staring at the white oil paints, trying to decide what will work best for Irwin's angel wings, it occurs to Harriet that Mrs. Rivera's visions were no less real than Mr. Blake's. Mr. Chubak said when Mr. Blake was on his deathbed surrounded by people pleading with him not to die, he jumped up and sang, "Angels! Angels!" He was happy because he was going with the angels and ditching the humans. By not believing in Mrs. Rivera's or Mr. Blake's visions, Harriet is flattening her world based on her past experience and seeing things only thro' the narrow chinks of her cavern. She is turning in the same dull round while Mrs. Rivera is on the other side with golden fingernails, playing harp with the saints and spooning *halo halo special*. Suddenly eternity pops open above Harriet, even though she's indoors. Angels and saints swoop around her, singing "What a Wonderful World" with silky voices, and she feels enlightened, as though she has gotten to the bottom of everything. The Titanium White glows like angel wings, and the Zinc White offers a soothing softness, while the Sevres Blue and Ultramarine shimmer like oceans. She holds the tubes in her hands, knowing they cost more than she can afford, but she *must* have them to paint Irwin—to become herself. The Sap Green beckons to her for mountaintops, and the Azo Lemon Yellow offers rays of heavenly light. Six tubes of paint at $4.95 each. She has $12.65. The tubes become sweaty in her grip. Without looking around for security cameras, she slides two tubes in each of her front pockets, easy-squeezy.

"What on earth possessed you to steal?" her mother asks while Irwin lurches around the cramped, windowless office because standing still isn't something he does. "Why?"

Harriet has sat quaking on the broken office chair with the store detective's bulgy eyes on her for over an hour. She banged her infected toe on the steps and watched fresh crimson mixing with the burnt umber of her pus.

"Technically you're under arrest," he told her. He didn't look like a detective but wore a Batman T-shirt, skateboard shorts and shoes. He explained that he was undercover. When she pleaded that she'd made a mistake, that she would never do it again, he responded, "I still have to call it in," and speed-dialled the police.

Sweat splotches Lynne's tank top even though she hasn't been running. "Why, Harriet? Tell me why you took those tubes of paint."

"Because I wanted to paint Irwin."

"She's going to give me angel wings," Irwin explains.

"Why didn't you ask me for money for paints?"

"Because you wouldn't give it to me. You *never* give me art supplies."

Lynne became repulsed by her paintings after Harriet discovered Hieronymus Bosch, Pieter Bruegel and Francis Bacon. Before Irwin was born, when Harriet was into the Impressionists, Lynne thought it was cute that her little daughter's favourite pastime was leafing through the library's art books. But after Irwin turned three and Harriet realized he would never turn into a normal little brother, and Trent moved into Uma's house,

Harriet began figurative paintings of subjects unrecognizable to anyone but herself.

The tubes of colours lie exposed on the desk in front of the store detective.

"How did you become a store detective?" Harriet asked him to turn the attention away from herself. This works at school; a teacher will ask her a question she can't answer and she'll ask the teacher about something vaguely related to the original question.

"I went to security guard school," the skateboarder said. "This isn't permanent. I want to be a cop."

Irwin leans against Harriet's knees because standing for long periods tires him. "You *stole?*" he asks, his mouth forming a circle, his head listing to one side.

"I am so disappointed in you," Lynne says, snapping open her purse and fishing for a Kleenex to wipe Irwin's nose. "As for you," she says to the detective, who is scribbling on the form with Harriet's name, address and birth date on it, "was it really necessary to call the police? She's just a child."

"It's procedure, ma'am. The officers should be here shortly." His knees bounce constantly as he sits in the chair, and he repeatedly clicks his ballpoint pen.

"I'm staaarved." Irwin pulls on Lynne's hand, dropping his butt to add leverage.

"We'll get you something in a minute, peanut."

Harriet stops trembling finally. At first when the detective asked to see the contents of her pockets, she felt the floor growing spongy and the world as she knew it orbiting farther and farther away from her. Even now her mother and brother seem alien, a billion miles away. Dee has told her about juvie, that most of the girls there are dykes and force you to eat them out, or eat you out, or shove things up your snatch. Harriet will jump in front of a subway car before anyone sends her to juvie.

"Surely the police won't charge her," Lynne says. "She's a *child.*"

The store detective clicks his pen. "Attempted theft is attempted theft, ma'am. A lot of these juvenile shoplifters get around without their parents knowing about it. I'm not saying your daughter's lying, ma'am, but I can't take her at her word given the circumstances."

Sickening shame pulses through Harriet. When the police finally arrive, they tower over her in hats and epaulettes. "Have you ever been in trouble with the police before?" the ginger-haired one asks.

"No."

He stares down at her. She's afraid to look at either of them.

"Of course she's never been in trouble with the police," Lynne says. "She's eleven years old."

"Crime has no age requirements, ma'am. Just give us a minute." He gestures to the store detective, who grabs his forms and follows the cops out.

"I can't believe this is happening, Harriet. It's Darcy, isn't it? Does she steal? Does Buck know?"

"It's got nothing to do with Darcy. I wanted to paint Irwin and I didn't have enough money."

"That's no excuse for stealing." Lynne slumps against the desk. "I can't believe this is happening."

"It'll be okay," Irwin says. "Stop fighting. Harry doesn't have to paint me. We'll give the paint back."

The Titanium White no longer glows and the Zinc White looks flat. The Sevres Blue and Ultramarine appear drab against the dirty grey desk, and she can't believe she even wanted the gaudy Sap Green or Azo Lemon Yellow. She never wants to paint ever again.

The cops and the detective return and surround her, but only the ginger-haired cop speaks. The other cop, who looks like he shoots people, crosses his hairy arms and stares at her.

"Okay, Harriet," the ginger-haired one says. "Tell me something I don't know. Explain it to me so I can understand it." Harriet dares to look up at him. His badge says P.C. Dandy. "Come on, kid, talk to me. We checked and you have no record, so this is a first offence. Explain it to me."

"I needed paint to paint my brother. He's sick and might die before the end of the week."

"What?" Lynne sputters. "What are you talking about?"

Irwin stands uncharacteristically straight. "I'm not dying."

"Me and Darcy did Ouija, and Grandpa Archie said Irwin would die in a week."

"Oh for god's sake," Lynne says, covering her face with her hands.

"Take it easy, ma'am," P.C. Dandy says. "Okay, Harriet, so you wanted to paint your brother. Vince here says you paid for some of the paint."

"I had enough for two tubes plus tax. I bought the whites for angel wings." The cops exchange solemn looks. Lynne keeps shaking her head and mumbling, "I can't believe this is happening."

"Well, Harriet," P.C. Dandy says, "can you promise me you will never steal again?"

"I promise. And I will never paint again either."

"Thank god for that," Lynne says. "I'm sick to death of this art thing, Harriet. You have to get over it, read about vampires or boys like normal girls."

"Ma'am, go easy on her. You can see she's sorry for what she did."

"Harriet's never sorry for what she does. Otherwise she wouldn't keep doing it."

"Are you sorry for what you did, Harriet?" P.C. Dandy asks.

Harriet manages to nod even though she feels like vomiting and sliding to the floor and never getting up again.

"Well, *I'm* satisfied if my partner's satisfied." He looks at the killer cop who's playing *Call of Duty* on his smartphone. "You okay with not charging her?" P.C. Dandy asks. The killer cop, without looking up from his game, nods. P.C. Dandy ruffles Harriet's hair. "Don't believe that Ouija stuff. There's always some smartass moving it around. Okay, you're free to go, but if you do it again, you'll be charged. You name is tagged in the system so we won't let you off so easy next time. Understood?"

"Yes."

"Good." As they leave, both cops glance at Lynne's legs. "Good day, ma'am," P.C. Dandy says. "Go easy on her, she looks a little raw." Harriet would rather go with P.C. Dandy than stay with her irate mother.

"Let's go," Lynne says, ignoring the store detective. She lifts Irwin onto her hip and grabs Harriet's hand, yanking her out of the chair so hard it hurts Harriet's shoulder.

Eighteen

They don't bother trying to keep it down in the kitchen. "What have I been saying about her all along?" Gennedy bellows. "There's something *wrong* with her."

"She's been through a lot."

"Irwin's been through a lot, you've been through a lot. That girl does what she wants when she wants. Nothing stops her. I've never seen anything like it—it's sociopathic."

"Are you calling my daughter a sociopath?"

"She lies, she steals, she tries to poison her brother, she feels absolutely no compassion for anyone, refuses to obey school rules. How many times have you been called in to talk to her teachers? Do you realize how close she just got to having a criminal record? The cops gave you a break this time. It won't happen again."

Lynne ordered Harriet to watch Irwin. She sits with him on the cratered carpet by the flying machine. His clumsy movements mean he's tired.

"When will they stop fighting?" he asks.

"Soon."

"I have a headache." He gets headaches when his shunt is infected.

Harriet grabs some plastic animals. "Find them seats." Irwin carefully arranges the animals in the egg carton cabin.

"I'm saying," Gennedy bellows, "she needs professional help. She has a personality disorder. She needs medication."

"I'm not drugging my daughter. And we can't afford a therapist, you, of all people, should know that."

"Shrinks are covered if a doctor orders it."

"Theo won't send her to a shrink. He thinks she's artistic. All he says is keep her off the red dye and MSG." Theo, their GP, is an old hippie and smells of dirt.

"Well," Gennedy says, "all I can say is we're on a slippery slope here and something must be done. She's a danger to herself and everyone around her. Seriously, I think she's capable of harming Irwin."

"Gennedy hit me!" Harriet screams, startling Irwin. He drops a giraffe and stares wide-eyed at her. She listens for sounds from the kitchen.

"Don't listen to her," Gennedy says. "She's vengeful."

"He hit me in the face yesterday," Harriet shouts. "All the seniors saw how red my face got."

Lynne trudges wearily out of the kitchen and leans against the wall. "Then why didn't you tell me yesterday?"

"Because you wouldn't have believed me. Just like you don't believe me now."

"The timing's a little convenient, Harriet." Lynne treads back into the kitchen where Gennedy is cursing the "badly designed" can opener. According to Gennedy, anything he has difficulty operating is badly designed.

"Did you hit her?" Lynne demands.

"Don't you see what she's doing? She's using diversion tactics. Divide and conquer is her *modus operandi*. It's sociopathic."

"Did you hit her?"

"I cut myself."

"What?"

"On this fucking can opener. Who designed this thing?"

"*Did* you hit my daughter?"

"She was running out to collect garbage or scrounge money off the old folks. I tried to stop her because Irwin was crying, but as you know, nothing stops her. So I slapped her."

"How dare you slap my child."

"It got her attention."

Irwin topples onto his side. His eyes close and his arms and legs stiffen. Harriet gently nudges him. "Bud?"

"I can't believe you would do that," Lynne says. "I mean, how could you do that? She's just a child."

"That's no child."

"She's eleven years old and you're scared of her. What kind of man hits a defenceless child?"

"She's not defenceless, and the longer you insist on seeing her as innocent, the more harm she will cause."

Harriet kneels beside Irwin and carefully shakes him. When he doesn't respond she suspects he's about to seize and that she should call her mother. But this will only lead to more torment for Irwin. They will pull down his pants and shove Diastat up his ass. It probably won't work and he'll have to go back to the hospital because his shunt is malfunctioning again. The doctors will shave some of his hair before they cut open his head. Last time they did this it left a scar in the shape of a question mark. Mindy's sons Conner and Taylor called him the Riddler because the Riddler has question marks all over his head. Irwin hated being named after a bad guy. Sometimes, when the neurosurgeon revises the shunt, he cuts holes in Irwin's neck and abdomen to pull out the infected shunt and put in a new one. If the infected shunt is slimy with bacteria and breaks, the surgeon leaves it there and sticks in another one. Sometimes he even leaves the valve in the abdominal cavity. Irwin's body is a silicone dumping ground. And every time they operate they make more scar tissue that obstructs his bowel. To fight infection they'll dose him with cocktails that will give him diarrhea, turn him yellow and destroy his appetite. He'll get even skinnier and weaker. It seems to Harriet he'd be better off dead. Before he died, Mr. Tackett in 611 had really bad arthritis, walked funny from a stroke and couldn't see properly because of macular degeneration. Mr. Tackett often said he'd be better off dead.

If Irwin's body turns blue and stops moving, the real Irwin, the shoo-in for angel wings, will be freed from earthly torment. That's what Mrs. Rivera called living after she'd been almost dead with the saints. "I'm so tired of this earthly torment, *anak*," she'd say, reaching for more morphine.

Maybe right now Irwin is between life and death, singing with the saints or superheroes or angels. Maybe right now he is developing superpowers and, in seconds, will be able to breathe on any planet, even Pluto. As abruptly as his limbs tightened, they soften and he lies inert on his side. Harriet sees a bright, silvery glow around him and knows he has escaped.

Gennedy squishes towards her. "What's going on here?"

"Nothing."

"What do you mean 'nothing'? What's with Irwin?"

"He fell asleep."

"On the carpet?" Gennedy tenderly sweeps hair from Irwin's forehead and holds his palm against it. "He's warm. What happened? You were supposed to be watching him."

"I was. He just fell asleep."

"Bullshit, you deceitful child. He seized, didn't he? Lynne, get in here." He lifts Irwin onto the couch.

"What is it?" Lynne asks.

"Harriet sat back and watched while Irwin had a seizure."

"I did not."

"She would never do that, Gennedy. Stop accusing her. Is he okay?"

"Seems a little warm. Get the thermometer." Lynne scrambles to the bathroom.

"I know what you're up to," Gennedy hisses, "even if your mother doesn't. You tried to kill your brother."

"I did not."

"Live with it for the rest of your life, you little bitch. But if you try it again I'm calling the police no matter what your mother says."

Lynne returns with the thermometer. She pulls down Irwin's pants and shoves it up his ass. He wakens and starts to cry. Harriet wants to shout at him to stay dead, to stay free, that he mustn't be scared and that it's way better on the other side.

Lynne pulls out the thermometer and reads it. "False alarm. If he had one he's over it, my sweet baby boy." She holds him to her breast and kisses him. "Everything's going to be all right, baby. Mummy's here."

"Did I fall asleep?"

"You did, sweetheart."

"Have you stopped fighting?"

"Yes, peanut, no more fighting. We're all here, and it's all fine."

It isn't and Harriet can't stand the lies. She goes to her room, closes the door and wedges a chair under the doorknob. "Mortality weighs heavily on me like unwilling sleep," she mutters. She tramples *The Leopard Who Changed Her Spots* and *And I Think to Myself, What a Wonderful World*. She slides her window open, pulls out the busted screen and tosses the mixed media into the parking lot, relishing the smash as they land on the tarmac. She carefully unfolds Mr. Chubak's scraps of poetry and reads the verses quietly to herself. Hard tears prick her eyes. She got to the bottom of everything only to find there is nothing there, just her own difficult, selfish, greedy and compassionless self. She got to the bottom of everything only to realize that everything they say about her is true. Behind Lynne's back Gennedy pointed two fingers at his eyes then one at Harriet and mouthed, "I'm watching you."

She lies down in her tomb like Tutankhamun.

Her mother pushes against the door, opening it a crack. "Harriet, we need to talk." Harriet remains motionless, feigning sleep. "What have you got against the door? I think she's wedged a chair against the door."

"The criminal mind at work," Gennedy bellows.

"Stop saying that. Help me open it."

"Get *her* to open it. She's an innocent child. She'll do as she's told."

"Harriet? Take the chair away from the door, please. I just want to talk."

Harriet's done with talking. She's an actor pretending to be dead, trying not to breathe or move her eyelids while people simulate grief around her, grasping her lifeless hands and throwing their heads down on her unmoving chest.

"You're wasting your time," Gennedy says. "I promise you, get her a psych assessment and she'll turn up a sociopath."

"You're not helping."

"I've been helping for too long, Lynne. I'm tired of it. She's got you right where she wants you."

"Please go and watch Irwin and leave us alone."

"With pleasure."

Harriet hears her mother slide down the wall and sit on the floor. She talks into the crack in the door permitted by the chair. "Please tell me Gennedy's wrong about you."

If she needs Harriet to tell her, the game's over, as Grandpa Archie would say.

"I really want to believe he's wrong about you, bunny. But you're not making it easy for me. You behaviour is . . . is crazy. You're doing bad things and nothing I say stops you. You run around who knows where, jumping into dumpsters, hanging out with all kinds of low-lifes, collecting garbage. You're out of control, and I guess it's partly my fault because I've kind of turned a blind eye. With Irwin and everything, and the bookkeeping, I just haven't been paying attention."

Harriet's nose is itching but she can't scratch it because she doesn't know how much Lynne can see through the crack.

"I know it's been hard on you, having a sick brother, but you have to understand that life is full of challenges and we must face them, not run from them."

All her mother's ever done is run from challenges, first into Trent's and now Gennedy's pasty white arms. A challenge would have been to let Irwin die when the doctors said they should, to let nature take its course instead of dragging him through earthly torment.

"Gennedy says sociopaths don't know the difference between right and wrong. Please tell me you know the difference."

Harriet's not sure she knows the difference. One person's right is another person's wrong. One person's wrong is another person's right. She wiggles her nose quickly to stop the itching.

"I'm glad you're quitting the painting and the garbage picking. I really don't think it's been healthy for you, I mean, the toxins alone are a concern. But you can't steal again, ever. Gennedy says a criminal record stays with you for life. It'll affect university, job applications, everything. It's no joke."

Harriet never said it was. She wishes her mother would go away. Her legs are starting to cramp.

"I have to tell your father about this. Then we'll decide what action to take."

What action? They never *do* anything. They run around in circles, pretending to be grown-ups when they're just big babies.

"Babe?" Gennedy calls. "Irwin wants you." And off Lynne goes. Harriet jumps off the bed and shakes out her arms and legs. She turns on her glue gun to make a crucifix for Mr. Rivera. The Riveras have either a crucifix or a Virgin Mary in every room, but Harriet wants to make him a small one he can put in his shirt pocket with his reading glasses. She digs in her wood scraps box until she finds suitable pieces. After sanding and gluing them, she selects beads from her bead collection to decorate the cross. Mrs. Rivera loved sparkly, brightly coloured jewellery she bought in Chinatown. Harriet chooses the brightest and most sparkly beads for Mr. Rivera's crucifix.

"Harriet?" her mother says through the door. "Have you been taking your pills? You're supposed to have them with food. Please come and have some dinner. Do I smell the glue gun? Harriet? Oh for god's sake."

After a moment her mother flip-flops back to the kitchen, where she resumes squabbling with Gennedy. Irwin must be sleeping. Harriet eats the red Twizzlers Mr. Hung gave her because he doesn't know she's not allowed red dye. When they tire of bickering, Gennedy turns on *News World* to find out if he needs to call an emergency meeting of world leaders.

Harriet hears the rumble of Buck's truck and leans out the window to wave at him, but he doesn't look up or get out of the cab. She suspects her mother has forgotten they were supposed to meet for a run after dinner. If Harriet leaves her room to remind her, Gennedy and Lynne will corner her and she's too exhausted to fight. Her forehead feels clammy and she's thirsty. She doesn't understand why they don't go into their bedroom. Usually Gennedy has important reading to do, and Lynne has to catch up on Hollywood gossip. Harriet blows on the crucifix to dry the glue. She sniffs it, wishing the glue were toxic, and eats another piece of licorice, hoping the red dye and fumes will free her of the shifting hatreds, doubts and resentments chained inside her. Gennedy says she does what she wants when she wants, but it doesn't feel that way. He says he'll report her to the police if she tries to kill her brother again, but it didn't feel like she was trying to kill him. She's not sure what's really going on anymore. All she knows is that Gennedy will always be watching her, hitting her, scraping bits of food off his plate, squishing around the apartment, leaving tea stains on countertops. Her mother will never give him his marching orders. Her mother is weak. It doesn't matter that Buck is ripped and fun and employed, Lynne will tie herself to the loser because that's all she knows. That's all she feels she deserves. Just as Harriet believes she deserves no better than to wake up each morning filled with dread. Her self-loathing has surpassed Gennedy's disdain for her. She cannot make good. Grandpa Archie used to speak fondly about people who made good, and Harriet always wanted to be one of them so he would speak fondly about her. But she lies and steals and tries to kill her brother.

Finally she hears movement in the bedroom, then the radio. Gennedy listens to news shows while doing important reading. She carefully slides the chair from under the doorknob and soundlessly opens the door to look down the hall. TV light flickers. Lynne, like Gran, falls asleep in front of the TV. Even if her mother is awake, she'll be lying on the couch with her back to the apartment door. Harriet grabs the crucifix and creeps stealthily down the hall and out the door.

The curtain is drawn in Buck's cab. The stereo blares and the engine is running to power the air conditioner. Harriet knocks on the door to tell Buck there's been a family emergency and they won't be able to meet for a run. She climbs onto the rocker panel and raps on the window, hoping Buck will call her Ranger and offer her a Pepsi, play "Thriller" and coach her on her moonwalk.

She spots one of his bare feet poking out from under the curtain. Its toes spread as the foot moves back and forth rhythmically. On the floor of the passenger side Harriet sees flip-flops. They're jelly green like her mother's. At first she tells herself they can't be her mother's, but the imprint of Lynne's foot in the foam is unmistakable. The ball of her foot wears out flip-flops faster than her heels. Harriet stares at the compressed foam while Buck's speakers pound through her. This is not what she and Dee strategized; the 'rents were supposed to date and fall in love before shagging. Now her mother is just another fuck buddy. Harriet yanks on the cab door but it's locked. She hammers on the window with both fists.

Buck's foot disappears. He draws back the curtain while pulling up his running shorts. Lynne also pulls up her shorts and adjusts her tank top. Her face, when she sees Harriet, looks like a Francis Bacon painting. Buck quickly closes the curtain and opens the door. "What's up, Ranger? You ready for a run?"

"You disgust me," Harriet says. "You *both* disgust me." She jumps off the rocker panel and kicks one of the massive tires. "And you're polluting just so you can rut." She runs across the parking lot, ignoring the scorching pain of her toe. Her mother's pleading cries mean nothing to her.

"I am so happy to see you, *anak*," Mr. Rivera says. Relatives pack his apartment, eating *pancit bihon*, drinking *calamansi* juice and playing bingo. Harriet sees the roast pig on the table with its hind legs twisted behind it and its front legs bent forward as though it's begging for mercy. Chunks of flesh have been cut out of it, and the tail is missing.

"You look sad, Harry, is everything okay?"

"I'm fine. May I please use your comportment room?" Mrs. Rivera called bathrooms *comportment rooms*, or *CRs*.

"Of course, *anak*."

As she wends her way through Riveras of all ages, they say, "Hi, Harry, so happy to see you. Are you going to sing for us tonight?"

She opens the medicine cabinet. No NyQuil or cough syrup but there's a bottle of Mrs. Rivera's liquid morphine, as well as non-drowsy allergy pills. That Caitlin sack of shit said taking them was like being on speed. Harriet wants speed and pain relief, although she's not sure if what she's feeling is pain. Heat blasts through her at unpredictable intervals and then waves of cold. Trapped between fire and ice, she can't go backwards or forwards.

She measures the morphine in the little plastic cup like she did for Mrs. Rivera, and swallows it with six allergy pills. Dee advised her that a bat-shit-crazy high is M mixed with booze and Red Bull. Maybe M stands for morphine, and non-drowsy allergy pills have similar ingredients to energy drinks. Harriet needs energy, but also to stop the hot and cold blasts. She must find booze. Mr. Rivera's male relatives drink San Miguel beer. If she pours one into a glass, the Riveras will think it's ginger ale. This is her criminal mind at work.

She sits on the plush toilet seat cover because suddenly her legs feel leaden and her feet clamped to the floor. She hates her mother more than she has ever hated anybody. The bubble-assed slut left Harriet alone—in the apartment with the abusive loser—to run off and shag a pothead. After the fuckfest, she'll drag her horny ass back to the deadbeat, and they'll go on telling Irwin everything will be all right while they shove things up his butt and make him sicker and sicker. Harriet should kidnap Irwin. She can lift him easily. She could feed him Turtles, take the bus to the lake and go swimming with him. He always wants to play in the water but Lynne won't let him, even if the green flag signals that the water is safe. Harriet could pull him far out into the lake, hold him close so he feels loved, then quickly drag him under. With his fluid-filled lungs, it will be over in seconds, and she'll hug him the whole time.

"The tygers of wrath are wiser than the horses of instruction." This is another thing Mr. Blake said that she doesn't really understand but enjoys saying. Mr. Chubak told her Mr. Blake said to see the infinite in all things. "Whatever you do, Harry," Mr. Chubak said, "you don't want *mind-forg'd manacles.*"

"Mind-forg'd manacles." Harriet's lips tingle from the m's in mind and manacles.

The black and white tiles in the Riveras' bathroom are tiny squares and rectangles. The rectangles form a pinwheel around the tiny black squares. The squares pop out at Harriet, spinning, making her dizzy. She stops staring at them and instead looks up at the Virgin Mary gazing sorrowfully down at her. "It must've been horrible having your son strung up like that," Harriet says. "Especially wearing a crown of thorns. And the nails must have really hurt." The Virgin Mary doesn't nod because she's not a complainer. "It seems weird that he had to die for *our* sins," Harriet says. "I mean, that blows. Why should anybody have to suffer for everybody else's sins? That sucks rocks." The Virgin Mary remains contrite, and Harriet says, "You mustn't be crushed by duty. You must become who you are. Otherwise you'll never get to the bottom of everything. *I* got to the bottom of everything and I'm evil, and I'm okay with that. Somebody has to be evil."

She hopes the Virgin Mary will offer a sign that she is not evil but she doesn't, and someone's pounding on the door. "I gotta poo," a boy says. Harriet stands, surprised that her legs no longer feel leaden but light, and washes her hands to remove any traces of Buck's truck.

The boy pounds on the door again. "Hurry up, I need to go!"

Harriet opens the door and the little boy, smelling of smoked *bangus*, charges in and slams it in her face. To avoid bumping into Riveras, Harriet slides along the wall to the kitchen where the sink is full of bottles of San Miguel. She grabs a glass from the dish rack, and the bottle opener on the counter, and opens a bottle. She manages to pour its entire contents into the glass before Lauro and Remus, two of Mr. Rivera's sons, come into the kitchen for more beers. She slips into the hall and gulps from the glass. Mr. Shotlander says Canadian beer tastes like horse piss. She doesn't know what he says about San Miguel, but it tastes like horse piss to her. She ducks into the Riveras' bedroom. It's already occupied by teenaged Riveras showing off tattoos and piercings their parents don't know about. They panic when they see Harriet. "Your secret's safe with me," she assures them, stepping back into the hallway. Little Riveras run wild around her, playing games she doesn't understand. A teeny boy, chewing on pig skin, bumps into her and says, "I'll kill you last."

The old aunts who prayed with Mrs. Rivera beckon to Harriet. Lined up on the couch, they drink Diet Coke. "Harry, so good to see you. Did you have *puto bumgbong*?" All the old ladies have rice bowl haircuts and are eating *bicho bicho*. "Come sit with us, Harry." She sits on the edge of the couch while they discuss what an old parish priest did to get kicked out of his order. Harriet feels the hot and cold blasts mellowing into tropical breezes, even though she's never been to the tropics. Her toe has stopped hurting and energy simmers at the back of her neck—a gestating superpower. Behind her, Mr. Rivera's son Remus says, "I've been getting hate messages all day long and it's like, what do you want from me?" It comforts Harriet that Remus, who dances better than anybody and is always nice, is getting hate messages. If it's possible to hate Remus, maybe Harriet isn't so hateful, and maybe not even evil. Her legs feel sprung as she walks over to the table laden with sweets. She chooses Mrs. Rivera's favourite desert, *kutsinta*, a sticky rice flour cupcake steamed and served with coconut. Lauro, a law student and the pride of Mr. Rivera, is eating rolls of sticky rice. He dips a piece in coconut while talking to his cousin Luis about the Greeks and the original democracy. "It was a benevolent society," Lauro explains, as coconut and sticky rice fall onto the rug. "In the Greek system, the prosecutor says, 'I know all about you. I love you, but you're going to die.' There's something really beautiful about that."

This is what Harriet wants to say to Irwin, and it *is* really beautiful. She leans back on the couch, gazing up at the Happy Birthday banner and the helium balloons gently nudging the ceiling, and becomes transfixed by the mass of purples, blues, yellows, pinks, oranges and greens. The banner and balloons merge into a massive, glistening jellyfish while the old aunts talk about people they know who have died, and whether or not they were good Christians. This reminds Harriet about the crucifix. She pulls it from her pocket and goes in search of Mr. Rivera. She finds him in the bedroom, now empty of teenagers, on his knees praying again. "What are you praying for?" she asks.

"I'm praying to God through saints and patrons that whatever is good for me and my family will be done."

"Here." Harriet hands him the crucifix.

"Oh it is beautiful, *anak*. Thank you."

"If it's totally up to God what happens to you, why do you have to pray so much?"

"I pray for us sinners, now and at the hour of our death, amen."

"Do you pray for me?"

"Of course, *anak*."

"Do you miss Mrs. Rivera?"

"Always."

Harriet tries to think of someone in her life she'd miss if they died. "She's with the saints and angels," she assures Mr. Rivera, which is way better than being with humans. Humans disappoint and betray, but this no longer matters to Harriet with morphine, non-drowsy allergy pills, red dye and San Miguel in her blood. She doesn't understand why she allowed humans to matter. They are not infinite, whereas Harriet is beginning to see the infinite in all things. She touches Jesus' bleeding feet nailed to the cross beside Mr. Rivera. "I feel you," she tells the Son of Our Lord.

Ramiro, the 102-year-old uncle who only eats fish and rice, summons Mr. Rivera. "Pedro," he calls, "time for a prayer."

"We already prayed," the wild children protest.

"So, we pray again," the grown-ups say.

They all kneel and Ramiro says a novena to the patron saint Joseph, the infant Jesus and blessed Mother Mary and the Sacred Heart of Jesus. Then Ramiro talks about what a good man Pedro is, and asks God to bless him. Next Ramiro asks Holy Mary, Mother of God, to pray for us sinners, now and at the hour of our death, amen. All the Riveras repeat this phrase ten times, then say the Lord's Prayer and ten Hail Marys. "Now," Ramiro commands, "all the children must go to Pedro and make *mano*." One by one the children take Mr. Rivera's hand and fidget while he holds it against their foreheads. "God bless you, my child," he says, and they run away.

"Harry," Ramiro says. "Make *mano*."

Harriet takes Mr. Rivera's hand and holds it against her forehead. It feels soft and healing, and a confidence shoots through her she has never felt before.

"Will you sing 'My Way' with me tonight, Harry?" Mr. Rivera asks.

"Damn straight." She scoops maraschino cherries from a bowl. "After I use the CR."

Munching cherries, she measures more morphine into the little cup and swallows more non-drowsy allergy pills. She's never felt so good about not belonging in the world. Floating and free to drift, the infinite in everything shimmers around her. She practices some Michael Jackson moves in the big mirror but she can't see her feet. Gripping the shower rod, she stands on the edge of the tub to check her footwork in the mirror. She starts singing about Billie Jean not being her lover but another wild child bangs on the door.

The adults squeeze onto the couch and easy chairs to watch the karaoke. The ones who can't fit on the furniture lean on the arms of the couch and chairs, or against a Rivera perched on the arms of the couch or chairs. Lauro, the law student, sings "Don't Stop Believin'," passing the microphone from hand to hand and scrunching up his face during the high notes. When he finishes, the Riveras applaud and shout "Good job!" even though he only scores sixty-two percent on the karaoke machine. "That machine sucks, man," Lauro says. "No way that was a sixty-two."

Next, Christy, Mr. Rivera's daughter who looks exactly like Mrs. Rivera in her wedding photo except she has blonde streaks in her hair, sings "My Heart Will Go On." Harriet recognizes this song from *Titanic*, a movie Lynne watches when she can't sleep. Christy scores ninety-two percent, and the other Riveras applaud even more and shout "Bravo!" Next up is Remus singing "Livin' on a Prayer." He wiggles his hips when he sings and tips his head back on the high notes. He only scores fifty-seven percent, but the Riveras applaud him anyway. Mr. Rivera takes the microphone and beckons to Harriet. Without hesitation her sprung legs lead her to the microphone. Mr. Rivera takes a second microphone from the machine. All the Riveras say, "Go for it, Harry," and "You can do it, *anak*." And Harriet has no doubt that she can. Mr. Rivera selects "My Way," the music swells, the words appear on the screen and Harriet sings them in a clear voice she has never heard before, that doesn't even feel like it's coming from her, more like it's the voice of a saint. Mr. Rivera steps back to watch her, smiling encouragingly as she sings about the end being near and facing the final curtain and doing what she had to do. The Riveras, squeezed on the couches and chairs, sway with the music. Harriet sings that she bit off more than she could chew, but when there was doubt she ate it up and spat it out. And she knows she is freed of the shifting doubts and hatreds and resentments chained inside her. She faced it all, took the blows and stood tall, and she did it her way. She scores ninety-four percent, and the Riveras stand up to applaud and shout "Bravo!" Mr. Rivera hugs her and says, "Thank you for everything you have done for us, *anak*." She doesn't know what he means but she knows he means it and hugs him back. The aunts offer her *halo halo special* in a sundae glass and stroke her like a cherished pet. Harriet eats more maraschino cherries and sucks on the straw. The coolness from the shaved ice soothes her dry mouth and throat. Mr. Rivera says he's tired and going to bed but insists everybody party anyway, and they do, singing and dancing and drinking San Miguel.

Out the sliding glass doors to the balcony, Harriet sees the sun setting beyond the low rise across the street—pink, orange and violet radiate above the dull concrete, fanning into a cloudless sky. She leans against the railing, moving closer to the radiant light. *"'Tis very sweet to look into the fair and open face of heaven,"* she says. Then she hears the singing again. At first she can't see the wings, just their dark silhouettes against the fuchsia and apricot sky. She climbs onto the railing for a better view, and stands looking upwards, gripping Mrs. Rivera's clothesline for balance. The angels sing to Harriet that she is not evil or a sociopath, or lacking compassion, or selfish, or negative, or uncooperative, or difficult, or deceitful. "I tried to steal," she confesses. "And tried to let my brother die. I've even been thinking about drowning him."

"You mean well," the angels answer back. "You want to save him from suffering. We forgive you. You are a good person, *anak*." This is what Mrs. Rivera used to say, and suddenly Harriet misses her so much tears ooze out of her again only this time she doesn't mind crying because the angels sing "What a Wonderful World" to her with silky voices. They sway above the building in flowing white robes like the Riveras swayed on the couch. Harriet too starts to sway and sing about the colours of the rainbow being so pretty in a sky of blue. The angels reach down to her like her mother did when she pulled her out of the pool at the Americana. Lynne wrapped her in a big soft white towel and held her close. "My sweet baby girl," she whispered into Harriet's ear. When the angels reach down to wrap her in their wings, Harriet reaches up to them like she did for her mother.

AFTER

Nineteen

"Your mother tells me you've stopped taking your meds." Theo removes the blood pressure cuff from Irwin's arm.

"What makes her think that?" Irwin stares at Theo's hippie grad photo. Now Theo has hair everywhere but on his head. His shaggy eyebrows hang over his eyes.

"Your mother knows you better than anybody."

No she doesn't. She stopped knowing him. She scares him. He can do nothing right.

Theo leafs through Irwin's encyclopedia-thick file. "Your neuro says you're doing well. No revisions or seizures. So we just need to treat the depression."

"Who says it's depression?"

"What do you think it is?"

"I'm just sad."

"Sadness passes. How's the internet addiction?"

"Who says I'm addicted?"

"Your mother says if she doesn't force you off it, you'll be on it all day."

It bugs Irwin that they talk behind his back. When he turns eighteen he will find his own doctor. "I quit. Cold turkey." Facebook torments him, compelling him to stalk happy people. He can't stop looking at their smiling photos at parties and on vacations, with girlfriends and boyfriends. He checks the status of every kid he's ever known and they're all in a relationship. Sometimes he makes friend requests but they never reply.

Irwin's only comfort is masturbation, picturing Sydney, their boarder, in her shiny, skin-tight workout gear. She complains that the receptionist job at LA Fitness is making her fat, but Irwin loves her rolls and curves. On meds he can't jerk off. He doesn't admit this to Theo because he's ashamed. The truth is, medicated, Irwin can't feel anything, can't laugh or cry. It didn't matter to him when his little sister's puppy got hit by a car. Heike cried for days. Her face and eyes became so puffy she could hardly see. On autopilot, Irwin handed her Kleenexes.

Theo's shaggy eyebrows merge. "We can try another medication."

"They give me headaches and make my eyes itchy. And I'm always thirsty."

"Yes, but you're *functioning*, Irwin. At least you can get out of bed. That's big."

Theo often says "that's big" about things Irwin does. When he was little, he believed him.

Theo jots something down in the file. "All drugs have side effects. The important thing is that you've stopped crying and aren't as anxious. Your mother says you're even delivering a paper."

"Just the *Mirror*. It's volunteer."

"But it's a responsibility and you're handling it, at fourteen. That's big. You're managing to swallow the liquid Prozac okay?"

Irwin nods although he has been pouring it down the sink, avoiding Lynne as she rushes to and from the bank, complaining about how some new hire got promoted. "I have way more experience but kissing ass is what it's all about these days." His mother has become all jagged edges and explosive moods. She spends hours on the balcony sucking hard on cigarettes. At the bank she wears a nicotine patch.

"There is no easy fix for grief," Theo says, as though Irwin doesn't know this. "The medicine is there to help you through it. That's all. When you're through it, you won't need it anymore."

It rained for two weeks after Harriet fell. The parched grass turned green and the wilted flowers pulled themselves upright, flushing colour into their petals. Irwin resented their unfeeling determination to thrive while Harry lay with only a flicker of life behind her eyelids.

Irwin pushes himself out of the chair. "I have to pick up my little sister from camp."

In the community centre, waiting for Heike, Irwin succumbs to his addiction and checks his Facebook account. He never puts photos of his freaky self on his timeline, instead searches for vintage images of superheroes he can post. This is why he was invited to the Marvel Comic Tumblr meet-up. His friends on Tumblr thought the illustrations were *awesome*☺. They messaged frequently until they met him and couldn't stop staring at his head. After that, they quit tagging him in their status updates, and he no longer got notifications. Today, as expected, no friendship requests have been made or accepted; he has not been tagged in anyone's status update, nor received any notifications. Loneliness pummels him and he vows, once again, to quit Facebook. Cold turkey.

Out in the yard, he leans against the chain-link fence. From a distance his little sister looks like Harriet: the same muddy blonde hair and coltish limbs. Up close the similarities fade because Heike believes anything is possible. Energy sparks off her. She is a super brain, skipped grade two, and, at age seven, is already a member of Mensa. She has decided to be a detective and carries baby powder in her backpack to check for prints, as well as a magnifying glass, pocket binoculars and a notebook filled with clues printed in tidy letters.

She flicks through her notebook. "My deductions were correct. My mother *is* dating again."

"How do you know?" Irwin unlocks her pink scooter.

"I saw a pattern and tailed her."

"Where did she go?"

"Starbucks. He looks dorky. I'm telling Dad."

"It's none of his business, is it?"

"Maybe not, but no way is that dork sleeping over."

"How will you stop him?"

"I have my methods." She straps on her tiger helmet. "What's the plan, Stan?"

"Forbes and me are delivering flyers."

"Sick." *Sick* in Heike's vocabulary means *awesome*.

Off Prozac, Irwin is surrounded by dense clouds, making it hard to think clearly and, sometimes, even breathe. His tremors are slightly worse and, without warning, nausea hammers him, forcing him to vomit or lie down. Forbes in 305 tells him these are withdrawal symptoms. Forbes was on SSRIs after he got shot, as well as narcotics. The docs turned him into a junkie, he says. It was only when he broke through the membrane into his alternate universe that he was able to stop the meds. In his alternate universe, Forbes isn't an incomplete paraplegic and still has all his teeth.

When Irwin has pounder headaches, Forbes offers him a blunt, but Irwin's afraid of pot. He's noticed that Forbes gets louder when he smokes, and thinks he's being profound when he's not making any sense. Forbes says smoking pot isn't required to enter an AU. Every morning, after Lynne and Sydney leave for work, Irwin tries to break through the membrane into his alternate universe where he hopes to have a normal head and a friend, and see Harriet.

"Any breakthrough yet?" Heike asks.

"No." She is the only one, besides Forbes, who knows he's trying.

"Maybe it's a bunch of bunk." She sails off on her scooter. Irwin was never allowed a scooter because Lynne feared he'd fall off it. Heike is capable of all the things he could never do: team sports, track and field, skating, skiing, tobogganing, wind instruments. Math. "Quit dragging your ass," she shouts over her shoulder.

They find Forbes in the lobby of the Shangrila, hunched over his laptop. He has thousands of Facebook friends, many of them incomplete or complete paraplegics he meets online. He says he connects people who are afraid to make the connections themselves. Forbes moved into the Tumicellis' apartment after Mr. Tumicelli choked to death on a ciabatta and Mrs. Tumicelli was put in a nursing home with a lock-up. Forbes lives on disability and runs Bingo Night for the seniors. Lynne calls him a low-life.

"I wish you'd quit hanging around with that low-life," she says. "That's how your sister got into trouble." She only mentions Harriet when she's cautioning Irwin not to do things. She never calls her by name, just says *your sister*. For years Lynne seemed to be looking for Harriet. She'd see Irwin, then glance around as though about to ask, "Where's your sister?"

Forbes high-fives Irwin. "It's Spidey, and the Private Eye too. Must be my lucky day."

Heike bounces on the balls of her feet. "Can I ride the gimpmobile?"

"Of course, ace." Heike hops onto his lap and he wheels them out onto the street.

Before the drive-by shooting, Forbes played amateur baseball. When he pitches rolled-up flyers at doorsteps, his arms, muscular from navigating the wheelchair, flex and extend like a real pitcher's. On the rare occasions he misses, Irwin trots up the walk to retrieve the flyers and place them on the doorstep. For this Forbes gives him twenty percent of the take.

"Can I throw the next one?" Heike asks. "Please please please? I bet I can do it better than you." Perched on Forbes's lap, she pitches the flyers perfectly, one after another. She can do anything better than anyone. Irwin can't understand how Uma, who cries all the time and can't get a job, and Trent, a bankrupt IT consultant who can't commit to anything but bike meets, could produce a miracle like Heike. "There was a mix-up in the lab," Lynne says.

That Heike insists Irwin be her after-camp babysitter baffles him. Uma disapproves, he knows, because she rarely leaves her laptop to acknowledge him when he brings Heike home. Uma is working on another thesis, which is why she can't have Heike home after camp.

"Slide it through the goddamn door handle," an old man, wearing a ball cap with *Number 1 Grandpa* on it, shouts. "How the dickens am I supposed to bend down and pick that up?"

Heike skips back up the walk, hands the old man the flyers with a flourish then curtsies. "My apologies, sir."

"Aren't you a cutie? Thank you, lovey."

Heike makes everybody love her. Lynne says Irwin did this when he was little. "You used to light up a room," she says. "Everybody loved you." He knows she wants him to be little again, lighting up rooms. "You always used to laugh," she says. He tries to laugh, and do the things she asks, like vacuuming and cleaning. When he calls her at work to make sure he's doing it right, she grows irritated. "What's the matter with you?" she says. "Use common sense."

Forbes spins his chair around to look at Heike. "Where'd you learn to curtsy like that?"

"Ballet. I'll teach you. You only really need one leg."

Forbes can stand for short periods on his right leg, although it doesn't sense hot or cold and sometimes goes into spasm. His left leg hangs lifeless when he uses his crutch to move around the apartment. Balancing is a challenge. If he turns his head quickly, it can throw him off, making him crash to the floor. Irwin has witnessed several falls and been alarmed by the change in Forbes, who thrashes about cursing his leg. Eventually, his fury spent, Forbes lies still and silent. After a few minutes, Irwin helps him to a chair.

Heike demonstrates a deep curtsy. "All the weight's on my right leg, see?"

"Hmm, must try it. Way snappier than a bow."

A yellow dog charges out of a house, barking. Unperturbed, Heike holds out her hand for it to sniff. "Easy, boy."

Dogs frighten Irwin. Forbes says too much frightens him, and that when he breaks through the membrane Irwin will stop being afraid because he will see that humans are just interacting particles. "Reality splits up into a set of parallel streams," Forbes explained, "each representing a different possible outcome, just like we split up into multiple selves in a multiverse."

Irwin doesn't understand quantum field theory. But the multiverse makes sense to him because why would there be just one universe if the cosmos is infinite?

Heike pats the yellow dog's head. "Nice doggy." Irwin takes the flyers from her and leaves them at the door.

When suicidal thoughts taunt him, Irwin goes to his room and jerks off, thinking of Sydney, even though he's afraid of her too. Her eyes change colour daily. Sometimes they're violet, sometimes green or blue. He knows she's wearing contact lenses but still the bright colours unsettle him—especially if he meets Sydney coming out of the bathroom after her shower. Knowing she is naked under the terry robe stiffens his penis but, when he looks at her eyes—minus the coloured contacts—he almost doesn't recognize her. She looks washed out and worn. By the time she leaves for LA Fitness she has her lenses in and makeup on and he can resume jerking off. It prevents him from searching for somewhere to hook the end of his belt.

"Beep beep beep, big brother, you're holding up traffic." Irwin steps out of the path of the wheelchair and into a flowerbed.

"My roses," a woman in a muumuu squawks from her porch.

"Sorry," Irwin mutters. Heike says he has to stop apologizing all the time. "It's not like *everything's* your fault," she tells him.

But it feels that way. Harriet falling, Gennedy leaving, Lynne smoking.

Heike does a cartwheel on the sidewalk. "Were my legs straight?"

"A little frog-like, ace," Forbes says.

"No way."

"Yes way."

She does another one. "How was that?"

"A little better. Point your toes next time."

They stop at Mr. Hung's for freezies. He doesn't speak to them, hasn't spoken to customers since his wife died. People new to the neighbourhood think he can't speak English.

At the Shangrila, Mr. Shotlander talks to himself while doing the crossword. "Now what dang word is that? Come on now, you *know* that word." As Mr. Shotlander grows deafer, he talks louder. "Forty-one down, five letters. Wild dog of Australia. You *know* that word."

"Dingo," Heike says.

"For the love of Mike, you're right. Dingo." He quickly writes it into the crossword then jabs a finger at Irwin. "Where's my dang *Mirror*?"

"They haven't been dropped off yet."

"You come by for a Coke when you bring it."

"Will do." Irwin enjoys visiting the seniors because they talk about Harry.

Once Forbes is in his apartment, he grabs his crutch and levers himself out of the wheelchair. Heike, clenching her freezie between her teeth, demonstrates curtsies. "You can go really deep, or just kind of bob. You should probably just bob."

Forbes, standing on his right leg, bobs.

"Excellent. Now hold your hand out. Kind of sweep it across." Heike gracefully sweeps her hand sideways as she bobs.

"He's tired, Heike," Irwin says. "Teach him some other time."

"No prob, I'm on it." Forbes manages a wobbly bob and a sweep before steadying himself against the wall.

"What's your favourite animal?" Heike asks.

"Elephants."

"Snap. They are sooo civilized. The females anyway. The males are jerks."

"Like the males of most species," Forbes says.

When Harriet was in a coma, Irwin asked repeatedly what her favourite animal was, even though he knew it was a capybara. He asked her many things in an effort to wake her. Lynne and Gennedy wouldn't let him visit long. "Don't disturb her," they said. But the ventilator was more disturbing than Irwin could ever be, blasting wind in and out of her. He had to speak very loud for her to hear him. When she didn't answer, he would answer for her, sometimes incorrectly, hoping she'd get mad and correct him. "What's your favourite colour?" he'd ask, knowing she didn't have one because colours changed in light and she could never pick a favourite. "I bet your favourite colour is black," he'd say, expecting her to sit up and tell him black is not a colour. "Who's your favourite superhero?" he'd ask, knowing she thought only derps were into superheroes. Gennedy would put his hand on Irwin's shoulder. "Time to go, little man."

Irwin talked to Harry every day until they told him she had passed. Irwin knew kids only died on vents when their parents said it was okay to take them off. "You took her off the vent!" he cried. "You *killed* her! She was getting better. I saw." He screamed until his insides felt bloody and a nurse gave him a needle. When he woke up he was at home and convinced it was all a horrible nightmare. He scrambled to the kitchen, where they sat slumped over cereal. "Let's go see Harry," he said. "I want to talk to her *now*."

His mother poked her spoon at the Shredded Wheat. "She's dead, baby."

"No she's not."

"I'm afraid it's true, champ." Gennedy tried to pull him close but Irwin started screaming that they were murderers. Mrs. Butts banged on the door to find out what all the commotion was about. Irwin wailed for thirteen hours then couldn't stop crying. They took him back to the hospital to get hydrated. He insisted on taking Harry's pillow because it smelled of her. Hooked up to an IV, he pressed his face into the pillow, soaking it with so many tears it didn't smell of Harry anymore.

Heike pokes a finger in her mouth. "I have a wiggly tooth. That means *another* toonie from the tooth fairy."

"You're going to bankrupt the poor woman," Forbes says.

"She's not a woman, she's a fairy. What happened to *your* tooth?"

"I broke it."

"How?"

"Undoing a zipper."

"What zipper?"

"On a pair of jeans."

"Why were you undoing your zipper with your teeth?"

"It wasn't my zipper."

"Whose was it?"

"My ex's."

"Why were you undoing *her* zipper with your teeth?"

"Guess my hands were busy."

"You're not making any sense." Heike always says this when she doesn't understand, as though it's the other person's fault that she doesn't understand.

"Heike," Irwin says, "check your phone to see if Dad's called." They're supposed to have dinner with Trent, but he cancels if he's running late or has a bike meet. Heike checks her cell. Lynne stopped buying Irwin phones because he kept losing them and she's not made of money.

"He says to meet us at the fish and chips place," Heike says. "Sick. Mum's going to be super pissed."

Irwin is uncomfortable around his father because he looks at him as though he wishes he were someone else.

Forbes hobbles to the balcony door and slides it open. Heike pulls her notebook from her backpack. "I have a lead on the guy who exposed himself to that little girl."

"Not that little, ace, she was older than you."

Heike reads from the notebook. "Suspect between five-foot-six and five-ten, with spiky hair and a big nose."

"That's no lead," Forbes says. "They said that on the radio."

"Me and Irwin saw a guy who fits that description at the SOC."

"Which is?"

"The DQ. He did it in the DQ parking lot."

"So why didn't you call it in?"

"He took off. But I'm starting to see a pattern. I'm going to stake him out."

"Not by yourself you're not," Irwin says. Uma gets hysterical when Heike does stakeouts on her own.

Forbes collapses on his armchair, immediately slipping until his ass is half off the seat. Irwin used to worry he'd slide right off until he figured out Forbes grips the arms of the chair between his upper arms and ribs.

Heike practices more curtsies. "Tell us another orifice story."

Forbes was an emergency room orderly before he got shot. That's how he figured out before anyone else he was paralyzed. The shooter didn't know Forbes. Forbes was eating burgers in the wrong place at the wrong time. "What was the last orifice story I told you?"

"The lady who swallowed three quarters, two dimes and a nickel."

"Did I tell you about the guy who swallowed magnets? They looked like candies. He swallowed them at different times so the magnets sought each other out, screwed up his guts."

"Eww," Heike says.

"Then there was the guy with the glowing gut. What do you think he put down there?"

Heike, looking puzzled, fondles her lucky horseshoe pendant.

Irwin likes Forbes because his body is as out of control as his own. People who can control their bodies lose patience with those who can't. Forbes never loses patience with Irwin and doesn't seem to notice his head or ears or clumsiness. He never stares at the shunt pulsing under Irwin's skin or at the scars on his scalp or his shaking hands. Most people try not to stare but end up staring anyway. And they always keep their distance. The last seat on the bus is always beside Irwin.

"I'll give you a clue," Forbes says. "What glows?"

Heike scrunches up her face. "A light? What kind of light fits in your gut?"

This makes Irwin think of his own gut. The neuro showed him the X-rays. The broken tubes looked like snakes. When he can't sleep, he feels them slithering around inside him.

"No light can fit in a gut," Heike says. "He'd have to swallow it and it would be too big."

"A minor detail, my dear Watson. Guess again."

"He swallowed a glowstick?"

Forbes wiggles his eyebrows. "There are other orifices besides the mouth."

Heike sucks on her freezie then gasps. "You mean he stuck a glow stick up his *bum*?"

"A flashlight."

"Why would he do that?"

"To see better."

Heike, unconvinced, stares at him, narrowing her eyes like Uma.

Forbes winks at her. "Did I tell you about the cockroach crawling into a guy's ear?"

"We have to go," Irwin says.

While they wait for Trent at the fish and chips place, Heike dusts for prints. "Mum says they never clean these tables and there's germy prints all over them." Uma carries plastic bags in her fanny pack and slips them on like gloves to open doors or press elevator buttons. Operating ATMs wearing the bags is difficult. People line up behind her, growing irritable. Uma doesn't notice.

Heike gently blows on the baby powder. Most of it sticks to the table's greasy surface. "As I suspected." She hops over to the scarred woman at the cash register. Mr. Chubak told Irwin the cashier is from Afghanistan and had a jealous husband who threw acid on her face. She looks annoyed all the time. Irwin would never have the nerve to speak to her. "Excuse me, ma'am," Heike says. "Would you be so kind as to wipe our table? I have to be careful about germs." Heike coughs to demonstrate her sensitivity to germs then smiles apologetically, revealing the gaps left behind by baby teeth. "Sorry, I don't want you to go to any trouble."

The lady smiles back, although, because of the scars, only one side of her mouth lifts up. "Not to worry, miss. I'll take care of it."

"Thank you so much." Heike pulls binoculars out of her backpack and leans out the glass door to survey the street.

"Can you see Dad?" Irwin asks.

"Yellow helmet at six o'clock. ETA four minutes."

Forbes calls Heike a smooth operator and says he can't wait till she becomes prime minister. Watching Heike operate smoothly makes Irwin nervous. He fears one day she will go too far, like Harriet. She will be away from him, among strangers, operating, and he will lose her. He won't be able to stand it.

Twenty

"How's the dynamic duo?" Trent asks, pulling off his yellow helmet.

"Good." Heike fits her binoculars into her backpack. "Let's order, I'm starved." She looks at Irwin. "The usual?" He nods.

Trent takes the chair closest to the window. "Your mom will want you to have some veggies. Get a couple sides of slaw."

"Mummy told me not to have slaw here because there might be toxic bacteria in it."

Irwin knows Heike's lying because they didn't tell Uma they were going for fish and chips. This is Heike being a smooth operator.

"FYI, Dad," she says, "you've got helmet head."

Trent runs his fingers through his hair and glances at Irwin as though he wishes he were someone else. "How's it going, Irwin?"

"It's going." He knows his father finds it hard to look at him.

"How's your mother? Working two jobs, I take it."

"She's always working two jobs," Irwin says. "Does your going bankrupt mean you're poor now too?"

"Not poor, exactly, but we have to tighten our belts a little."

"Who's 'we'? I mean, you haven't been sending *my* mother any money. So it doesn't make any difference to us. Our belts are tight anyway."

"It's more to do with Uma. She's got expensive tastes. She's going to have to lower her standards a little."

Uma calls herself a perfectionist. Irwin doesn't understand why when she is far from perfect and can't get a job. Lynne calls her a lazy German sow.

Irwin watches Trent staring out the window to avoid staring at his head. He wishes Heike would come back with the order, but she's chatting happily with the scarred lady. Conversation with his father has always been difficult. Irwin knows he divorced Lynne because of him. He heard Gennedy and Lynne argue about Trent many times and Gennedy would say, "He left you because he couldn't handle a mentally and physically challenged son. What kind of coward is that?" Irwin doesn't know what kind of coward that is. Or what kind of coward leaves a wife and two children, and then another wife and one child. Children need their parents, Mr. Shotlander says. He believes Harriet fell because she didn't have a father looking out for her, just "that layabout." Irwin still visits Gennedy in the rooming house, despite his fear of the white Rasta boarder with floor-length dreadlocks. While Irwin waits for Gennedy to answer his door, the white Rasta talks at him with great urgency, saying things like "What a sweet nanny goat a go run him belly," or "Fire de a Mus Mus tail, him tink a cool breeze."

Finally Heike brings the food to the table. "Everybody has to say what their fish is shaped like."

"Mine's shaped like a fish," Trent says.

"No way, it looks like a torpedo. What about yours, Irwin?" She leans both elbows on the table and scrutinizes Irwin's fish.

"A flying carpet?"

"Flying carpets are thin and wavy. Your fish is thick, like a huge tongue."

"Can I eat it now?"

"*Mine's* shaped like a broken wing. See how it's bent?"

Trent tugs on her ponytail. "So how are things, Super Girl?"

"Good."

"What did you pirates get up to today?"

"We delivered flyers on the gimpmobile. Forbes let me throw them."

"Wow."

"And then I taught him how to curtsy."

"Cool." Trent says "cool" when he isn't listening. He keeps glancing out the window. "How's your mother?"

"Whose mother?" Heike asks.

"Yours."

"She's mad at the landscapers. She doesn't like the rocks they put in. I told her we don't need more rocks. There's no room for me to dig with those rocks all over the place. She said I shouldn't be digging in the dirt anyway, so I asked if I could have a sandbox. She said cats defecate in sandboxes and make them toxic."

"Wow."

"She's really stressed out about the landscaping. She wants the landscaper to change the rocks or give the money back." Heike pushes several fries into her mouth.

"Did you wash your hands?" Irwin asks. Uma tells him to make sure Heike washes her hands before meals. He never remembers to wash his.

Heike squeezes more ketchup onto her fries. "Of course I washed my hands, big brother."

"When?"

"After I ordered."

He suspects she's lying but can't be sure as he wasn't watching her the whole time. It worries him how easily she lies, and that no one notices.

A stocky woman in bike shorts and a purple helmet pulls open the glass door. "Trent Baggs," she says. "What a marvellous coincidence."

"Candace. What a wonderful surprise." Trent stands and offers her a seat. "Would you care to join us?"

"Don't mind if I do. Are these your beautiful children?"

"They certainly are. This is Heike, and this is Irwin. Kids, I'd like you to meet a very special lady. Candace Gittens."

Candace Gittens offers her bicycle-gloved hand for them to shake. Irwin shakes but Heike just eyes her, chewing on fish.

"You're not surprised to see my father at all," she says. "You were down the block waiting for him to get here. I saw you. This was a set-up."

"Heike," Irwin says, "be polite."

245

"It's not polite to pretend you're surprised to meet someone when it was all planned. It's time for full disclosure."

"Wow," Trent says. "Can we rewind a little?"

"I am *not* rewinding," Heike insists, spewing bits of fish. "Are you my dad's new squeeze? Do you know how many girlfriends he's had? Hundreds. And *two wives*."

"Heike, that's enough," Trent says.

"It is *not* enough. You think just because we're children you can fool us. Well you can't. And you know what? Mum has a new boy toy. They meet at Starbucks, and I bet he's parking his plane in her runway *right this second*."

"Wow."

Candace, still in her bike helmet, seems unable to take her eyes off Heike, who stares right back at her. "Blinking contest," Heike announces. "You blinked. I win."

Trent wipes his hands on a napkin. "Okay, kids, you're right. We did set this up only because we didn't want to upset you."

Heike shoves her notebook into her backpack. "We're upset anyway."

"*I'm* not," Irwin says.

"That's because you're on meds."

"I'm not on meds."

"You're not?" Trent asks.

"I forgot to take them. I'll take them when I get home."

"Listen, guys, I just wanted you to meet Candace casually. We didn't want to make a big deal about it."

"It *is* a big deal," Heike says. "Why do you have to have girlfriends all the time? Why can't you just be single?"

"I was single before I met Candace."

"For about five minutes after what's-her-face."

"More than five minutes."

Candace holds up her hand as if she's not sure she has the correct answer. "Heike, I completely understand where you're coming from. My parents divorced and met new people, and I had to adjust. It was really hard. But then I decided I wanted them to be happy. I knew they wouldn't be happy alone. Humans just aren't that kind of animal."

"They're selfish animals." Heike grabs her paper plate of fish and fries. "Let's bounce, Irwin."

"Heike!" Trent says.

"Stay with your new squeeze, Father. Don't let your *children* stand in your way."

Trent clutches one of Candace Gittens' gloved hands. "I'm so sorry, Candy."

Heike unlocks her scooter from a parking sign. "I like how he says sorry to her but not to us."

"You can't hold a plate and ride your scooter at the same time. We should go back in. We don't have to sit with them."

She hands her plate to Irwin and turns off her cell. "No way I'm going back in there. He called her Candy. Eww."

They eat their fish in the park. Heike studies the graffiti carved into the bench. "I wonder if Liam still loves Emily. Doubt it."

"I don't know why you get so worked up about your parents dating."

"They're supposed to be married."

"So, it didn't work out. Lots of people don't stay married."

"My parents aren't lots of people. They sacrificed a lot to have me. Mummy says she had to postpone defending her thesis because of me. If I'm so special, how come they're homewreckers?"

"I don't think it's any of our business what they do."

"You don't think *anything* is your business. Name one thing you think is your business."

Irwin feeds a fry to a squirrel, trying to think of something that he considers his business.

"Case closed," Heike says. "You can't think of anything."

"You're my business, babysitting you."

"I don't see why. She never pays you. If I were you, I'd be pissed she never coughs up."

"I like being with you."

"Not as much as with Harry. You wish I was Harry."

"That's not true." Heike has always been jealous of Harriet, and Irwin's never understood why. Harriet is dead.

"If you find her in your alternate universe," Heike says, "you'll never come back and I'll be all alone."

"I'll never leave you alone."

"People always do things they say they'll never do. Like getting divorced. And Dad said he'd never forget to call me and he always does."

"I'm not like Dad. I don't forget."

"Please take me with you to your AU."

"You can't take a person with you."

"Why not?"

"Because my alternate universe is different from yours. You can only visit *your* alternate universe."

"That doesn't make any sense." She pulls out her magnifying glass to examine the bench more closely. "You should have kept some of Harry's blood for DNA, then you could have cloned her. They're doing that to a frog. It's been extinct for thirty years and now they're cloning it because it's the only animal that gives birth through its mouth."

"Why? It'll just go extinct all over again. I mean, there are way fewer places for frogs to live than there were thirty years ago."

"Does that mean you think Harry would die all over again if she was cloned?"

"Of course not."

"Why not? It's a worse environment. She'd probably kill herself all over again."

"She didn't kill herself. She fell."

"Likely story." Uma says this.

"Why are you being so mean?"

"I'm not being mean," Heike says. "It's just everybody thinks she killed herself."

"Nobody knew her like I did. She wouldn't do that. She wouldn't have left me alone. She loved me. She took care of me. She would never do that." A rush of despair, freed from medical restraints, floods his chest and gushes up his throat. In seconds hot tears spurt from his eyes and onto his fish.

"How come you're crying again? You never cry on meds." She claps her hand over her mouth. "You *have* stopped taking them."

It bugs him that it's impossible to keep secrets from Heike. "I just forgot today. I'll take them when I get home."

She pulls out her notebook and pen.

"What are you doing?"

She kneels in the grass, using the bench for a writing surface, and prints carefully.

"What are you writing?"

"I'm keeping you under observation."

"Why?"

"Changes in your behaviour will indicate if you're off meds."

"Check your messages. See if your mum called."

Heike looks at her phone. "Three times. The woman needs to get a life. And Dad called to make excuses. What a doofus."

"We'd better get you home."

As soon as they step onto the porch, Uma flings the door open. "I've been worried sick. It's past eight. What were you thinking, Irwin?"

"We went to the park."

She turns to Heike. "Why am I paying for a cell when you always switch it off?"

"I don't *always* switch it off. We were watching a chess game and I didn't want to disturb the players." Another lie. "We lost track of time. I'm so sorry, Mummy." The smooth operator hugs Uma around the waist.

"Well, that was very considerate of the players, sweetie, but what about me? I worry when I can't reach you. Call me before you start watching chess next time. Okay, honeybun?"

"Okay."

Uma scowls at the decorative boulders and gravel spread out in place of lawn. "I'm so upset about these rocks. The grey is so nineties."

"What colour did you want?" Irwin asks.

"It's not about colour, it's about tone."

"Mummy, I promised Irwin frozen yogourt." Heike didn't promise him anything.

"That's okay," he says.

"No, Irwin," Uma says resignedly, "come inside and have some yogourt with us."

He knows she doesn't want him inside but Heike pulls with all her might on his hand. "Banana Split, your favourite."

"Wash your hands," Uma orders. "Both of you."

Irwin believes in ghosts when he's in Uma's house. Her dead parents and brother lounge on the antique furniture, speaking German. Uma's grandparents brought the furniture over from Hamburg in a ship. Uma makes her cleaning lady polish the mahogany to keep it shiny like her mother did. The living room remains as it was when her parents and brother were alive, so there is no reason for the ghosts to leave. The only major house renovation has been the kitchen, which is full of stainless steel appliances and granite surfaces. Uma had a granite-topped island built in the centre of the kitchen. Uma and Heike live on this island and leave the rest of the house to the Germans.

Uma sets out two bowls. "How was your father?"

"Good." Heike takes the frozen yogourt out of the freezer.

"Where did you eat?"

"The fish and chips place."

Uma groans. "He does it deliberately to irritate me."

"It was really good. I talked to the scarred lady. She says I'm so lucky to be able to go to school because boys threw rocks at her when she tried to go."

"How did Trent look?" Uma always asks how Trent looked after they've seen him.

"Good." Heike spoons frozen yogourt into the bowls. "He introduced us to a very special lady."

"What lady?"

"Her name's Candy. They pretended like they just ran into each other, but it was a set-up. I saw her hanging around down the block with my binoculars."

Uma grips the counter the way she does when she's about to tear up.

"I should go," Irwin says.

"Wait a second, big brother, I didn't tell you my tomato joke. It's really funny. There's this family of tomatoes, and they're walking down the street and the son is really slow, like, he's just not keeping up. Guess what his father says?"

Uma yanks Kleenexes from a box and dabs her eyes.

"Guess," Heike repeats.

"I give up," Irwin says.

"Ketchup. Get it? Catch up? Ketchup. Isn't that hilarious?"

"What did this Candy woman look like?" Uma asks.

Heike takes her spoon out of her mouth. "Booby-liscious. A total bike babe."

"No she wasn't," Irwin says.

"She was too."

Uma shakes her head and sighs. Trent tried to get her on a bike but she refused because she fell off one once and is afraid of spinal cord injuries.

"Mummy, did you know you can stick a flashlight up your bum?"

"Did you get her last name?" Uma asks, bunching up her teary Kleenexes.

Heike spoons more ice cream. "Gittens, rhymes with mittens."

Irwin suspects Uma plans to check out Candy Gittens on Facebook. Sydney stalks her ex-boyfriends on social media and says their new girlfriends look like slutty hags.

"If you turn the flashlight on," Heike says, "it lights up your gut. I want to try it for Halloween."

"Do *not* try that," Uma says vehemently. "People *die* from putting things up their bums."

Heike's eyes widen. "What things?"

"I can't believe I'm being forced to have this conversation. Who have you been talking to?"

"Dad."

"Are you saying your father told you people put flashlights up their rectums?"

"Up their whats?"

Uma shudders. "That man has completely lost it. I don't know what's got into him."

"Mummy, what kills you if you put it up your bum?"

"All kinds of things, sweetie. Sharp things, dirty things, vegetables that go rotten. Your rectum is not a plaything. Do not try to put anything in it, do you understand? And do not let anyone else put anything in it either.

Or your vagina for that matter. Your private parts are not to be touched by anyone. Do you understand?"

Heike, who rarely looks confused, stares saucer-eyed at her mother while Banana Split dribbles down her chin. "Why would people put vegetables and dirty sharp things up their bums?"

"Promise me you will leave your rectum alone, Heike. And your vagina. Promise me."

"I promise."

"That's my girl." Uma wraps her arms around Heike and kisses her repeatedly. "I don't want anything bad to happen to you, ever, ever, ever. I love you very, very, very much, honeybun."

Irwin longs to be loved this much. It would be like always having a protective coating. No matter how cruel people were, it wouldn't stick. Meanness would just slide off the coating. He believes Harry loved him this much.

Mr. Shotlander invites him in when he delivers the *Mirror*. "My dang CD player's on the blink again. More newfangled nonsense. We never had these problems with LPs."

"CD players aren't new," Irwin says loudly to Mr. Shotlander's good ear. "Did you vacuum it?"

"Why the heck would I vacuum it?" Mr. Shotlander tugs up his trousers.

"Last time this happened I vacuumed it, remember? Sometimes it's just a speck of dust that screws things up."

"Who ever heard of vacuuming a dang record player? We just used to wipe the vinyl on our sleeves, and pick the dust off the needle with our fingers."

"Do you want me to vacuum it? It'll just take a second."

"Sure, sure. I'll get our Cokes."

Irwin pulls out the Dustbuster and vacuums the player inside and out. He puts the Doris Day CD back on. Doris sings "Qué Sera, Sera."

"Sounds spiffy," Mr. Shotlander says. "What would I do without you, Irwin? You and that sister of yours." Sometimes Mr. Shotlander forgets that Harriet is dead. Or he sees Heike and thinks she's Harriet. He croaks along with Doris and sits on the couch, tapping his feet. "I bet you think everything started with Elvis."

"Not really."

"Everybody thinks 'Heartbreak Hotel' was where it all started, but I'm telling you, before Elvis the Pelvis we had Kay Starr and Dean Martin, Perry Como, Pat Boone. Those folks knew how to sing." He picks up the remote and tries to adjust the volume but presses the skip button. "Oh for the love of Mike, why can't they make things simpler? I can't even see the dang buttons."

"You don't need to use the remote. Just press the buttons on the player."

"Can't see those either. Here you go." He hands Irwin a Diet Coke. "I used to play the trumpet. How do you like that? Louis Armstrong was my idol. Do you play anything?"

"I tried drums for a while."

"What happened?"

"I sucked." Lynne bought him a set three years ago because he said he might like to try drumming. He quickly learned that he had difficulty maintaining a rhythm but, because she'd bought him the drums, he felt obliged to keep trying. He hated practicing and would only make a show of it when Lynne was around. She noticed he wasn't improving. "You keep making the same mistakes," she told him. "Join the school band and learn properly." But the school band didn't need a drummer. The leader, Mr. De Jonge, must have felt sorry for Irwin because he let him play the glockenspiel. When Irwin had trouble with that, Mr. De Jonge let him play the timpani. When he had trouble with that, he let him play the triangle.

"You don't get good without practice," Mr. Shotlander says.

From then on whenever Irwin expressed an interest in trying anything that cost money, Lynne would say, "What about the drum set? Don't think I'm sponsoring your every whim. I'm not made of money." He stopped expressing interest in anything for fear that she might think it was a whim he wanted her to sponsor. She sold the drums for a quarter of what she paid for them. It was around this time she started getting angry all the time and talking about his hormones hitting. "It's the hormones hitting," she'd say whenever they had a disagreement. He avoided her by lurking on

Facebook, watching happy lives. For extra income Lynne rented Harriet's room and complained to Irwin about what inconsiderate slobs the boarders were. She blamed Trent for their financial difficulties. "If that asshole hadn't quit the bank, we wouldn't be in this situation."

Mr. Shotlander pokes his finger in his ear and wipes the wax on his polyester trousers. "It's good to play an instrument. Good for the soul."

"What happened to your trumpet?"

"Didn't have the pipes for it anymore. Gave it to my son."

"Does he play it?"

"Heck, no. Kids never do what you want them to."

Getting Harriet's room ready to rent took weeks. Lynne insisted on doing it alone. She would go in after work with an empty box and sit on the bed. An hour later Irwin would find her still on the bed, gripping the empty box so tightly her sweaty fingers left prints on the cardboard. He offered to help but every time he tried to put something in the box Lynne would say, "Not that."

"What then?"

"I'm getting there, Irwin. Don't rush me."

She threw out the glue gun but let him take Harry's artwork. He hammered nails into his walls and hung up her scary paintings. After six weeks Lynne filled three boxes with clothes and two boxes with art books Harry had bought at yard sales. She stacked them by the front door where they remained for another three weeks. Finally she called the Diabetes Association to pick them up. The boxes were heavy and Irwin had to carry them one by one to the lobby. Lynne taped them closed and ordered him not to open them. He sat beside them until the truck arrived. The scraggly haired driver grabbed the boxes and shoved them into the truck. Irwin wanted to ask him to be more careful but was too afraid. As the truck drove away, Irwin felt Harry dying all over again. Mr. Chubak and Mr. Shotlander called him over and fed him Cracker Jacks, but he choked on a kernel and couldn't stop sobbing. Mr. Chubak took him upstairs to Lynne, who was smoking on the balcony and put her arm around Irwin. The cigarette smoke nauseated him and he went to his room to try to feel Harry in the paintings. Laying his hands over the paint swirls, whorls and daubs, he felt nothing. After a while Lynne came in and hugged him. She felt bony and smelled of cigarettes.

Lynne taped two other boxes closed and wrote *HARRIET* in black marker on them. She put them in a corner of her bedroom. She has instructed Irwin to vacuum the tops of the boxes when he does the broadloom.

"Too bad about that little girl," Mr. Shotlander says, looking at the front page of the *Mirror*.

"What little girl?"

"A three-year-old got hit by a garbage truck. An eyewitness said the driver was so shocked when he got out of the cab his legs went rubbery. It's these one-man-operated trucks, I'm telling you. He can't see a dang thing driving that hulk all by himself. This wouldn't have happened in the days you had guys hanging off the trucks." Mr. Shotlander often talks about things that wouldn't have happened in the days before cell phones, self-serve registers, ATMs, voicemail and online everything. It makes Irwin pine for the simplicity of those days.

"My son got laid off again. How do you like that? They told him he wasn't a good fit. What is he, a shoe?"

Mr. Shotlander was an electrician and advised his son to learn a trade. Now he advises Irwin to learn a trade. "Nobody can manage without plumbers and electricians." Irwin would learn a trade if he could, but he can't learn anything. His mother winces when she looks at his report card.

"Have you heard anything from Mr. Zilberschmuck?" Irwin asks. They wheeled him out strapped to a gurney last week. Mr. Zilberschmuck insisted on finishing his JD and a cigarillo before they put him in the medical transportation van. "Till we meet again," he said to the other seniors, who avoided his eyes. In Irwin's experience, the ones wheeled out almost never return.

Mr. Shotlander shakes his head. "The place just isn't the same without the old lothario." He sips his Coke. He keeps forgetting to go to the barber and his tufted white hair is matted at the back. "It's only a matter of time, Irwin. For all of us." He eases himself off the couch and rummages in the kitchen. "Where's that dang sister of yours? I'm right out of chips."

Irwin delivers Mrs. Chipchase's *Mirror*, and she invites him in for fig bars and milk. She is working on another jigsaw puzzle of a cathedral. She and Irwin have been doing puzzles together for years. She taught him how to pick out the straight-edged pieces first, to find the corners and to build up the four sides. She taught him to sort the colours next, and to construct areas of the picture. They use the image on the box for guidance, although Mrs. Chipchase admitted that the die-hard puzzlers consider this cheating.

"Well," Mrs. Chipchase says, "I can't see by the colours anymore. I've done all the bright ones, let's go by the shapes now."

Near the end of a puzzle, Irwin inevitably panics, convinced that certain pieces are missing. Some blue sky with a wisp of cloud, or a piece of tree, that should occupy a space can't be found. Mrs. Chipchase tells him not to worry, that the piece must be somewhere, but anxiety tackles him and he falls down on all fours and scours the floor. Sometimes he goes so far as to empty a vacuum cleaner bag. Mrs. Chipchase suggests he count the pieces and the spaces to make sure there aren't any missing. Irwin loses track and has to start over. When he determines that there is the right number of pieces for the spaces, he feels unusually calm knowing that somehow, some way they will finish the puzzle. Mrs. Chipchase always lets him fit in the final piece. As he presses it into the picture, savouring the soft click, an unfamiliar sense of accomplishment settles over him.

When Irwin asked Mrs. Chipchase if Harriet did puzzles with her, she said, "No, dear. Your sweet sister moved too fast for puzzles."

"Why did she move too fast?"

"She was looking for something."

"What?"

Mrs. Chipchase sipped her tea. "Love and approval."

"*I* loved and approved her."

"I'm sure you did, dear, but I don't think she felt safe."

"Why not?" Irwin knows that Gennedy hit Harry once, but lots of parents hit their kids. "Why didn't she feel safe?"

Mrs. Chipchase stared at her Persian rug. "Many, many people don't feel safe, Irwin. Even in their own homes."

"You feel safe in your own home, don't you?"

"I do now, dear."

Irwin doesn't feel safe in his own home with his mother all jagged edges, smoking and angry, and Sydney strutting around, changing eye colour and cursing her ex-boyfriends and their slutty hags. When he breaks through the membrane he will leave home, find Harry and stop her from falling.

Twenty-one

Lynne and Sydney are on the couch drinking wine again. When Sydney first moved in, Lynne complained to Irwin that she was a souse. Then Sydney started offering Lynne a glass of wine. Sydney would be sitting at the kitchen table, flipping through a *People* magazine, commenting on how fat and ugly the actresses looked in their candid shots, and she'd point to the bottle and say to Lynne, "Help yourself. It's a nice little Riesling. Have a taste." Lynne would pour herself a glass, take a sip and say, "It *is* nice." Sydney never calls wine wine, it's always a Riesling or a Merlot or a Shiraz. Lynne told Irwin she doesn't know how Sydney can afford it, but she drinks her wine anyway. "Syd and me are just having a little vino," she'll say to Irwin. He'll sit with them and watch Sydney's rolls and curves shift under her shiny workout gear. After a couple of glasses, they'll forget he's there and talk loudly about what peasants people are.

"Is that my baby boy?" Lynne calls. "Come here, peanut, give us a hug."

She grabs his hand and pulls him onto the couch between them. She smells of wine. "Did you hear about that little girl who got run over? What a tragedy. Oh my lord, you have to be so careful, sweet pea."

"I'm fourteen. She was three."

"Could happen to anybody," Sydney says. "Those trucks are humongous."

Lynne drinks more wine. "Can you imagine being the driver? I mean, how's he supposed to recover from that?"

"Drugs," Sydney says. "They'll send him for PTSD counselling and he'll end up on SSRIs that make his eyeballs vibrate and give him diarrhea. For real, it happened to a friend of mine." Sydney has many friends who have things happen to them.

"Imagine the child's poor mother." Lynne holds Irwin tight against her ribs. "So how was your day, angel?" When she drinks vino, she acts loving then suddenly attacks him about something he was supposed to do. She leaves to-do lists for him, and when he forgets something she says, "It was on the list. How could you miss it? What's the matter with you?" His hands start to shake and Lynne says she's sorry, it's just she's under a lot of pressure at the bank.

She sweeps hair out of his eyes. "How was dinner with your dad?"

"Okay."

"Did he have any new over-priced bike accessories?"

"I don't think so."

"*Entre nous*," Lynne says, because speaking French is another thing she does liquored up, "Irwin's father is the cheapest prick of all time, except where his bikes are concerned. I keep hoping he'll get cancer or something, or at least go bald. He's always biking in wine country and going to tastings. You'd think he'd have the decency to get a prostate problem."

"That happened to a friend of mine." Sydney's eyes are emerald green tonight. "He was a total bikeaholic. It scrunched his balls and his prostate got swollen."

"Cancer?"

"Some bladder thing. He had stones in his bladder."

"Did it kill him?"

"No. He pissed rocks for a while. I think he was bi. Anyway, he had a kid who turned out to be trans and had his balls cut off and his penis made into a vagina. Now he has to take female hormones for life."

Irwin shifts slightly away from his mother and closer to Sydney. She smells of the perfume she carries in her purse. Every morning, before she leaves for LA Fitness, she sprays her neck and cleavage with the perfume.

Irwin thinks it smells flowery, but Lynne says it makes her gag and they should declare the apartment a fragrance-free zone.

"I think that's criminal," Lynne says. "I mean, what kind of doctors do those operations?"

"Rich ones. It costs twenty thousand to get a penis turned into a vagina. Guess how much to turn a pussy into a dick?"

Lynne snorts. She only snorts when she's drinking vino. "Fifty grand?"

"A hundred."

"Oh my lord, who wants a penis anyway? Seriously, who needs the old twig and berries hanging around?" They both cackle. They've forgotten that Irwin's there. He leans a little closer to Sydney. Moist heat radiates off her, and her thigh presses against his as she reaches for the bottle on the coffee table. He feels his penis at half-mast and covers it with a seat cushion.

"Our masseur at LA Fitness is turning into a woman." Sydney tops up their glasses. "He's getting boobs, and the facial hair's fading away. Don't know how the desperate housewives are going to feel about George turning into Georgette."

"Is he hot?"

"Kind of androgynous, which pleases the boys *and* the girls because in their minds he could go either way. Only one way to go with boobs." Sydney shakes her breasts, grazing Irwin. He can see her nipples through her sports bra. His groin throbs and his penis pushes against the cushion. When he slinks off the couch and into his bedroom, they don't even notice.

After he thinks they've gone to bed, he gets up to find something to eat, but Sydney's at the kitchen table with her laptop. "Hey, junior. Couldn't sleep?"

"I haven't really tried yet."

"Don't try, that's the secret. Check out this peasant." On the screen a man wearing a goalie mask and bikini briefs points to his crotch.

"Is that one of your exes?"

"How did you guess."

"You deserve better than that."

"Thank you, Irwin. I couldn't agree more." She's in her bathrobe but not wearing lenses or makeup and has that washed-out look about her.

"Your mother took that little girl getting killed really hard. I'm a little worried about her, to be honest. I've never seen her cry before."

"She was crying?"

"Yeah, I think because it made her think of your sister."

"Which one?"

"The one that died."

"What did she say about her?"

"Just that she misses her and all that."

"Did she say her name?"

"Harriet."

Hearing Sydney say "Harriet" startles Irwin, as though she'd been speaking a foreign language then suddenly used an English word. "I haven't heard her say my sister's name in years."

"Yeah, well, I guess it's too painful for her. It sure opened the floodgates."

Irwin hasn't seen his mother cry since Harriet's fall. Before that she cried at his bedside during various hospital stays. He knew she thought he was asleep and would peek at her through partially closed lids.

"That's awesome that she donated her organs," Sydney says.

"What?"

"Yikes, maybe she doesn't want you to know."

"I knew," Irwin says, although he didn't.

"I really admire organ donors. I wish I had the guts to sign mine away, but something creeps me out about the whole deal. I mean, like, what if they put your heart in some peasant who abuses his wife and kids or something? It's not like they check character references. Someone needs a heart, they go on a list, a match is found and bingo, in it goes. Could be a pedo for all they care. They fix him up and he's back on the street messing with little kids. I'd do it if I could choose the recipient. That happened to a friend of mine."

"What?"

"Oh she had this baby with a heart problem and there was another couple with a baby who had something wrong with her brain, like, she was a vegetable. So they gave her heart to my friend's baby. It was awesome. Their video went viral."

The thought of Harriet's heart in someone else's body causes the dense, dark clouds to close in on Irwin.

Sydney swishes wine around in her glass. "It's a bummer she has to take heavy duty drugs all her life though."

"Why does she have to take drugs?"

"To stop her body from rejecting the heart. That's the part I can't get my head around. I mean, if the recipients have to take heavy-duty drugs that make the rest of their body sick, something's weird about the whole deal."

"Which of Harriet's organs were donated?"

"I didn't ask. How did she look at the end?"

"Asleep. She had casts."

"Okay, so probably her internal organs were intact, like the liver and kidneys. They probably took all kinds of stuff out of her. They can even transplant faces and eyes now. It's pretty amazing. Look," she turns the laptop towards Irwin. "That's my friend's kid. She's nine." The child stares into the camera with an anxious smile. "Modern medicine at its finest."

The girl looks bloated and pale and has dark circles under her eyes. She has fooled death and knows she should not be alive.

Irwin hurries to the bathroom and vomits into the toilet. He returns to the kitchen because he can't be alone with visions of Harry chopped up. He saw a movie about a corporation that sold organs for hundreds of thousands of dollars. When the recipients couldn't come up with the money after ninety days, the corporation sent repo men with knives after them to cut out the organs so the corporation could sell them all over again. After the repo men cut out the organs, they dropped them into Ziploc bags. Irwin can't stop seeing Harriet's organs cut out and dropped into Ziploc bags.

Sydney turns her laptop towards him again. "What do you make of this guy?"

"He looks okay."

"He just joined LA Fitness and asked me out. He's a computer programmer. Looks nerdy but you never know what's downstairs with those guys."

"What else did my mother say?"

"About what?"

"Harriet."

"Oh, just that she never really understood her and blames herself for her death. Which is pretty self-destructive. I told her there's no reason parents should understand their children. *My* parents don't understand *me* and I'm not planning to kill myself. It's like, let go already. Your kids aren't you, and you're not always going to like them, get over it."

"She said she didn't like Harriet?"

"Not exactly, but it's pretty clear they weren't close. I mean, she's never talked about her before. Just that little girl getting killed brought it on."

"What on?"

"Her talking about Harriet."

"What else did she say?"

"Okay, this is getting a little weird. I mean, maybe you should talk to *her* about it."

"If she cried, that means she misses her."

Sydney closes her laptop. "I'm calling it a night. You should too."

He sits on her chair, warm from her ass, and tries to enter his alternate universe. Forbes says what might be preventing him from breaking through the membrane is particles of matter clinging to three-dimensional spaces. It bugs Irwin that clinging particles are stopping him from entering, or even observing, his AU—particles he can't even see and therefore can't do anything about. It's not like he can Dustbuster them.

It has always consoled him that Harriet never had to endure surgery, that her body was never violated, that she never had physiotherapists twisting her limbs till they hurt. Sometimes he'd watch her perfect body— free of scars and pain—with envy, but it always comforted him that she was whole. Now he knows she was butchered. He has never felt hatred for his mother, but now it gurgles inside him and he fears it has always been there like some kind of sleeping sea monster.

Irwin drinks the wine left in Sydney's glass even though it tastes bitter. He runs his tongue along the rim greased by her lips.

"Let my universes collide," he chants quietly because Forbes told him chanting increases focus. Chanting and breathing. *In and out, in and out. Imagine how your universe might have turned out differently.* Irwin chants and breathes but his newly woken hatred for his mother snags his attention. How can he hate her. She is all he has. Heike will grow up and away from him and he will only have Lynne, smoking and drinking and angry all the time. He can't hate her. The wine loosens particles around him and suddenly he sees Harry sitting on the counter, swinging her legs, banging her heels into the cabinets to annoy Gennedy. Irwin tries to speak to her but she vanishes.

Sydney returns and sits across from him, putting her hand on his knee. Her breasts sway under the robe, so close he could touch them.

"Have you been drinking, junior? That's not cool, my friend. Time for beddy-byes." She takes his hand and helps him to a standing position. She smells of Herbal Essences shampoo. Sometimes he washes his hair with it to smell like her. She puts her arm around his waist and guides him to his room. Her curves and folds press against him and his erection struggles inside his jeans. She leads him to the bed, sits him down and takes off his shoes. He wants to press his face into her cleavage. "Feet up," she says. He bends his knees to hide his crotch as he lifts his feet onto the bed. She pulls the comforter over him. "It's going to be all right, junior."

He stayed in his room this morning until his mother and Sydney left for work. He presses the elevator button. Mrs. Butts' cane taps towards him. "Irwin, dear, would you do something for me? It'll only take a minute." Nothing only takes a minute with Mrs. Butts, but he helps her because she talks about Harriet; what a delightful girl she was, how she would do anything for Mrs. Butts.

"I don't know what I did," she says, as he follows her into her apartment. "I must have strained something because I can't lift the litter box and it's garbage day tomorrow. Would you be a dear and empty it for me and pour in some fresh. I ordered the large bag because it's cheaper, but I had no idea it would be so heavy. They should have told me it was so heavy when I ordered it. I'm a regular customer. They should know better, they know I'm not well."

Irwin empties the litter box. Lukey winds around Mrs. Butts' legs.

"You're a bad cat, yes you are, a *bad cat*. Badsy, badsy. What have you been doing to Lindy, you devil? She's not herself. Shoo! Now, Irwin, don't spill it like last time. You have to be more careful. Don't rush. Your sister never spilled a thing. She was always very careful."

The bag is full and bulky and he spills some kitty litter on the kitchen floor. "Now look what you've done," Mrs. Butts scolds. "Didn't I warn you to be careful? What a mess. You'll have to sweep that up. I can't bend down because of my back."

Irwin takes the dustpan and broom from the closet and sweeps the floor.

Mrs. Butts points to a few granules with her cane. "Look, you missed a spot. You're always rushing, rushing. You have to take more time like your sister did. That girl was a delight. She'd do anything for me."

When Irwin can see no more kitty litter on the floor, he puts the dustpan and broom back in the closet and starts for the door.

"Now just a minute, Irwin, would you do me a favour and take a look at this drawer for me? I don't know what happened to it but it falls down when I push it in. Can you kneel down and have a look under the counter? I can't because of my back."

When he does favours for Mrs. Butts, he feels closer to Harry. He imagines her handling the same dustpan and broom, and the same kitty litter box. He pictures her standing where he is standing. But he can't imagine her fixing a drawer. "I don't know anything about drawers."

"Just kneel down and have a look. Try pushing it in and see what happens."

He pushes the drawer in and it falls down.

"Now why's it doing that? Can you see anything?" Mrs. Butts stands over him, smelling of sour milk and cough drops. "It frightens Lindy every time it does that. I think that's why she's stopped eating. Pull it out."

"What?"

"The drawer. Pull it out and tell me what's going on inside."

Lukey rubs against Irwin, breathing cat food breath on him. "I'm allergic to cats."

"It'll just take a minute."

Irwin pulls out the drawer and it crashes to the floor.

"Now look what you've done. Why are you so clumsy? Your sister never dropped a thing."

He pictures Harriet in Ziploc bags again. "I don't know anything about drawers."

"Well, why didn't you say so? Now you've broken it. I'll have to get that nasty wog up here to fix it. Why didn't you tell me you didn't know anything about drawers? What's the matter with you?"

Irwin's having trouble breathing. He's not sure if it's because of the cats or Mrs. Butts or because he's off meds, but he feels about to faint. "I'm so sorry but I've got to go."

"And leave me with this mess? I can't clean this up. I'm not well. I bruised a rib last week. The doctor says I'm not to lift a thing. I requested an X-ray."

He uses the fire stairs exit to escape. Sitting on the top step he breathes—in and out, in and out—and focuses, trying to break through the membrane to where Harriet is whole.

He never saw her body dead, only her ashes in an urn his mother keeps on her bedside table. What was left to burn after they cut her up? Maybe it's not even Harriet in the urn. The seniors talk about how you never know whose ashes you're getting. Irwin smells cigarette smoke and hears Mr. Pungartnik's transistor radio. Ever since his wife died, he has sat for hours in the stairwell, chain smoking. He lives on the ground floor and could smoke out front, but he's afraid of Mrs. Rumph and her ferret. With Mrs. Pungartnik no longer around to dye and cut his hair, it hangs in greasy white strands to his shoulders. It doesn't seem fair to Irwin that all these old people are still alive while Harriet is stitched inside strangers' bodies. She always said mean and cheap people live forever and he didn't believe her.

He stumbles down to Darcy's because he agreed to be a model for a facial. Dee attends the Elite School of Beauty and needs heads to practice on. She uses Irwin because walk-in clients at the school tend to avoid her and go with the skinny-assed fuck tarts.

"First I'm going to steam your pores," she tells him. "It'll totally relax you. You're going to love it."

She always tells Irwin he's going to love things she's about to do to him, but he never does. When she plucked his eyebrows his skin burned for a week. But Dee was Harriet's friend and sometimes she tells him things he didn't know about her, like how she scared the shit out of some ho bag at the DQ.

Darcy places a warm, moist towel over his face. Immediately he can't breathe and tries to pull it off but she grabs his wrists. "Cool it, it's not blocking your nostrils. Just breathe normally. We've got to open your pores."

Last week Dee's boyfriend called the police and said she sexually assaulted him in his hatchback. The case is under investigation. This makes Irwin more wary of her than usual. With the towel over his face he can't see what she's doing. He hears her moving around, and she frequently bumps against him. She is five-three and 173 pounds, which makes it difficult to avoid bodily contact when she's doing beauty work on him. He's never heard of a man being sexually assaulted by a woman and can't imagine how it would work. Her boyfriend, Wyck, is tall and skinny with pimples. Dee refers to him as "the stick insect" and says he was a virgin when they met and should be grateful she popped his cherry. She told the police she didn't do anything Wyck didn't want her to do. She told Irwin that the stick insect is scared to try anything different. "Like, he hasn't even heard of the *Kama Sutra*." Irwin hadn't either, but Googled it later. The positions looked uncomfortable, and he could see why Wyck didn't want to try them.

With the towel still over his face, he hears Dee opening the fridge. "Want a Diet Sprite?"

"Please."

The Korean prodigy is playing piano next door again. Everybody in the building is excited about Kwan because he wins competitions and is only six years old. His mother attaches extensions to the piano pedals so Kwan can reach them. Sometimes the extensions slip in concerts and she has to crawl in her black dress under the piano to reattach them. Darcy and Nina can't stand listening to piano 24/7 and want Kwan and his mother evicted. Mr. Hoogstra, in the apartment on the other side, thinks Kwan's terrific. "That little tiger is going to put our building on the map," he says. "Just like Glenn Gould. There's a plaque outside Glenn's childhood home. We'll get a plaque just like it out front for Kwan. Terrific!" He and some other seniors organized a tasty treat sale to raise money for Kwan's piano lessons. Mr. Hoogstra appointed Irwin captain of the baking team. This was a great honour, except that Irwin didn't know how to bake. He tried baking cupcakes and cookies, but the cupcakes came out flat and the cookies melted together. Lynne said chocolate chips and butter don't come cheap and she isn't made of money. Irwin resigned as captain of the baking team. Mr. Hoogstra put him in charge of corn roasting on the barbecue. He only burned himself three times. They raised $286 for Kwan's lessons.

Dee puts a can of Sprite in Irwin's hand. "I'm going to murder that kid."

"Can I take the towel off yet?"

Dee whips it off and tosses it aside. "Okay, Charlie Brown, I'm going to squeeze your blackheads. It's going to hurt a little."

"Why do you have to squeeze my blackheads?"

"That's what facials are for, Irwin, deep cleaning. Suck it up, buttercup."

She yanks two Kleenexes from a box and, holding one in each hand, bears down on him, pinching his skin between the tissues. "Yuk, do you ever wash your face? It's a sewer up here."

"You're hurting me."

"No pain, no gain."

Irwin, accustomed to pain, has learned to endure it by thinking of something else, like Kwan. "Don't his fingers ever get tired?"

"You should hear Mommie Dearest screaming at him if he stops. Pretty soon you'll be baking cookies to pay for his therapy."

Irwin has been to therapy. His therapist wore ropey beads and nodded frequently. She told him to imagine his mother sitting in the chair across from him. "What do you want to say to her?" Simone asked. "Say what you can't say to her in real life." Irwin didn't see the point in saying to the chair what he couldn't say to his mother, but he liked Simone. She offered him gluten-free chocolate brownies. So he talked to the chair about Harriet, which seemed to please Simone because she kept nodding, fingering her ropey beads. During another session she showed him a broken chair and asked him how he thought the broken chair felt. When he said the broken chair probably felt sad, Simone nodded and said, "It's okay to feel sad." He saw her once a week for several months until Lynne, who was working two jobs to pay for it, said, "You're not getting any better." Irwin wasn't sure what she meant by this. He had stopped pulling out his hair and scratching his arms. And he stood up to Lynne when she wrongly accused him of making mistakes. "Did Simone put you up to this?" she'd demand. "Did she tell you to stand up to me? Is that what I'm paying her to do, make my son insolent? She's not even a real therapist, for god's sake, doesn't have a Ph.D. or anything."

"Then why did you send me to her?"

"Because of Theo. Theo's nuts about her."

"I like her too."

"You're not supposed to like your therapist."

Simone phoned Lynne repeatedly to arrange a private meeting, but Lynne was too busy working two jobs. When they finally met, Lynne came home and sat on the couch without taking her coat off. She stared morosely at the aquarium Irwin had forgotten to clean even though it was on the to-do list. Gennedy bought him two goldfish after Harriet died because Irwin was allergic to anything with dander. After Lynne's meeting with Simone, Irwin waited for his mother to ask if he'd cleaned the aquarium. When she didn't say anything, he sat on the couch beside her. They both stared at the aquarium. Betty and Bob—these were the only names he could think of when he was six—hardly moved and Irwin worried they were dying because he'd forgotten to clean the tank. Finally his mother said, "I want you to get better, but I don't want to be blamed."

"I don't blame you for anything."

She hugged him hard, squashing his nose into her down coat. It smelled of chicken. "I love you so much, my sweet boy. And I'm so, so sorry." He didn't know what she was so sorry for but didn't ask for fear of upsetting her. Now he knows she was sorry for chopping up Harriet, dropping her in Ziploc bags and letting doctors stitch her into any old peasant.

Dee squeezes more blackheads on his forehead. "Did you hear about the woman who won the forty million?"

"No."

"She's fat and fifty, been working at some shit job for, like, forever. Now she's taking her dream honeymoon in Hawaii with her deadbeat husband. If I were her, I'd dump him, get the fat sucked off me plus a face job, and welcome some new boys into the yard."

Irwin can't visualize the number forty million. He has always had trouble adding the right number of zeros. "How do you know her husband is a deadbeat?"

"Ninety-nine percent of husbands are deadbeats."

Darcy is furious with Buck because he married again and has two skinny-assed kids and never takes Dee out unless it's to his daughter's dance recitals. He tells Dee he wants them to be one happy family. Dee doesn't want a family. She wants her dad.

"What would *you* do with the forty million?" Irwin asks.

"Dip outta here."

"Where would you go?"

Dee pushes his head back to squeeze the blackheads on his nose, cramping his neck. "California. I'd drink Tequila Sunrises on the beach and enjoy the surfer boys." Irwin tries to scratch his nose but Dee slaps his hand away.

Kwan is playing a piece full of yearning and melancholy.

"Was Harriet sad?" Irwin asks.

"What do you mean 'sad'?"

"Sad. Was she sad?"

"Hell's bells, she was pissed off."

"Why?"

"Because people are sacks of shit."

"Not all people."

"You go, Charlie Brown, keep the dream alive. I'm going to do a cleanse now. You'll love it. Close your eyes." Irwin obeys as she sponges his face. Kwan's music rolls over and under him. He can't bring himself to tell Dee that Harriet was cut to pieces. Keeping quiet about it makes it less real.

"What people did Harry think were sacks of shit?" he asks.

"Most people."

"Me?"

"Not you."

"Who then?"

"She hated your mother's boyfriend."

"Why? He was really nice."

"To you, Chuck, not to H. He hit her for fucksake."

"Just once."

"Once is enough."

Irwin opens his eyes. "Did she hate my mother?"

"Close your eyes or you're going to get soap in them."

Irwin closes his eyes. "Did she hate my mom?"

"Nah. But she was mad at her."

"Why?"

"Oh come on, what am I, a shrink? Lots of girls are pissed with their mothers. It goes with the territory."

Irwin opens his eyes again. "Do *you* think she killed herself?"

"I don't want to talk about this shit. It's none of my business."

"It *is* your business. She was your best friend." He sits up and pushes her hands away. Simone always told him to look directly at people when he wants direct answers. He looks directly at Dee but she averts her eyes, rinsing the sponge. "I won't be your model anymore," he threatens, "unless you tell me if you think she killed herself."

"What's it matter, Chuck, it's over."

"It matters to me."

Dee grabs some Kleenexes and he's afraid she's going to start squeezing his blackheads again but she wipes her eyes.

"Are you crying?"

"It's the soap." She blows her nose.

"*Do* you think she killed herself?"

The redness in Dee's eyes makes the irises look a darker blue, almost like the sky in Harriet's painting of a tree with a scarred body for a trunk.

"You think she killed herself," Irwin says.

"No, I don't. I think she thought she could fly."

Kwan stops playing and his mother shouts at him in Korean. Irwin pictures Harry trying to fly, stretching out her arms and flapping them. He never saw her broken body on the ground. They wouldn't let him see her. "Maybe she did fly," he says.

Twenty-two

Irwin takes Heike to the pool to stake out the suspect who exposed himself to the little girl. Heike has a hunch he'll be there because he wasn't at the 7-Eleven. They hung around the parking lot for over an hour watching for a man between five-foot-six and five-foot-ten with spiky hair and a big nose.

"What happened to your face?" Heike asked.

"Dee gave me a facial."

"You look like you got stung by a jellyfish." She pulled out her binoculars and surveyed the street.

"See anything?"

"False alarm," she said, carefully printing notes in her notebook.

At the pool she insists they play Shark to give her an excuse to practice underwater surveillance wearing goggles. Before she submerges, he asks, "How are you going to recognize the suspect underwater?"

"Use your imagination, big brother." She always says this when he questions her investigative techniques.

Playing Shark requires Irwin to get his hair wet. This makes his head and ears look even bigger. The scars on his scalp and torso frighten children.

They run to their mothers and whisper in their ears. The mothers stare briefly at Irwin before looking away. They try to interest their children in juice boxes or Fruit Roll-Ups, but nothing is more interesting than Irwin soaking wet in swimming trunks. Heike calls him Exhibit A and says he shouldn't pay any attention to the spares who stare. She calls many people spares, and he doesn't really understand why. "What a spare," she'll remark about someone. He thinks it has to do with the person being just like everybody else, easily replaced, like a spare tire. Heike prefers people with sass. He feels her monkey grip on his ankle just before she pops to the surface. "Bro, you're not even *trying* to get away."

"Sorry. I forgot."

"Swim for your life," she commands, diving below again. Irwin goes under and swims as fast as he can but nowhere near as fast as Heike. Uma delivered her in a birthing pool and took her to swimming lessons when she was nine months old. Heike swims like a fish and can stay submerged longer than anyone. She grabs his ankle again and pops up. "You're not even *trying*."

"I'm tired."

"It's because you're off meds."

"I'm not."

"Yes you are. I've been keeping notes. You're tired all the time and hardly drinking anything and you're not rubbing your eyes. On meds you're always thirsty and your eyes are itchy and you're not tired all the time."

"I'm on different meds."

"Likely story."

"Why do you say that? Your mother says that. It's rude." He can't read her expression behind the foggy goggles.

"Suspect at five o'clock," she says. He wishes she'd just point. He closes his eyes, trying to picture a clock, then looks where the five should be, at a man with spiky hair slathering sunscreen onto his girlfriend's back.

"He doesn't have a big nose," Irwin says.

"Are you kidding me? That's a honker." Heike swims underwater towards the couple and pops up poolside. This kind of behaviour makes Irwin nervous. He clings to the side of the pool, watching her operate. Within seconds she is chatting energetically with them. The woman giggles while adjusting the strings on her bikini top. The man puts on wraparound sunglasses. The woman starts rubbing sunscreen onto his back. The whole time Heike is gabbing away, but Irwin can't hear a word because of the splashing and shrieking going on around him. He's too tired to swim over there, besides, he might sink. It's happened before. He just suddenly forgets how to swim. He used to enjoy going to the pool with Gennedy because Gennedy would rescue him if he sank. Irwin jumped off the board once when Conner and Taylor told him he was a chickenshit scaredy-ass. Mindy had slapped their heads and told them to leave Irwin alone but they wouldn't. So Irwin jumped and sank down and down into the forgiving coolness, forgetting what to do with his arms and legs. It was wonderfully silent, and when he looked up the sun sparkled in the turquoise water. He wanted to stay at the bottom of the pool where no one could stare at him, but Gennedy wrapped an arm around him and hauled him to the surface. Irwin expected him to be mad but Gennedy said, "Way to go, champ. That took guts." Gennedy badly wanted Irwin to have guts, and Irwin hated disappointing him. Gennedy volunteered as a baseball coach so Irwin could play. The speeding ball terrified Irwin. Gennedy put him in centre field, where the ball rarely went. The one time it looped down from the sky at him, Irwin held out his glove and miraculously the ball dropped into it. A second later it plopped onto the ground. Gennedy said, "What the fuck did you think you were doing out there?"

Irwin rubs his eyes, itchy from the chlorine. When he opens them, Heike and the man in wraparound sunglasses are nowhere in sight. The bikinied woman lies face down on a towel. Still clinging to the side of the pool, Irwin feels he can't possibly pull himself out or swim. All the activity around him causes unpredictable currents that resist him. He uses his arms to drag himself along the edge to the ladder but two old ladies, discussing arthritis, are hanging off it. "Excuse me," Irwin says. "I need to get by."

"Where's your manners?" the one wearing a flowery bathing cap demands.

The other old lady climbs on the ladder and holds out her lumpy knee. "See, it's less swollen. Don't you think it's less swollen?"

Irwin tries to dog paddle across the pool to the other ladder but gets bumped by swimmers. A foot hits him in the face, a hand jabs him, a head butts him and he forgets how to swim. He sinks down and down until he sees Harriet hanging on to a purple noodle. She's wearing her green bathing suit with the white stripe down the side. He tries to swim over to her and grab her ankle but she keeps flutter kicking, moving farther away from him. He desperately wants her to join him at the bottom of the pool where it's quiet and safe from stares. He opens his mouth to call out to her.

Heike is practising handstands in the shallow end. "Did you almost drown so the lifeguard would kiss you?" She has ordered Irwin to sit at the edge of the pool and watch to see if her legs are straight. "Did you?"

"What?"

"Fake drowning so the lifeguard would kiss you? She's booby-liscious."

"Where did you get that word?"

"I made it up. Watch this. Are you watching?" She does another handstand. "How was that?"

"You're supposed to keep your feet together."

"They were."

"They weren't. Don't ask me to watch if you don't believe me."

"I bet you faked being unconscious so she'd French you."

"That's not Frenching, that's CPR."

"Yeah, you keep telling yourself that, big brother."

It bugs him that Heike's figured out he let the resuscitation go on longer than necessary. He'd been in awe of the caramel-tanned lifeguard for weeks. She had smooth legs that hung down from her perch. Pink flip-flops dangled from her delicate feet. She painted her toenails pink and wore a silver ankle bracelet with a pink heart on it. When she leaned over to save his life, her breasts nudged his chest and her mouth tasted of Juicy Fruit gum. She looked surprised when he opened his eyes, and he suspected he was her first official rescue. He wished he'd been conscious when she pulled him out of the water. He imagined the feel of her breasts against his back. "You shouldn't swim across the pool when it's busy," she scolded. "Length ways only."

"I'm really sorry. Have you seen my little sister?"

"Here." Heike landed like a frog beside him.

"Can you sit up?" the lifeguard asked him. She put a hand behind his neck to help him sit up. "Do you think you'll be all right now?"

"For sure." He knew she found him repulsive and would never get this close to him under normal circumstances.

"It's your call," she said. "But stay out of the water."

Heike hands Irwin her waterproof camera. "Take a picture of my legs if they're straight." She does another handstand and pops up. "How was that?"

"Too fast. You've got to keep your feet up longer. And point your toes."

"Got it, I'm going to nail it this time, bro. Get ready."

He holds up the camera. She dives under and he takes the shot even though her legs aren't perfectly straight.

"Were they straight?"

"Close enough."

She takes the camera and looks at the photo. "They're not straight at all."

"Where did you go with that guy?"

"What guy?"

"The suspect."

"He's not a suspect anymore."

"Why not?"

"I questioned him. He's got an alibi."

"You can't just go off with strangers."

"I didn't just go off."

"I couldn't see you."

"That's because you were fake drowning. He was really nice. He gave me some gum."

"You took candy from a stranger?"

"He's no stranger. His name's Bertie. He can make fart noises with his armpits."

"You can't just start talking to anybody. I'll tell your mother."

"You just try that, big brother. Quit being so drippy. I'm going to play Marco Polo." She joins in with other kids splashing around. A boy with a buzz cut closes his eyes and shouts, "Marco!" and the other kids shout, "Polo!" The boy has to catch the other kids with his eyes closed. To tag them he must follow their voices. Unlike Harriet, Heike has no problem making friends and easily participates in what Harriet would consider dumbass games. Irwin knows that Heike thinks many of her peers are spares, but she makes them like her anyway. This is why she is going to be prime minister.

Irwin can't stop looking for surgical scars on people's bodies. If someone has a scar on their chest, Harriet's heart might be pounding inside them. If it's on their lower back, it could be her liver or one of her kidneys. He's not sure where they cut to transplant lungs. All the people around the pool have become just organs to him. Without skin, everybody looks the same. Even Heike, who's shouting "Marco!," would look like everybody else without her skin. Only Irwin, with his enlarged skull, would stand out. This doesn't comfort him.

In the lobby, playing euchre with Mr. Chubak and Mr. Quigley, Mr. Shotlander's talking about his dead wife's diamond ring, how it got nicked when she was bone thin from cancer. "We were just standing there in some dang piazza and a greaseball speeds by on a scooter and whips off her ring. How do you like that? There's Italy for you."

Mr. Chubak peels an orange. "You got to hide your valuables when you travel. I keep my cash in my socks."

Mr. Quigley gulps Gatorade. "Don't talk to me about travel." He just returned from his son's place in Minnesota. His titanium knee set off the metal detector again. "Those bastards had me down to my underwear and up against the wall."

"This never happened in the days before 9/11," Mr. Shotlander said. He notices Heike. "Hey, Harry, where've you been? I'm way down on chips."

"I'm not Harry." The only time Heike seems uneasy is when Mr. Shotlander mistakes her for Harriet.

"That's Irwin's *little* sister," Mr. Chubak says loudly into Mr. Shotlander's good ear. "Heike. You remember her."

"That's right," Mr. Shotlander says, looking like he doesn't. "What kind of name is that anyway? Kraut?" He has been more confused lately and won't stop adjusting the thermostat in his apartment even though Irwin has explained that it's summer and the heat is turned off.

In the elevator, Heike plays with the zipper on her backpack. "What's Kraut mean?"

"German." Irwin checks her swimming bag to make sure she packed her goggles and camera.

"Kraut doesn't sound very nice."

"He didn't mean anything by it. He's old and a little mixed up."

Heike sighs heavily. "I wish I was born before 9/11."

"Me too. Things were way nicer back then."

"There weren't any terrorists."

"Oh I think there were, just not as many. I mean, there were wars and stuff, war's like terrorism."

"I guess." Heike splits her granola bar and gives Irwin half. "Mummy says before 9/11 you used to be allowed to keep your clothes and shoes on when you went through security, and it took, like, three seconds. Mummy says everybody's a suspect these days."

Irwin takes Heike's hand when they get to Forbes' floor. "Mr. Shotlander says nobody trusts anybody anymore. He says trust went out the window with the twentieth century."

They find Forbes hunched over his laptop as usual. He offers them the cranberry juice he drinks frequently to prevent bladder infections.

"Forbesy," Heike asks, "what would you do if you knew the world was going to end *tomorrow*?" She often asks people this question and they never look comfortable answering.

"I'd stop worrying about being regular," Forbes says.

"Why do you worry about being regular? Who wants to be regular? I'd spend *all* my birthday money. Doing fun stuff Mummy won't let me do. We'd go to Canada's Wonderland, wouldn't we, Irwin. Irwin's not allowed to go because of his condition."

Heike convinces Forbes to practise baseball in the parking lot.

"Pitch it for real this time," she commands, swinging the bat. Forbes pitches underhand again. "That's a girly pitch, mister."

"That's because you're a girl."

"Overhand is dangerous, Heike," Irwin cautions.

"*Life* is dangerous. Don't mess, Forbes, I'm serious. Show me your fastball. I'll totally kick your ass."

"You're too little for a fastball."

"Try me."

Forbes wheels his chair farther back and pitches for real but slowly. Heike hits the ball across the parking lot. "I killed it!" She scampers after it.

Taj, the janitor, pushes open the back door. "No ball playing here. You hit a car or window, you pay."

"He's got a point," Forbes says.

"Boo hiss." Heike tosses the ball straight up in the air and catches it with one hand. Irwin could never do this.

They sit out front where Mrs. Rumph's new ferret is climbing all over her. Every time one dies she buys another one. Dee thinks she gets off on ferret contact "because human contact ain't going to happen."

Forbes offers them beef jerky. Irwin takes one but Heike says, "Meat is murder."

Irwin stares up at bruised clouds. He started a not-to-do list this morning, and one of the things listed was not to tell Heike about Harriet being chopped up. But because he can't stop thinking about it, it's hard not to mention it. Harry's blood drips in his mind. Last week Heike made him watch a documentary about a real crime scene with real blood in it. He had to keep reminding himself the police footage was real. The real blood on the floor looked exactly like the fake blood in movies.

"I'm going to play with Toodles," Heike says. She is the only one who talks to Mrs. Rumph, and the only one who wants to play with her ferrets. For this reason Mrs. Rumph is always delighted to see her. She has a squeaky voice and often says, "Oh my," to Heike.

Forbes nudges Irwin. "What's your damage, son?"

"What do you mean?"

"Something's eating you."

"Not really."

"If you say so."

Heike lets Toodles crawl all over her. Mrs. Rumph squeaks, "Oh my."

"Do you believe in organ donation?" Irwin asks.

Forbes bites his beef jerky. "If I needed an organ I would."

"My mother donated my sister's organs."

"Okay." Forbes often says okay when bombs are dropped. Heike pointed this out to Irwin. "It's like he's stalling to think about it," she explained.

Forbes scratches an eyebrow with his thumb. "So, you just found this out?"

Irwin nods, looking down at ants on the concrete. He crumbles beef jerky for them. They clamp their jaws around tiny pieces and march off in different directions.

"Who told you? Your mom?"

"She didn't tell *me*. She told Sydney."

"Which means your mom doesn't want you to know."

"I don't care what she wants. She cut up my sister." His drug-free despair bulks up in his gut and he's afraid he's going to vomit again.

"Okay," Forbes says. "Let's think this through. She didn't cut her up. She was already dead."

"No she wasn't. She was on a vent."

"Irwin, they don't take them off vents unless they're brain-dead. She wasn't Harry anymore."

"She was too. I saw her. She was asleep. She might have woken up."

"That doesn't happen, son. Only in the movies. And they're very careful when they harvest the organs. They stitch the body back together again so it looks normal and the family can see it."

"*I* didn't see it."

"I guess your mom thought it might upset you."

"I was upset anyway. One day she was there and then she wasn't. I never saw her. Just the urn, and she's not even in the urn. Just her skin and bones. She could be anybody."

Heike skips back and digs in her backpack for sidewalk chalk. "Time for hopscotch, boys. Whoever loses buys freezies."

"Don't step on the ants," Irwin says, pointing at them.

Heike looks down at the ants transporting the beef jerky. "Sick! Ants rock. They are, like, so organized. Way more than humans. Do you want to hear my ant joke?"

"Do we have a choice?" Forbes asks.

"It's really funny. There's these two guys on a plane and one of them's really scared of flying so he closes his eyes for, like, ten minutes or something. And when he opens them, he looks out the window and says, 'Gee, that was a really smooth takeoff. Look at the people. They look like ants.' The other guy says, 'That's because they *are* ants. We haven't taken off yet.' Isn't that hilarious?"

"Hilarious." Forbes chews beef jerky. Heike begins meticulously chalking a hopscotch grid. Irwin sees Buck pulling up in his SUV with his two kids, presumably to pick up Dee. She hates going out with them because they make fat jokes behind her back. Alyssa not only performs in dance recitals but is on a gymnastics team. According to Dee, Alyssa is an eating disorder waiting to happen. Dylan is five and into monster trucks. Buck drove him to Hamilton to watch a monster truck show. They stayed at the Sheraton and swam in the pool. Dee says Buck never drove her anywhere but Canada's Wonderland.

Since Harriet fell, Buck hasn't been very friendly with Irwin, or Lynne, and never let Irwin sit on his lap and steer his truck again. Years ago, if Irwin saw Buck's cab in the parking lot, he'd linger, hoping Buck would invite him up. But he never did. He'd give him a thumbs-up through the closed window.

Heike claps her hands. "Okay, team. Hop to it."

"I'm not feeling very well," Irwin mutters.

"It's because you're off meds."

"Who says he's off meds?" Forbes knows Irwin has been trying to keep it a secret.

"I can tell," Heike says. "I've been keeping notes. He's never thirsty and his eyeballs don't itch and he's drippy all the time."

"I am not drippy all the time. Just today."

"So why are you drippy today, big brother?"

"Do we always need a reason to be drippy?" Forbes asks. "I feel drippy for no particular reason on no particular day. Okay," he levers himself off the chair, "I'm ready." He's good at hopscotch if his leg isn't acting up. Irwin offers his shoulder to lean on as Forbes hops over to the game.

Buck's skinny-assed children refuse to get out of the SUV. "Come on, guys," Buck pleads, "we're all family here."

Irwin stays close to Forbes in case he loses his balance. Heike hands Forbes her lucky pebble to throw. It lands on four. He hops awkwardly, with his bad leg dragging behind him.

"Way to go, Forbesy," Heike cheers. "You are one cool customer." Forbes turns around, leaning on Irwin, and starts to hop back. From his heavy breathing, Irwin can tell he's exhausted. Heike bounces on the souls of her feet. "You're killing it, dude!"

"Get the chair," Irwin tells her.

Dee comes out of the building and starts arguing with Buck.

"Heike, get the chair."

"I've got this," Forbes says. "No worries. I'm all right."

"No you're not." Irwin steadies him. Heike spins the chair around and Irwin eases Forbes into it. He slumps and drops his head into his chest the way he does when he doesn't think he can endure being an incomplete paraplegic anymore.

Heike pats his shoulder. "You did great."

"I forgot to pick up the lucky pebble."

"Who cares, you got exercise. And you balanced. That was super duper awesome!"

"Let him rest, Heike," Irwin says.

"I hate resting." Forbes stares at his legs. "I rot when I rest."

Dee is getting loud. In the SUV behind Buck, Alyssa and Dylan make pig faces at her. "You think you can just show up whenever you feel like it and I'll jump?" Darcy demands.

"Dee, honey, I just want us to be one happy family."

"We can't be one happy family, you dick. Wake up. Your fucking kids hate me and I fucking hate them." She sticks her tongue out at the kids. When Buck turns to look at them, Alyssa and Derek stop making faces.

"They're your blood, Dee."

"I don't give a fuck about blood. The best thing about having no family is I don't have to hang out with sacks of shit just because we're related." She holds out her hand. "I need cash. I'm out of beauty supplies."

Buck reaches into his pocket, pulls out some bills and hands them to her. "Please, Dee, just come out with us for a bite. We'll go wherever you want. How 'bout the DQ?"

"Not in this lifetime."

Heike skips up to Buck and pokes him. "Don't you get it? She wants to be with just you, silly. Not them."

"Heike," Irwin cautions.

"Hey Irwin," Buck says. "Didn't see you there. How you doin'?"

"I'm doin'."

"You should take her someplace nice," Heike persists. "Like Canada's Wonderland."

"She's too old for Canada's Wonderland."

"She is not. She just doesn't go because you always take *them*. And they keep making faces at her. They're mean. I wouldn't go anywhere with them either."

"Glad we got that cleared up." Buck fiddles with his car keys, staring at Heike. "You look just like your sister."

"My sister's dead."

"She was an amazing girl."

Irwin grabs Heike's hand and tries to pull her back to Forbes, but she won't budge. "Dee, wouldn't you like to go someplace nice with just your dad?"

"Heike," Irwin says, "it's none of your business."

Dee takes her other hand. "Come on, H, let's go get freezies."

"*Our* dad had two wives," Heike says, "and three kids and it's a disaster." Uma often describes things as disasters. Irwin and Dee pull Heike towards Mr. Hung's. "A *disaster*," she repeats.

"I've got your back," Dee assures Irwin. "I can handle this. Go make sure Forbes is okay."

He is not okay. His good leg is in spasm and, from his contorted face, Irwin can tell his paralyzed leg is burning with phantom pain. Forbes stares at both legs as if they don't belong to him. "Fucking useless pieces of shit."

"You shouldn't do everything Heike tells you to do."

"Nobody tells me to do anything, Irwin. That's the problem. Nobody expects anything from me. She gets me off my ass, thinks I can do shit not even *I* think I can do. And doing it makes me feel like I'm not totally useless. I tell you what, when she makes me the first incomplete minister of foreign affairs, I'll let you fly around in my government jet." He pulls his water bottle from the backpack slung over the wheelchair and drinks. Mrs. Rumph waves excitedly at Clayton, who drives up in his beat-up Sunfire. He's a pizza delivery man and brings leftovers to his mother. He ignores Irwin and Forbes as he gets out of the car and slouches over to Mrs. Rumph with a pizza box. "Oh my," she squeaks.

When Buck drives off in the SUV, Alyssa flips Irwin the bird.

Forbes grips his twitching leg. "Wheel me over to the tree, son. I could use some shade."

It's not much of a tree. The city cut down the huge silver maple and replaced it with what Lynne calls a twig. She was home when the forestry men got out their chainsaws. She raced downstairs to stop them but they told her an inspector said the maple was diseased and needed to be cut down. "It doesn't look sick to me," Lynne protested. They turned on their chainsaws anyway. Lynne stayed in her room that night. Irwin asked Gennedy why she was so upset about the tree.

"It was your sister's tree," Gennedy said. "When they first moved here she drew it all the time. She lay on the ground under it and drew it. Your mother sat and watched her. She says after the divorce it was the only time Harriet seemed happy."

Irwin wheels Forbes across the patchy grass to the twig and tries to lean against it but it bends.

"Okay," Forbes says, "do you want to meet any of her organ recipients?"

"What? No way. That's creepy."

"I don't see what's creepy about it. Relations of donors meet up with recipients all the time. Facebook makes it easy."

Irwin's body tightens and he feels like he might explode. "I don't want to do that."

"Okay, son, I get it, take it easy. Nuff said." He offers Irwin his water bottle.

"Thanks." Nobody shares their water bottle with Irwin except Heike.

"How's the withdrawal going?"

"I still get dizzy and stuff."

"Any suicidal thoughts?"

Irwin hands the bottle back. "Not really." He can't admit that suicidal thoughts continually lie in wait, ready to ambush.

"You come see me if your mind goes that way, any time of the night or day. Understood?" Forbes empties his water bottle over his twitching leg and strokes it as though it's an animal that needs quieting. "There were these Russian ice dancers back in the nineties who kept winning gold medals. A husband and wife team, poetry on ice. Anyway, one night they're performing and he lifts her up but doesn't hold her in the air as long as usual. The commentators can't figure it out—he hasn't slipped, doesn't look injured, but he slows down, stops, and carefully sets her down on the ice. Two seconds later he collapses and dies from a bum ticker. An Olympic athlete. They had a little kid. Imagine that, Daddy goes off to ice dance with Mommy and dies. That's what I call tragic."

"If he died right there on the ice, he couldn't have got a transplant."

"No, but if he could have been saved, and I'd been brain-dead on a vent, I would have wanted to give him my heart."

"Harry wasn't brain-dead."

"She was, son, or they wouldn't have taken her off."

"Shut up about it. I don't want to talk about it."

Heike skips up with freezies. "Shut up about what?"

"I get grape," Forbes says.

"I know that, Forbesy. I remembered everybody's favourite flavour." She distributes the freezies.

"We should get you home, Heike," Irwin says.

"No way, José. I'm going to get Clayton to skip with me." She pulls her skipping rope out of her backpack and skips over to the pizza-eating Rumphs. Within seconds she has tied one end of the rope to Mrs. Rumph's lawn chair and handed the other end to Clayton who turns it for her.

"How does she get the mutant to do that?" Dee asks. "The guy's a total psychopath."

Irwin shrugs. "She can get anyone to do anything."

"Which is why she's going to be prime minister," Forbes says.

Half a block from Uma's house Heike pulls out her binoculars. "Holy smokes. It's the dorky guy from Starbucks."

"Where?"

"He's moving the rocks around. Mummy's not happy with the way the landscaper arranged them. She says it's a disaster." Heike continues to look through the binoculars. "The guy's a total spare. Gotta get rid of him."

"You can't just get rid of people."

"Watch me."

Irwin picks up the pink scooter. "Come on, we're late." Another thing on his not-to-do list is to let Heike boss him around.

"There you are, honeybun. I was starting to worry. I've been calling and calling."

"We were on the subway," Heike lies.

"You can't have been on the subway for an hour and a half. Honeybun, you have to start answering your phone. What if it was an emergency?"

"Who's this?" Heike says.

"My friend Donald. He's been helping me with the garden."

"That's no garden," Heike says. "That's a rock pile."

Donald adjusts his glasses on his nose made sweaty from all the rock arranging. Uma looks at him and smiles. She so rarely smiles Irwin almost doesn't recognize her. "My daughter and I have a difference of opinion regarding the landscaping."

"I gathered that," Donald says.

"Gathered what?" Heike says. "Rocks? What do *you* think about it, Donald? This is supposed to be a yard to play in. Would you want to play in it?"

"Good for climbing. It's fun to climb on rocks." Donald shrugs slightly when he says *fun*. Heike stares at him and Irwin knows she's thinking he's a total spare.

"Okay, enough chit-chat." Uma flaps her hands the way she does after using her laptop. "Let's have some stir-fry. It's ready."

"I promised Irwin he could stay for dinner." Heike didn't promise him anything, and he doesn't want to stay for dinner. "Please, Mummy? His mum's doing bookkeeping. He needs a healthy meal."

"I've got to get home." Irwin notices Donald trying not to stare at his head.

"No you don't," Heike insists. "There's nobody there except the boarder and she'll be getting liquored up anyway. Mummy, do you know what a Kraut is?"

"Where did you hear that? Where are you taking her, Irwin?"

"Just around the Shangrila. It's the seniors. She hears them talking."

"Mr. Shotlander always thinks I'm Harriet." Heike climbs on a rock and jumps off it.

"Who's Harriet?" Donald asks, tucking his white shirt—dirtied by grey rocks—into his trousers.

"Harriet's my big sister who fell off a balcony and died," Heike explains.

"Oh." Donald takes a step back as though she's spit at him. "I'm so sorry."

"Don't be. It's not your fault."

"Okay, everyone," Uma says cheerfully, as though a sister's death hasn't been mentioned. "Time to wash your hands."

They file into the house. While the others use the washroom, Irwin waits in the living room with the ghosts. He doesn't sit on the mahogany furniture. He tried that once and felt the Germans' hostility. After Harriet fell, Mr. Rivera felt ghost hostility. People in the corridor outside his apartment heard him begging the ghosts to leave him alone. "Have mercy," he would say in English, but often he'd plead in Tagalog. He shrieked as they chased him around the apartment. Finally his sons came and took him away.

"Irwin?" Uma calls. "Did you wash your hands?"

"Will do."

They sit on stools around the granite island. Donald looks as unenthusiastic about the stir-fry as Irwin.

"I used kale," Uma says. "Fresh from the farmers' market, packed with vitamin A and calcium."

The cubes of tofu are hard to swallow, but Irwin eats them to be polite.

Heike keeps an eye on Donald. "So what's your dash, Donald?"

"Excuse me?"

"She means the dash between your birth date and death date," Irwin explains. "On your gravestone."

"Oh. Interesting. Umm, I've never really thought about it."

"You should," Heike says. "*Everybody* should. Everybody should have a purpose."

"What's yours?" Donald tries to fit a kale leaf into his mouth.

"I'm going to make sure everybody in the entire world has clean drinking water and composting toilets."

"Oh. Very nice."

Uma smiles her unrecognizable smile. "Heike's always been a bit of a humanitarian."

Donald shrugs slightly again. "It's a dirty job but somebody's gotta do it."

Heike sprinkles soy sauce on her stir-fry. "Donald, do you know about flying toilets?"

"Should I?"

"People in Africa poop in plastic bags and throw them into the streets."

"Heike," Uma says, "is this suitable dinner conversation?"

"What's suitable? Donald doesn't know about flying toilets. *Everybody* should know. It's atrocious." This is another word Uma uses. "In India they have hanging toilets. That's where they dig a hole and people have to poop in it."

"Donald," Uma intervenes, "is a financial analyst. He knows all about economies all over the world. You might want him on your team, honeybun, as a consultant."

"My dad has a consulting business and it's a disaster."

"Oh. Really?" Donald adjusts his glasses on his nose. "What kind of consulting?"

"IT," Uma says. "He used to work for a bank but then went freelance."

"Freelance is tough," Donald concedes.

"Not as tough as shitting in a plastic bag."

"Okay, Heike, that's enough."

"Enough of what? Real life? Are you a climate change denier, Donald?"

Donald shrugs. "I don't know enough about the science to have an opinion one way or the other."

"Mr. Shotlander says fence sitters get 'rrhoids."

Irwin wishes he could talk boldly like Heike. He's so tired of being a loser and feeling that lives are something other people have. He's so tired of chronic pain and anxiety, and not wanting to get up in the morning because he'll only have more chronic pain and anxiety. He forgot to clean the aquarium again. It was underlined on Lynne's to-do list.

"Let me ask you something, Donald," Heike says. "When you analyze finances, do you ever notice that the billionaires are the climate change deniers? Not the people shitting in bags and holes."

Uma puts her fork down. "Am I going to have to give you a time out, Heike?"

"Well, what do *you* want to talk about, Mother?" Heike shoves greens into her mouth.

"Well, why don't you tell us about your day? What did you do in camp?"

"We played capture the flag and had a singalong with a total spare. She was holding a monkey puppet and pretending it was singing. It was totally lame."

"Then we went swimming," Irwin says to point out they did more than hang around the Shangrila hearing words like *Kraut*.

"And Irwin almost drowned so the booby-liscious lifeguard would rescue him."

"Then we had freezies and played Hopscotch."

"It was sick," Heike says. "I *love* Irwin. He's the best big brother ever." She jumps off her stool to kiss him on the cheek and suddenly, fleetingly, he feels he has a life.

Twenty-three

Irwin checks to make sure Forbes is all right. He's lying on his couch smoking a fatty with his laptop balanced on his stomach.

"Is your leg hurting really badly?" Irwin asks because Forbes is only supposed to smoke marijuana when the pain is intolerable.

"Come here, son. Pull up a chair. I want to show you something."

Irwin sits on the footstool Forbes uses for his bad leg.

"Check this out." Forbes scrolls through photos of people Irwin doesn't recognize.

"Are they your friends?"

"Nope. What do you think they all have in common?"

"Are they part of a fandom?"

"Kind of. They all look like normal people, right?"

"Sure."

"Every one of them is an organ recipient."

Irwin stands up so fast he knocks over the stool. "Gross, I don't want to look at that."

Forbes enlarges an image of a young freckled woman with curly red hair wearing nerd glasses. "She's had a lung transplant. She was born with cystic fibrosis and was supposed to die. But then someone gave her their lungs and she didn't. Do you want to watch her video?"

"No way. That's freaky."

"It's not freaky at all. She talks about how tough it is to know someone had to die for her to live."

"I don't care."

"The point is *two* people could have died. Her as well the donor. This way only one person had to die. Your brave sis saved a life, son."

"I'm going home."

Forbes closes the laptop. "Not till you have some ice cream. Chocolate chip, your fave. Go help yourself."

Irwin could use some ice cream after Uma's stir-fry. Heike tried to stop him from leaving before dessert. Uma cut up something she called dragon fruit that had spotty white insides and green skin with tentacles. She told them it was delicious with goat yogourt from the farmers' market. Donald, looking worried, adjusted the glasses on his nose. Irwin, having managed to swallow tofu and kale, excused himself, kissed the top of Heike's head and said he'd see her tomorrow.

He heaps a generous serving of chocolate chip ice cream into his bowl. Lynne never buys ice cream anymore because she says it makes him fat. When he was little she let him eat bowls of it to put weight on. Now that the hormones have hit, she wants him to take weight off.

He sits on the footstool with his ice cream. "Do you think I'm overweight?"

"No way, dude. You need a little extra padding for emergencies." Forbes pinches the fat around his own middle. He is talking louder, which means he's getting stoned.

"I think I might have broken through the membrane," Irwin says.

"No shit. What'd you see?"

"Harriet. She was sitting on the kitchen counter, and then she was in the pool when I was swimming."

"Slick."

"I might have imagined her."

"Was she active?"

"What do you mean 'active'?"

"Was she doing something or was it like a snapshot?"

"She was swinging her legs the way she did to annoy Gennedy. And then she was swimming with her noodle."

"You're on your way, man. Congrats." Forbes inhales on the spliff and holds the smoke in his lungs.

"Do you mean, for it to be real, she has to be doing something?"

Smoke drifts from Forbes nostrils. "Yep. Like it's not freeze-frame, you know what I'm saying? Freeze-frame's like a flash, right. Like a memory flash. Next you got to get in there and interact with her."

"That would be amazing." Irwin sucks on a chocolate chip.

"It'll happen, man. Just keep working on your focus." Forbes saying "man" frequently indicates he's getting really stoned. "I was just in my AU as a matter of fact. With a hot chick. She was hairy all over, which you'd think would be a turnoff but she was so ripe, you know what I'm saying, like, she wanted me *so* bad the hairiness didn't matter. It was kind of exciting because I couldn't see what she looked like under all that hair. I had to move my hands all over her, like, really *feel* her, and she was making these noises, oh man, it was juicy." He takes another toke, holds it in his lungs and squints at the coffee table. "You know what drives me nuts is how we think we know what stuff is." Smoke drifts out of his nose and mouth. "Like, we think that's a table, right, but who says it's a table, who came up with the table word in the first place? I mean, why do we have to *label* everything?"

Irwin shrugs, eating his ice cream quickly because he wants to leave before Forbes makes no sense at all.

"It's a control thing, right?" Forbes squints at the table. "Like, I know what it is, therefore I control it. Kind of the I-think-therefore-I-am bullshit. Thinking sucks, man. Like, they're just thoughts. We treat them like they're meaningful and real and all that, but they're just *thoughts*, man. Like, what if I *don't* think that's a table. What if I just look at it and go, okay, that would be a good place to put my coffee down. You get where I'm going with this? And what if I *don't* think that's a chair." Forbes waves at the chair with the fatty pinched between his fingers. "Like, I just look at it and go, that four-legged thing would be good to set my ass down on, you know what I'm saying? Like, why's it got to have a *name*? We're fucking shackled by our thoughts, man."

Irwin finishes his ice cream and cleans the bowl in the kitchen sink. He washes the other dishes as well because washing dishes with only one leg is difficult. He hears Forbes coughing, which sometimes happens when he smokes pot. "Animals don't need *labels*, man, they just go around and say, okay, I'll eat this because I'm hungry. Okay, I'm tired and the sun's gone down so I'll sleep. Like, what's with the clocks? Clocks are doom, man."

The first thing Irwin notices when he gets home is the open wine bottle on the table. His mother and Sydney aren't in the living room but the balcony door is open. He picks up the plastic container from PetSmart that he remembered to set out with water and DE chlorinator this morning. Often he forgets this step which means he can't clean the tank because the water he puts the fish into should be room temperature. He puts the container on the bathroom floor then hurries to the aquarium to unplug the bubbler and the filter. He removes the tank lid, remembering he forgot to turn the tank lights off last night which means Betty and Bob couldn't sleep. He carries the tank to the bathroom, finds his net on the hook behind the door and gently scoops up the fish and places them in the PetSmart container. He's always wondered how they feel about this. They swim around briefly then stop, as though they've figured out there's no point in swimming around. He shakes some food flakes into the water to keep them busy. It saddens him that he has never bonded with Betty or Bob. When Gennedy first brought them home, Irwin sat on a stool watching them but didn't tap on the glass because that would be rude. He waited for them to swim over and acknowledge him, but they never did. They always look as if they're waiting for something to happen: escape, death, a new fish. It's only a two-gallon tank, not big enough for more fish. The important thing is that they get along. Some fish kill each other, Irwin learned online. Male bettas are really pretty, but they can't coexist with other male bettas or gouramis or male guppies. Flashy fish are killers. Betty and Bob are boring, but at least they don't murder each other. Although they do shit a lot and dirty the water quickly. Forgetting to clean the tank is cruel, Irwin knows. He's making them choke on their own shit.

He empties most of the water from the tank into the bathtub and scrubs the sides with a J-Cloth then gets out his gravel vacuum and sucks the muck out of the substrate. When he was little, to make Betty and Bob like him, he overfed them. This caused them to shit even more, and algae grew on the sides of the tank and all over the gravel. He had to do many water changes to get rid of the green slime. Now he only feeds them at night.

Next he grabs the old Ocean Spray bottle marked by Gennedy with two lines; one indicating the amount of conditioner required, and the other, the amount of water. He measures out the right amount of each and empties the Ocean Spray bottle into the tank. He repeats this procedure until the tank is full, periodically checking the water temperature with his thermometer. Betty and Bob barely move in their PetSmart container while they wait for something to happen.

"Oh, there you are," Lynne says. "Were you over at the German sow's again? How is the so-called intellectual? Spending more of the asshole's money no doubt."

"He says she has to tighten her belt and lower her standards a little."

"Oh, well, in that case, I'm sure the child support cheques will start rolling in."

It's easy to hate his mother for chopping up Harriet when she's smoking and drinking.

"Let me guess," she says. "She still hasn't paid you for babysitting."

"Can you get out of the way? I have to put the tank back."

"It's really great you remembered to clean it, peanut."

"Where's Sydney?" He lifts the tank and moves past her. She follows him.

"On a date with some computer geek."

"You're drinking her wine all by yourself?"

"She wouldn't mind."

"Did you ask her?"

"She's getting a deal here, Irwin. Four hundred bucks for a room plus full use of the apartment. Give me a break."

"It just seems rude to drink her wine without asking."

"You think everything's rude. I don't know where you got that from, Mr. Goody Two Shoes. Vino is the only thing that relaxes me. All day long I'm wound up trying to figure out the money thing. There's this tightness in my chest 24/7 from trying to figure out how we're going to make it. It's like this spring coiled up inside me."

She wouldn't talk like this without vino.

"And the spring," she continues, "coils tighter and tighter and I'm scared it's going to spring loose and blast me and you and everything else away."

"What's drinking Sydney's wine got to do with it?"

"It's got to do with the fact that I'm tense *all the time*. Surely a saint like yourself can allow me a glass of wine."

"I'm not a saint, and you've had more than one glass. It's not even yours."

"Where do you want this?" She waves Betty and Bob around in the PetSmart container. He didn't realize she was carrying them.

"Put it down," he says, more harshly than he'd intended. "You'll hurt them."

"You can't hurt fish. How old are these anyway? Seriously, how long do they live for? I'm going to go broke paying for fish supplies."

"Ten years. I told you that already. They can live for ten years."

"Oh my lord, what kind of life is that?"

"What kind of life is yours?"

"Excuse me?" She puts the hand that's not holding the wineglass on her hip. He can tell she's lost more weight because her skinny jeans sag off her.

"What kind of life is *yours*?" he repeats. "Smoking and drinking other people's wine, and hating your jobs and your exes, and feeling wound up all the time, and chopping up my sister." He did not mean to say this. He had no intention of mentioning it. The battered look on her face frightens him but he can't stop himself, just as he couldn't stop himself jumping off the diving board to escape Conner and Taylor. He wants to sink down, down into forgiving coolness, where it's quiet and no one can stare at him.

She grips her wineglass with both hands as though afraid she might drop it. "What are you talking about?"

"You know."

"No, I don't know."

"It doesn't matter."

"I did not chop up your sister. What are you talking about?"

"You let them cut her up and put her organs in Ziploc bags."

"Where do you get these ideas? From that low-life?"

"He's not a low-life."

"I can't believe Sydney told you. I knew I shouldn't have said anything. *Why* did I trust her? I should know by now not to trust *anybody*." She collapses on the couch and covers her eyes with her hand the way she used to when she didn't want Irwin to see her crying. He doesn't care. The hateful, gurgling sea monster inside him shifts its bulk.

He plugs in the bubbler and filter, carefully lifts the PetSmart container and pours Betty and Bob into the tank. He sprinkles a bit more food before fitting the lid onto the aquarium and turning off the light so they can get some sleep. "I'm going to bed."

"No you're not, young man. You can't accuse me of chopping up your sister and just walk away."

"If I die, are you going to let them chop me up too?"

"It's not chopping up, Irwin. They're very careful about harvesting the organs."

"Stop saying that word, it's not like she was a vegetable. And anyway, how do you know they were careful, were you watching? I don't want to be a donor. Don't make me a donor. Harry didn't know she was a donor."

"She did."

Irwin looks directly at her to make sure she isn't lying. When she lies, her eyeballs shift slightly. "She did?"

Lynne nods and her eyeballs don't shift. "Harriet didn't cling to life like the rest of us. Death didn't scare her, I guess because she saw so much of it. She understood why we were on donor lists. She saw all the sick kids in hospital. You didn't notice because you were little."

"I noticed they died when their parents took them off vents."

"She was brain-dead, baby, how many times do we have to go over this?"

"People can be in comas and get better." Just the other day he watched a movie where a guy got shot in the head, went into a coma and woke up perfectly fine a week later.

"Not in real life, sweet pea. Please come and sit with me."

"I don't want to. I'm tired. I'm going to bed."

"Please don't be like that. How do you think *I* feel about it? I live with it too, you know. Day in and day out I don't know where she is. I gave her away and now she's all over the place in bodies that reject her. That's the part I didn't understand. Nobody explained to me that the bodies hate other bodies' organs. They try to *kill* the organs. So my precious little girl is where she's not wanted, all alone, far from me, fighting for survival all by herself." She covers her eyes with her hand again. "I can't help her, can't protect her, can't love her. I'm a fuckup, a total fuckup as a mother, and as a wife, and as a provider. I'm a *total* fuckup. And I'm so sorry."

Irwin's noticed that when adults admit to making a mistake they start talking about themselves, and not the people or person they have wronged. His mother is waiting for him to say she isn't a total fuckup. She is waiting for him to feel sorry for her, and forgive her. That's not going to happen.

"Good night," he says.

"Irwin, you can't hate me for this. I did what I thought was right. Now I have to live with it. I'm sorry. I had no idea I would never stop worrying about her in strangers' bodies. But I do, all the time. It haunts me. I want her back so badly. I want to hold her and tell her how much I love her, and say that I just didn't understand."

"What?" He stares into her watery eyes in the same way he stares at Betty and Bob. He expects nothing.

"What do you mean 'what'?"

"What didn't you understand about Harry?"

"That she needed me. She always seemed so strong and self-reliant. She was independent and very stubborn. It was like she didn't even need a mother."

"You made her that way."

"What are you saying?"

"I'm saying she got that way because you were a total fuckup."

"It's because I was looking after *you* all the time, sweet pea. I was so worried about you. You were so sick, and we never knew if you were going to make it."

This is another thing he's noticed about adults. Even after they say they're sorry, they still pin the blame on somebody else.

"I should have died," he says. "I wish I'd died."

"Don't say that." She jumps off the couch and hugs him to her bony frame. "Never say that. I couldn't live without you, sweet pea. You're my miracle baby."

He pulls away from the smell of wine and cigarettes. "I'm getting a headache. I've got to go to bed." This will make her leave him alone because a headache could mean a seizure's pending.

"Okay, sweetie, do you want me to get you some hot milk or something?"

"No. I just need to lie down."

"Of course, baby. I love you so much, my sweet boy. And I won't donate your organs. I promise."

She seems so brittle and irrelevant to him standing there with her hands held out, begging for a love he can't feel. He can hardly remember who she was, or who he thought she was. He stares at the family photos on his dresser and mourns the loss of what she meant to him. She meant almost everything. And now she means almost nothing.

He tries to sleep, listening to her movements, waiting for her to go to bed. But she watches *Titanic*. When Céline Dion sings "My Heart Will Go On," all he can think about is Harriet's heart in a stranger's body that is trying to kill it. When Lynne finally goes to her room, he creeps to the bathroom to brush his teeth, determined to maintain good oral hygiene as per Dr. Du's instructions. Over the years, medications have made Irwin cavity prone. Every time Dr. Du finds decay, Lynne throws up her hands and shakes her head like Irwin did it on purpose.

He flosses and uses the Soft-Picks, considering taking meds to numb his feelings, but then he'll have itchy eyes and headaches. His muscles might start twitching and he'll start forgetting things. On Prozac he forgets entire incidents that other people remember, like Heike's birthday party at Laser Quest. "How could you forget?" she demanded. "It was the sickest thing ever." She told him his vest didn't activate so nobody could shoot him. "It was like you were bulletproof," she said. "You were walking around superhuman."

In the kitchen he sees the open wine bottle and his mother's half empty glass on the counter. He swallows the wine quickly, hoping it will loosen particles again, enabling him to see Harriet, maybe even interact with her.

His mother said vino is the only thing that relaxes her. All day long she's wound up, she said. There's a tightness in her chest 24/7, a coiled spring. This is how Irwin feels. He pours more wine into the glass because he can't remember what relaxing feels like. He pinches his nose as he swallows to reduce the vinegar taste. His face heats up and time slows down. The digital clock on the stove blinks minutes at him. Clocks are doom. He covers it with a pot holder. In a movie about men surviving a plane crash only to be eaten by wolves, one man said to another—who'd been mauled by a wolf—that death would be warm and slide over him. Irwin feels something warm slide over him, but he doesn't think it's death, although he wouldn't mind if it is. He feels rubbery, like someone could hit him and it wouldn't hurt. And tomorrow seems very far away and unimportant. Nothing's important except feeling rubbery and drinking more vino. He focuses on entering his AU. "Let the universes collide," he chants.

"What are you doing?" Sydney stands over him with violet eyes. Her lipstick, redder than her dress, is smudged, and silver teardrops dangle from her ears. "This isn't good, junior."

"I'm fine." She smells flowery.

"I can see that." She corks the bottle. "Who said you could drink my wine?"

"My mother opened it. I just had some."

"More than some. Christ. Does she know you're drinking?"

"She went to bed. She probably took one of my anxiety pills. How was your date with the computer geek?"

"Oh, just another one of those enough-about-me-tell-me-what-you-think-about-me conversations."

Irwin doesn't know what this means. All he wants is to look at her. Her tight skirt is very short and her thighs round. Lynne calls her a chub.

She throws her clutch purse on the table. "I'm so done with dating. It's, like, I really need to know that your eighteen-year-old cat who brought you so much happiness died, and you're really broken up about it and still paying the vet bills." She sits on a chair and puts her feet up on the other one. "As soon as they have a pet," she snaps her fingers, "it's game over. You know you'll always come second."

"But the computer geek's cat is dead."

"Even worse. He'll be talking about all the cute things Puss 'n Boots did for, like, forever."

"Did he really call it Puss 'n Boots?"

"Puss for short." Sydney uncorks the bottle and drinks from it.

"Did he have anything downstairs?" Irwin marvels that he has the nerve to ask this question.

"We didn't get that far. Savvy girls don't hook up on the first date, junior."

"When do you?" His penis lies flaccid in his jeans, liberating him. He can think or say anything and his penis won't betray him.

"Later. Guys like a chase." She kicks off her stilettos and he imagines sucking on her toes. "I don't get the status thing." She tips her head back and he watches a pulsing artery in her neck.

"What status thing?"

"Like, it's all about what he makes and what he owns. Like, when he's not talking about his dead cat, he's talking about his Merc or his condo reno or something. It's, like, didn't people just *talk* before?"

Irwin doesn't know.

"Like, I can't believe the first question people asked in the old days was 'So what do *you* do?'"

"You mean, like, before 9/11? Things were way nicer then. You could keep your clothes on at the airport." It's so wonderful conversing easily with Sydney. He has no fear of sounding stupid. "People trusted people back then. Everybody's a suspect these days."

Sydney pulls off her hair tie, allowing her sandy hair to tumble around her shoulders. Irwin can smell Herbal Essences shampoo. She stretches the hair tie between her fingers and flicks it across the kitchen. "I should have been born in the forties like Marilyn. I would have killed in those swishy dresses." She drinks from the bottle again and he imagines kissing her neck. "So, junior, I hope you didn't tell your mother what I told you."

"What?"

"About your sister."

"No." This is the first lie he has ever spoken. He can't believe how easily it spins off his tongue.

"Good, because she'd probably boot me out."

"I wouldn't let her do that." His boldness staggers him.

"You're adorable."

"I wouldn't."

"You let her rule your life, junior. It's like she's inside your head. For real. That happened to a friend of mine. He had this domineering mother, only she didn't act domineering, she was really coy about it, told him what a special boy he was and all that. But any time he made a decision on his own, she'd find some way to make him regret it. Especially if it had to do with girls. She didn't want competition, so any time he brought a girl home his mother would undermine her, make snitty comments like, 'She doesn't always talk like that, does she?' or 'She doesn't always wear her hair like that, does she?' He went through girl after girl, thinking one of them would please the old witch. Never happened. You know what he did?"

"What?"

"Tried to hang himself. The branch broke."

Irwin hadn't thought of this option—a strong tree limb. He'll look for one in the park. "My mother isn't an old witch," he says. For no reason he can understand, he feels protective of Lynne, and he's not sure he hates her anymore. She seems so inconsequential and defenceless.

"I know, junior. But at some point you're going to have to bust out. Trust me on this."

"My mother doesn't trust anybody."

"With good reason. Okay, time for beddy-byes. We won't tell her about the booze fest, okay?"

"Okay." He wants to press his face into her cleavage but feels himself shrinking back into Irwin. It's as though he was the Hulk and now he's Bruce Banner, his human weakling counterpart.

She helps him to his feet, puts her arm around his waist and guides him to his room. As her flesh rubs against him, he feels his penis tingling. She sits him on the bed and takes off his shoes. He pulls his knees into his groin and slides under the comforter.

"Sweet dreams, junior." She switches off the light. He rolls onto his side feeling the tension creeping back into him, the spring coiling tighter. He doesn't want to be Bruce Banner. Particles stick to him. He kicks off the comforter and shakes his arms and legs. He turns the light back on and stares at the beak and claw painting, trying to figure out if it's a bird, a monster, or part human. The creature looks angry and confused, as though it's not supposed to be there and wants to be somewhere else. This is how Irwin feels. Blood drips from the creature's chest and right talon, and Irwin doesn't know if it's the creature's blood or someone else's, if the creature has caused harm or is harmed, if it's a predator or prey. Irwin steps closer to the painting and stares into its eye.

Twenty-four

"It's a declaration of war," Darcy says. She promised the pedi wouldn't tickle but it does. Irwin tries not to squirm. Dee's steamed because the police came by to question her about the stick insect again. "Wyck just wants revenge for not being able to satisfy me. It's a typical limp dick hissy fit. I told the cops I can't believe taxpayer dollars are being spent on this fuckwad's whinging."

"Did you really say fuckwad to the cops?"

"What am I, stupid? Anyway, I think one of them is into me." Dee often thinks men are into her. "I'll bet you money he's got some skinny-assed wife who cut him off years ago. He's hungry for it. P.C. Babb. The boy wants it."

"What did he say when you talked about wasting taxpayers' dollars?"

"He said they have to investigate every complaint. Anyway, I'm going over to the fuckwad's to kick his mangy butt."

"That might get you into more trouble. He could get a restraining order like Mindy. Or charge you with verbal assault."

"I'd like to see him try. I bet he's a twinkie. He's always dissing fags, a sure sign he is one. Okay, I have to push back your cuticles. It might hurt a little. Then I have to scrape away the dead stuff."

It all hurts. But Kwan is playing something that sounds like a bubbling stream, and Irwin coasts merrily along. He didn't want to get out of bed this morning because his head hurt and the dark clouds were closing in, pressing down on his chest. He waited for Lynne and Sydney to leave for work. In his half sleep, he focused and chanted and broke through the membrane but didn't see Harriet. He saw the freckled, curly red-haired organ recipient in nerd glasses that Forbes showed him. Irwin asked her what it was like to breathe with somebody else's lungs, if she felt weird about having to make her body sick to stop it rejecting the stranger's lungs. She was doing stride jumps and looked healthier than in her photo. "I don't have somebody else's lungs," she said. That's when Irwin understood he was interacting in his AU. He was so excited he got up and ate four pieces of toast and jam.

"Did you understand Harry's art?" he asks.

Darcy makes a face. "Fuck no."

"Maybe we don't need to understand it."

"Fuck no. It's like you look at it and go, this is messed up. But in a good way."

"Did she have a boyfriend?"

"She wasn't into guys. Just her art. And making money off the oldsters. She would have made a great banker."

This morning the oldsters were in the lobby talking about the young nicely dressed couple currently robbing the seniors in the neighbourhood. The couple pretends to know the seniors then threatens to shoot them in the guts if they don't cooperate and give them their money and jewellery. They even force them to withdraw cash from ATMs.

"They wouldn't get far trying to get me to use one of those dang things," Mr. Shotlander said.

Mr. Quigley was icing his titanium knee with a bag of frozen peas. "Don't wear jewellery or fancy watches."

"Dress down." Mr. Chubak sipped from a juice box. "No designer togs."

"So you have to look like a bum to be safe," Mr. Shotlander said. "What a world."

Mr. Hoogstra scratched under his captain's hat. "I hear they make cameras so powerful now they can take pictures of your credit cards through your wallet."

"With telephoto lenses they can see your password," Mr. Quigley added.

Mr. Shotlander held up his hands in a helpless gesture. "What in blazes happened to going to the bank and talking to a pretty bank teller? *Signing* for your cash. A signature doesn't mean a dang thing anymore. They can rob you four ways to Sunday."

What nobody talked about was that Mr. Shotlander's son has a mass in his lung. The doctors don't know what it is yet. Danny is seeing an internal medicine specialist and having CT scans and other tests. Mrs. Shotlander died of lung cancer. Irwin knows this because Mrs. Chipchase told him and asked him to be gentle with Mr. Shotlander. "He's a very proud man," she said. "He won't show grief. But there's nothing worse than outliving your child."

Dee uses clippers on Irwin's toenails. "What about you, Charlie Brown, when are you going to get yourself a girlfriend?"

"No girls even look at me."

"That is a problem. I cannot lie. But you make up for it in niceness. Niceness is hard to come by these days."

"Niceness doesn't get girls."

"Not on the first round. But after they've been burned by a few bad boys, they'll be ready for you, Chuck. You just got to hang in there."

The seniors were also distressed about the murder that happened two blocks over in a basement apartment. Mr. Shotlander held up his hands in a helpless gesture again. "A twenty-year-old stabbing a seventy-year-old. How do you like that?"

"They say alcohol was involved," Mr. Hoogstra said.

All Irwin could think about was the dead man's organs, and if he was on a donor list, and if the organs were stabbed. Heike heard about the murder on the news and phoned Irwin because she wants to process the crime scene after camp to apprehend the suspect. "We're not doing that," Irwin said.

Dee wedges pieces of foam between Irwin's toes. "I need to practice French nails. So no way do you move."

"Why isn't your father nice to my mother anymore?"

"What do you mean?"

"When I was little they were friends and went jogging together."

"That's a long time ago, Chuck."

"I think it was because of me."

"Say what?"

"I think Buck didn't want me around, I mean, because I'm so freaky looking. I think he was embarrassed."

Dee carefully glues acrylic extensions onto Irwin's toenails. It tickles but he manages to hold still. "He let me sit in his truck once," he says. "Even let me steer. But after that he wouldn't even open his window to say hi."

"Why do you have to take things personally all the time? Like, maybe there were other reasons you don't know about."

"Like what?"

"Oh, Chuckie, you are such a baby. Part of me thinks it's cute and the other part thinks you'd better wise up or you're going to get eaten alive."

"Eaten alive by who?"

"The real world, *amigo*. Oh my god you are such a booby."

"I am not a booby. What reasons didn't I know about?"

"He screwed your mom, Irwin. They were humping in the truck the night Harry flew off the balcony. My dad said she caught them at it. He says he's never regretted anything like he regrets that night. Shit, you moved. I told you not to move." She grabs his foot and holds it steady. "What kind of lame-asses want French nails anyway?"

"I don't feel very well."

"You never feel well. Get over it. They were both adults and hot for each other. It happens. And as for the broke criminal lawyer, I'm not even sure if his balls have dropped. Like, what's with the Crocs? I don't think I ever saw him in grown-up shoes."

"I loved him."

"He was psycho to your sister so he's off my list."

Irwin is having trouble processing. Heike says this when something doesn't make sense. Why would a handsome man like Buck want Lynne? She's old. Buck's new wife is way younger and has no spider veins. He saw her once in a micro-mini when she was still pretending to like Dee.

Darcy's mother comes in and flings herself on the couch. "I am so sick of hairy shoulders," she says. "I had four apes this morning. Like, why am I being punished? Why?"

"It pays the bills, Mother."

"Is there anything to eat? Hi, Irwin."

"Hi, Nina."

"Sexy toenails."

"There's some of that low-fat turkey," Dee says. "Make sandwiches for all of us. Are you hungry, Charlie?"

"I should go."

"You've got an ingrown toenail here, bra. Harry used to get those." Dee squeezes his toe. "Does that hurt?"

It all hurts. Kwan is playing something that sounds like a thunderstorm.

"I have to cut the nail back a bit. You'll get an infection if we don't clean it up."

"Harry never said anything about ingrown toenails."

"Why would she? Nobody listened to her, Irwin. Don't you get it? Nobody cared."

"*I* cared."

"You were a little kid. You couldn't help her. She needed help."

"What kind of help?"

"We all need help," Nina says, stroking her cat. "And anybody who says they don't is deluded."

Irwin sits alone on a park bench in need of help. His toe throbs and disturbing images of Buck fucking his mother curl around his thoughts. The wrong universe spills around him, flooding his ankles and edging up his shins. The wrong universe is not sparkling turquoise like the pool but muddied. Fragments of conversations reach him as people who belong in the wrong universe move around him. Somebody says they have to stain the deck while the weather's good. Another person says we're always changing and growing as human beings, even when we're dead; we're electricity and you can't kill electricity.

It never occurred to him that Harry needed help. She was always helping him with buttons, zippers, shoelaces, and buying him Turtles and making chocolate pudding with marshmallows.

Two middle-aged men in plaid shorts sit beside him. "She pawned her wedding ring *three* times," the one closest to Irwin says. "I had to get it out of the pawn shop *three* times. But I couldn't give her up, with those long legs. Not many guys could walk away from a woman like that."

How could Irwin not notice Harry's ingrown toenails? How could he not see her sadness?

"It's stressful enough *being* with someone," the middle-aged man beside Irwin says. "If you can't trust her yah-yah-yahing, well, you're fooling yourself. My kids set me straight. Listen to your kids, they're more receptive, not cloudy, they know what's up."

Irwin doesn't know what's up. And he doesn't know what's down. He used to think his mother was the most beautiful, kind and smart woman in the world. This is why he couldn't figure out why Gennedy left. Maybe Gennedy found out about Lynne and Buck, although he didn't leave for almost a year. He and Lynne fought but it was always about Gennedy being the only criminal lawyer in history that's broke. Sometimes they argued about Irwin, but they never mentioned Harriet. Nobody ever mentioned Harriet. Irwin would say her name out loud to himself just to hear it. "Harriet," he murmurs. She needed a mother, the mother Irwin stole from her.

"Sometimes you just have to let things go," a woman in red jeans says to a woman in camouflage leggings.

Irwin can't listen to people in the wrong universe anymore. Its muddied reality is creeping up his torso. He stands and pushes through the sludge to a tree, spots a strong branch but can't figure out how to get to it, or if his belt will be long enough. Harriet would know what to do. He focuses and chants, trying to get her to interact. But he's too tired and his head hurts, and the pressure from the wrong universe stifles him. He crumples onto the grass as the muddied reality closes over him.

He feels wetness on his forehead and opens his eyes. A small boy with brown skin and pond green eyes stands over him with a squirt gun. "You spazzed out," he says.

Irwin rolls onto his side, away from the boy. He can't get up.

"Dude, why's your head so big?"

"It's a condition."

"Must mean you're really smart."

Nothing's changed, the middle-aged men in plaid shorts are still on the bench, the pigeons are still pecking at the overflowing trash bin, the clouds are still glued to the sky.

The boy steps around Irwin and squats, facing him. "They took your money."

"Who did?"

"Some dudes."

"I didn't have much."

"Well, they took it."

"Why didn't you stop them?"

"With what?" The boy squirts his gun at a sparrow and misses.

"Where's your mother?" Irwin asks.

"At work. What's your name?"

"Irwin."

"I'm Samuel." He offers his hand and Irwin shakes it to be polite, but he wishes Samuel would go away. "Can you sit up? Come on, man, sit up." Samuel helps Irwin to a sitting position.

"Why didn't those men on the bench stop the dudes from robbing me?"

"They don't give a fuck." Samuel hikes up his oversized shorts. "Anyway, they were fast, totally pro."

"How do I know *you* didn't take it?"

"If *I* took it, would I be standing here waking you up?"

"You should do up your shoelaces."

Samuel squirts at a squirrel and misses. "This pistol blows, man."

"Is it normal for you to be alone in the park?"

"Me? Totally. I'm the bull shark, man, hunting night and day, killing dolphins, sea turtles and even other sharks. Before I attack, I butt their heads." Samuel bends over as though about to butt Irwin's head. "That's how they know they're going to die."

As Irwin slowly gets up, Samuel prances around him. Irwin tries to pick up speed but it feels as though he is wading through Jell-O.

Samuel hikes up his shorts again. "I bet you thought the great white was the ocean's fiercest predator."

"Isn't it?"

"Fuck no. The bulls can beat the shit out of those pointy-nosed glamour boys. Besides, bulls can live in rivers *and* oceans. They got special kidneys and glands in their tails. They swim in the Amazon *and* the Mississippi."

"Cool," Irwin says. He can't tell his mother that he seized in the park and was robbed. He can't tell anybody.

While he waits outside Gennedy's door, the white Rasta with floor-length dreadlocks shambles towards him. "Cho!" he says. "Every hoe ha dem stick a bush." He flips his dreads and points to Gennedy's door. "Bald head is fayya buttu, a bong belly pickney, a bugu yaga." The Rasta pokes his finger into Irwin's chest. "I and I cut yai, craven choke puppy. Life is just a ketchy chuby game." He points at Gennedy's door again. "Bald head is a boderation, a downpressor. Fenky-fenky!" Irwin envies the Rasta because he seems certain what he's saying is right and necessary. Nothing Irwin says feels right or necessary. He knocks harder on Gennedy's door. He couldn't call ahead because Bell cut Gennedy's service. "It's me, Irwin."

The door opens. "Why didn't you say so, champ? I thought it was Bob Marley over here." He pulls Irwin inside. The room is even messier than the last time he visited. Stacks of newspapers, magazines, books and misplaced bookmarks collect on the floor, the bed, the desk. It seems to Irwin that everything about Gennedy is getting messier and wearing out: his clothes, his Crocs, his chipped mugs and plates, his teapot, his sheets, his towels. He sits at his cluttered desk and picks up a pencil, looking over something he has scribbled on a yellow notepad. Irwin rarely visits him anymore because he's uncomfortable about interrupting Gennedy's novel writing. Gennedy says he is driven to write, and that all those years spent in penury trying to build a law practice were wasted. "This is what I was meant to do," he insists. "This is what I am good at." Irwin never asks to read his novels because if he didn't think they were good, he would be relegated to the despised ranks of the cretinous publishers who have rejected them. Gennedy insisted that Lynne read the first one. Irwin saw her skip entire sections of its 631 pages. When she told Gennedy that she'd finished it and it was good, he wanted to know what she thought was good about it. "Give me specifics," he said.

"I don't remember."

"How can you not remember? You just finished it."

"I've had a lot on my mind. I'm under a lot of pressure at the bank."

"You're always under a lot of pressure at the bank. What about the ink stain? Wasn't that ingenious?"

"Ingenious," she agreed.

"There is no ink stain in the novel," he said. "You didn't even have the decency to read it thoroughly. I've supported you all these years. Whenever you've needed me, I've been there. Now it's *my* turn." He jabbed his thumb into his chest. "My turn." Next he started shouting, which he'd been doing more frequently since Harriet's fall. With Harry dead there was no one to shout at but Lynne. She told him he shouted at her because no one else would put up with him. "No one else can stand you," Lynne said.

The night she pretended she'd read his novel, he shouted about how she didn't respect him and treated him like a serf. Irwin didn't know what *serf* meant but understood it couldn't be good. To stop them arguing he announced he was going to have a bath. He was only six and still needed to be watched in case he seized in the water. Lynne sat on the toilet seat with her head in her hands. "He's right," Irwin said. "You didn't read it properly. I saw. You skipped all kinds of pages."

"Shhh," Lynne held her finger against her lips. "It was soooo boring. Never tell him I said that."

Irwin hated keeping secrets. There were many the year before Gennedy left. He and Lynne said hurtful things behind each other's backs then told Irwin not to tell the other what they'd said. He felt like a Ping-Pong ball being batted back and forth.

"What can I get you, champ?"

Irwin knows Gennedy can't get him anything besides tea because he doesn't have a kitchen, just an electric kettle. He's not hungry anyway. It feels as though there is something too big inside him trying to bust out—maybe the coiled spring.

"How's your mother? Still working two jobs?"

Irwin nods.

"That woman's thirst for cash will be the end of her."

"She has to pay rent and buy food and pay Bell."

"Yes, yes, yes." Gennedy waves his pencil dismissively. "There is more to life than paying bills."

"We couldn't live in one room like you do."

"The money will come, Irwin. It always does."

"From where? You get welfare but my mother says it wouldn't be enough for *us* to live on."

"Not in the style to which you have become addicted. I can't tell you how my life has improved since I got off the grid." Gennedy scribbles more words on the yellow notepad.

Irwin shifts his weight from one foot to the other. "I need to ask you something."

"Shoot."

"Why did you hit Harriet?"

"That's a loaded question."

"Can't you answer it?"

"I didn't hit her, Irwin. I slapped her. Two very different actions."

"How are they different?"

"A hit is a blow, very deliberate. A slap is spontaneous, unpremeditated."

"Why did you do it, though?"

"Because she took off without spending time with you, little man. You were crying you so badly wanted to see her, and she just left."

So Irwin is to blame again. "I didn't ask you to slap her. If I'd known you were going to hit her I would have asked you not to. I'd have stopped crying."

Gennedy scratches behind his ear with the pencil before jotting something else down on the notepad.

"Did you know my mother hooked up with Buck?"

"Where are you going with this line of questioning, Irwin?" He looks up from the pad with an avian stare, and Irwin recognizes the eye from Harriet's beaky and clawed creature.

"I want to understand what happened," Irwin mumbles. "Why Harriet fell."

"She was a tortured soul."

"Then why were you so mean to her if she was already tortured?"

"I wasn't mean to her. She was self-absorbed and uncooperative, and sometimes I lost my patience."

"I didn't think she was self-absorbed and uncooperative."

Gennedy taps his pencil on the pad and stands as though about to leave, but Irwin knows he has no place to go. "We're never going to agree about your sister, champ. And I've got to get back to work. This is all ancient history and, frankly, I've said all I'm going to say on the subject."

"You never said it to me. What did you say on the subject?"

Gennedy lifts his empty mug to his lips then sets it back down.

"Mum thinks Harry fell because you hit her."

"Eleven-year-old girls don't throw themselves off balconies because someone slapped them. She was mentally ill, Irwin. She was *sick*. She needed medical care. I always said she should have been seeing a psychiatrist, but your mother and her hippie physician insisted it was a phase, or a food allergy, that she was artistic yadda-yadda. Anything but face the fact that she had a personality disorder." Gennedy rifles through papers on his desk and uncovers a Spiderman T-shirt. "This is for you, champ. You had a birthday a while back."

"Thanks." Irwin takes the T-shirt, suspecting it's too small to fit over his hormone-hit girth. Even so, it's nice to be remembered. He's about to reach out for a hug but Gennedy picks up his chipped mug again, puts it back down and looks over his scribbling on the notepad. He grabs the pencil, scratches out some words then jots down another sentence.

"This is it," Heike says.

"You can't go in there. It's got police tape all around it."

"Who says I'm going in?" She pulls out her notebook and magnifying glass.

"We're going to get in trouble."

"The LEOs are long gone. It'll be a cold case in no time."

"They could come back."

"They're not coming back. Some old man was murdered in a basement.

It's not a top priority." She crouches down and examines a stain on the concrete with her magnifying glass. "Anyway, all *you* have to do is be the lookout. Just tell me if somebody's coming. A situation could suddenly erupt."

Irwin looks up and down the street, so nervous about a situation suddenly erupting that his bowels loosen. "I have to go to the bathroom."

Heike prints in her notebook. "I'm numbering this evidence. I'm starting to see a pattern."

A black man in an undershirt pushes open the door to the apartment building. "What you playin' at?"

Heike ducks under the tape. "Sorry, sir. I was just looking for my notebook."

"You get outta here. This is private property."

"Actually, I have a friend in the building."

"What friend?"

"A little girl."

"What girl?"

"She lives in the building. I just wanted to say hi, if that's all right, sir."

The man pulls his sweaty undershirt away from his body then lets it snap back over his potbelly. "You mean Amy in 2A?"

"Yeah, is she home?"

"How should I know."

"Is it okay if we check?"

"Just don't go messing with the crime scene."

"Is this a crime scene?"

"Can't you see the tape?"

"I didn't realize it meant it was a crime scene."

"Wise up, little girl. Get your butt over here."

"Can my brother come too?"

"I'm not going." Irwin knows he can't let her go in there alone.

"Suit yourself." Heike slips into the building and disappears behind the man. Irwin hurries after them but, once inside, can't see either Heike or the man. A dog barks behind one of the apartment doors. The stairwell smells of fried meat.

"Heike?" He hears footsteps and the bass beat from a stereo. He doesn't know whether to go upstairs or down. "Heike?" To suppress the urge to shit, he sits on the stairs. Behind a door a man and woman argue. "He's three years old," the woman shouts. "You're making him into a hockey star when he's three years old?"

"It's ten bucks for half an hour," the man shouts back. "This coach knows his stuff. I've seen him working with the five-year-olds."

"Ten bucks for half an hour? Are you out of your fucking mind? That's an entire meal for us. A pizza for fuck sake. Forget it, no more hockey shit."

"Don't tell me how to fucking raise my son."

"Get out and take your fucking dog with you."

Heike skips down the stairs. "Amy's not home," she says loudly. "What a bummer." She holds her index finger against her lips and points to the basement. Irwin shakes his head and tries to grab her hand, but she's halfway down the stairs already.

The man in the apartment shouts, "Don't dis my dog!"

"Just get him out of here for fuck sake. His drool makes me sick."

Irwin follows Heike into the gloomy basement that smells of cat piss and mould. He finds her on the wrong side of the police tape. "That's against the law," he tells her but, as usual, she ignores him. He hears a door open and the clacking of a dog's nails on the linoleum.

"What is it, boy?" the man says.

Irwin holds up the police tape with one arm and yanks Heike to the right side of it with the other.

"You're hurting me," she yowls.

The dog charges her before she has a chance to say nice doggy. Seeing the dog's jaws clamp around Heike's calf causes an internal scream in Irwin. Simone, the therapist, told him to let out his internal scream. He does, scaring the dog. It releases its hold and sprints to its master.

"What are *you* doing here?" the man demands. He has a handlebar moustache, tattoos and Indian braids.

"We're friends of Amy's," Irwin says. "We were just leaving." He grabs his little sister and throws her over his shoulder. He did not know he had the strength to do this. She starts to bawl. Each step he takes causes a hiccup in her cries as his shoulder pushes into her stomach.

"*She* provoked the dog," the moustached man yells. "Don't go thinking you can get him put down. You were trespassing and she provoked him."

"Definitely. We're really sorry."

"I'm not sorry!" Heike wails. "Your dog should be on a leash."

"Shut up," Irwin commands. He has never said this to Heike. It seems to work, although he can't see her face. Her calf is bleeding onto his arm. He doesn't want her to see the blood.

"I'm going to barf upside down like this," she says.

"Suck it up, buttercup." This is what Dee said.

"My leg hurts."

Irwin dreamed last night he was riding the bus to school with no pants on, trying to pretend this was normal. Similarly he tries to pretend it's normal to have a howling, bleeding seven-year-old girl slung over his shoulder.

"This is the meanest thing you've ever done," Heike moans. "And I'm going to make you pay."

"You do that." Having her completely under his control has freed him of the urge to shit and he realizes how stressful loving her is, how bad it is for him. Why love someone you can't control, who makes situations suddenly erupt? Who makes coiled springs and big things swell inside you? Because she is life itself. Uma said this. Life itself is bleeding on Irwin's shoulder. The weight of her causes burning pain in his neck, forcing him to stare down at the sidewalk. He needs Harriet to tell him what to do. He focuses and chants quietly but particles block him from all sides.

The seniors swarm them outside the elevator. Mr. Hoogstra scratches under his captain's hat. "You better get her a rabies vaccine."

Mr. Shotlander tugs up his trousers. "Has she had a tetanus shot? I've told her a hundred times, if she's going to go around dumpster diving, she better get a tetanus shot."

"This isn't Harry," Mr. Chubak says loudly to Mr. Shotlander's good ear. "This is Irwin's *little* sister, Heike."

"What kind of name is that? Kraut?"

Forbes knows what to do. "Lay her on the couch and get her leg elevated. Use pillows. We have to stop the bleeding." He hobbles to the bathroom and returns with a clean towel. "Press it over the wound. Give it some pressure." Heike has become eerily quiet, but when she sees the wound, she starts to blubber like a regular little girl and Irwin has no idea what to do about it. Heike never cries like a seven-year-old. The corners of her mouth drag down, her bottom lip trembles, her face reddens and endless tears streak her cheeks.

"It's okay," Irwin tells her. "We're going to fix it."

"I'm going to get rabies and die. It happened to a raccoon in our backyard."

"You're not going to get rabies and die."

"How do you know? You don't know anything. I want Mummy."

"If we tell Mummy where we were and why you got bit, she's not going to like it."

This makes Heike sob even more, and he wishes he could free her of her suffering, absorb it like his own. Physical pain he can endure, watching Heike suffer he cannot. "It's going to be all right."

"You don't know anything."

Forbes sits on the couch and places his hand on the towel. "I'll keep the pressure on it. Go get the basin from under the kitchen sink, fill it with warm water and grab a clean face cloth and a bar of soap."

"I'm going to get rabies and die."

"No you're not, ace, but you've got to steer clear of dogs. They're animals with big jaws and sharp teeth. You're lucky he didn't go for your face. Dogs aren't cuddly toys."

Irwin returns with the basin. Forbes slides the towel under Heike's leg, lathers the soap into the cloth and gently wipes off the blood, revealing puncture wounds and bruising. "What'd you get in a dog fight for anyway?"

"I didn't get into anything."

"She was processing an SOC."

"Which one?"

"The basement stabbing in the apartment building."

"Oh now that's a good place to hang out."

"We weren't *hanging out*," Heike insists. "The murder victim deserves a proper investigation."

"Yeah, but don't you need backup when you're dealing with basements and dogs and stabbings?"

"Irwin was with me."

"I mean backup with guns and Tasers. Police stuff. You've heard of them. You dial 911 and they show up with all kinds of cool equipment."

"She thinks LEOs are useless," Irwin says because Heike isn't saying anything. She's staring wide-eyed at the tooth marks.

"I always thought dogs were my friends," she whimpers.

This is the beginning, Irwin thinks, of the end. He remembers this, when he became afraid after Harriet fell. When the world became shadowy and threatening and nothing—and no one—could be trusted. "Most dogs still are your friend," he says. "You just surprised that dog. You were in his territory and he was defending it."

"Why didn't he bite *you* then?"

This is a good question. Irwin was closer to the dog. Maybe the dog knew that Irwin wasn't a threat, just a big booby. "I don't think I scared him."

"*I* didn't scare him. I didn't even see him till he bit me."

"Their muscle fibres fire about a thousand times faster than ours," Forbes explains. "So if they decide to bite us, we don't stand a chance. What kind of dog was it?"

"I don't know," Irwin says. "Big."

"Do you know the owner?"

"No."

"You better ask him if the dog's up to date on vaccinations."

"I'm going to get rabies and die!" Heike howls.

"Take it easy, ace. It's just a precaution. Most people make sure their dogs get all their shots."

Irwin can't imagine the moustached man with tattoos and Indian braids making sure his dog gets all his shots. Vets are expensive. Mrs. Schidt continually complains about vet bills. "I'll go ask him."

"You can't do that!" Heike shrieks. "He'll kill you. He's *mean*."

Irwin fears, if the dog hasn't been vaccinated, Heike will require a rabies shot. Uma doesn't believe in vaccines. Heike has never been jabbed by a needle. The thought of her body being violated in this way pitches him into gasping darkness.

"I'm going," he says.

"Don't go!" she screams. "You can't go! Don't let him go!"

"We need to find this out, ace."

Irwin can still hear her cries as the elevator doors close behind him.

Twenty-five

His legs feel numb, like his gums when Dr. Du freezes them. He drags
them into the apartment building and knocks on the door. The dog barks
and Irwin knows he's going to lunge at his face, and that he mustn't jerk
away because the dog's fangs will tear through his flesh. When no one
answers, he knocks again. He can hear the TV, and the bass beat from a
stereo continues to pound through the building. He knocks harder. The
moustached man swings the door open with the dog drooling at his heels.
"I told you, you freak, you were trespassing and she provoked him."

"I agree." Irwin hopes he can be heard because he can hardly hear
himself.

"Then what the fuck are you doing here?"

"I just wanted to know if your dog is up to date on his shots."

The man starts to laugh as though Irwin has told a really funny joke.
His shoulders shake and his gut jiggles. Irwin rarely makes people laugh
and shifts his weight awkwardly from one foot to the other.

A straw-haired woman with a cigarette pinched between her lips peers
over the man's shoulder. "Who's this?"

"It's the kid who was with the girl that threatened Toto."

"She didn't threaten him," Irwin says.

"He wants to know if Toto's had all his shots." He turns his back to Irwin, blocking the woman's face from view. "Toto's had all his shots, hasn't he, honey?"

"Fuck yeah," the woman says. "He was at the vet's just last week getting shot up."

This makes the man laugh even harder as he slams the door in Irwin's face.

Back at Forbes' apartment, Heike is eating chocolate chip ice cream and asking Forbes if he would rather be killed by a shark or an alligator.

"A gator. Totally. Those jaws take you right out, you don't even see it coming."

Heike sucks on her spoon. "Same with sharks."

"Are you kiddin' me? Sharks keep tearing pieces off you—first an arm, then a leg. Meanwhile you're drowning and your blood's turning the water red, attracting all the other sharks. No thank you."

Irwin sits on the footstool.

"What's up, Spidey? What'd they say?"

"They say he got shot up at the vet's last week."

"They actually said 'shot up'?"

"I think they were lying."

"Why would they lie?" Heike asks.

"Because they don't want their dog put down."

"If you report it to the cops," Forbes says, "they'll have to show his vaccination record."

Heike sits up. "No way I'm reporting it. The LEOs will think I compromised a crime scene."

"Which you did," Irwin says.

"I did not. I didn't touch *anything*."

"Okay." Forbes scratches his eyebrow with this thumb. "Ace, you need to go home and tell your mom about this."

"I'm not telling Mummy *anything*."

"How else are you going to explain the dog bite?"

"We'll just say I scraped my leg."

Irwin shakes his head. "I'm not lying to your mother."

As they approach Uma's house, with Heike limping and Irwin's brain short circuiting from the stress load, Heike says, "We've got to get our stories straight."

"I'm not lying to your mother."

"We were in the park and the dog bit me. If you tell her what really happened, she won't let you babysit me anymore."

This hadn't occurred to Irwin. Without Heike—without life itself—he cannot function.

Uma, bent over her rocks, doesn't notice them right away.

"Hi, Mummy."

Uma remains bent over, her buttocks looming large. "Hi, honeybun, can you believe the litter collecting here? The wind blows it down the street into our garden and it catches on the rocks. It's a disaster." She stands up, holding empty chip packets and chocolate bar wrappers. When she notices the gauze and sterile tape on Heike's calf, she drops the garbage and clambers over the rocks to her. "What happened?"

"I got bit by a dog."

"Oh my god."

"It's okay, Mummy. It's had all its shots. It just wanted to play. We were in the park playing grounders and running and the doggy got all excited and tried to catch me."

"Oh my god." Uma crouches down and examines the dressing. "Who did this?"

"Forbes," Heike explains. "He's an emergency room nurse. He knows all about dog bites. He even put disinfectant on it that made my skin orange, but it didn't hurt or anything. What's for dinner? Can Irwin stay?"

"I'm not staying. It's Bingo Night."

"Oh, can I come? Please please please?"

"Heike," Uma says, "we have to get you to the hospital."

"No way. It's all good. Forbes fixed it."

"I'm sure he did his best but you may need some medication."

Irwin knows Uma means shots and antibiotics. He has experienced too many of these treatments and the thought of doctors doing them to Heike intensifies the zapping in his brain. He releases her hand in an effort to walk away, but she grabs him around the waist. "I'm not going to the hospital without Irwin."

"Irwin's busy. I think you've seen quite enough of him for one day."

"I never see enough of Irwin. He's my big brother and I hardly *ever* see him."

Irwin pushes her away while the big swollen thing inside him crowds his lungs.

"I'm calling a cab," Uma says, pulling on Heike's wrists.

"Irwin!"

"I'll see you tomorrow after camp."

She starts to cry like a seven-year-old again. He staggers down the street while her sobs grow faint behind him.

At Mr. Shotlander's—set up for Bingo Night—Mr. Chubak talks about bonobo monkeys on the left bank of the Congo River. He believes if bonobos ruled the world, we wouldn't be in the mess we're in. "The females dominate," he explains, squatting on his three-legged stool from Nepal. "No such thing as alpha males with the bonobos. And the females are fertile all the time so the males don't kill each other over them. They have sex when they feel like it—it's communication to them, no big whoop. Sometimes the girls have sex with girls, and the boys with boys. It's all about giving pleasure. Nothing to do with power. That's the trouble with humans, everything's about power. The bonobos couldn't care less about power. They just want to eat, sleep and have sex."

"Very sensible," Mrs. Chipchase says, knitting on the couch.

"Terrific!" Mr. Hoogstra jabs a toothpick into his gums.

"With humans it's all a pissing contest," Mr. Shotlander concludes.

Forbes spins the bingo ball cage again and calls out a number and letter. Those with N56 place their markers, but nobody shouts bingo.

Irwin shakily pours pop for the seniors, although Mr. Quigley brought Gatorade along with his skipping rope. He said he missed his workout today and has to skip for twenty minutes to make up for it. "What's the matter, Irwin?" he asks. "You look beat."

"I'm all right." Irwin has been trying to think about other things than what's happening to Heike in the hospital. Seizing in the park should be foremost in his thoughts as he hasn't had a seizure for two years. And Gennedy claiming Harry was mentally ill and had a personality disorder. Rufus in 609 is mentally ill and hears voices. When he first moved in, Irwin assumed he had a tiny phone hidden on his person because he was always talking to somebody. Heike once asked him whom he was talking to, and Rufus said loudly, "Bee, this isn't your hive," and swatted the air in front of her face. "Buzz off, bee."

Harriet never heard voices.

The more Irwin tries not to think about what doctors are doing to Heike, the more he sees men in white coats jabbing her with needles and making her cry like a seven-year-old.

"Pass the chips around, Irwin," Mr. Shotlander urges. Forbes keeps spinning the bingo ball cage and calling out numbers and letters, but nobody says bingo.

Between placing his markers, Mr. Quigley skips rope. "Did you hear about the carjacking attempt?"

Mr. Shotlander scrutinizes his bingo card. "What carjacking attempt?"

"The thief couldn't drive stick shift. He forces the driver out of the Porsche, gets in and can't work the clutch. He keeps stalling the car. So the thief gets out and the driver gets back in."

"Terrific!" Mr. Hoogstra scratches under his captain's hat.

Irwin pours Mr. Shotlander's Coke and sits in the fold-out chair beside him. "Do you know anything about organ donation?"

"What about it?" Mr. Shotlander fingers his bingo markers.

"I just wondered if you knew anybody who got one, or gave one."

"Chubak, who was that fellah got a heart and swore they put it in wrong?"

"Borts. Nice guy till he got that heart."

"What happened when he got the heart?" Irwin asks.

Mr. Chubak sips Orange Crush. "He was always cussing it. It was like the heart was his arch-enemy."

"The doc told him he'd had to sew the dang thing in deeper than his old heart," Mr. Shotlander explains. "That's why it felt higher."

"So Borts tracks down the donor family and finds out he got a black woman's heart."

"All hell broke loose," Mr. Shotlander says. "He said if he'd known they were going to put a coloured woman's heart into him, he would have refused the surgery."

Mr. Chubak scratches his bald spot. "He was from Alabama, a racist born and bred."

"He said he could feel it beating wrong and coming unstitched." Mr. Shotlander drains his Coke, and Irwin pours him another. "He tried to cut it out with a kitchen knife. Remember that, Chubak?"

"Do I ever. There was blood all over the place. They took him away in an ambulance. Poor old Borts. A nice guy till he got that heart."

"Did he die?" Irwin asks.

"We never heard another peep about him, did we, Shotlander? The next thing you know, the movers showed up. He had two beanbag chairs. I'd never have taken Borts for a beanbag man."

"Maybe he bought them after he got the coloured woman's heart," Mr. Shotlander says.

Irwin associates moving men with death, and dreads seeing their trucks parked out front. Seeing valued possessions transformed into junk distresses him. He avoids the lobby on moving days, sits in the apartment looking at the possessions that will be transformed into junk when he and Lynne are dead. Who will look after Betty and Bob?

"Bingo!" Mr. Quigley hurrahs.

"What the heck?" Mr. Shotlander says. "You're supposed to be skipping."

"I'm multitasking."

Irwin hands the toonies he collected from the seniors for prize money to Mr. Quigley.

"That fellah's got horseshoes up the yin yang," Mr. Shotlander grumbles.

Sydney's on the couch drinking wine again. "Why did you tell your mom what I told you?"

"I didn't tell her *you* told me."

"Gee whiz, I guess she figured it out all by herself."

"Was she mad?"

"She phoned me at the gym and called me a twat."

"I'm sorry."

"Means I can't trust you."

Irwin hadn't realized she'd trusted him. The loss of her trust causes puffs of dejectedness, forcing him to sit on the couch. "Is she making you move out?"

"Not likely. She's too desperate for cash. No way am I ever going to let myself get that desperate." When Sydney gets bombed, she imagines a future much grander than working reception at LA Fitness.

"How are you going to prevent getting that desperate?"

"Careful planning. I'm seeing that programmer again. He's got connections. It's all about making the right connections."

"But you didn't like him."

"I didn't say I didn't like him. I said I was tired of hearing about his dead cat." She curls her hand around her glass and brings it to her lips. Her eyes are Windex blue tonight. If he could lie down and rest his head on her lap, the oppressive clouds might disperse.

"I want a house with a private drive," she says. "A friend of mine bought a house with a mutual and it's, like, total war with his crazy neighbour all day every day."

"But the programmer lives in a condo."

"For now. Anyway, who says I'm interested in him? I'm just saying he's got connections. The problem with your mom is, she's got, like, nobody. It's like she's never figured out how to network."

Irwin shifts as close as he dares to Sydney. "She was looking after me. She didn't have time to network."

"Make excuses for her, junior, if it makes you feel better. The truth is she needs to get her head around the fact that networking isn't about time, it's about people skills. Your mom scores minus ninety at people skills."

"She was nicer before Harriet died."

"Okay, you know what, junior, it's time you stopped obsessing over Harriet. For real. I mean, are you going to drag this Harriet thing around for, like, forever? That happened to a friend of mine. Her two-year-old stuck a strawberry soap in his mouth and choked to death. My friend and her husband were watching the Academy Awards and didn't hear the kid gagging in the bathroom. Usually they closed the door so the toddler couldn't get in there. But this one time they forgot. So anyway her husband got over it, or through it, or whatever they call it. But Trish just couldn't. Mourning her baby became, like, her life. Dave took her to Arizona because their shrink said a change of scenery would be good for them. He got totally into the desert Indians and their crafts and history. He was, like, consumed by how fucked over the Indians were by white people. It was all he could talk about. Meanwhile it was driving Trish nuts and interfering with her grieving for Ashton. She started saying his name over and over to Dave so he would grieve too, and showing baby pics on her phone, and reminding Dave of the cute things Ash used to do until Dave was, like, just standing there holding some Indian artifact, and she said, 'You've left us.' And he said, 'I can't stay where you are.'" Sydney tips her head back on the couch. Irwin watches the pulsing artery in her neck. "You don't want to stay where you are, junior."

He doesn't. He is in the wrong universe.

Lynne comes in with groceries and doesn't acknowledge either of them. They listen to her shoving food into the fridge and cabinets.

"Are you okay, Mum?"

"Fine. Did you eat?"

"Yeah." He can't admit he pigged out on snack foods at Bingo Night. Lynne says snack foods make him fat.

Sydney, wineglass in hand, swaggers to the kitchen. "Are you ignoring me? Because I won't tolerate being ignored."

"You're impossible to ignore. You live here."

"Then what's with the silent treatment?"

"I'm tired, Sydney, bone and blood tired, like I can hardly stand."

"You need a drink."

Irwin hears wine being poured.

"I probably shouldn't be doing this," Lynne says.

"Sure you should. Look at the French. Bottoms up."

Irwin feeds Betty and Bob and sits on the stool watching the fish gobble the flakes. What goes on in Betty and Bob's alternate universe?

"Hinkle asked me out," Lynne says.

"No shit, the boss? Are you going to go?"

"He's old. And hairy. He has to shave his neck."

"So? He's the manager, hello."

"He's divorced with kids."

"So are you."

"I don't think I could do that to Irwin. Start that all over again."

"Getting out of this shithole would be good for Irwin."

They both stop talking, which means they're drinking more, and goggling at the kitchen tiles. Irwin knows they've forgotten he's in the living room. He is as tangential to them as he is to Betty and Bob.

"I don't know how I'm supposed to pay for college if he goes," Lynne says. "He won't get scholarships, that's for sure."

"Sounds like Hinkle could be just the ticket. Hairy can be hot. Think Mediterranean."

"He said he's looking for a mature relationship."

"There you go."

"Which means I'm old. How did I get old? The only men who want me are old and hairy and want mature relationships."

"Does he have pets?"

"A dog. Some kind of husky called Sophia. Hinkle says Sophia got him through the divorce. She's the sweetest soul, he says."

"Canine bitch competition. Could be trouble."

Irwin's brain won't stop zapping. He drags the Harriet thing to his room and lies on his bed trying to figure out why he can't get over it, or through it, like Dave did. He focuses on Harry's painting of a tree with a scarred human torso. This is the painting Lynne hates most. In his head he hears her saying, "I can't look at that. How can you sleep in the same room as that?" and he realizes that Sydney's right. His mother *is* inside his head telling him what to do, what to eat, what to think—ruling his life. Sydney said at some point he's going to have to bust out.

"There's no time like the present," Irwin mumbles. Mr. Quigley says this. Irwin throws off the comforter and tries to shake out his arms and legs but they're too heavy, swamped in the Jell-O of the wrong universe, and he's forced to flop back onto the bed. He stares at the ceiling, focusing hard. "Let the universes collide," he chants.

When he wakes he doesn't hear the women and sneaks to the bathroom. If he is able to brush his teeth, it means he's not depressed. When he's depressed he can't brush his teeth. Lynne sits on the edge of his bed and pushes Q-tips soaked in Listerine into his mouth.

Only the stove light is on. He pours himself a glass of water before noticing the wine. If he drinks a little it might loosen particles and stop the brain zaps. He sips from the bottle, wary that either of them could appear at any moment and catch him at it. What he's noticing is that everyone, not just his mother, tells him what he should and shouldn't do. Everybody has an idea of who he is. He has no idea who he is, so how can they know? At school Mrs. Aikenhead told them to make collages about themselves. They had to cut out images that represented who they were and stick them on bristol board. Irwin couldn't think of who he was. He glued bus transfers onto the board because he spends an hour a day on public transit getting to and from school. Next he stuck Band-Aids on the board to represent his surgeries. After that he couldn't think of anything.

"There must be *something* else about you that you can add, Irwin," Mrs. Aikenhead said, smiling as always. Mrs. Aikenhead smiled even when she was annoyed. "Irwin, isn't there something a little less gloomy about you you'd like us to know?"

He didn't want them to know anything else about him. They talk behind his back and call him spaz and reject. He'd blow up the school, if he could. He drinks more wine. The rubbery feeling spreads from his chest to his arms and legs, and it occurs to him that he could make a bomb. The instructions must be online because everybody makes bombs, although Irwin has trouble following instructions. Often, in gym class, Mr. Brint thinks he's being uncooperative when really Irwin is just overwhelmed by the demand to follow a sequence of instructions. He envies the other kids for being able to follow Mr. Brint's directions. Especially Kirk Cornwall, who is the best at everything and can even climb ropes. Mrs. Aikenhead smiling, tells the students, "We should never compare ourselves to others. We all have different strengths and weaknesses and nobody is better or worse than anybody else, just different." Mrs. Aikenhead talks about her husband and cute twins, and what fun in the sun they had on the weekend. Then she asks the class what *they* did for fun on the weekend. Once she asked Irwin and he couldn't think of anything. Kirk Cornwall said, "Duh," and made stuttering noises.

With particles loosening and the brain zapping subsiding, it becomes obvious to Irwin that he must follow bomb-making instructions. Harry could help him if she'd only interact with him. He wishes he had photos of her. Trent stopped taking pictures when Irwin stopped getting better. Lynne took shots with her phone but never printed them because she didn't have time to stand in line to print them at Walmart. When her phone got stolen she squalled about how all her babies' pictures were gone. Gennedy didn't take photos. He said he kept the good pictures in his head. Irwin couldn't imagine what the good pictures were, since Gennedy didn't like Harriet and Irwin kept disappointing him. The two family photos on Irwin's dresser were taken at Walmart, and Harry's only in one of them. She refused to be in the second because she insisted they weren't a family, that Gennedy wasn't legit. In the first photo, she looks as though she doesn't belong, as if she just happened to be there when the photographer took the shot. Gennedy and Lynne have their arms around Irwin, who's smiling as though the world is a wonderful surprise waiting for him. He had no idea that Harry was standing to one side, looking with centuries-old eyes beyond the camera into a world that wasn't a wonderful surprise—a world without a mother.

He hears the sliding doors to the balcony open. He jams the cork back into the bottle and grabs a banana from the fruit bowl.

"Oh my lord, you scared me," Lynne says. "What are you doing up?"

"I was hungry."

"I thought you said you ate?"

"I just wanted a banana."

"Were you at the German sow's? Did she lecture you on cold-pressed salad oils?" She washes her wineglass and sets it in the dish rack.

"You're drinking Sydney's wine again," he says, emboldened by vino.

"What I really don't need right now, Irwin, is an anal-retentive fourteen-year-old on my case. So I drink a little. Get over it."

"I can't get over it, or through it, or anything. Unlike yourself who can get over anything as long as you have a pack of smokes and Sydney's vino."

She faces him, apparently flabbergasted, crossing her skinny arms. "I can't believe you just said that."

"I can't believe you're over Harriet. She was my sister and you act like she never existed. You never say her name, you never talk about the stuff she used to do. There's no pictures of her anywhere, you hate her art." He rests his head on the table because he can't hold it up any longer. "You've left us."

"What are you talking about?" She sits beside him, placing a hand on his shoulder that he tries to shrug off. "I would never leave you, peanut. You know that."

"Why did you fuck Buck?"

"Since when do you say 'fuck'?"

"Since now."

She removes her hand. "Who told you that?"

"It doesn't matter who told me. Why did you do it?"

"Because I was sad."

"That's no reason to fuck somebody. How was Gennedy supposed to feel? That's why he left us, isn't it? I always thought he left because of me but it's because you fucked Buck." Irwin could never speak this way without vino. Everything seems clear to him now, but distant at the same time, as though he's looking through a telescope. Nothing can touch him. Nothing can scare him.

Lynne slouches in her chair. "He left for a number of reasons."

"No. He left because you fucked Buck, and because you blamed him for Harriet's fall."

"That is so unfair."

"Who said life is fair?" Mr. Shotlander asks this question frequently. "Mr. Shotlander's son might have cancer and you don't see Mr. Shotlander fucking people because he's sad."

"Who would fuck that old goat?"

She wouldn't speak this way if she weren't drunk. She looks sleepy. She is never sleepy sober. "Buck made me feel attractive, sweet pea. You don't know this yet but being desired is the biggest turn-on of all. And he was totally ripped." The dreamy look in her eyes disgusts Irwin.

"That's no excuse."

"Plus I was mad at Gennedy for hitting her. I'll never forgive him for hitting her."

"Then why didn't you stay with Buck? Harry liked him. Maybe if you'd hooked up with Buck sooner, Harry wouldn't have fallen."

"Maybe, maybe, maybe. Don't you think I go through the maybes a million times? All day, all night, year after year, I go through the maybes."

She's making it about her again, when it should be about Harriet. "We never talk about her," Irwin says. "It's like she never existed. We never celebrate her birthday. We never remember the stuff she did. It's like her name is a bad word. I want to talk about her. Talking about her makes it almost like she's here."

"No it doesn't. It reminds us that she isn't."

Harry is sitting on the counter again, swinging her legs and banging her heels into the cabinets, chewing red Twizzlers.

"You're not allowed to eat red candy," Irwin says.

"Bust me," Harry says.

"What's the matter, baby?" Lynne asks. Irwin knows she can't see Harry in his AU.

"Red dye makes you hyper," Irwin whispers.

"Who you gonna call?" Harriet says.

Lynne feels Irwin's forehead. "You're a little warm."

Irwin pushes Lynne's hand away. "Not talking about her makes us forget her." Harry's vanished again and his vino superpowers are fading. He is shrinking back into Bruce Banner. Lynne starts clearing the dish rack, noisily stacking plates.

"Peanut, is this about the donor business? I wish you hadn't told the paraplegic. He nearly ran me over in the hall to interrogate me about it. Why would you tell a stranger?"

"You put Harriet's organs into strangers."

Lynne turns on him, a plate in each hand. "What do you want me to do about it? It's over. It's done." She makes sweeping motions with the plates as though trying to brush the Harriet word from the kitchen. "Do you want me to track down the bodies and hack her organs out of them because, believe me, that's crossed my mind."

He rests his head on the table again.

"Look at me," she says.

He can't lift his head.

"Look at me. Irwin?"

He can't.

"Oh my lord, are you seizing?"

Twenty-six

The hospital comforts him. He can do nothing but wait for test results. No one is nice to him like when he was little, but he doesn't care. He wants to be left alone. Beside him, on a gurney behind the curtain, a boy plays computer games, making explosive sounds when he kills. This reminds Irwin of Heike's birthday party at Laser Quest, when his vest was inactivated and nobody could shoot him. He feels like this in the hospital. It has always been a place where people can't get at him. He stares at the dirty beige wall, making it vibrate, until Harriet is painting colourful stripes across it. "You're going to get in trouble," he warns her.

"I don't give a fifth of a fuck," she says.

"Is it a rainbow?"

"It's whatever you want it to be." She paints as though she's in a hurry.

"Why are you rushing? Please stay with me."

"Black isn't a colour," she says.

"I need you to help me make a bomb."

Then she's gone and only the wall remains, drained of colour. Lynne appears and strokes Irwin's forehead. "How are you feeling, baby boy?"

"Okay."

"You scared me. Do you have any idea what brought this on?"

"No." He wants her to stop touching him. He wants to interact with Harriet again.

"What's wrong, peanut?"

"Nothing. I want to sleep." He doesn't because he never sees Harry in his dreams. Sometimes she's just left and he sees things she forgot to take with her. He calls out that she forgot her hoodie or her mitts but she never comes back for them, and he's always afraid to go looking for her in case he gets lost.

A bushy-haired doctor Irwin doesn't recognize pushes past the curtain. He massages the back of his neck while looking at Irwin's chart. "Your blood work shows your liver enzymes are elevated. Do you have any idea why? Have you been taking your seizure medication?" The doctor has tiny eyes that look almost closed.

"Yes." Irwin doesn't admit he forgets to take them because he hasn't had a seizure for two years.

"Hmmm. That's odd. We may have to switch your medications."

"Why?" Lynne asks.

"Something's elevated his liver enzymes. Could be the drugs."

"That doesn't make any sense. He's been on the same drugs for years and never had a problem."

"Maybe so, but they might be harming him now. Something is damaging his liver. We'll find out more with a liver biopsy."

Lynne grips her chin the way she does when she's worried about what the doctors are telling her. "How do you do a liver biopsy?"

"Stick a needle into his liver. We'll do an ultrasound and a CT scan first, see if they tell us anything."

"Nobody's sticking a needle into my liver," Irwin says. "I'm fine."

"You're not fine, peanut. Your liver's sick and we need to find out why."

"I'm *fine*. Nobody's sticking a needle into my liver." He will no longer do what people tell him to do.

"Why isn't he wearing a MedicAlert bracelet?" the doctor asks Lynne, as though Irwin isn't there.

"He refuses to wear it, says he's too old for it."

"People with seizure histories are never too old to wear MedicAlert bracelets."

Irwin's glad they're talking at each other and not at him.

"What about alcohol?" The doctor's tiny eyes fix on Irwin.

Irwin scratches his arm. "What about it?"

"Have you been drinking?"

"He doesn't drink," Lynne says then looks at Irwin. "Oh my lord."

Irwin stares at the wall. If only they'd leave him alone, he might be able to make it vibrate.

"Irwin, were you drinking Sydney's wine again?"

Irwin doesn't answer. He's tired of answering. Nobody listens anyway.

"Who's Sydney?" the doctor asks. "Maybe you should ask him. In any case, I'll order the ultrasound and CT scan." He disappears behind the curtain and suddenly Lynne is shaking Irwin's shoulder.

"Were you drinking? Answer me. This isn't a joke." Harry's behind her making goofy faces, and Irwin starts to giggle.

"It's not funny," Lynne says.

Harry crosses her eyes and does rabbit ears behind Lynne's head, and Irwin starts to laugh. "Stop that," Lynne orders, but Harry wags her tongue and Irwin chortles even more. He'd forgotten how wonderful it feels to laugh. Harry pulls on her ears and touches her tongue to her nose. Irwin has never been able to do this but tries anyway, stretching his tongue up towards his nose. His mother slaps him. For a moment he's not sure which universe he's in.

"Oh my lord, I'm so sorry, sweet pea, but this is serious. I mean, liver damage is *serious*. Stop fooling around. Peanut, please look at me."

He does and sees messy hair and crumbling mascara, a coffee stained T-shirt, his mother twitching for nicotine.

"Is there something you haven't told me?" she asks. "If they have to stick a needle into your liver, it will hurt like hell."

She doesn't understand that physical pain doesn't frighten him anymore. "I'm fine, Mum. You look tired. You should go home and rest. I'll wait for the tests. You don't need to be here."

"Of course I need to be here."

"No you don't. I don't want you here." He immediately regrets saying this because her face collapses and she covers her eyes with her hand. "I know you're crying," he says. "It's okay to cry. Just please leave now. I want to be alone."

"You never want to be alone in hospital."

"I want to be alone now. Please go. I'll call you when they've done the tests. You should get to the bank."

Lynne looks at her phone. "You're right. I should."

"Go home and change."

"You're sure you'll be all right?"

"Sure. I'm in good hands here."

"That's right." She nods as though trying to convince herself. "You're in good hands."

He wants her gone. It's become hard to look at her. He has to squint as though staring into sun.

"I love you, peanut."

He knows she's waiting for him to say *I love you too*, but he can't. She hovers by the bed. He rolls onto his side, away from her.

"I'm so sorry I hit you," she says.

"I know. I'll call you later."

She kisses the back of his head and he can't understand how her caresses meant everything to him once and mean nothing to him now. When he hears the slide of the curtain rings, he flips back onto his other side to make the wall vibrate again. The doctors are doing something to the boy behind the curtain who was gaming and making explosive killing sounds. Gulping sobs, the boy begs them to stop, but they tell him it's almost over and that he's being very brave. Irwin's heard it all before and knows it's all lies.

He arrives early at the community centre and waits by the chain-link fence. Parents in SUVs, and nannies on foot, arrive to pick up the children swarming out of the building. Irwin shifts his weight from one foot to the other, watching the doors swing open as more children exit. When the doors no longer swing open, and all the children are gone, Irwin continues to wait. He tried calling Heike from the hospital, but he suspects her phone is dead. She doesn't charge it unless he reminds her. He called Uma but the service was on. That Heike is not here can only mean she is sick. Otherwise Uma wouldn't let her stay home because Heike interferes with her thesis work.

The drugs the doctors gave him have made him clumsy and worsened his tremor. He decides to stop taking drugs to please people. Not taking drugs upsets the nurses. During one of his hospital stays a pale boy insisted they were poisoning him and refused to take drugs. He called one of the nurses the spawn of Satan and made her cry. Irwin doesn't want to make anyone cry, but he will no longer take drugs for fear of upsetting them. It will be hours before they notice he is gone.

On the crowded bus, no one sits next to him. Behind him a woman with a gravelly voice says, "I bought some lunch and a pack of smokes and now I don't have enough to buy a phone card. What's so fucking difficult to understand?"

Outside Uma's, he waits behind the tree, staking out the house. It's still daylight and no lights are on. Burger King wrappers cling to Uma's rocks. Irwin tries to peer through the living room window to the kitchen, hoping to see them sitting around the granite island, but sunlight glints off the panes. He looks up at Heike's open window. He could try calling to her, although Uma is bound to hear and tell him to go away; she has no use for Irwin when Heike is sick. She only tolerates him, he knows, for the free babysitting. When Heike is sick, Uma pampers her, letting her eat ice cream instead of frozen yogourt, and drink ginger ale instead of unsweetened fruit juice. Heike occasionally pretends to be sick in order to eat what she wants. Maybe Heike is pretending to be sick now, except there's no school to avoid, just camp and Irwin. Is she avoiding *him*? Is she mad because he let the dog bite her? He was supposed to be on the lookout for erupting situations.

He climbs the wooden steps, startled by their creaking, and peeps in the small window on the door but can see only the coat rack. He rings the bell and waits. A squirrel squats on the porch railing and watches him. "I have no food," Irwin tells it, knowing that Heike feeds them. The squirrel twitches its tail. Irwin rings the bell again, leaning hard on the buzzer. Another squirrel sits on the railing, and Irwin feels they know something he doesn't, that they are conspiring against him. "Shoo," he tells them, waving his hand. The squirrels leap onto Uma's rocks. The door opens.

"What is it, Irwin?" Uma's hair, normally cinched into a bun, hangs messily around her shoulders.

"Heike wasn't at camp."

"She's not well. I'm sorry, I should have called you but it's been an intense twenty-four hours."

"Intense?" He wishes she'd let him in.

"Heike's had a reaction to the rabies shot."

"What kind of reaction?" Irwin has had many reactions to medications and knows this could mean anything: vomiting, diarrhea, rashes, headaches, weakness, difficulty swallowing, numbness or tingling—pain. More than anything, pain. The thought of Heike in pain sends cutting winds through him. "Why did you give her a shot? She didn't need a shot."

"She's going to need five in total over the next month."

"No."

"Yes. Thanks to you, Irwin, she requires rabies shots. Unfortunately, side effects are common."

"What kind of side effects?"

"Is that Irwin?" Heike calls weakly from upstairs.

"Honeybun, stay in bed. You don't want any more swelling."

"Irwin won't make me swell." She clambers down the stairs, gripping the bannister, wheezing from the exertion. Her face is red and swollen.

"Why won't you *ever* do what I say?" Uma demands. "Get back into bed."

"I want to see Irwin." She stands shivering in her Super Girl nightie even though it's warm. "I want to tell him a joke." She scratches her upper arm.

"Don't scratch the injection site, honeybun. How many times have I told you that?"

Heike makes a break for Irwin, grabbing him around his waist, but her hold is weak and her mother pulls her away easily, throwing Heike off balance. She stumbles. Irwin has never seen her stumble. She hangs limp and graceless in her mother's grip. "Are you dizzy again, sweetie?" Uma asks, feeling her forehead. "You're hot. This is ridiculous. Is your stomach hurting? Did you have more diarrhea?" Heike doesn't reply. Her swollen lids slide over her eyes. Uma lifts her into her arms.

"She doesn't need shots," Irwin protests. "The dog didn't have rabies."

"Yes, of course, this mysterious, untraceable dog in the park. You don't know anything about that dog, Irwin. Rabies *kills*. I'm not willing to take that chance with my daughter. Don't come here again. Close the door behind you."

Irwin's feet feel bolted to the floor. "We're supposed to go to the comics convention. She's been looking forward to it for months."

"Mummy, please let me go to Comic Con. I want to see people dressed up as superheroes. I want to meet the man who draws *Daredevil*. Please please please?"

Uma carries her upstairs. "Irwin, close the door behind you."

"I want Irwin," Heike whimpers.

Desolation strikes him behind the knees, forcing him to cling to the coat rack. He can't desert her. She needs him. He tries to take a step forward but his legs tremble. He grabs at the handles on the glass doors to the living room and manages to stand, balancing between them, staring at the German ghosts. They stare back. The old man smokes his pipe. "Get out," Irwin tells them. "You're *dead*. This is Heike's house now. You don't belong here." His legs buckle and he lunges for the only mahogany chair unoccupied by the Germans. He knows he has no choice but to wait for the seizure to pass.

He doesn't open his eyes when he hears his father. "Wow. Oom, why didn't you call an ambulance?"

"He's *your* son. What am *I* supposed to do with him? Maybe one of your girlfriends can look after him."

"Do you really need to do this now?"

"I need you to get him out of here so I can take care of my daughter."

"Are the anti-whatever-they-are drugs kicking in yet?"

"Antipyretics and anti-inflammatories. He's awake."

"Irwin," Trent says. "What's up, kiddo? You're supposed to be at the hospital."

"I'm fine. I just fell asleep."

"I see that. Your mom said you had a seizure last night. They want to run some tests on you."

"I'm not doing any of that. I'd rather die." He knows his father hates hospitals as much as he does. When Irwin was little and asked Lynne why Trent never visited him, she said he'd had a bad experience in a hospital.

"Who has a good experience in a hospital?" Irwin asked. "I mean, everybody's sick in hospitals."

"Yes, peanut, but usually they get better. Your daddy had a friend who didn't."

"What kind of friend?"

"His best friend."

Irwin had never had a best friend but yearned for one. He tried to imagine what it would be like to have one die in the hospital. As much as he felt sad for his father, he envied him for having a best friend once. He knew that he, a sick and freaky son, could never fill the void left behind by the best friend. He stopped asking why his father didn't visit.

"Okay, kiddo, let's get you home."

"I'm not leaving till I see Heike."

"Oh for god's sake," Uma says. "What is it with these two?"

"They love each other. Just let him say goodbye."

"Make it quick. She's exhausted."

Trent steadies Irwin as he climbs the stairs. Irwin can't remember the last time his father touched him. The grip on his elbow is limp, and he knows Trent doesn't want to touch him. Irwin pulls his arm away and grabs the bannister.

Heike looks even more red and puffy against the yellow-striped pillow-case. Irwin sits on the edge of her bed the way his mother sits on his. He strokes Heike's forehead just as his mother strokes his. "You're going to get better and we're going to go to the comic con, and you're going to meet *Daredevil*'s artist and score lots of *Daredevil* comics."

She nods, looking unconvinced.

"You are," he says. "Daredevil got blinded and nobody thought he could do anything, but he became a superhero to make sure justice was served. You're going to get better and do amazing things."

"Like what?"

"Become prime minister and give everybody toilets."

"Can I tell you my joke?" Her swollen tongue slows her speech.

"Of course."

"Why didn't the cannibal eat the clown?"

"I don't know."

"Because it tasted funny."

Irwin tries to chuckle but feels he is losing her. She is drifting farther and farther away from him, beyond rescue.

"Can you stay with me, big brother?"

"Heike," Uma says, standing behind him, "you are very sick and need rest. This isn't the time for jokes."

"He could read to me."

Irwin hates reading out loud because it makes him stutter.

"*I* can read to you, honeybun. We'll have a nice read and a nap. Is there anything else you want to say to Irwin before he goes?"

Heike clutches his hands and holds them against her face. She feels hot, and her burning tears sting his fingers.

"Oh for god's sake, Heike," Uma says, "why this performance? He's not going far."

"Wow, Oom." Trent leans against the bedstead. "Take it down a notch."

"Don't tell me to take it down a notch, you idiot."

"I should go," Irwin says to stop them fighting. "Charge your phone and I'll call you." Heike has closed her puffy eyes and her hands have slid from his.

"Does it look like she can charge a phone?" Uma demands. "I've had it with this nonsense. Time to go. We'll call you."

In the Rover, a deadly electric current runs between Irwin and Trent that only Irwin is aware of. Trent is on what Lynne calls Planet Trent. That his son and daughter are dangerously ill doesn't register on his planet where people love bikes more than each other. Irwin looks out the window at earthlings doing normal things, and he hates them. When he was little he enjoyed watching normal people because he believed he would be like them one day.

Trent phones Lynne while he's driving even though it's against the law. "I'm bringing him home right now . . . he seems fine, a little dopey but no seizures." It pleases Irwin that his father couldn't detect he'd just had a seizure. But it also reminds him that his father doesn't know him at all. "No worries, we'll be there in twenty." Trent pockets his cell.

"What did your best friend die of?" Irwin asks.

"What's that?"

"Your best friend who died. What did he die of?"

"What best friend?"

"When you were little you had a best friend who died in the hospital, and that's why you hate going to hospitals."

"Who told you that?"

"Mum."

Trent stares straight ahead. A traffic light isn't working and a beefy cop stands in the intersection directing cars.

"Mum said that's why you couldn't visit me in the hospital. Because your best friend died there." Irwin waits for comprehension to brighten his father's expression, but Trent only frowns at the traffic. Irwin has never dared mention the dead best friend before, and is already regretting bringing it up. Mr. Shotlander says some stones are better left unturned. Irwin suspects this is one of them. "It doesn't matter," he says.

"I've been a lousy father to you, Irwin, and I'm sorry."

How did they get to talking about Trent? They're supposed to be talking about the best friend.

"I . . ." Trent scratches his leg under his bike shorts, "I didn't handle your condition very well. I think . . . I think maybe I was too young. It all happened so fast, and then it kept happening. It never stopped. I kept hoping it would stop."

"Me too. I'm really sorry your best friend died, but I wish you'd visited me in the hospital. I really wanted to see you. Sometimes I thought you hated me and that's why you didn't come, but Mum said it was because of your friend. Which makes sense. I mean, I've never had a best friend, but if I did, and they died in the hospital, I wouldn't want to go there anymore either."

Sweat drips from his father's temples even though the air con is on.

"What was he like?" Irwin asks.

"Who?"

"Your best friend."

"Oh. Wow. Umm, great, he was great."

"Did you play sports together?"

Trent scratches his leg again. "We totally did."

"Which sports?"

"Basketball. He was . . . he could sink those baskets like nobody's biz. An awesome player."

"I've always wished I could play sports."

"Oh, sports are overrated, kiddo. You do all kinds of other great stuff."

"Like what?"

"The stuff you do."

"I don't do anything."

"Sure you do."

"I don't. There's so much I'm not supposed to do, I don't do anything."

"Well, you're one top-notch babysitter, I'll tell you that."

"Do you think so? Even though she got bit?"

"These things happen, Irwin. You did the right thing getting your nurse friend to fix her up. How was anyone supposed to know she'd react to the shot?" Lynne has often complained that not only does Trent have the emotional maturity of a five-year-old, but that he sees himself as blameless in all things. Irwin envies this ability. He blames himself for almost everything.

"Do you think Heike will be okay?" he asks.

"Of course she will. That kid's a fighter. Just like Hal." Her nickname hangs in the air. Irwin hasn't heard his father say it since she fell.

"But Hal's dead," Irwin says. "I think maybe because she didn't want to fight anymore. I think maybe she was tired of fighting. I think she wanted to fly."

"Whatever she did, she was a fighter." Trent's voice sounds hoarse, and his Adam's apple bobs.

"I'm scared Heike will try to fly too," Irwin says. "She climbs crazy places. Like, not just trees but statues and stuff."

"Heike loves life too much, kiddo. Zest is that kid's middle name."

Irwin isn't sure what zest is, other than a soap bar in Nina's bathroom, but asking what it means would make him look stupid. "She really wants to go to the comic con at the convention centre. Will you take us? Uma might let us go if you take us."

"When is it?"

"Next week."

"I've got rides planned, weather permitting."

The hateful deep-sea monster inside Irwin rumbles, forcing words out of him. "You just said you were sorry that you've been a lousy father. Why don't you be a good father for once and take us to the comic con?"

Trent stares at some bicycles strapped to the back of a minivan. Irwin reaches through the deadly electric current and shakes his father's shoulder the way his mother shook his earlier. "Be a good father for once."

"Whoa, can we start over here for a second?"

"Yes. You can take us to the convention centre. Tell Uma you'll look after us. You won't have to—we can look after ourselves—but tell her that."

Trent meets his eyes then looks back at the bicycles. Irwin had forgotten the colour of his father's eyes, he so rarely sees them. They are hazel like Harriet's.

"Promise you'll take us."

His father often says he'll do things he doesn't. Lynne says as soon as the asshole says he'll do something, you can be sure he won't. "I didn't get to it" is his perennial excuse. But a promise is a promise. "Promise," Irwin repeats.

"Promise. If she's well enough."

"If she knows she's going to the comic con, she'll get better."

Trent drops him off outside the Shangrila. "I'm going to make myself scarce. Your mom won't want to see me."

The seniors are passing around TUMS and discussing Mr. Shotlander's son's cancer, even though Mr. Shotlander is not in the lobby. "Stage four," Mr. Hoogstra says. "That's serious business."

Irwin would prefer not to listen, but he has to wait for the elevator.

Mr. Chubak peels an orange. "They're doing another biopsy and another CT scan, a PET scan and an eGFR test."

Mr. Quigley, doing stretches in the corner, says, "Lord have mercy on him."

Irwin quietly opens the door to the apartment and hurries to the computer to look up reactions to rabies shots. Severe reactions include rash, hives, difficulty breathing and swallowing, swelling of the mouth, face, lips, tongue, hoarseness, joint or muscle pain, numbness or tingling—paralysis.

"Peanut, I didn't hear you come in. Are you all right?'

"I'm fine." The word *paralysis* has jammed his brain.

"You don't look good. Have you eaten? I made meatloaf with bacon on it the way you like it."

She'd stopped putting bacon on it because it makes him fat. She guides him to his chair and places a plate of meatloaf, potatoes and green beans in front of him. "I cooked all your favourite things but it's not that hot anymore, do you want me to heat it up?" In his head Heike says meat is murder. If she is paralyzed, he will hang himself from a tree. Lynne dollops butter onto his potatoes. "I even made chocolate pudding with marshmallows."

Irwin tries to eat a green bean. It takes forever to chew.

Lynne sits at the table, staring at him. "Did you hear about what happened to Mindy?"

He shakes his head, managing to swallow the bean, and jabs his fork into a chunk of potato.

"She took Brianna to her mother's for a couple of days, and Conner and Taylor had a party in the apartment. Their so-called friends got totally drunk and trashed the place. Then some older boys, who'd found out about the party on Facebook, crashed it and stole everybody's cells."

Irwin doesn't know why she's telling him this.

"The point is alcohol, sweet pea. Alcohol makes people do crazy things."

"Then *you* shouldn't drink."

"I'm not going to anymore. I told Sydney no more wine in the apartment. Alcohol causes seizures, peanut. Alcohol can kill you."

"So can falling off a balcony."

She inhales quickly, as though spooked. "I can't believe you're blaming me for that."

"Because it's your fault."

"It is not my fault. It's not that simple."

"What's not simple about it?"

She pushes her chair back from the table and stands gripping her forehead. He chews on potato, waiting for her to explain but she doesn't. She walks away from him. He hears the springs on the couch and knows she's about to turn on the TV. "What's not simple about it?" he almost shouts, which he never does. He hates shouting.

"There were a whole bunch of other factors, Irwin. Life isn't black and white. When you grow up you'll find that out, and maybe you'll be a bit more forgiving."

Relieved she is no longer forcing him to eat, he follows her. "What other factors?"

She stares glassily at Betty and Bob. "Your condition for starters." She's using him as an excuse again, just like Gennedy used him as an excuse for hitting Harry. She crosses her bony arms. "I've tried to move on. For us. So you could have a life."

"Stop saying you're doing things for me. You don't drink vino for me, you don't smoke cigarettes for me, you didn't fuck Buck for me, you didn't make Gennedy leave for me."

"I could never forgive him for what he did to Harriet."

"What about what *you* did to Harriet? Who forgives you for that?"

"Okay, where's Trent in all this? He *is* your father after all. Where's *he* been?"

Irwin can't understand how finding someone else to blame makes it any easier. Although blaming his mother is easier than blaming himself. "He's not my father. I never think of him as my father. Gennedy was my father." When he woke up and found Gennedy gone, and an empty space where his desk had been, he couldn't speak at first. Lynne was making French toast and acting like everything was normal. "Where's Gennedy?" he asked finally.

"He moved out. We didn't think all that fighting was good for you, peanut."

Once again things were happening because of him. "I didn't mind the fighting."

"We were never really married anyway. It's better this way. Just you and me, kid."

Irwin didn't think it was better that way. He wanted Gennedy to help him with his homework, and take him to superhero movies and buy him buttered popcorn. At first he still saw him on weekends but, as Gennedy grew poorer, movies became too expensive. They went to the park to watch community baseball games. Gennedy would sit in the bleachers shouting at players as if he were their coach until finally some man, usually bigger than Gennedy, would shout, "Shut the fuck up, asshole!" During the winter there was nowhere free to go except the library. They'd sit side by side looking at stuff online, but they didn't say much. Gennedy talked to the computer, cursing politicians, successful criminal lawyers and John Grisham. Several times he swore so loudly the librarian had to ask him to keep it down. Irwin pretended he didn't know Gennedy and immersed himself in online games. He started coming up with reasons why he couldn't go out with Gennedy. Lynne didn't want him spending time with him anyway, so it was easy to make excuses. Gennedy called less and less. Then Bell cut his service.

Lynne has slid down in the couch and closed her eyes. Irwin thinks she might be asleep but she says, "You know what my mother used to say to me?"

Irwin doesn't bother to reply because he knows she'll tell him.

"She used to say, 'You're special. Just like everybody else.' I was nobody, could have been anybody. My mother treated me like I was just like everybody else. I didn't want to do that to my kids. I wanted you guys to feel special. Not like everybody else."

"I've never felt like everybody else."

"You know what my mother said to me before she died? She said as far as she was concerned I murdered Harriet. She said, 'Don't bother coming to my funeral.'"

"We couldn't afford a funeral." He doesn't remember much about his grandmother except that she wore bright red lipstick and high heels. At Christmas, Lynne would take him to her apartment with presents Gran never liked. "What'd you get me this for? Don't waste your money. Take it back."

Irwin tried to discourage Lynne from buying Gran presents she didn't want. But Lynne was determined. "She's my mother," she would say.

"That doesn't mean you have to buy her stuff." When Gran tossed her carefully chosen gifts aside, Lynne's shoulders drooped and her hands hung at her sides until finally she'd pack up the unwanted gifts.

"Peanut, when you blame me for everything, it's like you're my mother. It's like it's happening all over again."

"What?"

Lynne still hasn't opened her eyes. "Rejection."

How did they get to talking about *her* again? "I don't mean to reject you," he says, although he doesn't know what he means. "I just want to talk about Harriet."

"What about Harriet?"

"Something you remember."

Lynne flinches as though it hurts to remember anything about Harriet. "The video store. We used to go before you were born, and she'd pick out a video with animals on the cover. Sometimes they had free popcorn and she'd grab a handful to feed the squirrels. She was so sweet and small and loving. And smart. She was printing three-letter words by the time she was two and a half."

Irwin pictures Harry sweet and small and loving, printing letters. "What words?"

"Cat, mat, sat. She loved Dr. Seuss, could recite all his books. And she was very picky about the colours she wore. She went through a pink phase, a turquoise phase, a purple phase, then lime green."

"I just remember her in old T-shirts and jeans."

"That's because she stopped caring." Lynne covers her eyes with her hand.

"Why did she stop caring?"

"I don't know. I wish I knew." She leans forward, resting her elbows on her knees and her head in her hands. "It was like she switched off. She'd been really excited about having a baby brother but then you stayed at the hospital."

It's Irwin's fault again. "I didn't want to stay in the hospital."

"Of course not, sweet pea, but there were so many complications, and then when you did come home, you couldn't do much."

"She was disappointed in me."

"Not in you, it was just all really . . . difficult."

Harriet was so disappointed in Irwin, she switched off. He tries to remember that far back. She seemed like a miracle to him. He couldn't take his eyes off her. She could do all the things he couldn't.

Lynne pulls absently at a thread in the worn upholstery. "I wish you'd eat something, peanut. It'd be better heated up. Do you want me to heat it up?"

It was just all really . . . difficult. That's his mother's excuse. He is so disappointed in her, he switches off.

Twenty-seven

"So what's the deal, junior? Your mom says you're still lying around all day." Sydney pulls Irwin's desk chair beside his bed and rests her bare feet on the frame. Her eyes are purple and her toenails green. He used to enjoy watching her remove nail polish and apply a different colour. He can't remember why. It seems like so long ago. Heike has not charged her phone, and Uma is not picking up.

"That happened to a friend of mine. For real. He stopped getting out of bed and got double pneumonia. You've to get your head around the fact that your lungs need exercise, junior, otherwise they fill up with crud, and you get some superbug immune to antibiotics and you die."

This is what he wants. He doesn't have the energy to climb a tree and hang from a rope. And he can't follow the bomb-making instructions. He tried but they were too complicated, more complicated than the school science project he failed.

"Why are you here?" he asks.

"Your mom had to go to work. She's scared if she takes too many personal days she'll get replaced by some ass-kissing new hire. It's my day off, so she asked me to keep an eye on you."

"Do you have any vino?"

"Very funny. Get off your ass and quit feeling sorry for yourself."

He is feeling sorry but he's not sure for what, exactly. Everything. Being born. He looked up *zest. 1. Invigorating or keen excitement or enjoyment. 2. Added interest, flavour or charm. 3. Something added to give flavour or relish.* Heike is all of these things..

"When *I'm* sick," Sydney says, "I like to watch TV."

"You watch TV anyway."

"Touché." She wiggles her toes. "But this is kind of dullsville, don't you think? I mean, your mom's not even here so it's not like you need to hide from her."

"I'm not hiding."

"She loves you, junior. She really does. You're lucky."

No matter how hard he focuses and chants, he is stuck in the wrong universe. Harry's taken off—like she always does—leaving him behind. He's starting to hate her too.

"Who's supposed to look after your fish, junior?"

"You."

"Not this century. Fish creep me out with their goby mouths and staring eyes. Like, why don't they blink?"

Irwin doesn't have the energy to clean the tank. Betty and Bob will slowly choke to death on their own shit. He must be depressed because his mother has been shoving Q-tips soaked in Listerine in his mouth, and spooning liquid Prozac into him, sitting on the bed, waiting for him to swallow. She's been feeding him his antiseizure meds on a spoon with honey. Nothing is black or white, just grey.

"Is that somebody at the door?" Sydney lifts her feet off the bed and heads for the hallway. Irwin rolls onto his side and stares at the beaky, clawed creature that has Gennedy's eye.

Forbes wheels in with his laptop. "Well, hello, son. I had to deliver flyers all by my lonesome again today."

"Sad face," Sydney says.

"It's way harder without my assistant. Spidey, I want to show you something." He flips open his laptop and sets it on the chair beside the bed. "Check this out." Onscreen are paintings of creatures bleeding from gaping wounds.

"Those are Harriet's," Irwin says. "How did you get those?"

"Are you sure they're Harriet's?"

"Who else's would they be?"

"Maybe somebody who sees the world the way Harry did."

Irwin sits up to look more closely at the pictures. The reds, oranges and yellows spring out at him. "Nobody can see the world like Harry."

"Maybe so, son, but you've got to admit, they are a bit Harry-ish."

"Who did them?"

"A boy named Oliver."

"Who is he?"

"An artist. I discovered him online."

Blues and greens blend into the aqua Harriet loved, making Irwin feel almost as though he is at the bottom of the pool, staring up at the sparkling water.

Forbes backs up his chair to look at the screen. "Seems to me there's a difference between Harry's and Ollie's work, though, what do you think?"

Irwin looks at Harry's paintings on the wall then back at the laptop. "Ollie's aren't as scary."

"That's what I thought. The creatures are wounded and suffering, but they're not evil."

Irwin scratches at his arms because Lynne isn't around to stop him. "Why are they wounded?"

"Your guess is as good as mine. I thought maybe we'd ask Oliver. He has a show on in his old high-school gym. He's hoping we'll get our arses over there before it closes."

"You met him?"

"Online. I friended him."

"Why does he want us to go?"

"He's an artist. Artists always want people to go to their shows."

"A friend of mine's an artist," Sydney says. "He can't even *get* a show. I keep telling him he's got to get his head around the fact that nobody gives a fart about art."

"I do," Irwin says.

Forbes closes his laptop. "Good, then come with me. I need back up with my wheels." His foot slips off the footrest. He lifts it back on. "Oliver's a pretty special guy. Just like you, he was born with a condition, only his was fatal. He was on a waiting list for a heart and lungs for years. When he finally got them, his body rejected them. He started to die all over again, could hardly move, had to stay near life support equipment and never leave the house. His mom home-schooled him till grade seven. This was long after she'd contacted the donor family and they'd all gotten together to celebrate what they thought was a successful transplant. When Ollie's immune system rejected the organs it was like the donor family had to watch their son get sick all over again. They stopped calling, and when another donation became available, they opened Ollie up and trashed the first donor's organs. Ollie's mom was too scared to contact the second donor family in case the new organs were rejected. She told Oliver he shouldn't either. But when he turned eighteen he could do what he wanted, so he used Facebook to find them, only they weren't looking for him."

"Maybe they didn't want to find him."

"Maybe they didn't realize how easy it is on Facebook. In the old days it was way more complicated, you had to go through the hospital and write letters and such."

"Is he still looking for them?"

"Nope, because he found me. We matched up stats, hospitals, dates and OR times, and guess what? Harriet was his donor, son. He's got Harriet's heart and lungs inside him."

Irwin is flung into intergalactic darkness. Black cold engulfs him.

"Ollie says his body loves Harriet's heart and lungs. He says he's in love with her heart and talks to it, calls it H for heart. He's off the antirejection meds. Harry's heart is happy inside him, son. She's doing great and making him create weird art. He does all kinds of crazy stuff, mixed media just like Harry. His parents are pretty freaked about it. He was supposed to be an engineer and now he's messing around in art school. He's doing what Harriet wanted to do. He's living for her, son."

Irwin crashes back to earth, robbed of his ability to see Harriet whole. He can't think of her in a boy's body, can't think of her as a heart and lungs.

Forbes flips open his laptop again. "Check out Ollie's Facebook page."

In the photos, a tall, thin young man with wild dark hair stands in front of paintings that resemble Harriet's. He's wearing jeans and a T-shirt that says *IT WASN'T ME*.

"He could use a haircut," Sydney says.

"You okay, son?"

"Does my mother know about this?"

"Not unless you tell her."

Irwin scratches his arms some more. "He wants to meet me, really?"

"He's dying to meet you."

"Wrong word," Sydney says. "He's *eager* to meet you."

"Did you tell him about my head?"

"I showed him pictures I snapped when you wasn't lookin'."

No one is ever dying to meet Irwin, especially after they've seen his head. "What did he say about my head?"

"Why's it always got to be about your head, junior? For real, I mean it's not *that* freaky. You act like you're the Elephant Man or something."

"He didn't say anything about your head, son. He told me he's always wanted a brother."

The big, swollen thing inside Irwin finally busts out but doesn't rip him apart. He sinks back on the bed, freed of its burden.

"So," Forbes says, "are you in? Do you want to go tomorrow? His show closes tomorrow."

"What the frick, that's the door again." Sydney heads for the hallway.

"Seriously, Spidey, do you want to go?"

"I don't know."

"What don't you know?"

"It might be weird. I don't know if I'm ready."

"Ready for what? How are you supposed to know if you're ready when you don't know what it's like to meet a guy with your sister's heart and lungs inside him?"

Dee bustles in clutching her Elite School of Beauty bag. "What's this about not getting out of bed again, Charlie Brown? You promised you'd let me practice waxing on you."

"I'm too tired."

"All you have to do is lie there, you lazy ass. *I* do the work. We'll start with the pits." She plugs in her wax warmer. "If you don't cooperate I'll hypnotize you." Dee took a hypnotizing tutorial online and has been practising hypnosis on Nina's cat.

"All you can hypnotize is cats," Irwin says.

"You are wrong, Chuck. I hypnotized the stick insect."

"No shit," Forbes says. "What'd you make him do?"

"Suffer." Dee pulls out waxing strips, applicator sticks, baby powder and coconut oil.

"Practice waxing on *me*," Sydney says. "I have to shave constantly. It's a total drag."

"You're on. Move over, Charlie, she needs to lie down."

Irwin moves over, embarrassed but excited at the prospect of sharing his bed with Sydney. Her softness presses against him. Fortunately the Prozac subdues his erection.

Lynne comes in. "What's going on here?"

"A waxing party." Sydney stretches her arm back so Dee can spread some wax on her armpit. "What are you doing here, Lynne? You're supposed to be at work."

"I left early, and a good thing I did. I trusted you to look after him, not host a party. Irwin needs rest."

"No I don't. I need you to leave us alone."

"I should be going anyway," Forbes says.

"No, don't go," Irwin pleads. "I want you to stay."

Lynne sags against the doorframe. "So you're saying you want them to stay, and me to go?"

"That's right." It astonishes Irwin that he is able to speak to her this way without the assistance of vino. "Go smoke on the balcony."

"Irwin," Forbes says. "Take it easy, son."

"Let me tell *her* what to do for once. She's always telling *me* what to do."

"Hold still, Syd," Dee commands. "I have to figure out if your hair grows up or down then pull the strips off in the opposite direction."

"Fine," Lynne says. "I won't stay where I'm not wanted."

"Good."

"That's mean, junior."

"She's mean to *me*." He hears Lynne banging the kitchen cabinets, probably searching for vino.

"Okay," Dee says, "get ready. I'm tearing a strip off."

"Ow," Sydney yelps.

"The price of beauty."

"She always says that," Irwin says.

"There's this dingus at LA who's got an armpit fetish since he hit himself on the head with a dumbbell. All he talks about is licking hot chicks' armpits. He says, since he hit himself in the head with a dumbbell, he can screw all night long."

Dee lays another strip. "Cheaper than Viagra."

"When you hypnotized Wyck," Irwin asks, "did you make him drop the charges?"

"More than that. I made him think helium balloons were pulling his arms up. The stick insect was standing there with his arms stuck in the air. I considered leaving him like that but I'm too nice."

Lying with Sydney beside him, listening to Dee and Forbes, Irwin feels a part of something, he's not sure what, but he's comfortable in it whatever it is. Sydney, Dee and Forbes don't blame him for anything, don't tell him what to do, don't mind his big head. They might even be his friends. And there's a young man out there who still wants to meet him after seeing his picture.

His friends urge him to talk to his mother. They say it hasn't been easy for her, that she did the best she could. "That's all any of us can do," Sydney says.

"But how do you know what your best is?" Irwin asks.

"You can't think of anything else to do, junior. You've tried everything you can possibly think of."

"Everything you can think of that's possible." Dee tears another strip off Sydney, who yelps again.

"You've done your best when you're up against the wall, son. I'd say your mom's been up against the wall more than most."

"She calls you a low-life," Irwin says.

"I've been called worse. Cut her some slack, Spidey. She's kept a roof over your head, put food in your belly and clothes on your back."

"And she loves you like crazy," Sydney says.

After they leave, he studies Harriet's fierce and bleeding creatures and tries to understand why they had to be this way, why they couldn't have been vulnerable and suffering like Oliver's. Harriet's creatures seethe with vengeance. Vengeance is a waste of energy, Mr. Chubak says. Vengeance causes wars and everybody loses in war.

When Irwin ordered his mother out of his room, he could see she was hurt. He'd gotten his revenge. Now it lies lifeless beside him, a waste of energy.

He finds her on the balcony. She isn't smoking but leaning over the railing, staring morosely at the parking lot and Irwin's afraid she's going to jump, that she's vulnerable and suffering and too tired to fight anymore. Suddenly he can't imagine a universe without his mother loving him like crazy, and he grabs her around the middle the way Heike grabs him.

"What is it, sweet pea? What's wrong?"

"I love you."

"I know that, peanut."

He releases his hold and guides her away from the railing, easing her into a lawn chair. She's losing energy, as though her batteries are dying. When he was little, she bought him a mechanical blue poodle that barked and wagged its tail. The noise irritated Gennedy so they didn't replace the batteries, just watched the poodle slow down until it couldn't bark or wag its tail anymore. Irwin holds his mother's hand, alarmed at how small it feels in his. When he was little, her grown-up hand covering his gave him courage. Now her hand feels as though it will break if he squeezes it.

"You have to stop getting skinny," he says. "It's scary."

She doesn't respond, just stares at the cluttered balconies across the parking lot.

"Promise me you'll eat," he says.

"Cook me something. If you cook me something, I'll eat it."

"Is it okay if I make sandwiches?"

"Whatever you make, I'll eat."

"Promise?"

"I promise."

A promise from his mother is a promise. He strokes her hand gently, as though it's an injured animal. She rests her head on his shoulder. She has never done this before. He kisses the top of her head the way she kisses his.

Irwin hasn't seen Mr. Shotlander in the lobby for two days and is beginning to worry about him. He takes the *Mirror* up to his apartment and knocks several times. "It's me," he says through the door. "Irwin. I've got your paper."

When Mr. Shotlander answers, he looks shrunken. "Thanks, Irwin. You're a good kid."

Irwin waits for him to offer a Coke but Mr. Shotlander starts to close the door.

"Can I come in?" Irwin asks.

"What for?"

"A Coke?"

"A Coke?" Mr. Shotlander looks as though he doesn't know what a Coke is.

"A Diet Coke," Irwin clarifies.

"Oh right. Of course." He steps back from the door. He's been forgetting to tug up his trousers and they droop from his hips, revealing his diamond-patterned boxers. "Help yourself."

"Can I get you one?"

"Sure, sure. You've got to get that sister of yours to go to Mr. Hung's for me. I need chips. Barbecue."

The other seniors are concerned about Mr. Shotlander because a complete stranger managed to get a $500 cheque out of him for cancer research. When Mr. Chubak asked Mr. Shotlander what the stranger's organization was, or if he'd offered a receipt, Mr. Shotlander told him to mind his own business. Mr. Shotlander has never been known to write cheques for anybody. Not even for his son when he needed his wisdom teeth out. "The old tightwad got rooked," Mr. Chubak said.

Mr. Shotlander adjusts the thermostat.

"It's summer, Mr. Shotlander," Irwin says loudly to his good ear. "The heat's not on."

There is only one Coke in the fridge. He hands it to Mr. Shotlander, who sits on the couch holding the can as though he doesn't know what to do with it. Irwin takes it, flips the tab then hands it back to Mr. Shotlander. He doesn't drink any. "Get one for yourself," he says.

"I'm okay."

News about his son's tests has not been good. The cancer spread beyond his lungs into the adrenal glands and the abdomen. The oncologist recommended four months of chemo. His first treatment is next week. Mr. Hoogstra couldn't understand why it's going to take five and a half hours. "Who the hell gets chemo for five and a half hours?"

Mr. Quigley, doing sit-ups, said, "Somebody with stage four lung cancer."

Mr. Shotlander wanted to go with his son to the treatment, but his son said it wasn't necessary.

"Of course it's necessary," Mr. Quigley said. "It's his *son*. When my son was in for a kidney stone, I was right there with him. He should go regardless of what Danny says."

Irwin thinks it's strange that all the seniors talk about Danny and his cancer to each other but not to Mr. Shotlander. The only reason they know anything is because Mr. Shotlander's computer is on the blink and he has to use Mr. Quigley's. Mr. Shotlander is afraid of forgetting his password again and told it to Mr. Quigley. Mr. Quigley checks Mr. Shotlander's Gmail frequently to make sure he doesn't miss any important emails from Danny.

"Why don't they talk on the phone?" Mr. Chubak asked.

"For crying out loud," Mr. Quigley said, "what century are you in? Nobody talks on the phone these days."

Irwin sits on the couch beside Mr. Shotlander. "Can I get you anything else?"

"Not a thing."

Photos of Mr. Shotlander's dead wife and Danny at different ages are spread on the coffee table. "I guess you must've taken all those pictures," Irwin says. "Since you're not in any of them."

Mr. Shotlander feels in his pockets for change. He does this often now, for no apparent reason. Last week he sideswiped a minivan and rear-ended a CAA towing truck. He told the police he suspected the cause of the collision was that his automatic transmission was improperly engaged and failed to go into reverse. The police suspended his licence. The other seniors think it's time to surrender the Cavalier, but they don't say this to Mr. Shotlander.

"Don't let me forget to drive Danny to the hospital," Mr. Shotlander says. "The twenty-fifth, eleven a.m. Don't let me forget. I don't want him taking the subway after they drip poison into him. Elizabeth used to get so woozy from the stuff I had to carry her out of there."

"He can always take a taxi." Irwin does not want to remind Mr. Shotlander that his driver's licence has been revoked and his car impounded. "It's really hard to find parking around hospitals." Irwin knows this because Gennedy would circle SickKids many times before finding a space.

"Run along then, Irwin. Tell that sister of yours to come see me. I need her to look at my dang computer. It's on the blink again. Tell her I'll even pay her a fiver."

Irwin doesn't want to remind him that Harriet is dead. He has done this before and Mr. Shotlander, initially shocked by the news, becomes incensed, ranting about that layabout.

"*I* can get what you need from Mr. Hung's."

"No, Irwin, I'm a loyal customer. She needs the cash. She's got big plans, that one."

"What plans?"

"Escape money. She's going to escape that crumb-bum layabout."

"She told you that?"

"She told Chubak. She wants to eat seals, carve soapstone and learn Eskimo."

This is news to Irwin and can only mean she was saving money to abandon him. "Harry's dead," he blurts, suddenly wanting to hurt as he has been hurt.

"She's what?"

"She's dead, and her heart and lungs are in a guy named Oliver. He paints just like Harry."

Mr. Shotlander stares vacantly at him then feels in his pocket for change again. After a minute he gets up and checks the thermostat.

Irwin sits on the fire stairs, trying to forgive Harriet for wanting to leave him behind. Nothing is black and white, and he has to learn to forgive a little.

After she died, they found $95 hidden in her art books. Lynne stared at it like it was illegal. "Where did she get all this cash?"

"From the seniors," Gennedy said.

"But why wouldn't she put it in the bank? She loves the bank."

When they discovered that Harriet had $228 in the bank, Lynne closed the account and took the money. Irwin didn't think this was right, but couldn't think of what else to do with it. Now that he knows it was escape money, it feels even more wrong. Maybe, if he'd asked her, Harry would have taken him with her. Maybe she thought he'd want to stay with Gennedy and Lynne. This makes sense because she knew he loved Gennedy. Besides, she probably thought he was too little to travel. Maybe she was going to send for him later.

"Irwin, what you doing there sittin' like Tom Thumb?" Mr. Quigley climbs up and down the fire stairs when it's too rainy to run outside.

"Nothing."

"Nobody does nothing. Everybody's up to something."

"I'm worried about Mr. Shotlander. He seems really confused."

"That he is, but there's nothing the likes of us can do about it. Don't sweat the stuff you can't fix. Come on, kid, do some stair climbing with me. Two at a time on the way up. On your mark, get set, go!"

Irwin climbs with him because he can't think of what else to do. After two flights he is out of breath and has to stop. Mr. Quigley jogs on the spot. "How do you feel, sport?"

"Tired." Although for the first time in weeks he feels connected to his legs, and the heart and lungs pumping inside him.

"That's the stuff. One more then we'll do some stretches. You stick with me and you'll be in fighting shape in no time."

The idea of being in fighting shape appeals to Irwin, even though Harriet was tired of fighting and wanted to escape. Irwin has never fought, except for his life in the hospital. This isn't the same as what Mr. Quigley calls fighting the good fight. The good fight would be fighting for Heike and Lynne. Mr. Hoogstra told Irwin he's the man of the family now.

After stretches Mr. Quigley makes him do knee push-ups. He can only manage eight.

"It's a start, sport. Same time tomorrow?"

"Same time."

It's when he's cleaning the fish tank that Heike phones. "Why didn't you call me?" she demands.

"I've been calling and calling. You didn't charge your cell and your mother never answers when I call."

"Phooey."

"Are you better?"

"Way better. I ate an entire pizza today. I made Mummy order it with processed cow cheese and pineapple chunks and I ate it. Half for lunch and half for dinner. Mummy was totally grossed out. It was sick."

"Do you have to have more rabies shots?"

"No way, José. The doctor says I could get really sick from them. I Googled rabies and there's no way that dog had it. He was, like, totally normal. I want to go to the comic con."

"Call Dad and ask him to take us. I already asked him. If *you* ask him it'll be harder for him to say no."

"Eww, I don't want to go with him, he's too drippy."

"It's the only way your mom will let you go. She won't let you go with just me."

He hears Uma giving orders in the background.

"Gotta go, big brother. Chillax, I'm on it." She hangs up and joy blasts through him. Heike is better. Life itself is back.

They take the subway and two buses to get to Oliver's school. Forbes uses his crutch to climb on and off the buses while Irwin manages the chair, folding it to keep it from obstructing the other passengers. Dee offers Forbes an arm to grab if he loses his balance. Irwin's stomach feels jammed up against his ribs because he's afraid Oliver won't like him. He couldn't eat any of the waffles he toasted this morning. Lynne, at Irwin's request, ate two. Sydney ate seven then said, "I disgust myself. I'm going to have to spend, like, ten hours on the treadmill."

The school gym smells of stale sweat and old running shoes, and there aren't many people looking at the artwork hanging below the windows. Sun spills above the paintings, providing a heavenly glow, softening the blood and gore. Harriet never painted on large canvases. Enlarged, the creatures' suffering is more visible. Many seem to be running from something but losing energy, just like Lynne. After breakfast his mother didn't do the dishes but sat on the couch staring at Betty and Bob. Irwin considered telling her that he was going to meet the boy who'd received Harriet's heart and lungs, but he feared it would upset her.

Forbes spins his chair around. "I don't see Ollie. That's weird. Maybe he took a smoke break. Just kidding. By the way, son, all the proceeds from the show go towards promoting organ donation awareness. Guess I'll go take a leak." He wheels out the gym doors.

Dee stands back from the paintings. "These are fanfuckingtastic, like, they're practically alive."

"What are they do you figure?" a wizened man in a frayed sports jacket asks.

"Our fears," Dee says. "Our pain."

Irwin stares at a hoof that looks cracked. "Harriet always said her art is whatever you want it to be."

"Who's Harriet?" the man asks. "Didn't a boy do these? I'm thinking of signing up." He pats his chest under his frayed sports jacket. "I may be old but my ticker's still good to go."

Irwin stands closer to a painting and thinks he sees Harry in a creature that looks part monkey. She was good at monkey bars, could swing across them skipping rungs and hang upside down from her knees. Irwin wasn't allowed to do any of these things. He'd sit in the sandbox, trying to imagine what it would feel like to swing from your hands and hang upside down from your knees.

"Hey, Irwin," a gentle voice says. Irwin turns and sees Harry in Ollie's eyes. This glimpse of her causes his jammed stomach to soften. Oliver is tall and gangly. His wild hair tumbles over his round face, reminding Irwin of a puppy whose fur and limbs have grown faster than the rest of him.

Ollie's puppy excitement is contained in the same way Harry's was when she found treasures for mixed-media projects. She would handle them carefully, giddy with anticipation, her eyes riveted to what just seemed like garbage to Irwin. Oliver looks at Irwin as though he is a found treasure and not a freak. When he holds out his long arms for a hug, Irwin folds into them, pressing his head against the young man's narrow chest. On the other side of Ollie's ribs, Irwin hears the familiar rhythm of Harriet's heart. It pulses through him and he feels he can never let go. He grips the thin young man, expecting to feel resistance and the removal of his arms, but Oliver doesn't break the embrace. He holds on to Irwin and rests his cheek against his head. "It's going to be all right," he says.

Cordelia Strube is an accomplished playwright and the author of nine critically acclaimed novels, including *Alex & Zee*, *Teaching Pigs to Sing*, and *Lemon*. Winner of the CBC literary competition and a Toronto Arts Foundation Award, she has been nominated for the Governor General's Award, the Trillium Book Award, the W.H. Smith/Books in Canada First Novel Award, the Prix Italia, and longlisted for the Scotiabank Giller Prize. A two-time finalist for ACTRA's Nellie Award celebrating excellence in Canadian broadcasting, she is also a three-time nominee for the ReLit Award.